DORIS LANGLEY MOORE

ALL DONE BY KINDNESS

With an introduction by

Sir Roy Strong

DEAN STREET PRESS

A Furrowed Middlebrow Book
FM41

Published by Dean Street Press 2020

Copyright © 1951 Doris Langley Moore

Introduction © 2020 Roy Strong

First published in 1951 by Cassell & Co.

Cover by DSP

ISBN 978 1 913054 59 5

www.deanstreetpress.co.uk

DORIS LANGLEY MOORE
ALL DONE BY KINDNESS

Doris Elizabeth Langley Moore (*née* Levy) was born on 23 July 1902 in Liverpool. She moved with her family to South Africa when she was eight. She received no formal education, but read widely, under the influence of her father.

Moore moved to London in the early 1920s, and wrote prolifically and diversely, including Greek translation, and an etiquette manual. In 1926 she married Robert Moore, and they had one daughter, Pandora, before divorcing in 1942.

She published six romantic novels between 1932 and 1959, in addition to several books on household management and an influential biography of E. Nesbit.

Moore was passionately interested in clothes, and her own clothes formed the basis of a collection of costumes, to which she added important historical pieces. Her fashion museum was opened in 1955, eventually finding a permanent home in Bath in 1963.

In addition to books, she also wrote a ballet, *The Quest*, first performed at Sadler's Wells in 1943. Moore also worked as a costume designer for the theatre and films, and designed Katharine Hepburn's dresses for *The African Queen* (1951).

Doris Langley Moore continued to write books, with a particular emphasis on Lord Byron. Her last novel, *My Caravaggio Style* (1959), about the forgery of the lost Byron memoirs, was followed by three scholarly works on the poet.

Doris Langley Moore was appointed OBE in 1971. She died in London in 1989.

TITLES BY DORIS LANGLEY MOORE

Fiction

A Winter's Passion (1932)
The Unknown Eros (1935)
A Game of Snakes and Ladders (1938, 1955)* **
Not at Home (1948)*
All Done by Kindness (1951)*
My Caravaggio Style (1959)*

* available from Dean Street Press and Furrowed Middlebrow

Selected Non-fiction

The Technique of the Love Affair (1928, reprinted 1999)
E. Nesbit: A Biography (1933, expanded edition 1966)
The Vulgar Heart: An Enquiry into the Sentimental Tendencies of Public Opinion (1945)
The Woman in Fashion (1949)
The Child in Fashion (1953)
Pleasure: A Discursive Guide Book (1953)
The Late Lord Byron: Posthumous Dramas (1961)
Marie & the Duke of H: The Daydream Love Affair of Marie Bashkirtseff (1966)
Fashion Through Fashion Plates, 1771-1970 (1971)
Lord Byron: Accounts Rendered (1974)
Ada, Countess of Lovelace: Byron's Legitimate Daughter (1977)

** Published in 1938 under the title *They Knew Her When: A Game of Snakes and Ladders*. Revised and reprinted in 1955 as *A Game of Snakes and Ladders*. Dean Street Press has used the text of the 1955 edition for its new edition.

To

DEAR PANDORA

INTRODUCTION
By Sir Roy Strong

"I was the first writer to take the reader through the bedroom door". That announcement to me by Doris Langley Moore (1902-1989) has always stuck in my mind. I only came to know her late in her life, in the mid 1960s when I was involved in establishing The Costume Society. I already knew her work for I was early on fascinated by the history of dress and consumed her pioneer volumes *The Woman in Fashion* (1949) and *The Child in Fashion* (1953) while I was still at school. I had also travelled down to Eridge Castle in 1953 where Doris opened the first version of her Museum of Costume which was to find its resting place in Bath some ten years later in what is now called The Fashion Museum.

She later became a friend, a formidable one making me quickly grasp why she had gained a reputation for being difficult. She was. But any encounter with her tended to be memorable providing fragments of a larger mosaic of a life which had been for a period at the creative centre of things. Later encounters were remarkable like the one when she took me out to lunch at The Ivy so that I could sign her passport photograph as a true likeness when transparently it had been taken through a gauze! This was the occasion when she suddenly volunteered that she had been the handsome Director of the National Gallery Sir Philip Hendy's (1900-1980) mistress.

If the material existed Doris would be a good example of the new emancipated woman who burst on the scene in the 1920s flaunting convention. She, of course, rightly takes her place in the *New Oxford Dictionary of National Biography* but what we read there raises more questions than it answers. Here was the Liverpool born daughter of a newspaper editor who, having passed most of her childhood in South Africa, suddenly arrives on the scene with a translation from the Greek of *Anacreon: 29 Odes* (1926). Two years later came the even more startling *The Technique of the Love Affair* (1928) under a pseudonym 'a gentlewoman' of which Dorothy Parker wrote that her whole love life would have been different if she had had the good fortune to have read this first. It has apparently stood the test of time and was reprinted in 1999. Two years before Doris had married and, although she did not divorce her husband until 1942, one would conclude that that marriage rapidly went on the rocks. Indeed I recall being told that her husband had gone off with the nanny of her only child, a daughter called Pandora. She never married again.

Doris was an extraordinarily multi-talented woman who moved with ease within the creative art set of the era. She was closely involved in those who were to become the Royal Ballet and, in 1943, wrote the scenario for a patriotic ballet *The Quest* to get the future Sir Frederick Ashton out of army. The music was by William Walton and the designs by John Piper, and Margot Fonteyn and Robert Helpmann dance in it. Again I recall her telling me that the members of what were to become our Royal Ballet at the opening of the war were all up in her house in Harrogate. And, after I married the designer Julia Trevelyan Oman, she took us out to dinner with William Chappell, the designer of Ashton's *Les Patineurs*. Then there were connexions with the Redgrave family who appear dressed in Regency and Victorian costume in her books. Vivien Leigh also figures in these books, again Doris remarking disparagingly of Olivier's part in the famous break up.

Between 1932 and 1959 she wrote six romantic novels, appreciated today by a readership which scours the Net for copies. All of this sat alongside a sharp academic mind which she applied in particular to a life long obsession with Lord Byron. Again I recall her opening a lecture on him describing how she had fended off a young man trying to kiss her at her first ball by drawing back and saying "Have you read *Childe Harold*?" Her first book *The Late Lord Byron* (1961) revolutionised Byron studies and two more of equal importance followed, *Lord Byron, Accounts Rendered* (1974) and *Ada, Countess of Lovelace* (1977).

But her greatest legacy must be The Museum of Fashion in Bath. Doris was obsessed by fashion and details of dress. I remember her noticing the way that I followed in town the correct gentleman's etiquette of wearing one glove on the hand which held the other. She herself followed fashion and indeed her hats were the subject of a Sotheby's sale. Why was her contribution in this area so important? Doris was the first person who moved the study of dress out of the antiquary's study into the land of the living. When it came to wheeler dealing with historic dress she had no equal. To her dress was vivid visual evidence of the attitudes and aspirations of a whole society. In that she ranks as an original enabling others to follow in the path that she blazed. She began collecting in 1928 and was to campaign for a museum for some twenty five years until at last it came to rest in the Assembly Rooms in Bath. And, typical of Doris, it embraced the new from the outset inaugurating the annual Dress of the Year Event which took off with a Mary Quant mini-dress. But then we can still see her in action for we can go on line and watch her in the first ever BBC colour television programmes from 1957 on the madness and marvel of clothes.

Roy Strong

ONE

IT WAS on the 10th of February, 1946, that Dr. George Sandilands all innocently did the deed which was to result, a few years later, in one of the most vigorous controversies and gravest scandals that ever shook the art world of Europe and America. Indeed, to speak only of 'the art world' is to understate, for the excitement rippled out to a much wider sphere, being given front-page status on several occasions by the Press.

If the delinquencies revealed were less startling than the theft of the Mona Lisa from the Louvre in 1911, less sensational than the Van Meegeren forgeries exposed in more recent times, they were nevertheless sufficiently interesting to draw into art galleries large numbers of people who had always steered clear of such places, to increase strikingly for a time the attendance at picture sales, whether at Christie's or the Portobello Market, and to inspire a great many ludicrous speculations and perhaps a few delightful discoveries.

Had it been revealed to Dr. Sandilands, as he stopped his car at the gate of the Old Rectory that grey and cheerless day, that he was about to commit an imprudence which would not only affect his own mode of life, but would have repercussions far and wide amongst art dealers, collectors, keepers of museums, experts, critics and amateurs of all descriptions, he would have received the prophecy with disbelief at its most absolute. He himself was so far from having any pretensions to being an amateur that he could not even claim to know what he liked.

Sometimes he seemed to like one thing, sometimes another. In his boyhood he had liked 'The Vigil' by John Petrie and almost anything depicting knights and soldiers, and as a young medical student about 1910, he had decorated his room with photogravures of the interesting problem pictures by the Hon. John Collier, 'The Fallen Idol' and 'The Confession'; while later, when just qualified, he had shared the general admiration for ' September Morn', so stupidly banned in America by the evil-minded Comstock. After the war, the First World War, his tastes had advanced and he had begun to appreciate Frank Brangwyn, Glyn Philpott, and even the gypsies of Augustus John, reputed to be a most Bohemian character. His wife had been more conservative, preferring 'The Cries of London' in mezzotint and the better-known works of Burne-Jones and G. F. Watts. And these too he had, in a passive way, found rather pleasing. A framed lithograph of 'Hope' hung on their bedroom wall.

And now there were his children growing up, and his second daughter favoured Gauguin and Van Gogh, and really, after the first shock of seeing the three big reproductions in the dining-room, he was growing quite used to them; liked them in fact. There was no telling what he might like next.

Not that he usually devoted much attention to such matters. He was a busy man, an overworked man, and his few hours of leisure he spent in reading travel books, or listening to something good on the wireless, or, when the weather was pleasant, taking a nice walk with one of his children.

Art was as far as anything well could be from Dr. Sandilands' mind as he opened the squeaking, rusty gate and began to pick his way up the neglected drive, overgrown with weeds and very uneven to the tread. He had left his car outside because it would have been troublesome to open the iron gate to its full width; and his thoughts were all on the poor old lady who occupied the deteriorating house.

She had been old when he had first settled in Charlton Wells twenty-five years ago, or so she had seemed to him in those days when he was only a junior partner in the practice; and now she had become the very personification of all that was time-worn, venerable, remote from the world and its passions. Like some ancient ruined building, some stricken tree, she was gracious and dignified in decay, yet life had not, on the whole, treated her kindly, and now in these last few years, which should have brought her gently, comfortably, to the end of her long journey, she had experienced nothing but poverty and difficulty.

Dr. Sandilands glanced about him at the little wilderness, eerie in the winter twilight, that had once been a garden, and recalled the time when a gardener could always have been seen there, digging or mowing, planting or pruning, lovingly tending all that had since gone to seed. And at this hour of the day, there would have been a parlour-maid drawing the curtains, replenishing the ample fires, lighting the gas in the hall and passages. Yes, gas! It was quaint. . . . Mrs. Hovenden had never had the Old Rectory electrified, had not been able to afford it he imagined.

After all, Dr. Sandilands himself, who was only fifty-six—a good three decades younger than Mrs. Hovenden—could recall the time when electric light installed in an old house had been suggestive of opulence. She had certainly not been opulent, even before the two Great Wars had eaten up her capital; though there were many evidences that the family had once been well provided for.

Unfortunately, Dr. Sandilands reflected as he reached the shadowy stone porch, the sort of possessions well-to-do people used to acquire when Mrs. Hovenden was young had little value in today's market. The massive sideboards and towering bookcases, the pictures of tremendous size by forgotten Academicians, the carved Oriental screens and overmantels and bric-à-brac in general—no one could be induced, even under the boom conditions now prevailing, to purchase them at a tithe of their original cost. The offers of the local dealers had been quite insulting. Some of the smaller pieces of furniture, old-fashioned and despised in their owner's girlhood, had sold well and enabled her to pay the rates and keep the house going in a modest way: but all the best things must have gone by now.

He jerked the metal bell-handle two or three times and waited somewhat anxiously. Lately Mrs. Hovenden had enjoyed so little of the care and service needful at her great age that he felt distinctly apprehensive for her. It was for this reason that he made a habit of calling whenever he happened to be anywhere near the Old Rectory—a fact he had concealed from his elder daughter, Beatrix, who sent out his professional accounts.

There was no sound from within the house, and he rang again and knocked as hard as he could with the brass knocker. Too bad, he thought with an unwonted gust of indignation, too bad the way old people were disregarded nowadays. No doubt in the past over-much stress had been laid on the respect due to old age, but the pendulum had certainly swung too far in the opposite direction. Several of his patients in Charlton Wells were dragging out their last years in such loneliness and discomfort as must have been rare in the days when the more acute problems of housing, catering, and domestic labour had darkened the lives of only the very poor. Now there were all these new schemes for the welfare of the young, and the old were looked upon—though no one said it aloud—as so much human lumber. Why couldn't people see the pattern of life whole? Youth, maturity, and age, they were all equally entitled to the opportunities for happiness.

At last, when he had begun to wonder whether he should reconnoitre or retreat, the door was slowly opened and he saw Mrs. Hovenden herself framed in the gloom, a touching figure standing against the weight of eighty-eight years like a frail tree that struggles to hold its ground in a piercing wind. A thousand little wrinkles disguised impenetrably whatever the former character of her face had been, beautiful or ugly, reserved or open, grave or merry. The pale silver hair, the faded tints of eyes and skin, made it impossible to guess whether in youth her colouring had been fair or dark. There was only one quality the hand of time had not obscured, had perhaps even intensified, a quality of sweetness, uncloying sweetness as one might find it in a wine from which, in the course of long, cool years, the rich body has departed, leaving behind a soft and delicate ghost.

This sweet face was turned towards the visitor with a gaze which seemed to focus itself slowly and from far away. Then the thousand wrinkles were deepened by a smile. A hand, faintly pink, and seemingly as fragile as a sea-shell, was raised to welcome the outstretched hand of the doctor. A voice, slightly tremulous, pronounced his name.

'Dr. Sandilands! This is kind.'

'I looked in as I was passing to see how you're going along. You don't mean to tell me you're alone in the house again?' He raised his voice just a little above its normal tone and she heard him perfectly.

'Yes, doctor, yes. But you mustn't worry about me. I'm not a bit lonely.'

She pulled one of the two little cords attached to the gas-bracket, and the mantel in its engraved glass bowl slowly flickered into incandescence, shedding a rather grudging light on to the mahogany stand for umbrellas and coats, the vast console table of ebony and marble, and the bust of a late-Victorian pierrette on a black pedestal—that bust about which the town's one art dealer had been so extremely scathing when Dr. Sandilands had tried to prevail on him to buy it.

Mrs. Hovenden put out her hands for his coat, but, remembering the customary temperature of the house, he managed to retain it.

'Do you mind,' she asked, 'if we go to the housekeeper's room? I have a fire there. A fire but no housekeeper.' Her laugh was creaky but not uncheerful.

The drawing-room, with its portentous furniture and green serge curtains, was not nearly so cosy as the small parlour which, until a few years ago, had been part of the servants' quarters, and he was glad to leave its big oak door unopened. In the housekeeper's room there were light walls and paintwork, armchairs covered with flowery cretonne, and an efficient firegrate. But as he took the chair opposite Mrs. Hovenden's for the little chat that was always part of these benevolent visits, he looked with concern at the glowing fire, thinking how helpless she would be in an accident.

'I use this room every day now,' she said. 'So much nearer to the kitchen . . . easier to get my meals.'

'But what's happened to the woman you had last time I was here?'

'She had an offer of another place—better wages, nearer the town. They never *have* liked it out here, doctor, not even when we got the bus service after the war—I mean the other war, you know, the first one. No one dreamed of motor buses, of course, when my husband was rector. They weren't invented.'

He brought her back to the point. 'So this woman went off, and you're alone?'

'Yes, she gave me a week's notice. They all get paid by the week nowadays, and that means they *can* give a week's notice. It's legal, you see.'

'And you haven't been able to get anyone to replace her?'

'To tell you the truth, doctor, I haven't been trying. You understand—you know my affairs so well . . . I really can't afford it.' Her voice quavered apologetically, for she had never quite grown used to the post-Edwardian custom of talking openly about money. 'Two or three pounds a week they ask these days—you can't get anyone for less—and then they always put up the household bills so much. I'm making do with my nice Mrs. Potter. She comes along every morning and gets through the heavy work. You mustn't worry about me.'

'But you must have someone living in, Mrs. Hovenden, you simply must. It's absurd for an old lady like you to be left alone in this house. Quite absurd! I can't allow it!'

'You're always so kind, Dr. Sandilands, but you mustn't worry. I should be nervous if I were in London where there are so many burglars—always have been, you know, ever since I can remember, and it's getting even worse from what I hear—but in Charlton I feel quite safe.' The creaky laugh sounded again wholly free from bitterness. 'Everyone knows, in any case, that the plate's gone and my jewellery's gone, and there's nothing of any value that could be carried away. Such pretty jewellery! Most of it was my mother's.'

He did not like to tell her that he was thinking, not of burglars but of her feebleness and the unpleasant contingencies that might arise from it, and he let her ramble off a little about the jewellery while he pondered the deplorable situation which she bore with so much fortitude. Hers were the sort of problems that strangers, knowing nothing of her character or special circumstances, could dispose of with the briskest solutions. Local sympathizers glibly asked him why she did not sell the house and use the proceeds to move to one of those rest homes where the elderly are cared for, and when he explained that it was not her absolute property but was to pass on her death to a descendant of her late husband by his first wife, their reaction was almost one of irritation. Why then, they would inquire impatiently, did she not let off a portion, or take lodgers? But to divide the house up, costly alterations would be necessary (it had received its last touches of modernization in the 'eighties); while, as for letting lodgings, a woman of substantially over eighty could hardly take such a course as that without adequate and reliable domestic service.

Domestic service! The doctor sighed, for he heard these words so often on the lips of harassed patients. It had always been a trying business in Charlton Wells. The war, of course, had increased the difficulty tenfold, but it was by no means a new one. The town was a spa with a season lasting from spring to autumn, and, although the owners of private houses had once found it easy enough to get what help they needed in the winter, there was a tendency as soon as the season began for the young women to migrate to the hotels and boarding-houses where life was more exciting and wages constantly augmented by tips.

Since the war even the hotels were hardly able to attract employees in sufficient numbers, and a whole wing of the Cottage Hospital had been closed for want of staff, so there was little hope that any girl or woman would long be content with a single-handed post in an inconvenient old house two miles from the nearest cinema. For the Rectory, which was ecclesiastically obsolete, stood on the very outskirts of Charlton Wells in a district from which all vitality had ebbed away many years before.

Its disadvantages had been a boon to Mrs. Hovenden when a Government department had taken over practically the whole town in the first days of the war, requisitioning with the highest of hands all the best hotels, and mercilessly billeting in private houses several thousands of employees evacuated from their London homes. Two compulsory guests had been so housed in the Rectory, and she had done her best for them; but luckily the bad bus service, the gas-brackets, the shocking hot-water system, and the 'eighties furniture had soon inspired a petition for a change of quarters, and Dr. Sandilands himself had called on the billeting officer to ensure that no further demands would be made on an old and overburdened woman who would never plead her own cause.

She was intrepid, that was what he liked about her. In an entirely unobtrusive fashion of her own, she braved everything. He had watched her standard of living decline, had seen her forced to part with her treasures, had known her suffer that disaster inevitable to the very old, the loss by death of her most cherished friends, and never had she shown a sign of faltering. His admiration for a spirit that succeeded in being both high and humble had made her well-being a matter of importance to him. He was determined not to leave the house without finding some way of helping her.

'My husband's family never went in much for jewellery,' she was saying. 'What little there was went to my stepson's wife. I didn't begrudge it. My own things—from my mother, you know—seemed so much nicer. She had a prettier taste.'

'Your stepson, Mrs. Hovenden,' he struck in purposefully, 'he was the father, no doubt, of this young man who is to inherit the house?'

'Yes, doctor. The "young man"'—she quoted the words with a smile—''was born in 1888.'

'Good gracious! Two years before me! And he's your husband's grandson?'

'Yes, I was nineteen years younger than my husband. That was quite an ordinary sort of marriage in those days. Nobody thought anything of twenty years difference in age—as long as it wasn't the wife who was older. My husband was born in 1840. More than a hundred years ago! Isn't it strange?'

'You're certainly a link with the past, Mrs. Hovenden. Now this step-grandson of yours, you don't think, do you, that as he's going to get the house, he'd do anything to assist you in any way? Pay some of the expenses of running it, for instance, or take it off your hands and find you somewhere else to live, somewhere more suitable?'

Slowly and very decisively she shook her head. 'He's been in New South Wales for I don't know how many years. I haven't met him since he was a child. I don't see why he should do anything for me. He's entitled to look on me as a great nuisance for living so long.'

It was a forlorn hope. He had known it, and he knew the next question too was little better than a way of gaining time while he went on thinking. 'You haven't any relatives at all of your own? Not even distant cousins?'

'Distant cousins!' she repeated scornfully. 'There may be distant cousins for all I can say, but I don't know them and they don't know me, so why should I ask them favours?' This seemed conclusive, and he remained silent, frowning into the fire.

'My son,' she went on in a lower voice, 'was killed in the war, the Boer War that was. He was just turned nineteen. My daughter died in 1920 in this house.'

'And she left no children?' It was a ruminative statement rather than an inquiry, for he was well aware she had left no children. He had heard on several occasions of this regretted daughter and her marriage to a man who had done no good to Mrs. Hovenden's fortune.

It was futile to go on probing. The idea that some forgotten relative would turn up to save the situation, like a lost half-crown in a hungry man's pocket, was simply childish. What was he to do for her? Send her to a home? But she would never consent to share a room with four or five other old women, and she could not afford the luxury of privacy. Why should she not be enabled to end her days as she desired? He was not in favour of uprooting old people if it could be avoided.

'How are *your* children?' she was asking with her characteristic eager politeness.

'All well, thank you. I had a most amusing letter from my boy yesterday. I wish I'd brought it for you to see. It would have made you laugh. My eldest, Beatrix, is feeling a little sorry for herself, poor girl. She's suffering from your trouble, the housekeeping problem.'

'How very nice when a widower has his daughter to keep house for him! Your home is much more up-to-date, naturally. But we thought this was wonderfully modern, you know, when we had it done up soon after our wedding. Our shower-bath was the talk of Charlton. And the stained glass came all the way from London. Clayton and Bell supplied it.'

Once again he let her wander away into her memories, a kind of aerial perspective which, reversing the usual order, grew more vivid with distance. The mention of his daughter had brought to mind a possibility—yes, a very distinct possibility. Only today at lunch-time, Beatrix, groaning to him as well she might about the trouble she was having in finding a cook-general, had mentioned a rather embarrassing application from a married couple—local people whom he knew quite well—who were willing to accept low wages for the sake of the accommodation, but whom she had been obliged to turn down because they could not be made to fit in with the domestic scheme. She wanted one person, not two, and in any case she had thought them much too elderly. There was some circumstance—he had forgotten what—which had rendered this respectable pair homeless and out of work at the age of sixty or more. Suppose, now, that he were to ask Beatrix to get hold of them this evening! What seemed like decrepitude to her would be sprightly youth in comparison with Mrs. Hovenden. And at their time of life one might surely expect a readiness to settle for a while in one place, even though it should be on the outskirts of the town. The Old Rectory was at its best 'below stairs'.

'Mrs. Hovenden,' he said firmly, just as she reached the laying of the tiled pavement in the front hall, 'if I could find you a married couple with good recommendations and all that, how would it suit you?'

'I'm afraid it would be beyond me.' She looked at him pitifully, as if appealing to him not to lay bare the full unsightliness of her difficulties.

'No, the wages would be moderate.' He explained all that he knew of Beatrix's applicants.

'I dare say it would be very nice,' she conceded doubtfully, 'but you see I'm behind-hand, months behind-hand, with the rates. They're beginning to worry me for them. And twenty pounds I owe for that business last November—or was it October! You remember—when the chimney stack blew down and broke the roof. I shall have to practise rigid economy.' Her worn old mouth could only pronounce the words with a stumbling effort, her hands fluttered anxiously into a work-basket at her side and produced, quivering, the unseemly evidence, the accounts rendered and re-rendered. 'This is the first time I've ever been dunned, Dr. Sandilands, and I'm eighty-eight.'

It was then that he found himself saying the impulsive words destined to have consequences so wildly beyond prediction.

'If you'll let me see about getting someone in to look after you, my dear lady, I'll settle these bills.'

'You mean you'll lend me the money?'

'Yes, if you like to put it that way.'

'I couldn't pay you back.'

'I'm not worried about that.'

But even as he spoke, the doctor was conscious of his rashness. The two accounts which she had put into his hand came to fifty-four pounds, four shillings and threepence, and his income was by no means equal to benefactions on so lavish a scale. Indeed, if he were to do his own family justice, it was scarcely equal to any outside benefactions at all. He was faring no better than anyone else under the tide that was threatening to wash away the prosperity of the middle classes. His responsibilities were many, the years of productive capacity that still lay before him were few. Until faced with the more stringent need of his patient, he had supposed himself to be uncommonly hard up, and here he was proposing to give away fifty pounds!

She sat deliberating, her mouth working a little, and with a twinge of guilt he half-hoped that she was about to refuse his offer; but at length, in the manner of one who wishes to be perfectly clear on a somewhat abstruse point, she ventured: "If you settled the two bills, I could use my own money to pay the servants. Is that it? Perhaps I could manage that out of my little income, my annuity.'

He nodded, seeing there was no retreat.

'I wouldn't like to *borrow* the money,' she continued with an unwonted vigour, a disdain for the word she emphasized. 'I've never been a borrower, you know that. But if you would take something in exchange, something that you thought worth the amount, then I should be very happy to accept your great kindness.'

His heart sank. There was nothing in the house it could give him the faintest gratification to possess, nothing, that is to say, but a carpet or two and some objects of daily utility which it would be out of the question for him to remove. In the last two or three years, she had sold almost everything that could be considered an asset. He himself had acted for her in several transactions, even approaching dealers in Elderfield, the industrial city fifteen miles away, when offers in Charlton Wells had not proved adequate.

All that was left represented the anathema of household appointments to one who had been forming his taste in the first quarter of the twentieth century. If he did not know what he liked, he knew what he disliked, and, fond though he was of Mrs. Hovenden, he regarded her house as a Chamber of late-Victorian Horrors.

'My dear lady,' he assured her almost vehemently, 'such a bargain is quite unnecessary. You will pay me back if you can, and if not—'

'No, doctor, no. I cannot take the money as a gift or loan.' Pride strengthened her voice and speeded her usually slow utterance. 'You must have a fair return. On that I insist.'

His mind's eye roved panic-stricken round the house, lighting now upon one well-remembered object, now another. The marble bust of the pierrette! The overmantel in the dining-room all divided into little fancy compartments with looking-glass backs, and on the shelves brass vases and tiny silver-framed photographs! The huge harmonium adorned with fretwork by the rector's own skilful hand! What would his daughters say if he brought that home?

Mrs. Hovenden's invigorated tones guided him back to the house-keeper's room. 'There are some trunks in the attic,' she said, 'which I haven't looked through for many, many years, old trunks, very old. Four of them—four or five, I can't say offhand. I haven't tried to sell them before this for sentimental reasons; but you—you're such a friend, you've been so good, it would be different with you. They're family things, things that have been put away from time to time—'

She left the sentence in mid-air and seemed to be trying to recapture some straying memories.

'I couldn't take your family things, Mrs. Hovenden,' he protested, but less earnestly than if she had pressed on him the gigantic brown and gold vases which had formerly always been filled with bulrushes, or the statue of an Italian peasant boy in the decaying conservatory.

'Then I couldn't take your money. If you don't have them, they'll only end in the auction room when I'm gone. Now let me see! In one of the trunks there's my wedding dress. It came from Jay's in London. Forty pounds it cost, and that was a lot of money in those days. It's ottoman silk and trimmed so beautifully. That will be something for your daughters, doctor.'

Dr. Sandilands could not imagine his three daughters making much use of a wedding dress sixty-five years out-of-date, but it would certainly be a nicer thing to take home than—say—the dining-room picture called 'Snowbound in a Yorkshire Dale' which he could scarcely look at without shivering.

'And then there's some linen,' she went on. 'Linen of better quality than you could get now.'

He brightened. They were very short of linen at home and it was expensive and on coupons. Beatrix would be mollified by linen.

'We had such large trousseaux in those days, more than we needed of everything. Then, there's all kinds of needlework and lace, and a few clothes it might be worth while to make over. The old materials were not like the rubbish you get today.' She paused again and fished up, as it were, more of these long-submerged treasures. 'There are one or two very pretty counterpanes, and my mother's best parasol with an ivory handle—a beauty. And you'll find some of my husband's things—though I don't suppose they'll be much use, the cassocks and surplices. The cloth is good, of course. And there are some embroidered waistcoats that must have belonged to his father. They are very old. A museum might be glad of them.'

A museum, yes, thought Dr. Sandilands dismally, but what about Beatrix? The hard-working, short-tempered Beatrix who had no time for anything at all unless it could be turned to practical account! What was Beatrix going to say to fifty pounds spent on cassocks and surplices and waistcoats and needlework?

'There are some pictures too,' Mrs. Hovenden brought out with a fresh effort, 'oil paintings that were in the rector's family.'

The doctor mentally, if not physically, recoiled. He had seen an oil painting handed down by the rector's family: it depicted a very waxy little boy sitting on the green mound of a grave, above which floated, pointing heavenward, a guardian angel with the most unbearable expression. He positively could not face Beatrix with any Hovenden oil paintings. As for his second daughter, the lover of Van Gogh and Gauguin, it was unthinkable!

'They are old pictures,' Mrs. Hovenden proceeded. 'My husband intended to have them examined by an expert. He used to say some of them might be Old Masters, but I shouldn't like to go as far as that. And restoration is a very costly business, I hear. Still, I think you might find it all worth fifty pounds, doctor. The lace alone must have cost nearly that. . . .'

'I'll write you a cheque,' he answered heroically.

'And I'll give you a receipt.'

'Oh, there's no need for that.'

'I don't agree. When you deal with people who are nearer ninety than eighty, you must never neglect anything of that kind.'

The pale eyes in the wrinkled mask smiled waveringly at him, and he was glad, after all, that he had not left her to her solitary struggle.

Thus was accomplished the transaction known to his four children as Sandilands' Folly. The cheque was signed and in due course cashed, the formal receipt was written, the bills were paid, and Mrs. Hovenden was enabled to buy the service and companionship she needed.

Dr. Sandilands was always delighted, seeing that the contents of the trunks turned out a rather acrimonious family joke, that the elderly married couple he succeeded in installing at the Old Rectory were a great comfort to her in the last few months of her life, and that they were permitted to remain on as caretakers after her death, pending the decision of her kinsman-by-marriage in New South Wales.

* * * * *

It had been impossible, of course, to conceal his purchase from Beatrix. At first he had contemplated leaving the things in the Rectory attic and saying nothing about them at home. But Mrs. Hovenden insisted on being business-like, and so that she should not be weighed down with his charity or suspect him of scorning her sentimental hoard—for he was a man of very delicate feelings in such matters—he gave instructions to the carrier and the things were fetched within a fortnight.

Five trunks there were—one fairly modern, bound with cane, one immense and excessively heavy Saratoga, two of japanned tin, and one quite interesting old round-topped, nail-studded box of cowhide, that might have made many a journey on a stage-coach. Only Beatrix and his second girl, Linda, were present at the opening, his son and the youngest daughter being away at their respective boarding-schools. Beatrix was not pleased but she held her criticism suspended, while Linda was optimistic, even excited.

The first trunk contained the needlework, a collection dating back to Mrs. Hovenden's mother and forward to her daughter, and illustrating with a certain pathos many vanished modes of employing a gentle-woman's leisure. But Beatrix could see no utility in the hair-tidies and watch-pockets. Tea cosies, handkerchief sachets, and nightdress bags—several of them embroidered with legends such as *Bonne Nuit* and *The Cup that Cheers*—were pronounced hopeless, suitable only to send to Jumble Sales; and some pieces of tapestry and cross-stitch work that might have been of use had been badly damaged by moth. The lace, though fine, was mostly covered with brown spots, and Beatrix's efforts, later on, to bleach it were too drastic, so that some of the best pieces were spoiled. In any case, lace was not in vogue at the time, and Miss Nuttall, who kept the good antique shop by the Pump Room, would only give five pounds for the remainder.

The clothes in the two tin trunks might be said to be corrupted both by moth and rust, for the moth had been feasting ruinously for years on the woollen garments, and the cotton things, including some beauti-fully embroidered waistcoats, were very much damaged by iron-mould.

The wedding dress looked exquisite, and the girls unfolded it rever-ently and with rising spirits, but on close examination by Beatrix, it was found that the silk had perished and would soon shred away when exposed to the air. There were three or four charming fans, but each had at least one broken stick. The act of opening the attractive parasol split its fringed silk canopy in three places.

The linen, on which Dr. Sandilands had laid great stress to concili-ate Beatrix, turned out to be the object of endless jests at his expense, since it was not table- or bed-linen as he had supposed, but under-wear, Victorian drawers, chemises and petticoats, all plain and sober as became a rector's bride. Even the sight of their coupon-free lawn and cambric did not reconcile Beatrix to her disappointment.

There was an eighteenth-century family Bible with a number of Hovenden entries, and a man's rose-pink suit of clothes belong to the same period, undoubtedly worthy of a museum. But museums, as Dr. Sandilands was not unaware, are seldom very generous in the prices they pay for minor acquisitions. The little round-topped trunk was full of assorted relics, such as old spectacles, a sealskin cigar-case, an anti-quated belt for carrying money, and a dented silver christening mug, engraved with the name of Mrs. Hovenden's long-dead son.

They had left the weighty Saratoga trunk till last, and even Linda had little heart left to open it, though both the girls well-meaningly kept up the game of lively raillery at his expense. The Saratoga had a tray, and on this was found a counterpane. It was of old-fashioned crochet work, and Beatrix called it 'the last straw'. There were also some pages of manuscript in what the doctor recognized as extremely illegible Greek bound into a very battered and dirty vellum book, and a few dark pieces of broken pottery wrapped in an Italian newspaper yellow with age. Under the tray the trunk was entirely filled with pictures on wood.

Naturally they looked at these with interest, hoping against hope that they might yet turn out a treasure trove; but they were a miser-able lot, all painted in the darkest colours and with little distinctness, and some in very bad condition. Several of them were worm-eaten, and two or three had actually fallen apart, while of another only incom-plete portions remained, the dingy figure of a woman being cut right through. The paint of this had cracked and was flaking off, and alto-gether it seemed fit only to throw away.

Nevertheless, they did not throw it away. Dr. Sandilands considered it would be rash to do so without taking another opinion. The pictures, he said, were unquestionably old, though he admitted that not everything old could be accounted good and these were in too dilapidated a state to be of value. Still, he intended to look at them some other time by a better light. To be on the safe side, he even wrapped up the broken sherds again, bravely ignoring Beatrix when she pointed out that no amount of gluing together would be of the slightest use as many of the pieces were obviously missing.

The Greek manuscript book he extracted and put in his consulting-room. There was a coat of arms stamped on the back which he resolved to look up one evening when he could borrow a library book on heraldry. After the removal of the moth-infected things, the trunks were stowed in the loft, to the great annoyance of young Geoffrey, who liked, when on holidays, to claim this fastness as his own territory.

Altogether Dr. Sandilands felt like Moses Primrose when he had sold his family's horse for a gross of green spectacles.

TWO

IF IT HAD not been for Mrs. du Plessis, Dr. Sandilands might never have discovered that, far from having sold a horse for green spectacles, he had, so to speak, exchanged a cow for a handful of coloured beans.

Mrs. du Plessis was a name the doctor first began to hear soon after Linda went to work in the Public Library. She was Linda's superior, spoken of sometimes with approval, sometimes with resentment, according to what had been going on in library circles, where it was evident that, for good or ill, she made herself felt. No one denied that she was clever and well-read, devoted to her work, obviously destined to be a chief librarian. The more earnest of the reading ratepayers always sought her out when in need of bookish information, and she was never known to fail them. She took up every inquiry as a challenge: that was her nature. Her fellow assistants were secretly rather proud of her, but this did not prevent a tendency to feel that she needed, as Linda put it, to be kept in her place. Mrs. du Plessis had a very bad habit of coming out of her place, a habit probably contracted in Rhodesia, whence she had emerged.

Linda had thought it strange at first that anyone with book-learn-ing should have come from Rhodesia, where young women might be supposed to spend their time armed with rifles, riding horses across vast tracts of country, or being paddled down the Zambesi on a croco-dile-hunt. But it transpired that Mrs. du Plessis could not ride and had never been in a canoe. She was convent-bred, had a university degree, and displayed no athletic prowess except—in a moderate way—at tennis and swimming. She was not even sun-tanned, having, in fact, the almost pallid complexion, tinged with the faintest pink, that some-times accompanies light red hair.

Mrs. du Plessis was a widow. 'My husband,' she explained to Dr. Sandilands at their first meeting, 'was one of the South Africans who was killed in the war that famous year when England was standing "absolutely alone", with only Canada and Australia and us and the rest of the Empire to hold out a helping hand.'

It was such an embittered and satirical remark that he quite saw why she was criticized as well as admired. But it did not take long to discern that, if her feelings were expressed with alarming honesty, fundamentally they were kind and generous feelings. And since moral courage was in him something of a deficiency he esteemed, though he remained alarmed by, hers.

No circumstance could have been slighter, more casual, than that which ultimately introduced 'Sandilands' Folly' to the notice of the one person in Charlton Wells who was likely to bring an active, intelligent, and probing attention to bear upon it.

One evening about four years after Mrs. Hovenden's death, Mrs. du Plessis, whom he had grown to know fairly well both as his daughter's colleague and as an occasional patient, was in his consulting-room seek-ing his professional advice on headaches. He had diagnosed eyestrain, had recommended an oculist, and had also written a prescription for a tonic.

Mrs. du Plessis cast over this prescription her ever-inquisitive eye. 'I suppose it must be true,' she said, 'that doctors have a special kind of illegible writing to baffle lay people?'

He caught her smile and answered with gravity: 'Oh yes, we have to take an exam, in bad handwriting, before we can qualify.'

'You must have passed with very high honours, Dr. Sandilands. I could decipher Greek a lot more easily than this.' How often afterwards the doctor was to marvel at the effects wrought in his life and many other lives by those chance words! What idle words they were to have set up such a chain of consequences! 'Decipher Greek'—there was the vital phrase, the phrase that brought into his head, for the first time in months or years, that grimy vellum book found with the tatterdemalion collection depictures. He had put it out of sight because its broken binding looked untidy among his neat rows of medical works, and since he was always busy and sometimes absent-minded, out of sight was liable to mean out of mind. Now his memory received a welcome little nudge.

'Talking of Greek, Mrs. du Plessis—if you've a moment to spare—I believe you're just the person to tell me what this can be. I don't know what to make of it.' He took from one of the drawers in his capacious desk the battered volume. 'It looks pretty old, don't you think? I've forgotten my Greek, such as it was, and anyhow it's not the sort of script I was brought up on.'

'Greek was never my strong suit,' said Mrs. du Plessis, handling the book with a familiar yet respectful touch, 'but I learned a smattering. I don't know if I could read this, though. It's very pre-Porson, isn't it?' She turned the pages slowly. 'Written beautifully on parchment! What a pity the front leaves have been torn away. It would really be a lovely manuscript if it were in better condition.'

'It came to me with a lot of old pictures,' he said. 'Not that it would have any connection. But it might be interesting to find out what it is exactly.'

'There's an escutcheon on the binding,' she observed, holding it close to the lamp on his desk.

'Yes, I once tried to identify it, but it isn't in Boutell's *English Heraldry*.'

'Of course it isn't!' The exclamation broke from her with happy eagerness. 'Look, it's unmistakable! Seven balls—the arms of the Medici! I'm sure I'm right.'

'The arms of the Medici? Isn't that where the pawnbroker's sign is supposed to come from? They were bankers, weren't they?'

'Bankers and rulers.'

He tried to find something sensible to say about the Medici, since she seemed so pleased with her discovery. 'I've always gathered they were rather a shady lot,' was all he could think of.

She flashed up from the book a shocked, reproachful glance. 'They were the greatest patrons of art and letters that have ever been known.'

'Oh!' He felt obliged to be as apologetic as if he had cast some slur on her own family. 'I must have been mixing them up with some other fellows.'

Reluctantly he directed his thoughts towards the patients still in his waiting-room. 'If you'd care to take the book home with you and have a good look at it, I dare say you could make out whether it's—well, anything in particular, you know. There's quite a trunkful of old pictures in the loft, as I was telling you, and I found it with them. I've always intended to have a thorough good look at them, but what with one thing and another, I've never got down to it.'

No, he had never got down to it, and it was a long time now since he had even attempted it. He had very little leisure—less than ever since all this National Health business—and the Saratoga trunk was heavy and had been stacked away in a position that greatly discouraged casual approaches. Moreover, he realized that his unaided judgment would have not the slightest value, and the only expert he knew personally was Morris, the dealer, who had shed such boundless contempt on Mrs. Hovenden's works of art when, years ago, there had been a question of persuading him to buy them. 'Just a lot of junk!'—those were his words, standing in the dining-room of the Old Rectory, gazing at the boy with the guardian angel, and though the doctor had privately concurred in his opinion, he had disliked his gratuitously insolent way of expressing it, and shrank from another encounter on the same terms.

If the girls had shown any interest he might have taken a little more trouble, but that fifty-pound cheque had been a sore point with Beatrix, who could see no reason for all her self-sacrificing economies as her father's secretary-housekeeper if he was simply going to waste the money she helped him to save: while Linda, as she grew up, tended to be more and more absorbed in things outside her home. The boxes had remained undisturbed in the loft except when Beatrix required a few gifts for a Bring-and-Buy Sale, or when Geoffrey annexed something that took his fancy, such as the belt for carrying money secretly, or a set of artificial flies concealing fish-hooks.

But Mrs. du Plessis fanned back to life the mild spark of curiosity he had once felt in his queer purchase, and even made him a little ashamed of the indifference with which he had treated it. For Linda brought him, within three days, this letter:

Dear Dr. Sandilands,

Your MS is a text of the Anacreontic Odes, apparently copied in the fifteenth century. I am almost certain it belonged to Piero de' Medici—Piero the Gouty, father of Lorenzo the Magnificent. I will show why I think so when I return the book. Piero, like Lorenzo, spent large sums in seeking out the lost works of classical authors and having copies written so that they could be handled with ease and circulated among scholars. This appears to be a copy from his own library.

Its value is unfortunately much less than it would be if the condition were sound. Quite a few pages are missing. Still, it is a sentimental treasure for anyone interested in the Medici.

Naturally it has aroused in me a great desire to see those pictures you spoke about, as I understand you found them at the same source.

I am borrowing some printed texts of Anacreon from Mr. Flagg of the College, and I shall compare what is left of the odes to make sure there are no verbal differences, my Greek being just about equal to that. When that's done, I'll bring round the book any evening you like to name, and if it did happen to be a time when you were free to show me the pictures, I should be most grateful.

> Yours with sincere regards,
> STEPHANIE DU PLESSIS.

If the doctor had no very keen aesthetic sensibilities, he was as fond as the next man of the idea of unravelling a mystery, and this communication encouraged him to believe that his pictures might be of more significance than he had been able at first to imagine. Yet he felt a trifle silly and open to the mockery she so freely, if so amiably, bestowed on him as he announced to Beatrix that he desired to invite Mrs. du Plessis to dinner, and that afterwards he proposed to show her the Hovenden panels.

Beatrix never prevented him from inviting anyone to dinner. Indeed, she liked these contacts with the outside world and the opportunities of showing how she coped with rationing difficulties; and, though she was inclined to make things uncomfortable behind the scenes, she well understood the arts of hospitality. But it needed courage to explain that he wanted to get the pictures down from the loft.

Beatrix sighed her patient little sigh, and smiled her patient and pretty little smile. 'It's going to be rather a bother, isn't it, turning everything in the loft upside down? And that trunk weighs a ton. Is Mrs. du Plessis supposed to be an expert?'

'No, but she's knowledgeable.'

'Is she trying to tell you the pictures are masterpieces?'

Supposed to be . . . *Trying* to tell . . . by such subtle turns of phrase she succeeded, quite unconsciously no doubt, in making people sound ineffectual and their activities absurd.

'Not at all, my dear. She hasn't tried to tell me anything about them. She merely expressed an interest in seeing them.'

'Wait till she does see them!' said Beatrix with a brief laugh. 'Does she know they're all on their last legs?'

Dr. Sandilands felt sillier still. He really had half-forgotten the shocking condition of the pictures. If a book was undesirable because it had some pages missing, how much more so was an oil painting in two halves!

'Well,' he said lamely, 'I can't refuse to show them to her—it wouldn't look very obliging—and since you say that Tuesday is a good evening as far as you are concerned, why not let's invite her?'

'Perhaps we'd better polish off one or two other people while we're about it.'

'Oh no, Beatrix, no, no! It would be most boring for our other guests to sit and watch us examine the pictures.'

'Shouldn't wonder if you were right about that!' she agreed in a manner which completed his deflation. 'Very well, let's have Mrs. Brainy du Plessis alone.'

Where did she get that manner? He had often wondered. Not from him, the most easily intimidated of men! Not from her mother, an earnestly optimistic woman who had never made a sarcastic remark or taken the wind out of anybody's sails in her life! He could only conclude—and the conclusion surprised him afresh as often as he reached it—that Beatrix had modelled herself on a nurse they had employed for a few years when she was a little girl, a nurse of excellent but irritating character whom they had kept on long after deciding to part with her, because they never could work up enough courage to give her notice.

Dr. Sandilands was the fondest of fathers, and he considered it a great privilege to have his house kept and his affairs looked after by a nice-looking daughter who was also strikingly efficient: but there were times when he asked himself with anxiety whether Beatrix's manner, so cheerful yet so caustic, so benevolent yet so belittling, might not be a drawback to her prospects of matrimony. She was twenty-seven, and though her appearance was, to his way of thinking, a distinct asset, there had never yet been a suitor. Of course, husbands did not grow on trees, and it was unwise nowadays —he could see that plainly—for girls circumstanced as she was to count on marriage, girls who would once have been provided with good dowries and all kinds of skilfully-engineered opportunities of meeting eligible men. In the middle walks of life the machinery, which had been geared to its highest perfection during his Edwardian youth, had broken down. Nevertheless, he did sometimes fear that Beatrix was unwittingly increasing the difficulties.

If he only had the strength of mind to tell her candidly how it sometimes struck him, that gay censoriousness echoing the facetious rebukes of the nursery! If only he could bring himself to answer vigorously back, like Linda! But he did so detest unpleasantness, and Beatrix was disarmingly fond of him. She did her very best for him, for her whole family indeed, even Linda who, at twenty-one, was going through a very unco-operative phase.

Linda's job outside her home with its independent income gave her a measure of freedom she was a little inclined to abuse. She took for granted all the comforts of home life .and was unwilling to contribute anything to them, going out evening after evening to the Tennis Club, the cinema, the houses of her friends, and the weekly dances at the Royal Hotel. She had certain manifest advantages over her domesticated sister, whose circle of acquaintances was necessarily more restricted, and, though not better-looking than Beatrix, it seemed she was endowed with more attractiveness.

The household was thus not without its frictions, and Dr. Sandilands, who could appreciate the merits and share to some extent the points of view of both his daughters, was often distressed by their incompatibility and inclined to speculate apprehensively on what might be in store for him when Geoffrey and Valerie, his youngest, entered the ranks of the adults in their turn.

But all was smooth politeness and cordiality when Mrs. du Plessis made her first appearance at the family table; at any rate, smoother and more cordial than on an ordinary evening. Linda out of courtesy stayed at home to meet their visitor, though she had been working with her all day, and Beatrix was as genial as the assurance that she had produced a good meal always made her.

'I hear,' she said with affability as she carved the chicken, 'that you've found out something thrilling about that funny old book?'

'Thrilling to me at any rate,' said Stephanie du Plessis.

'Daddy told us that it belonged to one of the Medici who suffered from gout. He ought to have come to Charlton Wells and taken the cure.'

'How did you know, by the way, that it was that particular one?' put in Dr. Sandilands.

'It was the coat of arms. In Piero's time, the blazon was seven "palle", and one of them was stamped with the fleur-de-lis of France, a special honour conferred by Louis XI. If you look at the binding of your book with a magnifying glass, you can see that little fleur-de-lis quite clearly. When Lorenzo the Magnificent became head of the house, one ball was removed from the blazon. So, if the manuscript had been made for Lorenzo or later, there would have been only six balls, and if it had been earlier, no fleur-de-lis.'

'How clever you are!' said Linda in her low, warm, caressing voice. 'I saw your name entered for the Tennis Tournament. I do hope you get into the finals!'

'Linda's mind is wandering as usual,' said Beatrix. 'Take no notice of her! Pass round the bread sauce and gravy, lazybones! I only hope daddy explained to you, Mrs. du Plessis, that his precious pictures were just bought among a lot of awful old bits and pieces and probably haven't anything to do with the book at all.'

'Yes,' said Stephanie, who had been told the story over a glass of sherry while Beatrix was assisting in the kitchen. 'But I shall still be interested to see them.' She sounded, however, a shade crestfallen. 'Didn't you ever meet the old lady again, doctor, after doing your good deed?'

'Oh, certainly, on several occasions.'

'And you never got to know anything more about the pictures?'

'Nothing helpful, though I did once ask her about them. She said, as far as I can remember, that they had come down to her husband with the family furniture, and that he'd found some of them one day in turning out a big coffer that he needed for the church. The rest, the bigger ones, just used to stand about in the attic till he tidied them away into that huge trunk.'

'If he thought they were good, why didn't he do anything about them?' Beatrix inquired briskly, as she cast her eye round the table to see that all wants were attended to.

'Apparently he did speak now and then of getting the Curator of the Elderfield Museum—there wasn't an Art Gallery then—or some other likely person to come and look at them, but, like me, he never worked up the energy. After all, experts aren't two a penny round Charlton Wells.'

'Sir Harry Maximer was here the other day,' said Linda, 'staying at the Royal.'

'And who might he be when he's at home?' Beatrix still kept a stock of the very phrases used with such exasperating effect by her old nurse.

'Sir Harry Maximer is the expert of experts, isn't he, Mrs. du Plessis? He writes books on Italian painting and all that. If you ever set foot in the Library you could see multitudes of them.'

'I believe he came up to open the Loan Exhibition at Elderfield,' said Stephanie.

'We ought to have invited him to open the Sandilands Exhibition tonight,' said Beatrix. 'That would have made him sit up. Really, I shall never as long as I live forget unpacking that cartload of Hovenden Horrors! We still have a text of *God Bless Our Home* embroidered with thistles and shamrocks and things, and a pineapple about three times life-size all done in woolwork for a firescreen or something. I didn't dare to give those even to the Jumble Sale. I'm sure the old girl knew exactly what she was palming off on us.'

'I don't care for you to say that, Beatrix,' the doctor had the temerity to object in a gentle aside.

But Beatrix would not be subdued. 'Now, daddy, how could she *not* have known that all those woollen garments would be riddled with moth, for one thing? Don't tell *me*!'

'At eighty-eight one may overlook such a detail. As a matter of fact, she was so sure I'd had a most wonderful bargain that I found the topic quite embarrassing, and that's why I preferred to avoid it. She asked me what my daughters thought of the things as if she'd been a fairy godmother to you both, poor old soul!'

'That embroidered suit with the knee breeches is nice anyhow,' said Linda. 'Daddy, would you let Norman Johnson wear it next time there's a Fancy Dress Ball? I'm sure it would fit him. I got it out when we were hauling the trunks round.'

'It's a museum piece,' Beatrix interposed. 'To wear it at a Fancy Dress Ball would be idiotic.'

'There you are! That's typical! The things are all old rubbish until *I* want one of them, and then they become museum pieces!'

'I suppose almost everything becomes a museum piece if it's kept long enough,' said Stephanie. 'Even your woolwork pineapple will probably be one of the valuable antiques of the future. You must just hang on to it a hundred years or so.'

'I'm surprised,' said Beatrix, rewarding this tiny jest with a laugh, 'that you're so interested in antiques, Mrs. du Plessis. There aren't many in Rhodesia, are there? Except native things, I mean, which don't count.'

'They count, but they're not the same. To most Europeans they're so remote that they're somehow rather unreal. What we like are the relics of our own history—that is, if we like history at all. I do. I love it. That's why I took to England like a duck to water. Perhaps, in a way, I get more out of it all than you people who've always had the past round you, whether you wanted it or not.'

'Don't you ever feel you must go back to Africa?'

'I can't say I do. I have no roots there now. My husband's dead, my parents are dead. Life suits me better here. My father was an Irishman by birth, you know. It was just a chance that made him go out to Rhodesia when he was about the same age as I am now.'

'And was it just a chance,' the doctor ventured, 'that brought you to Charlton Wells?'

'Yes. After my husband's death I took a war-time job with the Ministry—the Ministry the Charlton residents hated so much. I was billeted here, and I made a few friends and joined the Tennis Club, and so—and so when I was offered the Library post at the end of the war, I took it. I can have a better standard of living here than I could in London with the same income. That means I can save enough to go to Italy every year for my holiday.'

'Is that what makes you interested in pictures?' asked Linda.

'I've always been interested in pictures. My father was the Director of an Art School and my husband was an artist.'

'There, I said you'd be knowledgeable!' cried the doctor triumphantly. 'Only I fear,' he added, his voice almost comically sinking, 'that there may be a most disappointing evening in store for you.'

The big Saratoga trunk had been placed in his consulting-room, as it was agreed that a better light was required than anyone had thought necessary in the first instance; and the family set about the investigation in a very different spirit from that which had prevailed on the earlier occasion. Then they had unpacked the pictures in mutual disillusionment and fatigue, and had examined them with a predisposition to mockery; now even Beatrix, though she was still decidedly sceptical, was inclined to feel some curiosity.

But Mrs. du Plessis made very heavy going of it. First, after looking with an intent and frowning face at a number of panels, she suggested that the shade should be removed from the desk lamp. Then, having indulged in a further lengthy and perfectly mute inspection, she pronounced the surfaces to be so dirty that it was scarcely possible to see even what they were supposed to represent, and asked if she might be allowed to wash them over with soap and water. Beatrix could remember the fuss of some years before about the cleaning of certain pictures in the National Gallery, and she hinted broadly that, in case there did happen to be anything valuable, it might not be benefited by this drastic procedure, but she was met with such a cheerful obstinacy on the other side that it was impossible to persist, especially as Linda reminded her that, only a few moments ago, she had held the lowest opinion of the collection.

It would have been convenient to take the pictures to the kitchen for washing, but that was unthinkable while the cook and housemaid were busy clearing up after dinner, and so Beatrix was obliged to make the necessary preparations in the consulting-room, where fortunately there was running water. While she was fetching a piece of waterproof sheeting to protect the carpet, with cotton-wool and soft rags as tiresomely requested, Mrs. du Plessis laid out the two largest pieces of panel, which, as the doctor apologetically showed her, had formerly been part of a bigger picture. Though far from brilliant, they were less disfigured by dirt than most of the others, and the subject, or what was left of it, could be clearly distinguished.

She fitted them together on the carpet and stared at them with a degree of astonishment that silenced the two onlookers. Then she took the electric lamp from the desk and held it at an angle more favourable for her scrutiny. After that, quite rapt, she asked Linda and the doctor to hold the painted boards, and placed herself at a little distance from them.

'What is it? A Botticelli?' Beatrix demanded banteringly as she came in with the various cleansing materials.

Stephanie replied in a low, bewildered voice: 'It doesn't seem as if it could be by anybody else.'

'What's it supposed to be?' said Beatrix. 'Four and a half peculiar-looking women with two and a half cherubs! What on earth is she doing—the one who's been cut through? Blowing a sort of trumpet thing. And the one next to her is holding a flute or something. Must be a classical jazz band, I should think. The one in blue, sitting down, has a drum in her lap. . . .'

'It's a globe,' Stephanie corrected her decisively, 'and I think if we can get it clean, you'll see that she's wearing a crown of stars. The one with the flute has flowers in her hair.'

'I wish she wouldn't stick her tummy out,' Beatrix giggled. 'They need lessons in deportment, these wenches. The lady who's leaning against the rock, or what ever it is, seems to have taken a dose of nasty medicine.'

'That rock is a fountain,' Stephanie remarked, rather as if to cut short Beatrix's speech than to impart information. 'I think it's the Castalian spring. I think these women are Muses. The one with the globe and the stars is Urania, that's certain, and the other, with the tragic expression, is Melpomene. It must be! Look!' She peered at the figure with devouring eyes. 'She has a dagger in one hand—that's Melpomene all right!—and a rod or a sceptre in the other. We can see when it's a little cleaner.'

'You come and hold it while I have a look, Beatrix!' said Dr. Sandilands, who had been craning round the raised panels without being able to see much. But when Beatrix took his place, and he was able to study the painting by the light Stephanie held up for him, its battered and mutilated condition interposed between him and any appreciation he might have been capable of feeling.

'It's interesting, I can see that,' he said doubtfully. 'What a pity it's in such a perfectly hopeless state!'

'It's a pity, an awful pity, that there's only half, but it isn't at all hopeless otherwise. It will need joining up again and some restoring, I dare say, where the paint's been damaged, but I should think the rest of it will clean up beautifully. It's an extraordinary work! Extraordinary! I feel almost dumbfounded.'

Her manner was so strange, so elated, yet so awestruck and puzzled, that the doctor suspected the glass of wine she had drunk with her dinner might have gone to her head, a conclusion Beatrix had reached some time before. But she went on soberly enough: 'Shall we stand it against the wall while we take the top dirt off the others?'

The picture was moved into the dining-room, and Stephanie, selecting one of the smaller panels, began with a delicate and deferential touch to wash it, using wet cotton-wool and the household's only tablet of Castile soap.

None of them could help feeling interested and even a little excited as the dingy browns and greys in which the painting appeared to have been executed vanished inch by inch revealing what Beatrix described as 'a beefy baby with a sickly look on its face standing in a sort of niche thing'. The title, she thought, should be 'Lost, Stolen, or Strayed'.

'They did sometimes have a quaint idea of holiness in babies.' Stephanie's response was abstracted and apparently unamused. 'This one's a little Jesus, I dare say, or perhaps an infant St. John. Of course, when it's cleaned really thoroughly by experts, it will look immensely different from this. I shouldn't wonder if the colour's very clear and vivid when it's properly seen. Would someone ever so gently wipe this dry,' she commanded, 'while I wash another!'

Linda kneeled down with one of the old pillowslips her sister had provided, and dabbed warily, conscious of a critical eye upon her. Beatrix was of much too practical a disposition to stand by as a mere humorous commentator, and she also picked out a panel with the intention of washing it, but she checked herself, holding up the one she had chosen.

'It's no use wasting time on this. It's cracked from top to bottom and dreadfully worm-eaten at the back.'

'It can be repaired!' Stephanie announced authoritatively, 'pictures have found their way into art galleries in worse condition than that!'

'Art galleries! You'll be putting ideas into our heads if you're not careful!' But even Beatrix became a little infected with their visitor's gusto, and could not repress a murmur of satisfaction as her wad of cotton, soaked in one of her father's surgical bowls, transformed what had seemed the profile of a dusky ghost into an extremely life-like portrait of a young woman.

'It does look like an Old Master!' cried Linda. 'Honestly it does—just like one of those portraits in the books about Italian art!' And venturing for the first time to utter the idea that was in everyone's mind, she went on: 'Wouldn't it be funny if Mrs. Hovenden had let you have a treasure after all, daddy?'

'They might be fakes or copies, I suppose,' said Dr. Sandilands nervously. He was unwilling to trust himself to a belief so far-fetched and likely to lead to disillusionment.

'Yes, they might be.' Stephanie held up the painting on which she was now busy and noted how the removal of immemorial grime was bringing to light the countenance of a strong-featured man with a mane of dark hair. 'But if they're fakes, they're extremely old and extremely good fakes, and one would want to know a lot more about them. And if they're copies, what are they copies *of*? That's the point.'

'Pictures *you* haven't seen perhaps,' said Beatrix.

'I have a very good memory for pictures,' Stephanie rejoined meditatively.

'But still you haven't seen all there are in the world.' Dr. Sandilands could almost hear the sharp voice in the nursery rounding off the sentence with, 'Miss Know-all!'

The little arrow fell harmlessly on the armour of Stephanie's simple absorption in the problem. 'There must be very few good things,' she said, arguing rather with herself than Beatrix, 'that one never sees even in photographs—especially if one works in a library with quite a fair art section. So far there's nothing here that I've ever set eyes on before in any form.'

Beatrix, who was quick and dexterous in everything she did, had already handed over the profile portrait to Linda to be dried, and was attempting to deal with another panel, but it was warped as well as worm-eaten and the paint was peeling away.

'That one is beyond us,' said Stephanie urgently and imperatively. 'We must leave it to an expert.'

'The paint is frightfully cracked,' Beatrix's acquiescence was almost complacent. The fact that their over-knowing guest was so cock-a-hoop about the pictures gave her an irrational pleasure in their blemishes.

'It's the only one that's really bad so far. The rest are in simply miraculous condition.'

'They look awful to me,' said Beatrix. 'What about the wormholes?'

'Those haven't affected the painting. Of course, some repairs will be necessary. We shall have to take them to a specialist. They can do such unbelievable things—even transfer a picture completely from a panel to a canvas.'

The doctor gave an embarrassed cough. He had good reason to know that the restoration of old works of art was, as Mrs. Hovenden herself had told him, a costly business; there had been a big rumpus lately on the Town Council about the account for doing up some eighteenth-century portraits bequeathed for the adornment of the Pump Room. His artistic young patient's enthusiasm must not be allowed to lead him into expenses beyond his means.

To change the subject, so that he would not find he had committed himself out of hand to taking any particular course with the damaged pictures, he drew out from the trunk the broken pottery wrapped in newspaper.

'What do you think these could have been kept for, Mrs. du Plessis?'

Politely though somewhat reluctantly, she shifted from a kneeling to a sitting position, and accepted from his hand the little bundle of fragments. 'Were these with the pictures?' She turned over one or two of the pieces, holding them to the light. 'They're glass—very dark glass. I don't know a thing about glass.'

He too raised one of the fragments to the lamp, and he was able to see now that what had seemed on his former cursory inspection to be glazed earthenware was actually a barely transparent blue glass bearing a white decoration in relief.

'I say!' he exclaimed. 'Do you see what it is? It's the same sort of stuff as the Portland Vase!'

This discovery pleased him much more than what had been hinted about the pictures. They were altogether too much for him: he was out of his depth with them, and the implications, if they really should turn out to be valuable and important, were unthinkable. But these broken bits were interesting without threatening to involve him in hideous expenses or alarming controversies. Of course, he knew the Portland Vase was notable even though it had been smashed; but at least it was complete, whereas one could see at a glance that no whole object would ever be made out of this Hovenden relic. And that seemed to relieve his mind, where already there faintly stirred a premonition of the challenging future.

'I've never seen the Portland Vase,' said Stephanie.

'*Something* we've missed then!' Beatrix's pleasant little laugh was meant to turn her sarcasm into friendly teasing.

'It wasn't in the British Museum the only time I ever went there, in the early days of the war.'

'It has a kind of double-layer effect, exactly like this,' the doctor proceeded delightedly. 'I believe they actually coated the dark glass with white, and then they carved the outer layer in the style of cameos. You can see for yourself, Mrs. du Plessis. There are bits of carving on these pieces.' Stephanie was a little put out at being obliged to withdraw her attention from her work on the picture, but she assumed as much responsive appreciation as she could with the engrossing portrait growing clearer every moment.

'This may have been a copy of the Portland Vase itself,' said Dr. Sandilands. 'I shall look it up in my encyclopaedia. There'll probably be a photograph.'

He always enjoyed having occasion to consult reference books, and now, finding the illustration he needed, he sat down at his desk and started, as Linda said, to play at jigsaw puzzles.

Beatrix meanwhile was washing a panel which disclosed, in a somewhat imperfect state, an Annunciation.

'They must have got jolly tired, those old boys, of always having to do religious subjects,' murmured Linda, looking down at it with distaste.

'They did quite a lot of non-religious ones too in the Renaissance,' said Stephanie. 'What about those nine Muses in the dining-room?'

'You mean those four and a half Muses,' said Beatrix.

'And this portrait of a Florentine nobleman?' Stephanie continued unheeding.

'How do you know it's a Florentine nobleman?'

'Because I'm absolutely certain as I live and breathe that this picture is Florentine—or a marvellous imitation of the Florentine style—and as the sitter is shown with a superb background of marble columns, he obviously isn't a peasant. He's wearing simple clothes, but he has a book in his hand—'

'Bright lad!' commented Beatrix.

'And a sort of twisted gold cord round his neck. What a wonderful face!'

'I think it's as ugly as sin.'

The doctor made an uneasy half-turn in his revolving chair. He wished Beatrix would refrain from witticisms and flat contradictions which seemed intended to pinprick their guest. He also wished their guest had a better understanding of how to get on with Beatrix. He knew that her self-assurance was only a manner, just as Beatrix's jocular contrariety was a manner. She loved knowledge, and was always as ready to receive instruction as to offer it, but tonight her eagerness had made her forget the show of humility that convention demands, and she sounded didactic. As for Beatrix, she must undoubtedly be feeling as far out of her depth as he was but, unlike him, she refused to be at a disadvantage and sought to hold her ground by tiny impertinences.

He felt he must somehow cover up her discourtesy, and interposed, smiling despite his irritation: 'You look like three cats on a mat! Would it interest any of you to know that the cameos on my bits of glass don't resemble anything at all on the Portland Vase? But the shape of the thing, whatever it was, must have been very similar. Most curious! The Portland Vase is apparently a highly classical affair—a cinerary urn—'

'You can't even pronounce it, daddy!' said Linda, but her laughter, unlike that of Beatrix, was in fun rather than in mockery.

'An urn, my child, for keeping the ashes of the dear departed.'

'Oh, good gracious! Talking of the dear departed, I forgot to give you this. It was in one of the pockets of the pink embroidered coat, the "museum piece".' Linda drew from her pocket a yellowing half-sheet of paper inscribed in faded ink but a plain hand which Dr. Sandilands read aloud without difficulty:

'"This coat and breeches were purchased by my maternal grandfather, the Honble. F. S. Sanbourne, in the French metropolis when he was returning from his extensive travels in 1754. Their fashion is now so exploded as to appear risible, but I had it from his sister that he wore them to an entertainment given by the celebrated Mr. Walpole, afterwards Earl of Orford, and it was on that occasion that he met the lady he married some few months later, my late dear mother's mother, then Miss Fyshe. The coat, being too fine for the country, was never worn afterwards. My grandmother preserved it, doubtless affected by sentiment, my grandfather having met with an early and lamented death in 1759, twenty-four years before my birth." The signature is Artemus Hovenden,' the doctor ended. 'That was probably Mrs. Hovenden's husband's father, or more likely his grandfather. I'll look it up in the family Bible.'

But nobody took any notice of this, because Mrs. du Plessis was leaning back on her heels breathing: 'I knew it! The proof! The proof! I knew it! I was sure of it!' in a voice which, though quiet, very positively compelled attention.

'It's Lorenzo himself,' she went on. 'Lorenzo the Magnificent! I thought I knew that face, and now here's the proof! Wait a minute—I'll show you, Dr. Sandilands!'

She rose and rushed into the hall, returning instantly with a substantial book. 'I brought this—the first volume of Colonel Young's book on the Medici. I took it out of the Library so that you could see the coats of arms. Now look at these medallions of Lorenzo!' She turned the pages with excessive haste, overshot the mark once or twice, but at last was able to show one after another the two plates she was seeking. 'Do you admit,' she demanded, 'that's the same face or not?'

She held up the portrait, still glistening with moisture, and they all gazed at the half-length figure she had now fully unveiled.

'There is some likeness certainly,' the doctor agreed.

'You can't really see from little pictures of medallions,' said Beatrix.

'Oh yes you can, if you study them feature by feature, because I'll tell you what—these features are unforgettable!' Stephanie had become almost vehement in the ardour of her conviction. 'And there's the death mask too—you can compare it with that. And there's a portrait by Ghirlandaio, where he appears in a group . . . only that's not in this book. But if you'd once seen it, you'd know this is the same man. It isn't a face that resembles anyone else's.'

'That's something to be thankful for, at any rate,' said Beatrix genially.

'It's a most intellectual face,' put in the doctor, 'even though it isn't handsome.' He felt that Mrs. du Plessis deserved such protection from his daughter's persiflage as it was in his power to give.

'I think it's madly attractive,' Linda announced still more conciliatingly.

'Now look at *this*!' Stephanie pointed triumphantly to the representation of a marble bust on a pedestal which had been introduced conspicuously into the background.

'Well?' they inquired with varying degrees of curiosity.

'Well! That's Piero de' Medici, Lorenzo's father.'

They were all impressed, even Beatrix, when, turning the pages rapidly again, she produced a photograph of the same bust, plainly recognizable by what could be seen of the brocaded tunic as well as the distinctive head.

'Do you realize what it means?' she flung at them with increasing excitement, as they conceded the identity of the bust. 'The man shown here must be one of the Medici. Nobody else would have had himself painted with an important Medici statue practically leaning over his shoulder. I say that's Piero's son, Lorenzo, and if you really look well at the medallions and the death mask, you'll say the same. Now the vital point is this'—her words tumbled out headlong, but yet were coherent enough to hold the listeners intent—'Lorenzo the Magnificent was the flower of the Medici, and you'd think a portrait of him as good as this would be well known, reproduced all over the place. Certainly you'd expect to find it in every book about Florence, wouldn't you? I've looked through a lot of books these last few days, Dr. Sandilands, because your Greek manuscript set me going, but this picture is not in any of them. So it isn't a copy of an established work.'

'It might be an imaginary portrait,' said the doctor, summoning up with an effort vague memories of what he had heard and read about Old Masters and their habits. 'They did sometimes do that sort of thing, didn't they?' 'Yes, but why should it be an imaginary portrait when you have so many things which link it up with Lorenzo's own time? You've got a book which belonged to his father. You've got the remains of a classical vase which was just the kind of treasure the Medici collected before anyone else did. You've got a whole hoard of pictures which, as far as I can see, are all of them Italian Renaissance works.'

'Fakes perhaps,' said Beatrix, but not in her rallying tone.

'I don't believe they're fakes. Of course it's much too soon to be definite, but you've got to consider how you came by them. This old lady said they were handed down to her husband as part of the family furniture, and you think she was telling the truth, don't you, doctor?'

'Unquestionably.'

'Very good. Then they were probably acquired in the eighteenth century, when so many Englishmen were bringing back works of art from Italy. Oh, I know there was any amount of faking going on at the time, but it was faking of the things eighteenth-century Englishmen admired, which weren't this kind of stuff at all. Take that big picture in the dining-room which is so distinctly, amazingly, in the style of Botticelli! Nobody cared about Botticelli before the Victorians, the pre-Raphaelites. It wouldn't have been worth anyone's while to forge a picture in Botticelli's most utterly pre-Raphael manner. There would have been no market for it, especially badly damaged as it is!'

'The damage may have been done afterwards,' suggested the doctor.

'It may, and we shall have to weigh up every possibility after studying all the pictures with the greatest care.'

The doctor groaned in his spirit, for this sounded like hard work of a particularly uncongenial kind.

'But I'll tell you now,' she went on, 'what I think. I must! I can't keep it to myself! The Medici Palace was sacked in 1494, sacked and looted. Some of its treasures were destroyed, some of them were stolen and dispersed all over Italy. Suppose in all the turmoil there should have been someone who looted, or perhaps saved, fifteen or sixteen pictures, mostly small ones, by taking them out of their frames, and a few portable objects of value with them—books, an antique urn, other things possibly that may have disappeared since. Suppose this man, for good or bad reasons, hid what he'd taken and kept it hidden for a long time. Then suppose it finds its way to some cellar or lumber room in Italy, and nobody bothers about it till the eighteenth century, when the rich English begin to go picture-hunting. Then an ancestor of that old lady's husband travels in Italy and buys this little hoard. Perhaps he buys it cheap because it's what might have been considered at the time a fairly bedraggled and unattractive lot. But he brings it home intending, just as the old lady's husband intended, to get it all thoroughly examined one of these days, and then—'

'And then,' interrupted Linda, 'he falls in love instead, and gets married, and goes into the country, and stuffs most of the pictures into a coffer, and in a few years he dies!' She snatched from the desk the paper which had been in the pocket of the rose-pink coat and waved it above her head.

'It's all conjecture,' said Dr. Sandilands, frowning and shaking his head. 'All the merest conjecture, you know.'

'Yes, at the present stage that's true.' Stephanie's eager voice dropped, then lifted again. 'But this is a portrait of Lorenzo the Magnificent, and it's a contemporary portrait, that I'll swear. And what's more, I think everything we've looked at so far is a masterpiece.'

But none of them, not even Linda, dared to believe her.

THREE

SIR HARRY Maximer walked about his library smoking his after-luncheon cigar—an exceptional cigar, the gift of a tobacco-growing potentate in Havana, for whom he had obtained a charming Renoir. He himself did not go in for pictures later than the seventeenth century, but if one is at the very centre of the world where works of art are everyone's main concern, one knows where to lay hands on things.

Sir Harry's good nature, his resourcefulness, and the disinterested love of connoisseurship by which he had been the instrument of enriching so many famous collections, were as celebrated as his virtuosity. The room contained many pleasant tributes to them. There was the handsome case of cigars from which he had just made his selection; there were the Boulle liqueur cabinet and the set of crystal inside it, the gold fountain pen lying on his desk, the little bon-bon dishes he used as ashtrays, and many of the enviable volumes which filled his bookshelves. Through the wreaths of fragrant cigar smoke Sir Harry surveyed these mementoes with satisfaction, remembering all that he had done to earn them.

Then his gaze wandered more largely, swept over the whole room and its contents, and brought him with fresh relish to the conclusion he reached at least once every day of his life—that no self-made man in Britain, few in the world, could boast an apartment so fine. Fine in the completest sense of the word. There were others more resplendent, richer in gilded ornaments and sumptuous trappings, but none where the exuberance of wealth was so perfectly restrained by the discretion of taste, where—without any obtrusive suggestion of a 'scheme'—each object was not only admirable in itself but harmoniously related to its surroundings.

Sir Harry himself was indeed the only object not so related. His big, complacent, rather shapeless face, and the thick, awkward figure which defied the best cutters and fitters in Savile Row, were altogether at odds with the elegances of their environment. But he was well aware of the contrast, to which he would sometimes make reference with a touch of not unconscious pathos. He had been able, he would say, to gratify his love of beauty in everything but his own person.

When smoking a cigar in solitude, whether in his comfortable library or his awe-inspiring drawing-room, Sir Harry was in the habit of moving erratically about, counting, as it were, his visible blessings, and weighing the pros and cons of acquisitions yet to be made. On this gentle perambulation today, he paused critically in front of the panel which he had at last established in the art world as what he had always known it to be, a Boltraffio of some importance, and asked himself whether he really liked it, not merely as a painting but as a decoration for his room, and whether, since it would now command a much larger price than he had paid for it—substantial though that was—he would not be wise to dispose of it. The problem brought his thoughts by a roundabout track to a note on his desk-pad, and he rang the bell that communicated with his secretary's room.

It was answered by a woman of about forty, short and plump yet active-looking, and carrying, on a face which was still endowed with a feminine sort of prettiness, an expression of decided alertness and capability, an expression on the whole more alert than amiable.

'Mrs. Rose,' he said, 'I have that doctor from Charlton Wells coming—the doctor who has been so persistently asking me to examine a collection of pictures. As he is bringing the whole lot with him and may require help, it would be as well to see that Hudson is on duty to carry the things upstairs. The cabmen sometimes refuse.'

Mrs. Rose replied with a murmur of acquiescence.

'I think it's quite possible,' he went on, 'that this doctor may be eccentric or peculiar in some way. If I ring the bell, you had better come in and give me some excuse for getting rid of him.'

The secretary received these instructions without surprise, for there were many eccentric and peculiar people who were desirous of crossing that threshold.

Sir Harry sat down at his desk, projecting his fancy into the appointed interview. His high reputation, both as a writer on art and a collector, brought him many letters from strangers asking him to pronounce his opinion or offer a price for items about which they told various stories, true, false, or erroneous. Although these approaches were occasionally fruitful and he seldom felt justified in rejecting them out of hand, in general they were productive of nothing but exasperation and pained astonishment at the visual stupidity they so crassly exposed. The appalling rubbish he had been expected to certify as the work of glorious Old Masters!

But of all the extravagant claims that had ever been made, none surely was more startling, more bold and presumptuous than this provincial doctor's claim that he possessed sixteen masterpieces from the peerless collection of Lorenzo the Magnificent!

The odd thing was that there was nothing bold and presumptuous in the phrasing of the doctor's letters. They were tentative, constrained, even embarrassed in tone; and to begin with, the description of the pictures had been very guarded. The amazing challenge had only been flung—and oh! how apologetically and how confidentially flung—after Sir Harry had refused to pay a special visit to Charlton Wells to see the supposed treasure trove.

It would have been easy to conclude that the man was mad, or else that some kind of fraudulence was intended; but particulars readily obtained from the Medical Directory indicated that he was a physician of standing, and his hospital appointments made it, to say the least, improbable that he was insane. Therefore, his curiosity piqued, Sir Harry had consented to look at the pictures and pronounce a verdict, though he continued to decline the invitation to Charlton Wells.

And now this strange correspondent, with his extraordinary delusion—a delusion of grandeur if ever there was one, and yet expressed so humbly and so cautiously—had actually brought all the way to London his little gallery of forgeries or bad copies, or whatever they would turn out to be, and was about to submit them, if he spoke the truth, to Sir Harry's judgment.

Glancing over the note he had received to confirm this afternoon's engagement, Sir Harry refreshed his memory.

> Although there seem to be many convincing reasons [it ended] for believing that these may be Medici pictures, as described, I realize that what I have is purely external evidence. The internal evidence is a matter on which I will accept your guidance absolutely, since you are well known to be our leading expert on the subject.

Well, that was flattering certainly, and he very much liked being flattered on his authoritative position, about which he fully shared the writer's opinion. When he heard a taxi pull up at his door and, peeping out of the window from behind the curtain, saw emerge an elderly man of somewhat harassed demeanour, he resolved to let him down as lightly as possible.

He was half-amused, half-irritated to observe, standing on its end at the front of the cab, an enormous Saratoga trunk filling every inch of the space beside the driver. Nowhere in his choicely appointed flat would such a bulk of mid-Victorian unsightliness look appropriate, but it was he who had insisted that the mountain should come to Mohammed, and at any rate, it was not likely to be there long.

A moment later he perceived that the visitor had a young woman with him, who presently took charge of unloading the taxi, a labour which required the united efforts of the driver, the porter of the building, and his own chauffeur. Sir Harry turned from the window and hurried to his secretary's room, addressing her with some urgency:

'Mrs. Rose, I really think I may need you at this interview. As you know, there have been occasions when words have been put into my mouth which I never said, when I have been credited with authenticating some work which was not in fact genuine. This man *must* have some bee in his bonnet to have brought a trunkful of pictures all the way from the North like this. . . .'

'You want me to stay in the room, Sir Harry?' she asked with a slight smile.

'Well, if I ring for you. One must be prudent. You remember that old woman with the so-called Pinturicchio which she succeeded in palming off on the Duchess of Surrey, thanks to taking my name in vain?' Without waiting for her reply, he continued at a tangent, 'You look remarkably well this afternoon, Mrs. Rose. I'm glad you've followed my advice and left off that new-fangled hair style. You may trust my eye as to what suits you.'

He hastened away, and by the time Dr. Sandilands, following the trunk upstairs, had reached the library, he was standing behind his desk ready to shake hands with cordiality.

The doctor diffidently presented his eldest daughter. 'I would have let you know we should both be coming,' he explained, 'if I had known myself. But my daughter only decided at the last minute not to be left behind.'

'You came down from Charlton Wells this morning?' said Sir Harry, indicating chairs.

'No, yesterday evening, and we shall be going back today, by Pullman.'

'A very brief visit.'

'I wish we could stay longer, but even to leave my practice for two days has required a good deal of planning.'

'Do you come often?' Sir Harry proffered cigarettes which they both in their nervousness accepted, though they were habitually almost non-smokers.

'We have not been in London since the Victory Procession in 1946, I believe,' said the doctor, feeling that he was making a damaging admission. Sir Harry's small talk, though not unkindly meant, sounded like a cross-examination by a prosecuting counsel particularly bent on securing a conviction.

'And your purpose in making this journey was expressly to consult me about this mysterious cache of pictures which you inherited, I think you said, from a relative?'

'Not precisely. She was a patient, not a relative, and in a sense I bought them. I didn't really mean to do so.'

'You didn't mean to do so?' Sir Harry fixed him with a keen and, as Dr. Sandilands thought, an accusing eye. 'And now perhaps you have some idea of selling them?'

'If they are valuable—if they should turn out to be valuable, he stammered, 'they would be better in the hands of those who can appreciate them. I don't profess to be artistic in any way.' He gave a feeble laugh.

Sir Harry, for all his well-known benevolence, was an intimidating personality. There was not only his massive form but his resonant voice with its rather assertively beautiful diction. There was also his air, immediately perceptible, of taking a situation in hand and moulding it according to his own notion of the shape it should take.

Seldom as much at ease as she pretended to be, Beatrix was now quite mute and subdued, while the doctor was acutely conscious of the unfamiliarity of the ground he trod upon. Here even more than in setting out from Charlton Wells, they were sensible of the fantastic nature of their mission with its potentialities for making them look ridiculous, and they sat like small children in the presence of a large headmaster while Sir Harry addressed them gravely:

'Everyone is entitled to sell pictures he doesn't want to keep, Dr. Sandilands, provided there is no misrepresentation as to the nature of such pictures. That, of course, is the matter about which you desire my opinion. Before I give it, I should like to make my position perfectly clear.' Extending each of his big hands to the uttermost, he caused the tips of his fingers to meet with a very meticulous exactitude. 'In one of your letters to me you made some mention of a fee. I at once replied that I could not give professional advice or undertake professional valuations. It's true that I write books on art, for which I am happy to receive royalties, but otherwise I am an amateur, and I give my services in an amateur capacity.'

'I greatly appreciate it,' the doctor began, but Sir Harry, interrupting, proceeded emphatically:

'Since you have stated frankly that you wish to sell the pictures, I feel I must reiterate what I have already told you by letter. I am not a dealer.'

'I understood that from the beginning,' said Dr. Sandilands. 'But naturally before I attempt to dispose of them—'

'I buy works of art,' Sir Harry's round and relentless voice went on, 'solely for my gratification as a collector. I can certainly recommend you to dealers, I may say the foremost art dealers in London, but only if what you have to sell is of a quality to justify my recommendation. My opinion will be given with absolute candour, and it is one which I fancy will carry a little weight. But in no circumstances would I accept a fee, nor, even if I were able to certify that your pictures are what you believe them to be, would any question of my personal gain arise.'

Dr. Sandilands murmured again his deep sense of obligation.

'And now that we all know where we stand'—Sir Harry's tone suddenly dropped to one much less admonitory—'let me see these remarkable pictures of yours.'

'I have brought a list of them,' said the doctor, handing him a paper. 'I won't trouble you as yet with our reasons for thinking they belonged to the Medici family before 1494 because we are all agreed that you ought to decide first whether they are genuine. If you come to the conclusion, after seeing them, that they are as old as they seem to be, you will want to know more about them, and we have quite an impressive array of data.'

'Data, my dear Dr. Sandilands!' Sir Harry, who had just risen, drew himself up abruptly to his full height. 'How can you have data about the pictures when you don't even know yet that they are genuine?'

Out of sheer pity for her father, Beatrix broke her unusually long silence. 'It isn't *real* data,' she said conciliatingly, 'just some ideas of a friend of ours who's been delving into a lot of books and things.'

Dr. Sandilands felt somewhat disloyal in letting Beatrix refer thus slightingly to the ardent and ingenious researches of Stephanie du Plessis, but it would be time to speak of those when, and if, the oracle whose wisdom he had invoked pronounced a favourable judgment. To confront a specialist of Sir Harry's prestige with a quantity of extraneous material which was only significant if the paintings themselves were significant would be simply to antagonize him. This much Sir Harry showed at once by his reaction to Beatrix's words.

'Ideas derived from books—even my books—are of little avail when it comes to taking upon oneself the immense responsibility of saying "This is, or this is not, the genuine article!" For that, nothing will do but

long years of experience —experience of handling the work of masters
and the work of fakers and imitators.'

'That's what I've been saying all along,' Beatrix responded warmly;
and the statement, if not literally accurate, was true enough in
substance: her attitude towards Stephanie's pretensions as an art critic
had scarcely wavered from its original scepticism.

'Without experience of the most practical kind,' Sir Harry was
encouraged to continue, 'you may learn all the books in the British
Museum by heart and still be completely unqualified—no, no, that is
an exaggeration—and still be very poorly qualified to judge whether
a certain canvas is from the hand of a certain master or one of his
disciples or an honest copyist or a forger.'

He stood in a forensic posture and for a moment Dr. Sandilands
feared he intended to hold forth at some length, as was clearly his
habit. But as if realizing the hopeless weight of his listeners' ignorance,
he turned abruptly and said in his lighter manner:

'Well, sir, now to open this Pandora's box of yours and see what
comes out of it!'

Dr. Sandilands' hand was not perfectly steady as he found the key
in his pocket and inserted it in the lock. It was not merely that he was
overwhelmed with Sir Harry Maximer and his formidably tasteful
and distinguished room: he had been in an exhausted state of nerves
before his arrival, for, being less sceptical than Beatrix, he had known
the disturbing tremors of hope as well as the alternating phases of
pessimism.

For weeks Mrs. du Plessis had kept him at the secret forced labour
of building castles in the air, castles in which his children were provided
for, his old age rendered smooth und easy, and the most pathetic of
his elderly patients supplied with comforts in memory of Mrs. Hovenden. Then, just when he might be enjoying the sight of the new carpets
(chosen, of course, by Beatrix) or handing Mrs. du Plessis a fine gift in
a jewel box, the whole structure would come crumbling abjectly down,
and he would remember that he had nothing at all to go upon but fragments of evidence, perhaps quite misleading, collected by a headstrong
young woman from Rhodesia who had jumped to a wild conclusion.

Though the present occasion was an ordeal, he was glad, very glad,
that at last a competent authority was to adjudicate. Disappointment
would be painful but would relieve him at any rate from the struggle to
suppress those stealthily growing hopes of his. However hard he had

toiled to uproot them, the energetic Stephanie toiled harder planting them afresh, and with assiduous green fingers she would raise another crop. He no sooner seemed to have convinced himself finally that the whole business was a fantasy, an error, a sheer impossibility, than she came along with some newly unearthed fact to nourish and sustain her irrepressible theory.

Since the night of her 'discovery' she had devoted every hour of her leisure, and perhaps some hours when she should not have been at leisure, to her painstaking inquiry into the fate of the treasures dispersed from the Medici Palace four and a half centuries before. Every library from which it was in her power to obtain books had its resources taxed to the uttermost so that she might sift a mass of information on the nature of those treasures and ransack the biographies of Renaissance masters for descriptions of works known to be lost; until little by little and not without many a setback, she had reached a position where she claimed to have identified five of the Hovenden paintings, and was more than ever convinced that the remainder could in the course of time be traced to Florentine sources.

She had readily agreed that before their genuineness could be established they must be submitted to technical tests beyond her skill, but she was determined that no one else should bring off the great coup of demonstrating their provenance. The doctor could not bear to think of her feelings if the verdict went against her. It was not for his sake alone that his hands quivered as he raised the lid of the trunk and revealed the contents carefully packed with every protection Beatrix had been able to devise.

'I am sorry the ones in the tray are in pieces,' he confessed in embarrassment. 'They are the largest. The lady who is so enthusiastic about these pictures—'

'The one who has been delving into books?' said Sir Harry with a quickness which surprised them both, for he had seemed too intent on his own oration to pay much heed to the turn of Beatrix's phrase.

'Yes. She was anxious that I should have special cases made in which they could be fitted together temporarily, but I didn't want to go to too much expense when it might turn out that the things were worthless—let alone the upheaval we've already had in the house.'

'Quite so,' said Sir Harry, removing the top covering.

'It seems they haven't really been cut up. They've just come apart where the joins were originally. Mrs. du Plessis, the lady I spoke of, thinks one of them is a Botticelli and another is by da Vinci, but that's flying high, I admit.'

'Now daddy, you said you weren't going to try and put any of *those* ideas into Sir Harry's head,' Beatrix interrupted scornfully, observing that the connoisseur's face had frozen into alarming disapproval.

'I'm afraid my head is impenetrable, my dear young lady, to any ideas except those which are conveyed to me by the merits or demerits of an artist's conception and execution, and I am not likely to be influenced by the views of Mrs. This or Mrs. That.'

Dr. Sandilands congratulated himself that he had withheld from this overbearing man the dossier of Mrs. du Plessis' findings, since it was plain that nothing would have exasperated him more.

As if to show how little he was allured by the prospect of Botticellis and Leonardos from Charlton Wells, Sir Harry lifted up the tray, placed it on the floor at some distance, and turned his back on it. Then he extracted from the trunk the first of the smaller works, a Madonna and Child, which he carried over to the window. For some minutes he silently examined it, holding it, now at arm's length, now unpainted side uppermost, his face expressionless: then he laid it on the window-seat and came back to the trunk for another panel, pausing by his desk to ring the bell.

This time he had taken the profile portrait of a young woman which it had fallen to Beatrix's lot to wash.

'It's got a bad crack in it,' said Beatrix, 'but that could be repaired, couldn't it? I mean, if it was worth it,' she added to show that there was no undue presumption.

'If it was worth it—oh, very probably.'

The secretary now entered, holding her shorthand book.

'Ah, yes, Mrs. Rose, please stand here! I want you to hold this curtain right away from the window. We need light.'

After a prolonged inspection of the profile in the fullest light he could bring to bear on it, he looked up with an agreeable smile of apology. 'I'm sorry this is such a slow business. Nothing to what it can be though—eh, Mrs. Rose?'

'No, Sir Harry.'

'We could really leave the trunk here for you to go through at your leisure,' the doctor suggested. 'If the things are good, I shall have to sell them in London in any case. If they're no good, perhaps you would very kindly get them sent back to Charlton Wells at my expense.'

Sir Harry, without at once replying to this proposal, set the portrait aside and lifted up a protective cloth which had been made from one of Mrs. Hovenden's cambric chemises, gazing impassively down on what lay beneath it.

'We shall see,' he answered enigmatically, 'we shall see! You can spare an hour or so now, I hope?'

'The Pullman leaves at five forty-five, and we must pick up our luggage at Trapp's Hotel.'

'Ah! That'll give us as much time as we'll need, I dare say. Would you hold that curtain a little further over, Mrs. Rose?'

He immersed himself in the study of a canvas which seemed to give him what Dr. Sandilands hoped was pleasure but Beatrix thought was amusement. 'And what did your friend, Mrs.—I didn't catch the name—what did she say about this? To what great master's hand did she ascribe it?'

'I don't recall that she mentioned anyone in particular,' The doctor wished he had not uttered a single word about Mrs. du Plessis and her opinions. It was absurd to have done so: he could see that now in the presence of the authority that Sir Harry seemed to exude like an aura and of Sir Harry's pictures that were quite as splendid, even to their rich gilt frames, as pictures in a public gallery.

'You told me, I think, in one of your letters that you had not shown these things to anyone outside your home circle and this Mrs.—Mrs.—?'

'Du Plessis. No. I've had to be careful about that. The local press would be printing half a column in a trice if I let them get hold of anything. Then the Elderfield papers might take it up. It's not that I'm anyone in particular, but the doings of doctors are always regarded as news in the region of a big watering-place, and that sort of thing can be very awkward.'

'Daddy would never hear the end of it,' Beatrix amplified helpfully, 'if the story got about all round the town and then the whole thing fell to the ground with a loud bump.'

'A very wise attitude.' Sir Harry strolled over to his desk for a magnifying glass, and through it gazed long and earnestly at the faces and hands in the picture. Dr. Sandilands wished he would offer some comment that would relieve the suspense, but he only put another of his questions—questions asked, the doctor considered, in the same spirit as those of a dentist who endeavours to distract his patient's mind from the drill and the probe.

'And you didn't attempt to get a reaction from any of the local dealers? There is no one, of course, of the slightest consequence in Charlton Wells, but Elderfield contains a few people who imagine they know something.'

'We thought it would be a mistake to approach dealers until we had a report that was perfectly disinterested.'

'It never occurred to you to try the Director of the Art Gallery at Elderfield, young Arnold Bayley? He's inexperienced but not altogether a fool.'

The doctor had no doubt that he was making another of his damaging admissions as he rejoined scrupulously: 'Well yes, we did try to see him, as a matter of fact, but he'd just gone away for his holidays.'

'So you decided to consult me instead?' said Sir Harry dryly.

Beatrix came again to her father's rescue: 'No, no, it wasn't like that!' Her pretty smile was all appeasement. 'We didn't want to bother you until we'd made sure we shouldn't just be wasting your time.'

Sir Harry impassively took another picture.

'We would have waited for this Mr. Bayley to come back before writing to you,' she went on, 'but the house was so horribly littered with pictures, and it was all so unsettling, I couldn't bear it any longer. I made daddy write. We've got to get it over one way or another.'

Sir Harry produced a not unsympathetic muttering, but his attention seemed to have wandered, and after a moment he said: 'Mrs. Rose, it must be exceedingly boring for our visitors to sit and watch me doing this. I think they might like to see the drawing-room, and the medallions, and the—the little Primitive I haven't hung yet.'

It was apparent that their absence would be a relief to him, and, though his manner had so far been dampening, Dr. Sandilands hoped this was a good symptom: he had perhaps reached the point of wishing to scrutinize the pictures without the necessity of making conversation. The one in hand happened to be the supposed portrait of Lorenzo the Magnificent by which Mrs. du Plessis set such store.

The doctor was on the verge of pointing out the resemblance, which by now she had made familiar to him, and the highly interesting bust of Piero de' Medici in the background, but, recollecting the icy reception that had been accorded to his mention of Botticelli and Leonardo da

Vinci, he pulled himself up and submissively followed Mrs. Rose from the room with his eager words unspoken.

The drawing-room tended to depress him. It was nothing less than a private art gallery with some sumptuous furniture. The pictures, which were all in the most superb condition, artfully hung, and lighted by special devices, bore little gilt plaques with such names as Bellini, Correggio, Titian, Perugino—names which, as he was well aware, stood for art at its most expensive and rarefied height. And both he and Beatrix were profoundly impressed to recognize that more than one of these treasures was a known masterpiece, reproduced in books and on calendars. After the sight of such splendours as these, it was nearly as hard for Dr. Sandilands as for his daughter to go on sharing any vestige of Mrs. du Plessis' faith in their own shabby and anonymous hoard.

Mrs. Rose acted as guide and entertained them with anecdotes about the acquisitions. This one had been a bargain, obtained for a modest three thousand pounds because Sir Harry alone had been willing to back his belief, when it was sold with the contents of Heminge Park, that it was really what it purported to be. That one, on the other hand, had come from the famous Caravia Collection, and Sir Harry had been obliged to off-load a large number of other items in order to make up the huge price it had fetched at Christie's. Here was the pretty little Luini which had been left to him by his friend, the great art critic, John Rennick, and here was the Spanish painting of doubtful attribution about which they had probably read in *The Burlington*, where it had been the subject of a long controversy.

The admission that they never saw *The Burlington* and the inward knowledge that they had never heard of Luini or the Caravia Collection or John Rennick completed their sense of unworthiness. By the time they had been shown the cases of medallions, a side-line of Sir Harry's, and the Primitive triptych to obtain which he had recently flown to Sicily and given the Treasury no end of trouble, and the portions of frescoes which appeared so museum-like at the top of the staircase, they were humbler even than they had been on their arrival.

They filed into the library, when Mrs. Rose had ascertained that the investigation was over, as if they themselves and not their pictures were on trial and they fully expected to be found guilty. Beatrix's demeanour was more jaunty than her father's because she had never allowed herself to fall under the du Plessis spell, but Dr. Sandilands could not forget the tempting visions by which he had been seduced—

the new motor-car, the bedroom suite for Linda, the allowance for his son Geoffrey who was to begin his medical studies next term—and he looked shamefaced.

Sir Harry Maximer received them with his pleasantest smile, which came near to redeeming the plainness and shapelessness of his broad face.

'I've ordered some tea,' he said. 'It will be here in a moment. I don't think you need bother to stay, Mrs. Rose. I know you're busy.'

He was packing up, as he spoke, the separate portions of the four and a half Muses, not failing to wrap them in the linen sheets with which Beatrix had conscientiously protected their surface though she was sure they had been grossly overrated by Stephanie. With equal care, he had refilled the trunk and now restored the tray.

'Please sit down,' he commanded them kindly when they offered to help him. 'It's all as good as done.'

He waited till his secretary had gone from the room and the tea had been brought and handed round before he made any reference to the object of their visit, and then his tone was as gentle as before it had been arrogant.

'Dr. Sandilands, a man of your profession must know all too well that there are moments in life when it is not pleasant to have to speak the truth.'

The doctor discovered that there still remained one sensitive green shoot of hope which could not be crushed without pain. He nodded, incapable at that instant of speaking a word, for the pain was surprisingly acute.

'The only consolation I have in performing this very disagreeable duty is that you appear—you *both* appear to be sensible and level-headed people who haven't been building too rashly on anything you may have been led to imagine about these pictures.'

Again the doctor bowed his head, and Beatrix, to break the tension, said abruptly: 'You mean they're no good?'

'No, Miss Sandilands, not precisely that. They're good, some of them . . . well, fairly good of their kind. But they're practically without value, and I think their value is the point at issue, isn't it? They're imitations—yes, imitations in the styles of various Florentine masters. And some of them are copies, frank undisguised copies, made probably in the eighteenth century. Can I give you some more tea?'

'So much for Stephanie du Plessis,' said Beatrix, handing over her cup. 'Didn't I say from that first evening, daddy, she was too clever by half?'

Sir Harry took no notice of this. 'I wish I'd been able to tell you what you wanted to hear, though there were a million chances against that! and to be candid, I feared the worst from the minute you brought up that awful Medici proposition. . . Oh, do forgive me, Dr. Sandilands! What you wrote was in perfectly good faith, I know, but it happens that the Medici are a kind of King Charles's head to—dare I say!—the half-baked, the would-be critics who have the little learning which can be such a dangerous thing. Lorenzo the Magnificent in particular seems to have quite a hypnotic effect on them.'

Beatrix broke in with a small staccato noise which fully conveyed her views of those who cherished fancies about Lorenzo the Magnificent.

'There is a portrait here,' Sir Harry went on, flicking his finger towards the Saratoga, 'which your friend, the lady with the Huguenot name, undoubtedly used as a starting-point for her theory.'

'No,' said the doctor, recovering himself, 'the starting-point was a manuscript that was found with the pictures, a book stamped with the Medici arms. It's the Odes of Anacreon in Greek, incomplete I'm afraid.'

'A manuscript?' Sir Harry seemed momentarily nonplussed, but after a brief pause while he sliced a Madeira cake, he continued: 'My dear sir, the faking of manuscripts has been a widespread practice, like the faking of everything else that could be sold for money. But even if it's genuine, it may have been put with the pictures merely to suggest exactly what it has suggested. The portrait is certainly a fake and a very effective one. If you could find some collector with more money than brains—which wouldn't be at all difficult—you might dispose of it quite profitably.'

'That's out of the question if it's not genuine,' the doctor said stiffly.

Sir Harry laughed. 'I'm joking, Dr. Sandilands. You surely know my reputation. I'm the worst enemy of fraudulence in every shape and form, and my campaign against the various kinds of trickery which, I'm ashamed to say, are so prevalent in the art world, has made me scores of enemies. Naturally you will not dream of trying to pass any of these spurious pictures off as genuine. If you tell the truth, that they are eighteenth-century concoctions which were probably foisted on to some tourist in Italy who wanted to bring home trophies, then you might get a hundred pounds, or so, for them.'

'A hundred pounds!' Dr. Sandilands brightened a little. After a report so destructive he had not expected to hear that his contemptible property was worth a single penny. 'That's at any rate substantially more than they cost me,' he said wonderingly. 'Who would pay it?'

'Someone could be found, I dare say. There are dealers who would furbish them up—the best of them anyhow, and put them in showy frames, and find homes for them at a good profit, which they would thoroughly deserve in view of the trouble they'd have to take.'

'Could you—?' Dr. Sandilands began, but before he could frame the words, Sir Harry had replied to them:

'No, doctor, I can give no recommendation for a transaction of that type. It's in a different sphere—a different sphere of action altogether.'

Dr. Sandilands thought of the august decorations in the drawing-room and was abashed; but Sir Harry proceeded courteously:

'I fancy you'd do better in your own district than here where we're deluged with this kind of thing. It's a mistake to bring everything to London. You're a man of position in Charlton Wells, and no one will dare to make you such a low offer there as they would where you're quite unknown.' He rose and pressed the bell. 'I'm going to order my car to take you to the station.' And as they both earnestly demurred, he insisted: 'No refusal! It's the least I can do after breaking such bad news to you.'

'It hasn't surprised me at all,' said Beatrix truthfully and almost with satisfaction. 'If you knew what I've gone through with this friend of ours hopping, round those miserable pictures like a cat on hot bricks!'

'Is she supposed to be an expert?' Sir Harry's inflexion was the same as Beatrix herself had used, asking the same question several weeks before.

'She's a Rhodesian who never came over here till she was grown up, and she's only about thirty now, but she thinks because her father taught in an Art School—'

She was interrupted by the entrance of Mrs. Rose, and while Sir Harry formulated his instructions for the chauffeur, the doctor took the opportunity to remonstrate mildly: 'Mrs. du Plessis will be more disappointed than we are, Beatrix. She wanted to make our fortune for us.'

'Well, she's given us a trip to London—at our own expense.'

He sighed. 'It was remarkably convincing, the way she worked it all out. And Sir Harry himself says the portrait of Lorenzo is very well done.'

Sir Harry turned back to them. 'Yes, it's well done; a number of them are well done. But oh! if you knew how well these things *can* be done and *have* been done for hundreds of years! Would you like to read a book on fakes? I'll lend you one to while away your journey.' He ran his hand along one of the bookshelves and extracted a volume. 'This is guaranteed to bring comfort to anyone who's been deceived by a bogus picture or a bogus anything else. You'll find the greatest museums and galleries in the world have been taken in; and your eighteenth-century stuff is particularly deceptive.'

Both Dr. Sandilands and his daughter agreed, as they followed their unwieldy luggage to the train at King's Cross, that, intimidating though he was and could not help being even when trying to be amiable, Sir Harry was fundamentally a person of the utmost good nature. This had been revealed unmistakably in the way he had behaved towards them when the pictures had turned out, from his point of view, worthless and without interest. They had, after all, wasted his afternoon and inflicted on him the embarrassment of having to make a very unwelcome communication, but he had treated them as considerately—of this they felt sure—as if they had really brought the trunkful of masterpieces of Stephanie's romantic imagination.

Dr. Sandilands read Otto Kurz's book on fakes nearly all the way to Charlton Wells, and succumbed by degrees to the conviction that he had probably never seen a genuine work of art in his life, except 'Snowbound in a Yorkshire Dale', the marble pierrette, the guardian angel, and those other items in the Hovenden collection which only a demented forger would have desired to reproduce.

FOUR

FOR SEVERAL minutes after the departure of his visitors, Sir Harry stood by the window reading with a smile the foolscap sheet on which had been set out the contents of the Saratoga trunk. The majority of the pictures were described in general terms with only such indications of their subjects and special features as might have been made by Dr. Sandilands or his daughter from their own observation; but towards the end of the list there appeared, in another handwriting, particularities which caused Sir Harry to raise his eyebrows.

'18. Portrait apparently of Pius II (Piccolomini)—perhaps made on his visit to Florence in 1460 when he stayed at the Medici Palace. . . .

'19. Portrait of the Emperor Johannes Paleologus when he attended the Council of Florence in 1439. The dress is the same as in the Gozzoli fresco. (If this is really by Masolino da Panicale, it must ante-date Gozzoli's work by some years.)'

The sentence in brackets brought Sir Harry's eyebrows down into a deep frown. 'Masolino da Panicale!' he repeated almost audibly. 'How in the world does he come into it?'

The character of his frown changed from one of disapprobation to one of perplexity. He folded the paper and tucked it into his breast pocket. Then, still frowning, he took the slightly unusual course of putting through a telephone call without troubling his secretary, and this although, on his first two attempts, the number was engaged.

Hearing at last a voice instantly recognizable, a quiet reluctant voice pitched on a low debilitated note, he inquired without wasting words:

'Are you going to be at home for the next hour?'

'Sir Harry, is it?' The voice seemed to struggle towards a livelier key. 'Yes, I'll be here.'

'Alone?'

'Yes, no one's likely to come in now. I can close the shop.'

'Very well. I'll be round at once. I'll jump into a taxi.'

Replacing the receiver, Sir Harry pulled open two of the numerous small drawers in his elegant but not unpractical Regency desk. These released the fastening, otherwise inviolable, of a chequered panel, behind which a bundle of pound notes was always kept in readiness for cash transactions. He put it in his pocket. At that moment Mrs. Rose came to the door.

'Is there anything you'd like me to do before I go, Sir Harry?'

He replied pleasantly, closing the drawers: 'Thank you, Mrs. Rose. If you'd very kindly ring up—No, no, don't bother! I'm too punctilious. What does it matter if one misses a cocktail party?'

'You're probably the chief attraction,' she remarked as a mere statement of fact.

'Come, come! Dame Bridget's drawing-room is a lions' den!' But the reproach, so briskly flattering, had its effect, and on his way to the lobby to fetch his hat, he called back at her: 'Well, I suppose I must try to turn up, if you think I ought.'

'Shall I 'phone and say you'll be late?'

'No, that would be making myself *too* important.'

If Sir Harry did not precisely jump into the cab, he entered it with a more springy step than the sight of his large and heavy figure would have suggested, and, giving the driver an address in Islington, sat back in profound but clearly genial meditation, as unaffected by the bustle of the roads and the hazards of the traffic as if he were floating on a cloud—as indeed he felt himself to be. The antique shop, more likely to be described by its customers as a junk shop, at the intersection of two dingy and undignified streets where the taxi ultimately pulled up, might have been the gateway to the Elysian fields, so buoyant was Sir Harry's tread as he approached the door.

But as, behind the name *E. Quiller* painted diagonally on the glass panel, he saw E. Quiller in person moving towards him from the shadows of bureaux and book-cases piled one above another, he toned down his elated expression and assumed one that was cool and business-like.

The door being unlocked to admit him, he took a path to which he was evidently well accustomed through a grove of pedestals, gilded mirror frames, and carved overmantels, and passed beyond another glass door into a small untidy office at the back of the shop. Here he stood for a moment, his eye wandering in an abstracted manner over the walls, on which, for convenience rather than artistic effect, a number of pictures had been hung.

'I'm afraid there's nothing to interest you, Sir Harry,' sighed the weary voice that had spoken on the telephone. 'I haven't had anything worth bothering you about for a long time.'

'I quite gathered that.' Sir Harry was bland yet firm. 'If you'd had anything, you would have offered it. I look at pictures from force of habit, wherever I see them.'

He sat down on a cretonne-covered chair which had been rapidly swept clear of a pile of books and a Spanish guitar, and clasping each knee with a big, unshapely hand, asked benevolently: 'How are you, Quiller? How are you doing?'

'You mean the business? It's poor.' Quiller dropped as if with fatigue into the swivel chair which belonged to his roll-topped desk. 'Not only this business,' he added defensively. 'The trade's just generally slack wherever you turn. Well, you know that even better than I do.'

'I don't see why I should,' said Sir Harry with a slightly injured air.

Quiller lowered his eyelids behind the thick lenses of his rimless glasses. 'It's just that you have such a good grasp of business.' His voice seemed to be dragged up, resisting, from the pit of his stomach. 'I don't know anyone whose opinion on a business matter would be worth more than yours.'

'And I don't know anyone whose assistance is worth more than yours,' Maximer responded handsomely. 'It's your assistance I require at this moment, my friend—your assistance in a very urgent affair.'

'Anything I can do—' Quiller passed his hand over his thin face in a gesture which conveyed that he made away with all thoughts that could distract him from Sir Harry's communication.

It began with a brusque query. 'Are you free to leave London for a few days?'

'I don't see why not, if my sister will look after the shop.'

'Your invaluable sister! How useful to be able to depend on her! Would you say you were known at all, Quiller, in Charlton Wells?'

'Known? To the trade you mean? I might be—a little. I've done a bit of buying there in my time.'

'Good. That may turn out an advantage. There's a man, a doctor, there who has some pictures I want. It's a question of your going up to buy them at the first possible moment. No mention of me, of course— not the faintest breath of a hint that I come into it anywhere.'

'Naturally. That's understood.' If there was any surprise in Quiller's inflexion it was only that the other had troubled to caution him.

'I know you're discreet, my dear fellow, but this is something exceptional, not just an ordinary case of keeping the price down. You could get the whole lot for a hundred pounds, or less if you were to haggle.'

The listener sat back and slowly folded one arm over the other, nodding attentively but without the eagerness of curiosity.

'Not that I want you to haggle, or at any rate no more than you must to make it convincing. I'd like him to feel he was getting a fair price. He's a nice old man.'

Quiller's myopic eyes blinked a little incredulously. Then he bestirred his languid voice to ask, 'How do I come into contact, so to speak, with these pictures—this doctor?'

'That's for you to work out. As long as I'm not involved, you can contrive any approach you like. It shouldn't be too difficult in a parochial town like Charlton Wells. You're a dealer. You happen to be scouring round the Elderfield district and you pick up some piece of gossip—genuine gossip if you can manage it—that puts you on the scent.'

'You'll give me all you can to go upon?'

'Certainly.' The grudging tone hardly accorded with the emphatic word. Sir Harry always detested the moment when he was obliged to lay bare the private beauties of his plans, beauties so liable to be gloated over in an unseemly spirit by profane eyes. Yet for Quiller the truth must undoubtedly be unveiled since without it he might make some blunder; and fortunately he had an impassive, in some ways almost indifferent, attitude that made it less objectionable to confide in him than in a more demonstrative man.

Sir Harry, whose good-natured actions always seemed to bring their own reward, had never had occasion to regret giving Quiller the backing to set up a modest antique shop after he had lost his job at Mandell & Strood's. Most men who had known, as he knew, that the great firm of auctioneers had found their employee out in an attempt at peculation would have declined, uncharitably, to enter into business dealings with him; but Maximer's ability to judge character was not inferior to his skill as a critic of pictures, and he had summed up Quiller as one of those individuals who became rash only under the stress of violent and unwonted emotion, such emotion as will not be aroused more than once or twice in a mature man's career.

The infatuation was not only over, it had left a powerful revulsion. For it happened that Quiller, to induce his wife to divorce him, had made a crippling agreement as to alimony, and that by the time the divorce was absolute, the object of his sacrifice had married someone else. The fact that he had so mismanaged his personal affairs, dooming himself to be permanently hard up even after Sir Harry had installed him in the Islington shop, was no disadvantage to his benefactor. His gratitude was buttressed by his needs, and he had proved an ingenious and loyal ally. No one else was allowed to suspect so much about the activities on which at least a large part of the Maximer Collection had been built—built all the more brilliantly because a façade of impeccable respectability protected the operations.

Not that Sir Harry, even under seal of secrecy, made any frank admission of malpractices. He spoke of rescuing works of art from unworthy hands, of profiting occasionally from fakes—well, not exactly fakes, but things that fell short of being genuine—in order to acquire funds for the purchase and preservation of masterpieces. But each was perfectly aware how much consternation the knowledge of such trans-actions would have inspired among Sir Harry's friends and admirers in the art world. Quiller's tact made him the most valued of the few, the precious half-dozen, scattered far and wide and all unknown to each other, to whom Sir Harry could turn for really private services.

Nevertheless, it was not agreeable to come as near as he now must to laying his cards nakedly on the table. To gain time while he decided how much it was essential to reveal, he said: 'First, I'd better give you the name and address,' and dictated them very slowly from Dr. Sandi-lands' writing-paper.

'There are sixteen pictures,' he began with a sigh which quivered both with joy and anxiety. 'You must get them all, Quiller.'

'Is there anything to check them by?'

'You're very astute.' Sir Harry's gratification was tempered by his ardent longing to keep to himself the information he must ultimately impart. 'I don't think for a moment you need fear that Dr. Sandilands will try to impose on you, but perhaps it would be a safeguard, in case of outside interference, to have a list of some sort. Before we part I shall dictate one to you.'

Quiller repressed a very faint and languid smile. Sir Harry's precau-tions against involving himself were so assiduous that not a scrap of his handwriting, except on matters that might have been investigated by the whole world, was in the possession of even his trustiest associate.

'You will also need money,' he continued. 'Cash, of course, from me to you, though there can be no objection to your paying Dr. Sandilands by cheque or any way you please. Your dealings with him will be abso-lutely open and above board.'

Quiller nodded, though not without a shade of confusion.

'Here are two hundred pounds.' Sir Harry took the bundle of notes from his breast pocket. 'Spend about fifty in the town to give colour to the idea that you're picking things up here and there. Whatever you buy, you can take into stock here for your own benefit.'

'Thank you, Sir Harry.'

'Pay your expenses out of the money, get the pictures for—say—a hundred and twenty, and bring them back yourself as personal luggage, and I'll see you don't, as the saying is, go short.'

'Suppose, after all, he won't part with them for a hundred and twenty?'

'My dear fellow, didn't I say you could get them for less if you haggled? I could have bought them myself not two hours ago for practically anything I might have offered.'

Quiller scorned to appear inquisitive, but he went so far in his increasing bewilderment as to scratch his forehead.

'It's no use making a mystery of it,' said Maximer, and in his effort not to show how much he would have preferred to do so, he became quite expansive. 'If I'd bought them myself, I couldn't have done anything at all with them afterwards. My hands would have been tied. Because, you see, having said they were fakes, I could hardly have gone back on it later and sold them, or even established them in my own collection.'

'And they're not fakes?'

'No, they're superlatively the real thing,' He laughed with unwonted nervousness, perceiving for the first time that his coup—so tremendous if he were to bring it off—might be classed by those who did not understand his praiseworthy motives as fraudulence on a rather considerable scale. He was not afraid; he had abounding faith in his own cleverness, but he was excited and a little overwhelmed at the daring of the steps he had already so coolly achieved, like a man who looks down from somewhere near a mountain top and wonders how he has succeeded, without losing his head, in scaling such a height.

He plunged, dizzy and exhilarated, into further confidence. 'If I had said they were the real thing, I should have been placing them—most of them—hopelessly out of my own reach. With extraordinary presence of mind, as I feel you'll agree, Quiller, when you've heard the story, I pronounced the whole lot to be—not worthless (that would have been too drastic)—but worth very little.'

Thus committed, he told as much as the other must inevitably know of the approach from the doctor and the outcome of their interview. There was no sense in trying to disguise the nature of the treasure. Quiller could not buy the pictures without looking at them, and though far less expert a judge than his patron, he was assuredly capable, after his twelve years' experience at Mandell & Strood's, of recognizing an important old painting when he saw one. If he was to be used at all, he must be trusted, there was nothing else for it. The only precaution Sir Harry took was to avoid mentioning the names of any particular Masters whose hands he believed he had traced: or to raise the question—as yet doubtful in his own mind—of Medici provenance.

Quiller listened with his usual stolid calm, but at the end his questions were more searching than he had ever ventured to make them hitherto, for the sense of his obligations usually stifled in him anything that could be construed as criticism.

'Your brain certainly worked quickly, Sir Harry—it always does—but don't you think these things are going to be pretty hard to handle?'

'Undoubtedly.'

'I mean, will you gain much advantage from not having bought them there and then?'

'My dear Quiller, I fancy you have hardly followed me.' Sir Harry's authoritative voice was suave but pained. 'If I had told this doctor and his ignorant but decidedly business-like daughter what the pictures really are, I would have been inflating their price to something beyond my means, beyond the means of any of our English collectors nowadays. Having, on the contrary, said they were of no consequence, I couldn't very well bargain for them myself.'

'That's true, you were in a cleft stick there. But I still don't see exactly . . . If you put them in your own collection, you'll have to keep them dark. If you sell them, well, you can't do anything to boost them beforehand. The sort of build-up you know so well how to give an item before you put it on the market—that's out of the question in a case like this.'

Maximer was tempted to tell the presumptuous fool to mind his own business, but realizing that this would scarcely bring out his best exertions on the mission before him, he replied instead with a disarming smile: 'Don't disturb yourself on my account. I have my plans, and in any event, there's one, one little pearl, that would make the whole effort worthwhile even if I had to keep it under lock and key for the rest of my life.'

'It must be a beauty to have that effect on you, Sir Harry. You've seen some pictures in your time.'

'I think I may safely say,' Maximer responded pleasantly, 'that no man living has more reason to trust his judgment in such an instance than I have.'

'You've got it all at your fingers' ends, there's no doubt of that,' Quiller conceded, striving to infuse some vivacity into his enervated tones.

Sir Harry spread out his fingertips and looked at them with complacency, as if he expected to see there some happy manifestation of his great critical abilities.

'I wonder,' Quiller went on, 'how you could risk letting them go off with such a hoard. They might have taken them straight to the nearest junk shop.'

Sir Harry laughed again in open relish of his own nefariousness as he explained how he had hurried the visitors to the station in his car after advising them on lines that suited his purpose but yet must leave him free from the smallest suspicion of personal interest.

'But you're perfectly right,' he added, growing graver, 'in assuming that the pictures are in very real danger unless I can get hold of them at once. You must go North tomorrow at the latest. Dr. Sandilands is feeling foolish and disappointed, and he'll want to wash his hands of the reason. His daughter, who is without the smallest vestige of aesthetic taste in any shape or form, dislikes having what seems to her to be merely a pile of battered panels taking up house room. I told them they might get a hundred pounds for the lot, and they won't lose much time, I'm pretty sure, in putting that to the test.'

'The things might be gone by the time I get there.' Even Quiller, phlegmatic as he was, had entered sufficiently into the spirit of the occasion to instil some urgency into these words.

'I am counting,' said Sir Harry, 'on the fact that a doctor, after leaving his practice, if only for a very short while, has an extra busy day when he gets back. Probably he won't be able to do anything tomorrow, and the next day you'll make contact. The moment you arrive—and by the way, it might be a good idea to arrive from Elderfield and not from London— you start your picking-up tour round the local dealers. You do a bit of buying and you do a bit of chatting. The doctor says nobody in Charlton Wells knows about his pictures, which is all to the good from one point of view; but it's to be hoped that somebody, if it's only a charwoman, has let a few words fall somewhere where you can gather them.'

'Otherwise it's going to be rather difficult to find an excuse for turning up,' said Quiller with a gloomy smile.

'You'll think of something,' Maximer rejoined cheerfully, 'even if you have to parade up and down outside his house crying 'New paintings for old!''

Quiller, who did not understand the allusion, smiled more gloomily still, and Sir Harry encouraged him with, 'Come, my dear fellow, you're always most resourceful! And only think what you'll be doing for the benefit of those who care about Italian art! Who knows what would happen without our intervention? Now I shall be in the most acute suspense till I know how you're faring up in Charlton Wells—'

'Shall I ring you up?'

'No, no, that would be indiscreet. I'll ring *you* up—from a public call box. Where will you stay? Charlton is very full at this season. Perhaps you'd better stay in Elderfield. It's more convincing in any case, and you can easily go to and fro by bus.'

The rest of the interview was devoted to the working out of tactics, and the dictation by Sir Harry of a brief catalogue of the sixteen works. For Quiller the one bright aspect of an embassy he regarded with profound distaste had been the expectation of a few days at the attractive spa; and now that he was commanded to stay in grimy and hideous Elderfield, his last hope of any pleasure in his employment vanished, and he could only look for profit.

Profit and pleasure occupied Sir Harry's mind equally as he strolled out into the cool September evening, and made his way by bus to his cocktail party. It would be a good while before he could expect any return for the trouble and large expense he was now undertaking, but he promised himself a most magnificently rich reward in the years to come. The paintings were worth a fortune. After thirty-five years of specializing in Italian art (for he had worked as a youth at the famous Quattrocento Gallery in Bond Street, and had never ceased to devote himself with all the tenacity of his powerful character to the ambition then formed of excelling in mastery of his subject), he had not needed even the one delicious hour he had spent alone with the treasure to bring him to the conclusion that it was a cache of superb Renaissance works in an exceptional state of preservation.

They would be taken, two or three at a time, to the wonderful craftsman in Paris who did his cleaning and restoring—the man whose inaccessibility during the War had been almost its greatest hardship to Sir Harry—and, at long intervals, those he could bring himself to part with would be sold, one by a highly reputed dealer on Fifty-Seventh Street, New York, another perhaps in Madrid or Rome, another under the hammer at Christie's or Sotheby's in London, yet another, it might be, by private treaty with a Johannesburg magnate or an art gallery in Australia—a series of transactions extending possibly over years and having no apparent connection with one another. The name of Maximer would appear nowhere in them, though his skill would have been used in devious ways to excite the interest that would ensure a proper price. He excelled in contrivances of this kind, and his acquaintance with the circles where valuable works of art change hands extended to seven capitals.

With few exceptions, those who helped him to dispose anonymously or pseudonymously of the masterpieces would be themselves persons of unimpeachable integrity: he was particularly adept at inveigling friends and fellow-collectors into supporting in good faith his most questionable dealings.

As long as he does not visibly belie it, a man will be taken at his own valuation, and Sir Harry Maximer not only claimed in an impressive manner to be a scrupulous critic and an amateur of the purest principles, but he waged an unremitting war on those who indulged in any form of shady dealing or misrepresentation. He had exposed a number of forgeries and false attributions, sometimes at the risk of making enemies in high places; his books were works of notable research; his kindness in assisting promising young scholars could be depended on; his possessions were the envy of connoisseurs. No one, in short, was more completely trusted even by those who found him arrogant and unsympathetic.

The knowledge that he had made money from spurious works and had always taken advantage of ignorance when he could do so without fear of discovery was spread very thinly among those who, being involved with him, were never likely to publish what they had learned.

In planning the future of the windfall from Charlton Wells, he counted happily on the artistic illiteracy of the Sandilands family. It was unlikely that they would keep any record of the pictures sufficiently detailed to enable them to be identified when, after a long lapse of time, they came to light, glorified beyond the recognition of such inexperienced eyes, in distant countries, and with skilfully invented histories. The probability was that neither the doctor nor his daughter was sufficiently alive to what transpired in the world of art ever to hear again about these paintings if they were handled adroitly.

It was a pity, of course, to break up the splendid collection. That was a necessity that weighed upon Sir Harry's conscience. It might well be that the panels had in fact hung in the Medici Palace and been removed together in one of the wars or civic disturbances which loomed so large in Florentine annals. He had not had time as yet to give attention to this theory, dismissed by him as fatuous when the doctor had diffidently mentioned it in his letters; and it was only with reluctance that he considered it now. Reluctance, first, because his vanity as an expert made him extremely resistant to theories that were not originated by himself, and second, because his sanguine visions were suddenly shadowed by a reminder of the one unknown quantity, Mrs. du Plessis.

He perceived that he was foolish not to have found out more about Mrs. du Plessis, for it was clearly she who had filled the humble and unpretending doctor's head with the notion that his pictures were important. She had not been mentioned in any of his letters, but the conversation—from which, preoccupied as he was, he had let nothing escape—had made it evident that, without her promptings, neither Dr. Sandilands nor his sceptical daughter would ever have dreamed of seeking out so great a man as Sir Harry Maximer. It might have been Miss Sandilands who had made her father write, 'to get it over one way or another', but it was their enigmatical friend 'delving into a lot of books' who must, in the first place, have given them the idea. How else could such a prosaic pair have conceived the fancy that their Saratoga trunk held riches beyond the dreams even of a collector's avarice?

A cloud passed over Sir Harry's hitherto beaming face, and he glowered alarmingly at a child kneeling on the seat in front of him. Perhaps, in making his swift and vigorous plan, he had not taken Mrs. du Plessis sufficiently into account.

Then he recalled more precisely the terms in which they had spoken of her, the doctor half-apologetic, his daughter scornful. She was a Rhodesian of about thirty with no qualifications that had succeeded in winning the confidence of Miss Sandilands. That meant nothing, Miss Sandilands being an unimaginative ignoramus, but it did at any rate suggest that her opinions would not be allowed to carry much weight after a famous authority had pronounced against them. And the pictures were not hers, so there was nothing she could do, no claim she could make, even if she should ultimately recognize one in an art gallery or an illustrated paper. Given a quite perfect identification, there would still be no grounds for suspecting fraudulence. Who was to say how many hands the works might pass through after the obscure dealer from Islington had acquired them? The worst Sir Harry could be accused of would be making a blunder.

He brightened again. Mrs. du Plessis was negligible. It might even be that her Medici attribution was a fluke based, not on knowledge, but on a naïve hit-or-miss romanticism. The scowl faded from his brow, and to the little boy in the next seat, who had been watching him with consternation, he became again a jolly old fat man.

He was thinking with surpassing delight of the portrait of Lorenzo the Magnificent, and of something even better, something in which he believed he had perceived quite unmistakably the rare and glorious hand of Masaccio.

FIVE

STEPHANIE du Plessis had been so profoundly, so overwhelmingly convinced of the genuineness of the Hovenden pictures that an adverse verdict had simply not seemed possible. A celebrated expert like Sir Harry Maximer must see that they were the real thing and would say so; and after he had produced his erudite judgment, based on a thorough and doubtless lengthy inspection, and taking into consideration all kinds of technicalities that were beyond her, Dr. Sandilands would send him the precious dossier containing the facts, small in themselves but marvellously sustaining one another, which she had garnered to support her belief that the hoard was a lost treasure of the Medici. She had often imagined his joy at the discovery, a scholar's joy, selfless and exalted.

The announcement in Dr. Sandilands' letter, brought to her by Linda's hand the morning after his return from London, fell upon her like a thunderbolt. Deprived of everything she had striven for during two months of the most intense activity, found guilty of having deluded those she had intended only to serve, she stood transfixed at the library counter where the letter had been delivered, and even Linda, who, though good-natured, was not a particularly sensitive girl, could guess that of the four of them, she was the hardest hit.

'It's awfully disappointing, isn't it?' said Linda, her voice soothing and friendly. 'I couldn't help hoping, though I told myself lots of times it was too good to be true.' Tactfully recalling that she must not lay too much stress on their dashed hopes, she added: 'Daddy says it's worse for you than for us really, because you'd got it all worked out so beautifully.'

'I can't believe it!' cried Stephanie, her eyes fixed fiercely on vacancy. And then: 'What's more, I *don't* believe it!' She turned and went about her library tasks, which at that hour of the morning were such as could be performed almost automatically, and this was fortunate, for her thoughts were entirely occupied with the problem of how a man of Sir Harry Maximer's standing could have made so appalling a mistake. Having recovered from the paralysing effect of the first shock, a complete and perfect contempt for Sir Harry's egregious pronouncement flooded her mind, and her belief in the pictures, which formerly had been based on aesthetic perception and a series of reasonable deductions, now renewed itself with the force of a religious conviction. Throughout the long and happy weeks of July and August, all her by no means feeble intellectual powers had been engrossed in reconstructing the probable history of those sixteen paintings, and she had built an edifice that would not crumble at one stroke even if that were delivered by so powerful a hand as Sir Harry Maximer's.

In one of the quiet interludes that gave a weekday morning in the Public Library an air of almost cloistral seclusion, she approached Linda, who was working at a card-index cabinet.

'I don't see from your father's letter,' she began, 'how Sir Harry could have spent more than an hour and a half at the most looking at the pictures.'

'Yes,' said Linda gently, 'but he's a most terrific expert, isn't he? I mean, he wouldn't need so long as just anybody.' Beatrix had prophesied that Stephanie would take it badly, and Linda, who had grown in her idle and casual way attached to her colleague, hoped that she was not going to make the prophecy true.

But her next utterance was ominous. 'Linda, I know your father was determined to abide by whatever Sir Harry told him, but you must—oh, my dear, you *must* persuade him somehow to get another opinion.'

'He won't, I'm sure of that.'

'He would if it were a matter of life and death for one of his patients.'

'But that's his profession,' said Linda reasonably. 'The pictures are so out of his line, once a specialist has told him they're no good, well, that's that! He's had it.'

'Linda, if only I could persuade you—'

'My dear Steph [so far had their intimacy progressed in recent weeks] you could persuade *me* of anything. You know what an infant in arms I am! But Daddy and Beatrix are another proposition.'

'I realize Beatrix has been sceptical from the first'—Stephanie by an effort infused regret into her sigh rather than the irritation she felt—'but don't you think if I went to see your father . . . ?'

'Honestly, I shouldn't if I were you! He's frightfully anxious now to forget about the pictures. They've been a bit of a strain on the poor old darling, you know. And as for Beatrix, she can't wait to get them out of the house.'

'Out of the house!' Stephanie's consternation was quite embarrassing to Linda, who was aware how much her father was longing to be left in peace now that the worst was known.

'Didn't he tell you?' she said lightly. 'He's going to take them down to Morris as soon as he gets a spare minute and try to sell them.'

'Morris? Who's Morris?'

'The man who has a picture shop on King's Parade. You know—on the next corner to the Pump Room.'

'Good God!' Her vehemence made Linda start. 'That's the shop of the Carousing Cardinals.'

Linda smiled with slow comprehension. 'Of course, he's awfully behind the times, and Daddy doesn't care for him much anyway, but he's more likely to buy our things than anyone else in Charlton Wells. Between ourselves, Daddy's heard that lots of his Old Masters aren't much good really.'

Stephanie was silent, for the prospect that the Hovenden collection would pass into the hands of so vulgar and grossly commercial a dealer filled her with sheer despair.

To bring what consolation she could, Linda went on in her warm and kindly fashion: 'Daddy wants to give you a picture as a souvenir. I thought he would have mentioned it in his letter.'

'I'm afraid I didn't read the end very carefully. I was so shattered.' She unfolded the letter again and saw that the offer by which the doctor had tried to soften the blow had indeed failed to register. He invited her to send a message by Linda to tell him which of the paintings he could reserve for her as a token of his gratitude for all she had tried to do. She turned away to hide the conflicting emotions that suddenly moistened her eyes.

'Which do you think you'll have?' Linda inquired with curiosity. Her range of tastes had shown little sign of growing beyond those awakened by an art mistress on whom she had had a crush at school, but such as they were, they were genuine and enabled her to feel a sympathetic interest in Stephanie's enthusiasm, though she could only faintly share it: the Italian Renaissance had been considered rather *vieux jeu* by Miss Upton.

'It will need thinking about,' said Stephanie steadying her voice.

'Well, don't think about it too long because Beatrix won't be fit to live with till she gets the blessed things out of the house. She loathes having that Saratoga monster lurking about, and there isn't anything else to keep them in.'

'I wouldn't accept such a princely gift,' Stephanie protested almost angrily, 'if it weren't that it'll save something from the dreadful wreck. Your father's not a millionaire to go round giving away such things! If I take even the worst—I mean, the least important—it'll be worth several thousand pounds.'

Linda was a little inclined to laugh, but the burning conviction couched in such practical terms was impressive all the same, and in spite of herself the thought arose: 'What a ghastly sell if Stephanie were right after all!'

She was glad to be released from a speculation so disturbing by the arrival at the counter of the young photographer who had recently taken over the business called the Portrait Studio nearly opposite the library—a business which was not engrossing his entire time, judging by the number of detective novels he managed to get through in the course of each week.

Stephanie, being nearest, moved forward to take the book he was returning, but observing that his eyes were fixed on Linda, she divined, even through her painful reflections on other matters, a motive for his frequent visits that went beyond his interest in crime and, as if recollecting an urgent task elsewhere, she turned away.

Linda was quickly engaged in the kind of conversation, bantering on the surface, flattering below, in which she was always able to hold her own with no more effort than was pleasurable.

Placid, complaisant, easily distracted, and of indolent habits, she was peculiarly unlike her tidy, emphatic, conscientious elder sister. Though less good-looking, her tolerance and amiability made her a more appealing person, and her ripe figure and plump, rather formless face achieved conquests denied to Beatrix's much better features. In an artless, unconceited way, she enjoyed these conquests, and they occupied more of her thoughts and energies than anything that took place in her home. Sometimes, when outside amusements were especially successful, she could scarcely conceal her view of home-life as a mere boring series of intervals, the descent of the curtain between the acts of an exciting play; a state of mind which was, not unnaturally, profoundly exasperating to Beatrix.

Even the affair of the pictures, which had lent colour to the domestic scene in recent weeks, could take but a secondary place when Linda's attention was claimed by an agreeable young man whom she suspected of desiring to flirt with her. Her disappointment, though much greater than she liked to admit, was consigned to some limbo where it could lie inert while she conducted him through the maze of the fiction shelves and, under the pretence of investigating his tastes, probed, in a manner which he was clearly far from resenting, into his life and circumstances.

Stephanie meanwhile, feeling a need for action so acute that it was a physical craving, almost tempting her to walk into the street and wander aimlessly to and fro, forced herself into immobility, and sitting on a high wooden stool beside the counter, rested her head in her hands and covered her eyes, the better to concentrate her thoughts.

No deed she had ever been called upon to do in her life had been so vital as this necessity of preventing Dr. Sandilands from committing an act of dire imprudence and benighted vandalism, but how to contend against Sir Harry Maximer she was at her wits' end to see. She herself had caused him to be brought into the lists, certain that he would be the pictures' champion. How could she put to rout so formidable an antagonist?

She had always realized that it was her ingenuity in building up a plausible historic background for the collection rather than his faith in her abilities as a judge of art that had prevailed on the doctor to let her encroach upon his busy life and fill him with unsettling and fantastic hopes. As for Beatrix, though not obstructive, she had hardly concealed her view that Stephanie's intellectual pride was destined for a fall. Why should either of them allow her to set herself up against an authority whose decision they had schooled themselves to accept as final? Dr. Sandilands had none of the gambling instinct that might have given him a sort of amusement in calculating on a thousandth chance. He had found no pleasure in being uncertain whether he owned works of art convertible into a fortune or some worthless copies. To him the suspense was sheerly a worry and from the first he had stipulated that a term should be set to it; while she for her part had expressed unquali-fied willingness to accept Sir Harry's ruling. How go back on that now?

'Have you got a headache, Mrs. du Plessis?'

She raised her eyes from her hand, which had been pressing hard upon them, and saw the Chief Librarian studying her with a look of solicitude. As if his speech had been a cue invoking a response already prepared, she answered unhesitating: 'I'm sorry. I don't seem to be very well.'

'That's bad. Not catching a cold surely in this weather?'

'I don't know what it is. I've got a sort of dizziness—a sick feeling.'

'Perhaps you've been eating something that doesn't agree with you,' said Mr. Hensby in his plain and practical way. 'What did you have for breakfast?'

'Nothing.' The lie sounded dreadfully downright, and she added quickly as a concession to her customary love of truth, 'Nothing that could have made me feel like this.'

'Perhaps you'd better go home. It's no use forcing yourself to work when you're poorly.'

'Oh, do you think you could spare me?' The compulsion to be free was no longer merely one of nerves. It was accompanied by an idea of action which had sprung into her mind almost full-fledged at the moment when she had taken advantage of his mistake.

'Yes, we can spare you. We shall have to spare you, shan't we, next week when you go off on your holiday? You've left it a bit late this year and you're run down, I dare say.'

She had postponed her holiday because she could not tear herself away from the pictures. It had been her intention, after Maximer had pronounced them genuine, and while their glorious destiny was under consideration, to go to Florence and continue her researches; but until Beatrix, the caretaker, had been taught at least the extrinsic value of the treasure, she would not abandon it.

Now less than ever was that to be thought of, and she said miserably: 'I may ask you to let me put off going, Mr. Hensby.'

'Again? Your plans upset as well as your tummy?'

'I'm afraid so. I'm not sure yet.'

Remembering the air of happiness that had surrounded her all summer, he wondered whether she had been engaged in some love affair that had begun to go wrong, and being a much more sensitive and kindly person than his bulky form and matter-of-fact North-country manner were able to suggest, he said a little gruffly: 'Well, we'll just deal with one trouble at a time, shall we? You're not well and you'd better go home. That's enough for one day.'

She thanked him gratefully, her scruples subdued by the urgency of her mission, and hurried from the building without speaking again to

Linda, who might be allowed for the moment to conclude that she had
given way to her annoyance and mortification.

The bed-sitting-room she occupied in the town was only two or
three minutes' walk from the general bus terminus, and within half an
hour of leaving her work she was in the queue waiting for the bus to
Elderfield, carrying under her arm the pink file that was known to her
and Dr. Sandilands as the Medici dossier. She took the risk of losing
Mr. Hensby's confidence completely if her deception should become
known, but such a consideration could only be a vague disquiet at the
back of a mind which had yielded itself up wholly to its impulse.

In Elderfield there was the Municipal Art Gallery directed by
Arnold Bayley, a man whom she believed to be highly intelligent and
full of initiative. His drastic revision of the collection and his new
purchases, though they had been the subject of much angry criticism
from newspaper correspondents signing themselves Beauty Lover, Fair
Play, and Rate-payer, were on the whole acknowledged to have made
the gallery a much more interesting place than it had been before his
appointment, while his loan exhibitions had already done much to lift
the heavy pall of provincialism. He had been the obvious person for the
doctor to consult before taking the Hovenden pictures to London and
she had looked forward eagerly to being present when he examined
them: but it had turned out unfortunately that he had left Elderfield
for nearly a month just at the time when Beatrix had grown impatient
for a final judgment. Her father had been persuaded to seek Sir Harry's
arbitration without waiting for an interim verdict, and the correspondence once opened and a meeting in the course of weeks vouchsafed, the
point of approaching Arnold Bayley had gone.

Now he must have returned. She had no very clear notion what he
could do or even whether he would consent to see her, but her sense
of the danger and the hopelessness of contending alone against the
defeatism of the Sandilands family fired her with an almost feverish
determination to win him as an ally if it were humanly possible. She
passed into the great smoke-blackened civic building in which the Art
Gallery was housed—a pile of architecture so obscured by grime that
only the most penetrating eye could have distinguished its qualities—
and found her way to the secretary's office, charged with the sort of
energy of purpose that communicates itself.

Mr. Bayley was engaged but might be free later. She was asked to
state the business on which she wished to see him, and wrote on a slip

of paper that she was the widow of Jan du Plessis, a South African artist of whom he might have heard, and that she wished to ask his advice about some pictures. She judged that her late husband's name, little known though it was in England, would at some time have reached the ears of one who was reputed to have an enthusiasm for contemporary painting, and that it would be a better introduction than a request that he should come to the rescue of a large hoard of Old Masters.

She was asked to return in half an hour, and wandered out to while away the time in the gallery. There her fever abated, and she was able in a few minutes to abandon herself to that positive and restoring calm which is always to be found in the presence of fine pictures well arranged and seen without the obstruction of crowds. An art gallery, like a library, is a little self-contained world, with its own atmosphere and system of time; and Stephanie had overrun the half-hour she had thought it would be hard to kill when she was accosted by a man of youthful appearance, with an unassuming and tentative manner that was rather at variance with his sharp, firmly modelled features. Almost shyly he tendered his hand.

'Are you Mrs. du Plessis? Would you come to my office? I'm sorry I had to keep you waiting.'

'How kind of you to come and fetch me! I was admiring, as I always do, the tremendous changes you've made here.'

'You knew it as it was before, did you?'

'Yes, it was one of the very few art galleries I got a chance of seeing when I first came to England. Of course, it was better than nothing, but you've made a wonderful clearance.'

'I had a lot of trouble about that,' he said as if he were still tired from the effort.

'I remember there was an awful fuss. But you had a great many supporters too.'

'It didn't feel like it. People who never visited the gallery from one year's end to another became tigers in defence of objects they hadn't even bothered to look at!'

'They were more tigerish still, weren't they, about the cleaning of the old pictures?'

'Ah, that!' His sigh expressed an unending mystification that made her laugh. 'Here in Elderfield where you'd think they'd be so glad to see a little clear colour they make out that the most beautiful thing in the world is dirty paint and brown varnish against a dingy wall!'

'At any rate, hasn't the attendance gone up?'

'Yes, quite a bit.' His smile hinted rather endearingly at his triumph.

She perceived that she had stepped off right foot foremost. The stormy reception of all his improvements had evidently been more than superficially unpleasant, and like most men who have had to fight their way, he had perhaps formed the habit of expecting hostility, so that her lively appreciation surprised and warmed him. He paused to show her how he planned to turn the huge oblong grey-green entrance hall into a pure white court for sculpture—a project so far thwarted on account of strong opposition to his moving the portraits of Lord Mayors and other dignitaries which were regarded as practically the basis of the institution. She was able to share his rueful amusement with a full response, and by the time she was sitting in his office armchair, it was no longer her impression that he was diffident.

'Cigarette?' He pushed a box across his desk towards her.

'No thank you. I gave it up two or three budgets ago.'

'How did you manage it!' he asked, taking one himself.

'Quite sordidly, by counting up what I was saving every time I resisted the temptation. No, I'm not a miser,' she protested, answering a slightly whimsical glance, 'but you see it's for a purpose. I go to Italy with what I save.'

'You have a feminine way of encompassing your purposes—little by little.'

'You think so?' She could not but laugh again at the prospect of his very rapidly revising that opinion.

'You've just as good as told me so.'

He seemed in no hurry to bring her to her business, and she was aware with a swift and delighted comprehension that not every day in the week brought nice-looking, easy-mannered, pleasantly dressed young women to consult the Director of Elderfield Art Gallery. The city was famous for its sombre and determined ugliness, and those who made their money out of its industries lived, if they could afford it, in outlying districts as far afield as Charlton Wells: the inhabitants who could not escape bore about them the drab shades of their prison house.

Stephanie was suddenly conscious that her brilliant hair and fine skin and the skilfully draped dress which had been the work of two week-ends before the pictures had stolen all her leisure made an agreeable impact on a man whose visual sense must be highly developed, and she resolved if need be to exploit the advantage. She resolved it all the more readily because Arnold Bayley was, to her way of thinking, an attractive young man. She could have wished that she had come to him with some less thorny problem, some story more assured of acceptance.

It was a long story, and she dared not let much more time pass in oblique approaches: yet it was desirable to establish in as many little ways as she could her being a rational and congenial person, before she endeavoured to enlist his interest in what might otherwise seem like an aesthetic gold brick trick or—almost worse—a delusion of bumptious ignorance.

It occurred to her to say, after he had puffed a cloud or two in a quite cosy silence:

'I heard of you in Florence.'

'You did?'

His voice had risen on a note of pleased surprise and she was glad that, in the fitfully lighted grottoes of her memory, this chance pebble had glistened just when it might be useful.

'You were one of the people sent over by the Army Council to protect works of art.'

'Sent over by the Monuments and Fine Arts Sub-Commission, to be exact. Yes, that was a great piece of luck for me—if it's a piece of luck to be Director here, and I suppose it is at my age. I more or less got the job on the strength of my good references from Italy.'

'You're certainly younger than I expected,' she found herself saying spontaneously.

'I'm thirty-four. Is that too young to give you advice about pictures?'

His sudden dart towards the subject of her message suggested a realization on his part too that time was being lost; and though she believed he would have been content, if he were free, to lose more of it in the same fashion, she took the plunge.

'Whom would you call the greatest authority on Italian painting?'

'In the English-speaking world? Sir Harry Maximer without question.'

'Would you say he was infallible?'

'Infallible? Good gracious, no expert alive is infallible. I should call him dependable—which is saying a great deal when there are so many opportunities of going off the rails.'

She looked intently first at the Medici dossier and then into the steady grey eyes which were fixed on her.

'You know him personally, don't you?'

'Yes, I've met him a few times. He came up to open our Summer Exhibition.'

'Is he, do you think, the sort of man who might give a rash judgment in haste, or out of caprice, or in a fit of prejudice? You know what I mean. . . .'

'I'm afraid I *don't* know what you mean.' There was an emphasis in his tone, despite its lightness, which told her clearly how he had come out victorious from so many tussles with the Council. 'I can give you advice about pictures, if it's in my power, but not about Sir Harry Maximer.'

'Then I'll come to the pictures,' she said submissively. 'In Charlton Wells there are sixteen which, I promise you—oh, I really promise you, Mr. Bayley, would go to your heart, they're so beautiful, so masterly. . . . Do you know Morris, the dealer, there?'

'Yes, indeed.' He picked up a pencil and began frowningly to draw a face in dots on his blotting pad. 'But I doubt whether I should think many pictures in Morris's shop beautiful and masterly.'

'Oh!' she cried, and her look of affront seemed to banish his frown. 'How can you imagine I could have come to see you about anything in Morris's shop? What I'm trying to tell you is that these superb, miraculous pictures, which the National Gallery would be overjoyed to get, are going to be sold to Morris for anything he'll pay because Sir Harry Maximer has said they're no good.'

With that, boldly and effectively, for she had been busy all the way from Charlton Wells selecting the essential points and arranging them in workmanlike order, she laid before him the outline of the story.

Arnold Bayley watched her closely as she talked, partly because he liked the look of her, partly because he was striving to assess from her demeanour what value he could place upon her words. Certainly, her descriptions of the paintings were fascinating, her deductions, even if based on false premises, could only be the fruit of diligent research, and her manner was altogether impressive. If it had not been for the overwhelming weight of Maximer against her, he would have felt assured there was something here that imperatively demanded investigation.

But to suspect for one moment that Sir Harry could be mistaken about no fewer than sixteen separate works was fatuous. One blunder was a possibility, perhaps two . . . or even, if for some reason he were bitterly prejudiced, three: but massive, wholesale error was an hypothesis which called for vigorous discouragement. And as, rounding off her recital, she offered him, with an eager, confiding gesture, the pink file, shabby from much handling, he spoke with regretful finality:

'Mrs. du Plessis, it's quite useless, candidly, for me to take this, though I'm sure I should find it full of most intelligent theories, and I sympathize immensely with your disappointment. But Maximer could have no conceivable motive for saying these pictures are not genuine if they really are, and once he's been consulted and has given a definite answer, I don't honestly see that there's anything at all I can do about it.'

'Then you do think he's infallible!'

He was dismayed to observe that tears were glittering on her eyelashes.

'No, but to be wrong sixteen times,' he said lamely, 'that's too much!'

'I should think it is too much!' She blinked away the tears with a sort of childish carelessness of appearances that touched him. 'How do you know he hadn't drunk a bottle of wine with his lunch! Or that he wasn't wearing the wrong glasses? Or in a tearing rage about something just when poor Dr. Sandilands turned up? The pictures are there for the saving. Do you mean you won't even look at them?'

Arnold Bayley glanced furtively at his watch, hoping that the Borough Surveyor, who was coming to discuss the new Loan Court, would be late, yet feeling obliged, in case he was not, to reply with succinctness:

'I can't make out what good I could do by looking at them.' He pressed his pencil incisively into the blotter. 'Maximer's a much bigger gun than I am.'

'You could offer to buy them,' she improvised.

'To buy them!' He laughed. 'To buy them at a fair price if they're really masterpieces! Do you realize I can hardly buy a Christmas calendar without the approval of the Finance Committee?'

'It would only be a way of gaining time—of making the doctor think twice about selling them to Morris.'

'Morris may not want them. They don't sound much in his line. Not nearly bogus enough.' He laid the stress on 'enough'.

'Then Dr. Sandilands will take them to a junk shop. His daughter will nag him till he gets rid of them.'

'I'm sorry,' He went on assiduously with his dotted drawing. 'As you think they're Old Masters with a tremendous history, I can quite understand how acutely you feel for them, but if you would try to believe, Mrs. du Plessis, that Maximer has a profound knowledge of these things, that—you must forgive me if this sounds rude—he's much more likely to be right about them than you are. . . .'

'I know, I know!' she almost wailed. 'But something has gone wrong! Won't you come and see for yourself? Think what may be at stake!'

He raised his eyes and found himself simply staring at her: the interview had reached a point of unconventionality when it seemed scarcely impolite to do so.

Dozens of times in every year, inhabitants of Elderfield and the district made their way to that room in the hope that he would certify some old canvas rummaged out of an attic or picked up at an auction sale as a find of enormous value and great artistic interest; only one such object in hundreds came anywhere near to justifying the possessor's hopes. He was accustomed to dealing with inquirers so ignorant that they imagined any picture old enough to have been in a family for a few generations must, by that mere attribute, be fit to adorn the walls of an art gallery, and he had grown to assume, as specialists will, that the estimates of lay people were generally unworthy of consideration. But here was someone who talked of Florentine artists, their styles and subjects and peculiarities, with a proficiency that made it impossible to class her with the usual run of those he was obliged to undeceive. He felt a real stirring of curiosity as to the works which could inspire such a fanatical faith in a person otherwise eminently gifted with reasoning powers.

Yet to accede to her request, if it meant an appearance of setting himself up as a check upon Sir Harry Maximer, was out of the question. He was preparing a reply which, though courteous, should be unyielding when his house telephone rang to announce the arrival of the Borough Surveyor.

'Ask him to wait a moment or two,' he told his secretary, and looked up to find his visitor already on her feet, taking up the rejected file with a humbled and despairing air that moved his compassion, as the qualities of her face and figure moved his admiration.

'I don't know where to turn,' she said wretchedly. 'You are the only person who could have helped.'

Instead of stepping forward to open the door for her, he stood motionless, full of indecision. Was their acquaintance to end thus, with his brusquely turning down her appeal, sending her empty away? Was she to remember him—this nice, attractive, clever, impassioned girl—only as the man who had proved callous, disobliging, deaf to

supplication? What debt had he ever owed the pompous, self-satis-
fied Maximer that he should put his prestige before the claims of a
particularly charming lady in distress—and distress of so interesting
a character?

'Look here!' he heard himself saying. 'Couldn't we talk it over when
the Borough Surveyor isn't waiting? Where are you going to have
lunch?' And as she paused, her face lighting up with relief, 'Why not
lunch with me at Quayly's? You know the place—in Market Street?'

'What time?' she asked joyfully.

'One-fifteen. Leave me the file! I'll try and dip into it before I come,
just for the fun of the thing.' He approached and coaxed it from her
hand with a movement that seemed to apologize for his former rejec-
tion. 'I might as well see what sort of detective story you've made of it.'

He always honourably admitted afterwards that, if it had not been
for quite extraneous factors like Stephanie's hair and something that
happened to captivate him in her manner, he would not for an instant
have concerned himself with the fate of the Hovenden collection.

SIX

IT WAS ONE thing to cajole Arnold Bayley into agreeing to see the
pictures and quite another to find a means of enabling him to do so.
They were, after all, only accessible by the courtesy of Dr. Sandilands
and Beatrix, who kept his house; and for Stephanie to behave as if she
considered herself to have proprietary rights would be, at this unhappy
moment, to court a rebuff. Though they might credit her with benevolent intentions, the fact remained that she was in their eyes the cause
of a great waste of time and trouble and the promoter of a delusion
which had, as they would see it, made fools of them. By dragging in the
young man from Elderfield without their authority, she would be flinging down the gauntlet in the most provocative fashion.

Moreover, she had faithfully promised the doctor not to discuss the
pictures at all outside his family, and although she considered herself
exonerated by his own interests, as well as by much higher issues than
the Sandilands' horror of 'getting into the papers', the discreet moment
for confessing the breach of confidence was certainly not today, when
her stock stood at lowest ebb.

She decided at last to resort to a subterfuge. She would ask Dr. Sandilands to let her see in her own room three or four of the panels she considered most impressive so that she might choose the one she would keep. These she would show at once to Arnold Bayley, and when he had acknowledged the absurdity of their condemnation by Maximer, she would have grounds firmer than her own unsupported opinion for pleading that the whole question of authenticity be reopened.

Arnold Bayley was pleased with this plan on account of its privacy. Without intruding on the unwilling Sandilands family, he would have the opportunity of demonstrating plainly to her intelligent eyes the technical points that would prove the falsity of the pictures—the points on which Maximer had doubtless based his findings. It would be painful, but surely much kinder in the long run than leaving her to the tormenting idea that great masterpieces were being squandered. He had no doubt at all, having dipped into her closely reasoned notes and listened to her enthusiastic but never illogical conversation at their luncheon, that he would find it possible to persuade her gently of her error without involving himself on the wrong side of a perilous controversy.

But it happened that Stephanie had made the same mistake in her calculations that Maximer had made in his: she had concluded that at least a day or two must elapse before Dr. Sandilands, making up the time he had lost in London, would find leisure to seek out Morris or any other dealer. That is to say, she had reckoned without Beatrix.

Beatrix was angry with the pictures, and she wanted to be rid of them. She felt that they had made her father ridiculous. The thought of Sir Harry's scorn at the naïve mention of Botticelli and da Vinci produced vicarious mortification of the most unbearable kind, the kind that grows worse in retrospect. Her father's silliness in listening to the fairy tales of Stephanie du Plessis was of a piece with his silliness in buying all that Hovenden rubbish in the first place. The things he did and continued to do for the most tiresome people—really, there were times when, knowing his financial position, one lost patience with him!

And Linda too! She had been a perfect fool, swallowing everything, secretly imagining no doubt that the overbearing Stephanie was going to make them all rich. She had even let fall in an unguarded moment some nonsense about buying a fur coat. And then, to complete her exasperation, Beatrix was not altogether sure that she herself had adequately sealed her ears against the siren voice. Mistrustful as her general attitude had been, she had found herself at times stealthily making calculations. Just in case. . . . One never knew. . . . Strange things did sometimes happen. Pictures quite as unprepossessing as theirs were for some reason prized by people who went in for that sort of thing, and she deserved a fur coat much more than Linda who was years younger and never did a hand's turn in the house.

Well, the dream had now gone up in smoke, and it was smoke that left an acrid savour. A hundred pounds for the pictures, which was the sum Sir Harry had thought within their reach, would repay the original price and, even after their London expenses had been deducted, leave them a small profit. To get that hundred pounds would be a kind of salve to the wounded self-respect of the family, soothing if not healing. And at the same time there would be a purge; the offending objects would be removed once and for all from sight, and Stephanie du Plessis would learn—so Beatrix in her harsh humour put it—where she got off.

Therefore, the very first day after their return from London, she took five panels that were small enough to lie flat in her suitcase, packed them with their layers of linen—for she was always neat and careful—and, while her father was engaged in his afternoon interviews with private patients, drove off in his car to Morris's shop.

For some reason she had never been able to fathom, there was a tendency on the part of certain people to make fun of Morris's shop. She did not confess her heresy aloud, but to her way of thinking, its windows were very much more attractive than those of the Elder-field dealer who frequently displayed things a child of five could have painted; and yet the Elderfield dealer seemed to stand in higher esteem. Morris, at any rate, went in for painting that was clever, difficult to do, and nice to look at too; not like Elderfield's puerile stuff.

Seeing through the glass door that there was a customer in the shop, she paused, unwilling to state her business before a third party, and gave her attention to the window display. In the corner window, there was the full-length portrait of a lovely blonde girl, unclothed but for a drap-ery which had been caught by the breeze so as to cover whatever might be objectionable to the prudish while gracefully revealing superlatively smooth limbs of the most flawless shape and delicate fairness. She was standing against a wonderfully real-looking marble wall with a richly decorated bowl of fruit held under one arm. Beyond the wall was a vivid stretch of blue water. The title of the picture was 'By the Aegean Sea.' Beatrix knew it extremely well, as it had been in stock for several years and was given a week or two in the window every few months.

Near it was a smaller but more crowded canvas representing the dramatic encounter in a tavern of a Cavalier and a Roundhead, recognizable at once by their contrasting costumes. They were in the act of drawing their swords, while all around rustic characters signified in lifelike attitudes their excitement or dismay. The fat ruddy landlord, swathed in an apron, rushed forward in consternation, and in the foreground a serving maid of striking beauty, carrying a pewter tankard, stretched out an appealing hand towards the Cavalier. A gilt plaque announced that the picture, which was by a famous late-Victorian R.A., was called 'Brothers'. Having seen this, it did not take Beatrix long to notice that there was a strong facial resemblance between the two angry men, who were evidently hostile members of the same family.

Two landscapes, which were of no interest to her, a nymph by W. A. Bouguereau, and the portrait of a pretty little girl in fancy dress by James Sant, R.A., completed this window.

The central position at the other side was occupied by a very striking work of a type which was Morris's speciality. Indeed, even Beatrix, who was not much given to speculation on artistic subjects, had wondered from time to time where he obtained his apparently inexhaustible supply of cardinals. Usually they were depicted in informal, not to say raffish moments, leering perhaps at a well-fed bishop over a decanter of wine on a table convincingly covered with lace, or playing cards with an air of genial furtiveness, or possibly grouped in some corner whispering in such a way as to suggest scandal. But today, as its lengthy title frankly proclaimed, the subject was historical and ambitious: *Giovanni de' Medici (Leo X) being made a Cardinal in Secret at the Age of Thirteen by G. Paganelli, 1889.*

Although she was impatient to get into the shop with her burdensome suitcase, Beatrix found herself unable to resist gazing for several minutes at the details of the colourful scene. A little puzzled-looking boy in a splendid scarlet robe was reaching out his hand eagerly towards a large object—could it be a hat?—which was being presented by a kneeling bishop magnificent in purple. The expressions—benevolent, crafty, amused, resentful—on the faces of the various high dignitaries taking part in the ceremony were in themselves an interesting study, doubtless full of meaning for anyone who had some knowledge of the event. There were all sorts of characters, all sorts of things to look at in the way of costumes, furniture, and burnished gold ornaments. It was a picture one could really, she thought, have lived with; and she quite shrank from encountering Mr. Morris when she remembered how dull and ordinary were the contents of her valise—just imitations of those hackneyed subjects which made the Old Masters (she could silently acknowledge it) so boring.

There were two or three Old Masters in Morris's window—at least, she judged them to be so by the conspicuous way in which they carried dated labels—but they were of the kind that modern eyes can enjoy, shepherds making love to shepherdesses, skaters on a frozen dyke in Holland, a large dark still-life of fruit and flowers.

Beatrix had quite exhausted the window, from 1639 to 1889, and still the customer showed no sign of emerging from the shop. She peered once more into the comparative darkness beyond the glass door and saw with annoyance that he was seated in a leisurely fashion chatting. Mr. Morris was smoking as he talked, and there was no sign of any transaction in progress. It was getting late and her father would soon need the car for his afternoon round, so it became plain that she must either return home or set aside her delicacy. Summoning the little smile she used when she was taking things in hand, she opened the door.

Morris, who could see at half a glance that she did not belong to the class of merchants' wives who had enough money to buy Marcus Ward or a bogus Cuyp, Boucher, or Van Oss, went on with his conversation, leaving an assistant to hurry from the inner room of the shop with 'What can I do for you, madam?'

On her stating that she wished to see about disposing of some pictures, the assistant's demeanour instantly changed from suavity to something near contempt, for Morris, being one of those tradesmen who remain stubbornly unaware that their livelihood depends as much upon those who sell as upon those who buy, always treated vendors with the scantest courtesy, and his staff followed his example.

'You'd better come back later,' said the assistant. 'Mr. Morris is busy.'

But Beatrix had a will of her own and she was under the delusion that, when Morris knew her to be Dr. Sandilands' daughter, he would behave with the politeness she was accustomed to receive from the local shopkeepers; so, still smiling sweetly but very, very firmly, she replied: 'He doesn't *look* busy. I might as well sit down and wait.'

She sank stolidly into a chair and the assistant, recognizing determination, turned and muttered something in the ear of Morris, who then, with a grunt intended to convey that he would make short work of this young woman, strolled nonchalantly across to her.

Morris, though he bore an ancient Welsh name, was very far from being a Welshman. His origin, in fact, was so darkly and deeply foreign that his best friend could not have stated with precision what his earlier nationality might have been. A youth of mixed blood, many frontiers, and obscure languages of which he now retained only tattered remnants, he had been washed up in England as jetsam on the tides of 1918, had joined forces with helpful relatives swept in on an earlier wave, had worked, settled, avidly taken root, been shrewd in business, surreptitiously gathered to himself a British name, and finally emerged after many vicissitudes as the owner of naturalization papers and a shop in a prosperous watering-place.

He had picked up a great deal in spite of heavy odds; he had even mastered, in a fluent if inelegant form, the English language; and he felt entitled to assert his superiority to circumstances and the majority of people by bad manners as nicely cultivated as good ones more often are. Consequently, his first brisk speech came as rather a surprise to Beatrix.

'Now then, young lady, what do you want to try and palm off on me? If it's something you painted yourself for a hobby, I don't buy it—not even if you went to an art school!' And while Beatrix hesitated, wondering how to counter such an opening, he called over his shoulder: 'Don't go, Quiller! I shan't be a minute.'

Beatrix took the opportunity of swiftly opening her suitcase as the customer, rising and moving towards the door, rejoined in a voice that sounded, she thought, like the croaking of a very tired frog: 'Thanks, but I might as well be getting on. I'd like to look in at one or two other places.'

'What about that ikon?' asked Morris pressingly. 'It's a nice piece. Cheap too. You can sell that kind of thing in London.'

'I'll think about it,' said Quiller, and with a slack wave of the hand he was gone.

Morris, assured that he had lost a sale, addressed Beatrix yet more brusquely than before. 'What's this? A cracked panel! No frame! I don't buy this kind of stuff.'

'It's a copy of an Old Master,' said Beatrix, outwardly at least unshaken.

'Copies are of no interest to me. I sell only originals by first-rate artists.'

'They're not copies of anything that anyone *knows*,' she was bold enough to declare, 'anyone but an expert, I mean. And they're awfully well done—just like the real thing anyhow!'

'Just like the real thing! This bit of junk!' Morris held up by a damaged corner the Madonna and Child which Stephanie had often lovingly mentioned in the same breath as Filippo Lippi. 'If you can kid yourself like that, you ought to be in the advertising business.'

Morris spoke in this vein, partly because on strict principle he always belittled goods he was being asked to buy, and partly in all sincerity because he was not accustomed, as he truly said, to dealing in that kind of stuff. His whole experience of genuine Old Masters was comprised in a visit to the National Gallery one rainy Saturday years before and an occasional glimpse in a London sale room, and he had probably never laid eyes on one that was not set off by gilded frame and thrice-gilded certification.

Affronted as she was by his rudeness, Beatrix was obliged to swallow her pride, believing him to be their only hope of a buyer in Charlton Wells. In an attempt to seem at ease in this objectionable situation, she began to protest half-facetiously:

'You might at least have a proper look at them before you say they're no good. These are only a sample. There are a lot more at home. My father, Dr. Sandilands, would like you to come and see them up at the house.'

'Dr. Sandilands! So that's your father, is it?' Far from appearing impressed, Morris slowly shook his head with every appearance of commiseration. 'I know Dr. Sandilands. He once tried to get me to buy some of the worst trash I ever saw in my life from an old dame on the outskirts of the town. He hypnotized Keeley into buying some old parson's library, and it was all sermons and Greek books. . . . Keeley was years getting them off his hands. He's a very nice man, your father, always got some lame duck up his sleeve. When I go broke I better come and get him to sell my old clothes for me.'

It was at this moment, when Beatrix was wincing at the obnoxious joke, that the customer named Quiller re-entered the shop. She had been greatly relieved to see him go, disliking as she did the prospect of offering her second-hand wares in front of an audience, and now she was proportionately annoyed by his return. Morris too was so much more unpleasant to deal with than she had anticipated that, if it had not been for the thought of her father's disappointment over her bungling, she would have ended the interview there and then. And she found it particularly irritating when the stranger came up and peered through his glasses at the half-unpacked contents of her suitcase.

'I've decided I'll have that ikon,' he said with a slight increase of animation.

'You will? All right! I'll have it packed and sent off to London. You got a bargain there, Quiller.'

'I'll take it with me. No hurry. I can wait while they pack it. I'll write you a cheque.'

When Quiller had walked out into the street two or three minutes before, having failed to pick up anything useful from Morris, nothing had connected the young woman and her valise with the treasure it was his mission to acquire. In Maximer's account of their meeting, Dr. Sandilands had been the prime mover, and Quiller's mind was fixed upon an approach, somehow or other, to him. A daughter had certainly been mentioned, but in terms which had vaguely conjured up a figure plain and *passée*; and the nice-looking girl who had interrupted his thankless conversation seemed to him, as apparently she had seemed to Morris, merely a likely exponent of crinolines and herbaceous borders in water colours.

But as he meandered off down King's Parade, trying to decide where to drop in next, his mind's eye screened, as it were, a vivid flash-back of a gesture seen from the door. She had been taking from the topmost picture a linen wrapper! Now Maximer, in describing the wonderful hoard, had spoken appreciatively of the series of happy accidents by which it must have been preserved, and had said something about coverings of fine soft linen. It was surely rather unusual to cover pictures with linen. Quiller turned back and, profoundly as he detested fakes, concluded that he had better buy the ikon.

What Beatrix had laid out on the silver-painted table that did duty for a counter told him he had not erred. Indeed, he felt his heart absolutely palpitating at the horror of so near a miss. And even now he was not out of the wood. Morris could not be such a fool as to let these pictures go!

'Do you mind if I rest my cheque book here?' He laid it down on a corner of the table, and very slowly brought from his pocket a fountain pen.

'Go ahead! Go ahead!' With none too gentle a movement, Morris pushed away the profile portrait of a young woman.

'Oh, there's plenty of room!' Quiller instinctively put out a protective hand. 'Don't let me stop you from getting down to business.'

'I don't do this kind of business,' said Morris. 'Copies faked up to look old! Artificial wormholes and cracks! This isn't my line at all.'

It was true enough, thought Quiller, that the forgeries supplied to the innocents of Charlton Wells never looked a day older than was becoming to them. To please Morris's clients, it was not necessary that pictures should be hung in chimneys to be darkened by smoke, or baked in ovens to crackle their surfaces, or scratched with palette knives to suggest the injuries of time. It was enough to affix a small gilt plaque saying simply *Wouvermans*, or *Corot*, or even, lately, *Monet* or *Berthe Morisot*. None of the people willing to buy these factory products were likely to question such attributions. A nice oil painting with a good label—what more could they ask in a shop like this? Bitterly Quiller glanced round him, recalling his twelve years at Mandell & Strood's when he had known the *élite* of connoisseurs, had handled the most coveted masterpieces. . . .

Beatrix was protesting with spirit: 'I admit they're copies, but they were done ages ago, and those wormholes and things are real. And they're not *all* worm-eaten—not badly at any rate. I just brought these because they're the smallest.'

Morris picked up a panel and gazed at it gloomily. It was a dead Christ. 'I don't know whether it's worth my while to come and see the rest at your father's place or not,' he sighed. 'I can't sell these religious subjects, not even when they're good. I don't say this is a bad one of its kind.'

Quiller trembled with apprehension for he knew the excellence of the picture must be of a most striking order.

'They're not all religious. Some are portraits—'

'Portraits of what? Portraits of who? Men or women?'

'Men, except that one.' She indicated the profile which Quiller, who seemed to be having trouble with his fountain pen, was leaning over with what she took for idle and impertinent curiosity.

'I can't sell portraits of men. Not unless it's some big celebrity like George Washington or Henry the Eighth.'

'We've got Lorenzo the Magnificent,' said Beatrix quickly.

'It's no use asking me to sell Borgias. They been done to death.'

'But he's a Medici.'

'It's the same thing. Unless,' he added on a more hopeful note, 'he's in his cardinal's robes.'

'I'm afraid not. He's in a sort of black blouse affair.'

'Doesn't sound very magnificent to me.'

'We've got a pope,' she remembered brightening. 'Pius the some-thing-or-other.'

'Popes are religious. You can't get away from it.'

'But so are cardinals, aren't they?'

'In a different way,' he remarked coldly, and took another panel. His gloom deepened with the sense of his problem. After all, it was unwise to turn down out of hand the opportunity of buying, at the very small price that would doubtless be asked, a batch of pictures which, even if not suitable for his own stock, he might trade with some other dealer; but Dr. Sandilands would want him to call in the evening, and this was a busy week. He had guests staying at his house; his wife was giving a bridge party; he lived some miles out of Charlton Wells and disliked having to come back when the day's work ought to be over.

'More religion!' he said, confronting the infant St. John with quite a dramatic groan. 'Babies I can sell, but not when they look like they've swallowed a prayer book.'

'That one *is* a bit soppy,' she conceded, growing easier, for she found herself so perfectly in sympathy with his opinion. 'But about half of them aren't religious at all—honestly! For instance, there's a Leda. You can't call that religious.'

'Might be a religious leader.'

'Oh, I don't think so,' said Beatrix. 'She's nude, standing against a rock. You know—the woman with the swan. It's a big picture.' She refrained from mentioning that it was in three pieces, or that, until yesterday, her father had almost allowed himself to be convinced that it was the lost original of a most important work by Leonardo da Vinci. That sort of nonsense must be buried for ever in decent obscurity.

'I can't sell nudes,' said Morris implacably. 'Not in Charlton Wells. As a matter of fact, practically no one buys nudes in England except for public buildings. Mr. Quiller will tell you the same. He's in the trade.'

Quiller, during this interchange, had managed to take possession of the dead Christ, and, as if to kill time while waiting for his package, was studying it well.

'That's right.' His voice was so limp and casual that no one could have guessed with what anxiety he was plotting his course. 'I've seen Ettys go for eight or ten pounds.'

'Nudes, popes, saints, men in black blouses!' cried Morris. 'If I go and see them it'll be because I know your father's doing it for charity—

though he ought to understand by now I don't run this business as a charity. What time will he be in tomorrow?'

'You couldn't come this evening?' Beatrix pleaded. 'The daytime's awfully difficult.'

'No, the evenings I can't manage. Two o'clock tomorrow afternoon, that's the best I can do. Surely your father don't see patients when he should be digesting his food?'

'A doctor has to do a lot of things besides seeing patients,' said Beatrix, but she was visibly hesitant. His voice had a take-it-or-leave-it note—she could not know that this was part of a buying technique acquired by years of practice—and she felt that perhaps it was as well to accept the proffered appointment even if her father were not able to keep it and she were obliged to deputize for him. It would be too weariful to have to begin all over again with another picture dealer; and there was none nearer than Elderfield.

'If you absolutely can't come in the evening—' she was beginning, when there was an interruption from the exasperating Quiller.

'Excuse me, Morris'—he had the air of a man who cannot repress what has occurred to him—'but how are they packing that thing? Did you tell them I wanted to take it with me?'

'Of course.'

'I mean, with me in the carriage. I don't want some big clumsy case that's got to go into the luggage van.'

'Well, I better inquire,' said Morris, moving towards the interior depths of the shop. 'You didn't say nothing.'

'Sorry. I ought to have thought of it. I've never trusted the luggage vans since the war.'

Morris gave some instructions to his assistant and returned a little preoccupied, as Quiller had intended he should be. Was it possible that the ikon was worth more than the ten pounds he had just obtained for it? That it was, in fact, not quite a fake? Funny, the way Quiller had come back to the shop, suddenly changing his mind like that. . . .

Quiller was examining the defects of the profile portrait, regardless of Beatrix's eyes chillingly fixed on him. 'If you want to buy this stuff,' he said, as if she were not present, 'I can arrange to get it doctored up for you. It wouldn't take more than a key or two at the back to hold in that crack. The painting doesn't need a lot of restoration. I've got a man who's worth every penny he charges for this kind of job.'

The reaction was one of Morris's most discouraging grunts, and Quiller, whose brain worked a great deal faster than could be discovered from his manner, was heartened to a further effort: 'I might find you some frames for them too—'

'I got plenty of frames,' Morris informed him testily.

'Yes, plaster and gold paint, but you'll want some nice carved wood with old gilding for pictures like these, after you've laid out money on them.'

'Who said I was going to lay out money on them?'

'They're not worth having as a gift if you don't.'

Both Morris and Beatrix shot him glances of considerable antagonism, but he was unperturbed. Indeed, he felt absolutely cheerful because he no longer regarded his mission as an unsavoury one. He was rescuing the pictures from Morris rather than procuring them for Maximer.

'In Bond Street,' he continued, 'I've seen stuff not much better than this fetch a lot of money, but that's because it's had money spent on it—big money sometimes.'

'Bond Street and Charlton Wells are two different places,' said Morris with increasing irritation. He felt confused. Quiller's ill-timed suggestions must have some purpose. He was either hoping to cash in somehow on doing up old junk, or else—could he be trying to distract attention after giving something away about the ikon? There was no more demand for ikons in Charlton Wells than there was for nudes or for cardinals who had been promoted to popes, and the one in question was the unwanted part of an auction lot. Morris had not dared to pretend it was genuine to a man who had been on the staff at Mandell & Strood's, and he had been surprised at the interest the other had displayed in it. (It happened to be the only item at as low a price as ten pounds that could evoke even a pretence of interest in one who liked his deceptions to have a certain verisimilitude.)

What if he had missed some virtue that Quiller's more experienced eye had seen? He had a strong temptation to go and get another glimpse of it before they nailed up the box.

But was there anything he could do even if he did discover that he had practically given away a really good old piece?

In consequence of this disturbance in his mind, he became—as he easily did at all times—contumacious, and resolving not to be bounced into some costly scheme of renovations doubtless meant to benefit no one but Quiller, he spoke up curtly:

'I know what I can sell and what I can't sell. If I put them in carved wood frames worth ten times more than the pictures, and have them cleaned and restored till the man who painted them wouldn't know them, I still can't sell Old Masters in this style.' He banged forcefully with his knuckles on the dead Christ.

Quiller restrained his desire to seize a mock-Gainsborough that was displayed on an easel and strike Morris down, and instead persisted brilliantly:

'But the young lady's not pretending they're Old Masters and I don't suppose she's asking an Old Master price.'

'That's got nothing to do with it. There are some things I can't sell at any price. London's quite a different market. You might be able to dispose of them. I can't.'

Beatrix flashed at the impervious Quiller a most withering look. Thanks to his tactless intervention Morris was apparently going to back out of the half-made appointment. And in an endeavour to restore and, if possible, improve the position, she committed the indiscretion she had strictly intended to avoid.

'We showed these pictures, all of them, to a famous expert, and he said they were very good indeed. *He* seemed to think you'd be able to sell them all right.'

'Who, me? He *must* be an expert if he knows my business better than I do.'

'No, I don't say you were mentioned personally. And he did tell us they'd have to have things done to them—repairs and everything; but even so—'

'Even so—he didn't want to buy them himself, eh?'

'We were only asking for his advice.'

'And who, may I ask, is this wonderful expert of yours?'

Beatrix herself was adept at the deflating tone, but that is not to say she cared to be the victim of it. She was aware that to answer his question would be to advertise the extravagance of the hopes her family had entertained, and she would have much preferred to leave Mr. Morris imagining she was making a charitable effort on behalf of one of her father's 'lame ducks', but his sneering incredulity took her off her guard, and she could not resist flinging back at him the name that was in so many circles a word of power.

Its effect was not at all what she had foreseen. Among the class of dealers to which Morris belonged, that name, so far from being a talisman, was anathema. For a score of years Maximer had heaped ridicule on their wares and done everything possible to injure their business. His occasional articles in the popular press, exposing unethical practices in the lower reaches of the picture trade, caused a perceptible decline in sales. There was positively no name calculated to have a more excoriating effect upon Morris's temper.

'Sir Harry Maximer!' he repeated with the least endearing of smiles. 'Is he a friend of yours?'

'An acquaintance,' she felt it not dishonest to reply.

'And you showed him these things, and this is what he advised you do to with them?'

'Yes.'

'He thought I could sell them?'

Bewildered by his evident hostility she replied: 'Well, you or some other dealer who'd take the trouble to get them cleaned and all that.'

'You better tell him to think again,' said Morris, angrily stacking the five panels together without troubling to put their covers over them. 'I don't buy rubbish because wise guys like Maximer want me to, thank you very much.'

There was in his insulting refusal a double satisfaction: not only did it prove his contempt for a hateful enemy, but it testified his knowledge that there was nothing worth having in the entire hoard. Maximer would not have allowed anything of value to slip through his fingers. He could safely let the whole lot go.

But oh, if only he had examined that ikon more closely before his deal with Quiller! Even now perhaps it was not too late to make certain. If the packer had been held up by having to move it to a smaller and lighter box, there might still be a chance, before the lid was tacked on, of reassuring himself.

'Excuse me,' he said abruptly and turned on his heel, leaving Quiller and Beatrix unattended; thus having saved the day for Maximer as effectually as if he had been under a pledge to assist him.

Quiller, while preserving the lethargy of his voice and body, which was by no means a pose, lost not an instant. 'Let me put these back in their wrappings for you,' he said helpfully. And Beatrix was so stung by the humiliation of Morris's rudeness that she let the grievance of a few moments before fall into abeyance, the more readily as Quiller poured balm upon her wounded dignity by remarking: 'I'm afraid our friend has almost as much to learn about politeness as he has about pictures.

Of course, he may be right when he says he can't sell anything but tripe here. If you'd like me to come and see what you've got, I might be able to make you an offer.' He handed her one of his business cards. 'I've better facilities for dealing with this kind of stuff than a provincial firm.'

She read the name and address on the card cautiously, wondering how her father would take it if she confronted him not with Morris but a stranger from London; but he gave her doubts no time to take root.

'Early this evening would suit me if it's all right with you. I'm staying over at Elderfield, and the transport isn't too good after eight o'clock.'

It occurred to Beatrix that his intervention, tiresome as it had seemed, might after all be providential. A transaction with a London man who was not even staying in the town was less likely to give rise to 'talk': Beatrix had a thoroughly self-conscious woman's almost superstitious dread of 'talk', and a highly irrational notion as to its causes and effects. And then, Quiller evidently understood what could be done with the pictures by taking some pains with them, just as Maximer had suggested; and once they were in his hands, the stupid episode could be forgotten completely, whereas in Morris's stock they would have been bound to make mocking appearances from time to time.

Accordingly, she showed him her address on the label of her valise, and invited him to call immediately after 'surgery'. It would mean putting back dinner, but that was worth it for the sake of getting the business settled.

She was already depositing the valise back in her father's car when Morris came up from the basement of his shop. He had been able to glance again at the ikon and now he did not know what to make of it. The way it was mounted certainly indicated falsity, but then the thing itself might be genuine despite its faked setting. Quiller would know a lot about ikons. He had handled two or three which had fetched sensational prices at Mandell & Strood's. . . . It was best to be on the safe side and get it out of its concocted frame.

'I'm awfully sorry, Quiller,' he said. 'I seem to be in a bit of a mess about that ikon. My damn fool of a bookkeeper has just pointed out that a deposit's been paid on it. It seems it was sold by my other assistant—the one who's now on holiday.'

Quiller succeeded in looking downcast as he received back his cheque, but there was an unwonted jauntiness in his step as he moved towards the street door that was vaguely disquieting. It was fortunate for Morris, as he stood scornfully watching Miss Sandilands drive off in the shabby little car, that he was not given any prophetic vision of the price at which the five panels in her suitcase were ultimately destined to change hands.

SEVEN

WHEN SIR Harry Maximer telephoned to the Station Hotel, Elderfield, at ten o'clock that night, his most optimistic hope was that Quiller might have laid hands on some thread that would lead him with due appearance of guilelessness to Dr. Sandilands; and the news that the pictures were already acquired gave him a shock of joy which, after the first spontaneous outburst of enthusiasm, he hastened to calm down with the sedative of too-good-to-be-true. He looked forward nevertheless to being contradicted, but Quiller's drowsy voice came back along the wire with an unwelcome strain of acquiescence.

'Well, yes, there's a snag. There always is. The doctor is keeping one back. Fifteen are yours, bought and paid for. As for the sixteenth, I'm afraid I just couldn't shift him.'

'But which? Which is it?' cried Maximer, his bliss ungratefully clouded by the blackest fears. He had studied his list of the treasures again and again, and there was now scarcely one on which his prehensile longings had not firmly closed their grasp.

'I don't know. Neither does he. It seems he's promised one to some woman, some friend of the family, and he doesn't know which she'll choose. That's why I may not be able to bring them tomorrow.'

'Not bring them tomorrow? Did you say you couldn't bring them tomorrow? Speak up, Quiller! The line's crackling.'

The line was crackling only with Sir Harry's excitement and anxiety, as Quiller recognized, but he spoke up obediently enough:

'He won't let me take them away till this woman has chosen the one she wants. There was no arguing with him about it. He'll try to get hold of her as soon as he can, and until then I shall have to cool my heels.'

'But my dear fellow, she may choose anything! *Anything!*' Maximer's voice was pitiable, for he realized that the woman was likely to be none other than Mrs. du Plessis—Mrs. du Plessis who, as he had perceived at once on closer inspection of the document, must have written those two brief but knowledgeable notes identifying the portraits of Pius II and Johannes Paleologus.

'Well, what could I do?' Quiller reasonably grumbled. 'He wasn't under any compulsion to sell. If I'd made too many difficulties, he'd have shown me the door. As it is, you've got fifteen items for a hundred guineas.'

'My dear man, don't for a moment think I fail to appreciate your magnificent performance, but if it was a question of money—Ah, those accursed pips! I'd forgotten I was in a public box. Wait, operator, wait! Don't cut me off!'

The operator had no sooner accepted the tribute of silver than Quiller began with unaccustomed vigour to answer what he had evidently taken for a challenge:

'It's not a question of money. He'd promised to give away this item and it was quite plain that he wasn't going to be talked out of it. Besides, I had to be careful how much fuss I made. Fusses put ideas into people's heads.'

'True! True!' sighed Maximer. 'Well, we can only hope for the best—I mean, hope that the lady's taste is of the worst, though I fear not. If it weren't for the suspense I should feel happier. But you were wise no doubt to buy on the spot even with this condition hanging over your head.'

'I thought you'd want me to make sure of them.'

'Of course. You've done an admirable job, Quiller, an admirable job. I congratulate you. And the bargain, so to speak, is signed and sealed?' Such deep solicitude betrayed itself through the complacent tone that Quiller, who was a humane man, was glad to give a positive assurance:

'I've paid the money and taken a receipt.'

'Superb! Then there's no going back on it. Fine work!'

No going back on it! An hour before Maximer knew his good fortune from Quiller, Stephanie had heard Dr. Sandilands pronounce these same words, so dismal in their significance to her that her strength of purpose seemed almost to fail her. She felt a sense of loss too poignant to be contended against, and had it not been for the question still outstanding—the choice of her infelicitous souvenir—she might have abandoned the struggle. But the effort to decide which picture was best worth saving brought her afresh to the conclusion that, if there was one faint, shadowy hope of saving all, she must pursue it to the end.

Among the various apprehensions with which she had called on the doctor, the last was that the pictures would already have been sold. Had she dreamed of such an eventuality she would, at whatever risk of seeming clamorous and tiresome, have made her visit earlier, but Beatrix's intervention had been unforeseen even by Linda. Dr. Sandilands' communication, made with embarrassment and apology, seemed to deprive her even of breath to protest, and it was while she sat thus dumbfoundered that Beatrix, in a spirit of slightly nervous defiance, explained how she herself had visited Morris's shop and what the upshot had been.

'We had to take our opportunity, you know,' she went on with the bright severity of a well-meaning nurse who tells her charge that some distasteful remedy is unavoidable. 'A hundred guineas is not to be sneezed at, and, judging by my experience with Morris, there aren't so many people who'd be willing to pay it as Sir Harry seemed to think— not in this district anyhow.' And as a sugar plum offered to disguise the bitterness of the medicine, she added, kindly enough: 'Daddy insisted that you were to have one of the pictures, absolutely whichever one you want.'

'Thank you,' said Stephanie. 'All thanks are quite inadequate for such a gift.' She gulped as if she had literally taken some pungent dose. 'I have a hundred guineas,' she began, twisting her fingers together with an awkward constraint wholly foreign to her. 'I naturally wouldn't have dared to offer you so low a price, but if—'

It was then that Dr. Sandilands informed her that there was no going back on his bargain.

'In any case, we should be simply taking advantage of you now that we've had Sir Harry's report,' he said with a regretful smile, 'to let you spend your money on these things. Especially since Morris and this man Quiller have fully confirmed, in their different ways, what Maximer thought.'

'I believe Stephanie would throw away her entire savings to show she was right and all the experts wrong.' Beatrix's laugh was rather edgy though meant to be one of good-humoured raillery.

'Don't you think it would be worth it,' Stephanie asked wanly, 'if I could?'

'Whatever faith may do in the way of moving mountains,' said the doctor, 'I'm afraid it really won't turn these pictures into what we hoped they were.'

There was a silence broken only by the light clicking of Beatrix's knitting needles. Then she rose and said: 'I'll go and get some more coffee, Stephanie, while you decide which one you want.'

Stephanie, knowing there would no longer be anyone on duty in the kitchen and that Beatrix would have to make the coffee herself, supposed she ought in politeness to refuse it, but the desire for Beatrix's absence was stronger than the desire to appear considerate, and she watched her take the tray out without protest.

'The pictures are unpacked in my consulting-room,' said the doctor. 'We didn't put them back after this Quiller fellow had gone because we thought there was just a chance you might come round this evening and want another look before you chose.'

'Thank you,' she repeated numbly. 'Is he in a great hurry to get them away?'

'Well, not a great hurry, but he's going back to London in a day or so, and it would certainly be a convenience to us if he took them with him, as he's quite willing to do.'

Getting up, Stephanie went towards the window, whence she stared into a darkness glossy with new-fallen rain. She was inclined afterwards to think that the black glitter of the leaves and the fresh smell of the earth stimulated her dejected mind to an exertion it would otherwise have been incapable of, and that, had it not been for the well-timed shower, she would have found nothing to do but make the choice they were awaiting so impatiently and be gone.

One thing now grew clear, her plan of selecting three or four panels for Arnold Bayley to see had become imprudent. All that would happen was that the fortunate Quiller would be free to go off to London as soon as he pleased with the remainder, leaving her favourites to be dealt with later. Indeed she must not acknowledge any favourites, but must rather make a bid to hold back the entire collection until . . . Until what? She could see no further than the necessity of gaining time—gaining time and convincing Arnold Bayley. Her pride demanded that she should convince him, since she had persuaded him against his judgment to take her story seriously: but she believed too that, if he became once a whole-hearted ally, he would prove a redoubtable one.

'Would you like to go and look them over again?' said the doctor coaxingly.

She turned and shook her head, summoning all her courage; for in the sensitive nothing needs more courage than to take a course that opposes the one socially required of them: 'The more I look at them, the harder it'll be for me to choose. Must I make up my mind at once? I should so much like to have a little while to think about it.'

The doctor, who felt that, considering the dance she had led him for two months, she was being rather unaccommodating, cleared his throat and said with a sort of mild desperation: 'We don't want to hurry you, of course, but now that we've actually sold the things and been paid for them, we should naturally be happier if they were out of the way.'

'Yes, I do see that. But as this is going to be much the most valuable object I've ever possessed in my life, it's a very big decision for me. I want to go home and weigh it up carefully.'

'You're mistaken about its value, you know.' He had been hoping most earnestly to avoid argument on what had become an altogether vexatious topic, but it seemed necessary to remind her. 'This London dealer came independently to practically the same conclusion as Maximer.'

'I dare say he did, seeing what he has to gain by it.'

'Maximer had nothing to gain by it.'

She frowned. The fact that Maximer was above suspicion certainly rendered her situation more difficult. 'Perhaps,' she said, groping towards the only explanation that took a plausible shape in her own mind, 'he's hidebound—professional critics and connoisseurs often are—and he simply couldn't believe his eyes when he was faced with anything so fabulous as a whole huge trunkful of Renaissance paintings. After all, he's made such a point of repudiating things, he's probably got a bias by now against accepting anything as genuine.'

Dr. Sandilands' brow contracted into even deeper lines of perplexity than Stephanie's. Her obsession threatened to be worrying. It had a sort of contagion about it, and it was a contagion he must not, dare not, risk taking again, for the pictures were sold. He had locked his desk drawer on one hundred pounds in notes, and Beatrix had put five in her purse for a bonus. The subject must be closed, closed beyond any possibility of renewing its disturbing effects upon the peace of his household.

'I think you're wrong,' he reproached her gently, 'to persist in believing what can only lead to another disillusionment—'

'I've had no disillusionment—except in Sir Harry Maximer.'

'Then you've got one still to come, I'm afraid. I've resigned myself. At least, I thought I had, but you won't let me. Are you being quite fair? We agreed to be guided by Maximer—it was your own suggestion if I remember rightly—and now it's too late to repent of it.'

She checked an impulse to persist, to vindicate herself. A rapid calculation showed her that there was nothing at this moment to be gained by it, and indeed she was not at all sure she had done wisely to throw such candid doubts on Sir Harry's authority. It might have been more politic to make a feint of acceptance.

So far as she could, she retracted. 'I'm sorry if I'm being a nuisance. I love the pictures—whether they're genuine or not.' The pretended misgiving almost stuck in her throat, but she went on resolutely: 'Whatever they may really be, to me the choice is enormously important, and since you've been so generous, I don't want to regret afterwards that I decided in a hurry.'

'How long will you want?' he asked in what was for him an uncommonly point-blank tone.

'Couldn't you give me two or three days, at any rate?'

He paused, suppressing a sigh of pure weariness before rejoining, 'We shall have to ask Mr. Quiller. They're his property now, my dear Mrs. du Plessis, and he's already made one concession.'

He was tempted, since she was proving so troublesome, to let her know how extremely reluctant Quiller had been to agree to the subtraction of one unspecified panel, and how much firmness it had taken on his part to impose the condition, but it was not easy even under provocation to overcome a lifetime's habit of kindliness, and he did sympathize very much with the disappointment which must have shocked her out of the complaisance he had certainly thought due on such an occasion, and clouded her mind with selfishness.

When Beatrix brought in the tray of coffee a few moments later and learned, with the exasperation Stephanie had so perfect a knack of inflicting on her, that there was to be no conclusion tonight to the maddening business, she gave a comic groan that was like a true word spoken in jest. 'Oh, my dear, just when I was telling myself that tomorrow morning Mr. Quiller would be able to fetch away that *hideous* trunk! Two months it's been cluttering up the house, and wherever I put it, it looks worse than it did in the place before. You are a terror, Stephanie, you and your Old Masters!'

'I'm dreadfully sorry.' Stephanie found herself laughing nervously at the idea of Beatrix still being saddled with the hated trunk, which could not but be a most unwelcome encumbrance to any housewife.

It had been out of the question to return it to the loft while Stephanie's researches were in progress, glad as Beatrix would have been to do so; and she could not take the pictures out and arrange some other storage for them because Stephanie had thought it risky, in the scanty state of their knowledge, to keep them anywhere but where they had for years successfully been kept. There was in any case little cupboard room available during the summer holidays when Geoffrey and Valerie were home. Moreover, these younger members of the family were not taken into the secret of the hopes that Stephanie had implanted, and this had meant still more bother for the guardian of the Saratoga, who was obliged to let it remain accessible and yet prevent its unsightly presence from arousing curiosity.

After all these weeks it was hardly remarkable that Beatrix had developed what might, in a more highly strung person, have been called a neurosis on the subject of large and cumbersome boxes, and she considered that her father, by yielding to Stephanie's pleas for delay, had shown an absurd indulgence to what was manifestly affectation of a most irritating character.

At least, however, they were freed from any compulsion to go on treating the miserable trunk as if it contained the crown jewels. It was with a distinct touch of satisfaction that she announced, after Stephanie had reiterated her meaningless apologies:

'Tomorrow morning I shall call all hands on deck and have the thing moved out to the garage. That'll be one stage further on the way to getting rid of it.'

'We mustn't take any risks,' said the doctor, 'especially since they're no longer ours to risk, my dear.'

'I don't suppose they'll come to any harm in a thoroughly dry garage with a concrete floor and brick walls. They'll only be there a day or two at the most.' She looked challengingly at Stephanie, who began to stir her coffee with an air of perhaps excessive concentration.

The garage, as she remembered it, was full of an oily kind of dust, but that would not affect the pictures while they remained enclosed. Certain vague foreshadowings of the advantage that might be gained from their removal were gathering together among her more sanguine and venturesome thoughts, and it was her attempt to bring them into focus and not, as Beatrix thought, her mortified pride at the inglorious climax to all her fantasies, that kept her gazing silently into her coffee-cup until, pulling herself together, she offered to help in repacking the Saratoga, and took care, knowing how little her advice would now be regarded, to throw out a hint that it ought not to be sent to the garage.

When, a little after ten o'clock, she set out on her homeward journey, she paused at the gate by the side of the house, intending to cast over the outbuildings a daringly speculative eye. To her embarrassment that glance lighted instead upon two figures withdrawn against the still glistening wall just within the gateway. They were not embracing, but their murmuring voices and a sort of coquetry in the attitude of the backward-leaning girl suggested that at least the desire to embrace was understood between them and might presently pull them together like an invisible cord.

She was about to walk on, hoping to remain unnoticed, when a familiar giggle and the sound of her own name called softly after her on a little splutter of laughter informed her that it was Linda whose flirtation she had interrupted and who evidently supposed herself to have been recognized.

She hastened with an exaggerated start to dispel the impression that she could knowingly have intruded and, explaining deftly that she had stopped because she thought for a moment there was a book of hers left behind in the house, she was hurrying away when Linda, in a confusion of friendliness and bravado, said:

'Do let me introduce Mr. Kenneth Dyer—though it's quite unnecessary as you've met him any number of times!'

Reluctantly no doubt, but making the best of it, there stepped from the damp shadows where he had been hovering the young photographer who had lately been such a frequent visitor at the library, and they greeted each other in the slightly facetious manner that the occasion seemed to call for.

'What do you think I've been doing?' Linda demanded, covering up with her customary good humour the awkwardness they were all feeling. 'It's a secret. You mustn't tell the others because it's going to be a surprise for Daddy's birthday. I've been having my photograph taken!'

'What a good idea!' Stephanie was too well accustomed to Linda's ready sociability to feel much surprise at the progress she had made with her new acquaintance since this morning. 'Of course Mr. Dyer has the Portrait Studio.'

'Worse luck!' said Kenneth Dyer sepulchrally.

'Why, don't you like it?'

'As a place to work in it's not bad, as a business proposition it's not good.' A reply so perfectly succinct made her smile despite her preoccupation.

'The inhabitants of Charlton Wells probably have a horror of seeing their own faces,' said Linda. 'Do you wonder?'

'Not much, but I wish someone had told me before I sank my all in a studio for taking their portraits.'

'Never mind! You've got mine now,' Linda remarked with a flicker of the eyelids that showed on what an easy footing they already stood. 'It won't bring you any money, but just imagine what a thing of beauty it'll be!'

'I wouldn't be too sure. Yours is a jolly difficult face.'

'I like that—when you suggested doing it yourself!'

'I wanted something hard to practise on.'

'It was a lot harder for me than for you, let me tell you! The time you took, and the way you made me stand under those frightful lamps until I felt like a waxwork that was being melted down! I'd just as soon have been at the dentist's.'

'When shall we see the result?' asked Stephanie, who had decided to linger long enough to avoid the appearance of pointedly doing what was tactful.

'I'll get on with them in the morning, unless the local press gives me something to do. It's practically my sole support at the moment—that and my daily crime story.' He spoke after a manner he had cultivated during a shy phase of his adolescence, quite directly but as if it were immaterial whether anyone heard him or not, like an actor who has been told to 'throw away' certain lines. 'I might have some prints tomorrow evening,' he confided to one of the gateposts.

'Oh, how lovely!' Linda's voice when she was pleased had a purring quality that was very endearing. 'When shall I know?'

'I'll drop in at the library some time during the day.'

'Don't forget it's a secret, Steph! Talking of secrets, you'll be awfully shocked when you hear what I've done this evening. I've told Mr. Dyer—Kenneth, all about the pictures! I had to get it off my chest to someone, and after all, it can't affect us any more.'

'I'm not shocked,' said Stephanie gratefully. 'I told someone myself this morning.'

'This morning? When you were supposed to be sickening for some deadly disease! I thought you were up to something.'

'If you come to work a bit earlier tomorrow I'll let you know what I was really doing . . . but don't breathe a word, will you?'

'Oh, do tell me now! Kenneth doesn't matter. I mean,' she laughed, 'he's in the secret. I say, shall we move away from the house? We'll have Beatrix popping her head out of the window in a minute.' She walked off, briskly at first, in Stephanie's homeward direction and, as the others caught up with her, said encouragingly: 'Kenneth is by way of being a sympathizer.'

'A sympathizer? *Are* you?'

Her inflexion was so eager that he felt obliged to make a disclaimer. 'I only said that, if it had been me, I should have taken another opinion before I'd have sold those pictures.'

'You know then what's happened about them?'

'I dashed home to change,' Linda replied elliptically. 'I must admit it gave me a slight wrench when I heard the deed was done. But Beatrix was terrifically pleased because she'd got what Sir Harry Maximer believed they were worth and a bit over.'

'That was what made me think,' said the young man.

'Think what, Kenneth?'

'Just "think".'

'Now you're not to be mysterious, *please!*'

'If it was so easy to get that much money from the very first chap who came along, perhaps there were other chaps who would have been willing to give a lot more.'

'What a grim thought! And yet Sir Harry surely ought to know, oughtn't he?'

'I don't see why he should,' said Kenneth Dyer with a sudden forthrightness of tone that rang in Stephanie's ears like a herald's trumpet. 'Being an expert about the technical side of something isn't the same thing as knowing its commercial value. And anyhow, experts differ. They're always at loggerheads. In the firm I worked for in London we used to take photographs for some of the art journals. I've been to these collectors' houses and heard the sort of things they say about each other—worse than politicians some of them! I'd never be satisfied with the word of one expert. Another thing,' he went on, having wound himself up to a pitch of uninhibited eloquence, 'a hundred guineas seems to me a pretty tricky price to pay for a bunch of old paintings. Either they're junk, in which case no one would give that much, or else they aren't junk, and you can take it from me, if there's a man willing to pay a hundred there could just as well be another who'd pay a thousand.'

Linda, not having been present at the fateful interview in London, found this reasoning more impressive than it might have appeared if she had shared her sister's disadvantage of hearing the forceful and persuasive voice of Maximer first.

'Oh dear,' she moaned, 'why on earth does Beatrix have to get in a flap about everything? Now you've made me quite certain she's done the wrong thing. Daddy would never have taken such a turn against them if she hadn't fussed him.'

Stephanie, who guessed that a few words from a new admirer would weigh more at this moment than a whole discourse from herself, had refrained from interrupting even to acclaim his wisdom; but now, her plan having gradually achieved, not perfect focus, but sufficient outline to suggest what shape it would ultimately take, she made a diplomatic passado.

'I do wish Mr. Dyer could see the pictures for himself, don't you, Linda? As he's photographed such things, it would at least be interesting to hear his views.'

'Yes, it would,' Linda agreed with mournful cordiality, 'but Beatrix would only make one of her fusses, and anyhow, I think the man who's bought them is taking them away tomorrow.'

'Not tomorrow. That has been postponed for a day or two. And Beatrix is going to have them moved out to the garage.' She pronounced the word with emphasis and paused before continuing: 'I went this morning to Elderfield Art Gallery and spoke to the director, Arnold Bayley. He would very much like to see them too.' She apologized silently for a misrepresentation which she hoped would one day be freely forgiven by its victims. 'Don't you think it would be worth while if we could manage somehow or other to show them . . . without troubling Beatrix or your father?'

Linda stifled a little gasp at the audacity which she was very well able to detect beneath the seeming innocence of this proposal. 'Do you mean we should creep into the garage at dead of night, you and me and Kenneth and this perfectly strange art gallery man, and hold a Private View?'

'No, not the garage. The light's not good enough, and there's no room for seeing anything properly. We'd have to get the pictures out and take them somewhere else.'

'But my dear Steph, what could we do about it even if it turned out that they were worth their weight in diamonds like the Aga Khan? They've been sold, s-o-l-d—sold! You don't seem to grasp it.'

'Still, there *are* things we could do. Most decidedly there are!' Her bold and ready utterance conveyed so clearly the sense of her having considered the problem well and knowing what measures to take that

Linda, accustomed as she was at the library to regard her colleague as a prodigy of efficiency, found her faith in her pleasantly stirring again. It had never been as ready to yield itself up for destruction as that of her father, who was easily abashed, or Beatrix in whose nature scepticism was deeply rooted; and the fact that a young man of hourly increasing congeniality had expressed misgivings about the transaction quite independently of Stephanie's influence had already profoundly shaken her.

'Well, I suppose it would be sensible—in a way—to hear what someone else besides Sir Harry Maximer has to say about them,' she acknowledged as they strolled along slowly towards the avenue where Stephanie lived, 'though it won't do us much good to be told they're not junk after all unless we can induce Daddy to hang on to them. He's actually been paid, you know.'

'Bit of a coincidence, wasn't it?' said Kenneth Dyer in one of his elaborately casual asides.

'What was a coincidence?' Linda took her cue happily, for she enjoyed being forced to question him.

'On Wednesday in London this picture fancier says to your father, "You might get a hundred guineas for them". On Thursday in Charlton Wells along comes another picture fancier—from London too—who's got just a hundred guineas in his pocket.'

'You read too many detective stories. We'll have to put you on to Science or Biog, or something. The man didn't come from London, though he has a shop there: he came from Elderfield. And he offered a hundred guineas because my father asked for a hundred and twenty pounds, so there's not much of a coincidence about that!'

'I call it a coincidence for him to turn up at all.'

'Linda's sister found him; he didn't find her,' said Stephanie, who was anxious to press on with her plan, and feared to be led away on a trail that must surely prove false. 'She went out to sell the pictures and she came across a man who would buy them. It isn't very remarkable considering what they are,' she added bitterly. 'He'd seen five of them to begin with.'

Kenneth, with a brief grunt of disappointment, surrendered the argument, and she proceeded artfully: 'I have an appointment to meet Arnold Bayley tomorrow night. Did you know he'd held an important post in Florence at the end of the war, taking care of works of art? He has really very good qualifications indeed for advising us because he must have specialized in the Florentines.' She had no idea whether her description of his activities was accurate, but on an occasion so vital the letter of the truth must be sacrificed to expediency. 'What's worrying me is—where can we take the things once we've got them out of the garage?'

'My goodness! Isn't it a case of first catch your hare?' Linda interrupted, but with a gaiety that was heartening. 'How do we get them out of the garage! That trunk's not exactly invisible, my dear, and it weighs about as much as a grand piano.'

'We can't leave them in the trunk—'

'Beatrix keeps it locked.'

'Then you must steal the key!' The command was spoken with an echo of Linda's own playful note, whereby Stephanie hoped to present the scheme in the light of an escapade, a lively little adventure such as young people of high spirits might take in their stride. 'You can get hold of it and put it back after you've undone the lock without anyone being the wiser. Then tomorrow evening you say you're going out; you meet me; we wait till it's dark and we quietly bring out the pictures and take them where Mr. Bayley—and Mr. Dyer of course—can see them.'

'How do we carry them? On our heads?'

Stephanie was aware that Linda's flippancy augured not badly for the project since it was one that she was more likely to support in fun than in sober seriousness, and she strove to keep her reply in the same key: 'In wheelbarrows or perambulators if we can't get anything better. Or wouldn't it be possible for Mr. Dyer to meet us at the corner with a taxi?'

'So you want to implicate me, do you?'

Though jocose, his tone was not without a shading of expostulation, and she cast round feverishly for some means of quieting his scruples, for she feared that Linda, even if well-disposed, would never work up the energy or the courage to act without him.

'Why, we're absolutely depending on you!' she exclaimed. 'The panels are oak more than an inch thick. Linda and I will be wrecked if we handle them alone.'

'Isn't your Elderfield curator going to help? It's more his line than mine.'

She had no intention of disclosing at so critical a stage how necessary it was to conceal from Arnold Bayley measures against which he was certain to set his face, and there was nothing for it but to grow more daring in mendacity. 'I'm afraid he can't get over in time to be of much use. He has to have dinner with someone first.' And to circumvent his further question she continued rapidly: 'Have you ever seen him, Linda? It came as a great surprise to me that he was such a young and attractive man. That's the last thing one expects to find in Elderfield.'

Involuntarily she sighed. It was with her he had planned to dine, and she could not sacrifice the prospect without a keen-edged regret. Now the engagement must be put back to an hour when she could count on having secured the pictures, and he might never again invite her to the Royal Hotel, where she could have worn her new hat and had a long talk about other things than Renaissance art to convince him of her sanity.

'Young and attractive!' Linda inevitably giggled. 'You didn't mention *that* before! *Now* I see what all your plotting is about! *Now* you've let the cat out of the bag!'

Stephanie's first impulse was earnestly to deny the aspersion, but a sounder instinct warned her in time that she had stumbled on the one infallible means of gaining Linda's whole sympathy, without which nothing was possible. The more she could give this enterprise the colour of a manoeuvre on her part to bring her into contact with a man who appealed to her, the nearer she would be to bringing it to Linda's own plane, a plane on which the affairs of the heart were the most important business in life and it was friendship's paramount duty to smooth the path towards a new attachment. Conspiring to preserve Old Masters was an activity in which she could never feel completely in her element, even though the family fortunes should depend on it; but doing a good turn to a friend who was angling for a particular young man was a cause not open to dispute. For that she was prepared to throw her bonnet over the highest windmill.

So instead of defending herself, Stephanie laughed as if she had been found out, protested ineffectually, and murmured something to the effect that Linda really ought to have a look at him.

The ruse served a double purpose, for Kenneth, mistaking the nature of Linda's evident interest in Arnold Bayley, decided not to be left out of an occasion from which, but for this stimulus, he might have preferred to remain prudently aloof. It turned out too that he could bring a car.

'I have to have one,' he explained at large to anyone who might be listening, 'because of carrying round lights and cameras when I do my outside work. I share it with a friend who's in digs with me, a reporter.'

'You'd better not let him report this,' cried Linda.

'He won't know anything about it. Not that it would make much of a story. You take some pictures out of your father's garage one evening, and you put them back! I wouldn't call it precisely a scoop, would you? ... If you do put them back!'

'Of course! Do you think we're going to steal them?'

'We still haven't decided where we can take them,' said Stephanie. 'There's my bed-sitting-room if the worst comes to the worst, but it's very small for four people and sixteen pictures, and my landlady always hovers round when I bring anyone in.'

'I suppose you're hinting that you want the studio?' Kenneth Dyer kicked a pebble off the sidewalk and into the gutter as if he were disposing of some last reluctance. 'Well, as long as you honestly don't intend to steal them, all right! I can give you plenty of light at any rate.'

'Oh, Kenneth, you are a saint!'

Warmly, cosily, Linda slipped her arm under his, and Stephanie deemed it was time to let him take up their conversation where she had caused it to be broken off.

Walking alone down Jubilee Avenue, she felt the exhilaration of her own persuasiveness dismally subsiding. Her thoughts now seemed to reflect only the faint gleams of light caught by the moisture still lying on the black surface of the road. The responsibility she had taken upon herself, had even thrust in some lesser degree on others, weighed heavily upon her, and though she realized that circumstances had favoured her and was glad of the presence of mind that had enabled her to turn them to advantage, she still faced far too many hazards to be at ease. For all her air of being prepared for every eventuality, assumed to inspire confidence in the others, she had exhausted her ingenuity, and her furthest horizon was now the moment when Arnold Bayley would pronounce his judgment.

EIGHT

ARNOLD BAYLEY, for his part, reached the same hour of the evening in an almost equally obsessing quandary. He had taken home the Medici dossier through which, during his working day, he had only been able to glance superficially. His motive was rather one of courtesy towards a young woman in whose eyes he hoped to be agreeable than a desire to know the intricacies of her delusion, a delusion he trusted himself to have cured completely within twenty-four hours; but as he read it was borne in upon him once again, and more forcibly than before, that he had under his hand a piece of research that must compel attention. The immense labour she had devoted to pursuing the evidences of lost Florentine paintings was itself impressive, and the comparison between known features of missing works and corresponding features in the paintings owned by Dr. Sandilands had been made in such an eminently rational style that he could not read her descriptions of the five she thought she had identified without the strongest curiosity to see them with his own eyes.

The more, in short, he considered the whole story of this singular cache of pictures, as it emerged from her neatly arranged papers, the more unlikely it seemed that a person who had so intelligently set about probing their mystery could be quite deceived as to their nature, and he began to ask himself whether, after all, it were possible for Maximer to have erred.

The upshot of his various conjectures was that next morning, as he finished dictating letters to his secretary, he suddenly demanded, with very little conscious volition:

'Have we any file for Sir Harry Maximer, Miss Bosworth?'

Miss Bosworth, who had served the Art Gallery efficiently for twenty-four years, looked at him in slightly pained and yet perfectly respectful interrogation. It was not the least part of her efficiency that she had the happy faculty of feeling respect for each successive director though no two had had the same policy in running the gallery and each new one appointed had turned out several years younger than his predecessor.

'A file?' she repeated. 'If there's a correspondence there's bound to be a file.'

'Could I see it?'

'Certainly, Mr. Bayley. I'll go and get it.'

The folder when it came was disappointingly slender. He hardly knew what he had expected, but the letters and carbon copies dealing with the opening of the summer exhibition and, before that, with the hanging of certain valuable canvases which Sir Harry, during the war, had lent for safety to provincial galleries, made him feel a shade foolish; and it was with only an idle sort of persistence that he asked Miss Bosworth later in the morning:

'So Sir Harry has never concerned himself in any of our transactions here?'

'Do you mean—have we ever consulted him about buying something? Oh, yes, I'm sure we have, Mr. Bayley, though I can't remember when offhand.'

'There's nothing in the file.'

'No, we have separate files for purchases.' She spoke apologetically, in case it should seem to be any reflection upon him that he had let this detail escape him.

'Of course. I'd forgotten—those box things! But one has to know the year.'

'Well, there's the catalogue of purchases. That would save time in tracing the year.'

'Provided we knew what had been purchased.'

'Yes,' said Miss Bosworth after a sympathetic pause, while she tapped her pencil on her lips. 'We've got an index of the people we've bought things from, but that wouldn't be much help because Sir Harry isn't in it. I know we've never bought anything from him direct, though I'm sure he was instrumental in getting something or other.'

'It would be something Italian. That narrows the field. We're not what you can call rich in Italians at Elderfield.'

'Italian, and bought within the last fifteen years or so,' Miss Bosworth reflectively took up the unrevealing file. 'Before that Sir Harry hadn't quite the reputation he has now.'

'Yes, he's by way of being unique, I suppose—an asbestos magnate who's made himself an authority on art. If he wrote his autobiography it ought to be well worth reading.'

Miss Bosworth's previous employer, Mr. Sinnett, had never discussed anything with her except the weather, and she had admired him for his reticence; Mr. Bayley, on the other hand, often conversed with her for five or ten minutes on end in the easiest manner, and she admired him too, for his affability. Encouraged by it now, she replied, delving into a long if vague memory:

'I heard once that he began as office boy at the Quattrocento Gallery in London. He rose to quite a responsible position, and then there was some unpleasantness between him and the owner and he left. But one of the clients who was an important business man took him on as secretary or something of the sort. He must be very clever because he kept up his interest in art and learned all about business too.'

'I'll bet he did,' said Arnold, who had received a vivid impression of Maximer's capacity for learning anything it was to his advantage to know.

'And there's some story, but I've half-forgotten it, of an asbestos mine in Australia that was being badly run and making a loss, and Sir Harry—Mr. Maximer he was then, of course—was sent out there to look into things. He got it all sorted out and reorganized, and I think they gave him some shares, or perhaps he bought them when they were very low. Anyway, that was how he first got connected with asbestos, and now he more or less controls that huge company.'

'One wonders,' Arnold threw out, as a fisherman might throw a line without any idea of what sort of fish is to be caught or whether there is any fish to be caught at all, 'one wonders how he finds time for all his other activities, or even money to collect pictures on such a scale, taxation being what it is.'

'I suppose when you get to the very top of the tree, you don't have to sit all day with your nose to the grindstone.'

'That's probably why people climb to the tops of trees, Miss Bosworth, if you come to think of it.'

'As for the money,' she continued with a slight uncomprehending smile, 'Sir Harry has such a flair for buying things that he keeps a few years and then sells again at a higher price that perhaps his collecting isn't such an expensive hobby as it seems.'

He picked up his paper-knife and gazed at it for seconds on end entirely without seeing it. Then he asked unhopefully: 'Well, bring me the catalogue of purchases, Miss Bosworth, and I'll skim over it.'

The same respectfulness which prevented Miss Bosworth from asking why the information was needed convinced her that it was needed for some good reason, and it was a point of pride with her to be of service in such a matter if she could. Consequently, when Arnold, after checking over the gallery's few Italian pictures and their sources, had more or less decided to abandon a quest which, in any case, he had undertaken without a very clear idea of what he was looking for, she remained diligently turning over in her mind all her recollections of Sir Harry Maximer, until she lighted on one that took her back to the director's room.

'Mr. Bayley, if you've got a few minutes to come down to the Cemetery with me, I might be able to find the picture Sir Harry recommended. I should remember it if I saw it.'

Since their last conversation, he had received a telephone call from Mrs. du Plessis putting back the hour of their appointment that evening from seven-thirty till nine, cancelling, in fact, the dinner which, tasted in anticipation, had lent a zest to his search for knowledge that might serve her. The excuses she gave for postponing the hour had not even sounded genuine, and his enthusiasm had been so dampened that he no longer thought of Maximer, or the Medici dossier, but only of the casual way in which, after all that cajolery of yesterday, he was being treated, and whether he should not have stood on his dignity and refused to go altogether.

The invitation to accompany his secretary to the part of the building known as the Cemetery, however, revived his interest in the morning's problem; for it was here that were kept the gallery's failures, the works that had been acquired but were never shown. Maximer having so remarkable a flair for judging whether a picture would appreciate in value, it would be a strange thing if a purchase sponsored by him should have turned out unfit for exhibition. A strange thing and one worth knowing when the question was whether a verdict of his could be called into dispute! He sent to the public rooms for an attendant and followed Miss Bosworth downstairs.

The basement store-room was large, airy, and well lighted, partly by daylight and partly by electricity. Under the present regime, racks had been built to hold the canvases, and great care was taken to preserve them without deterioration, since Arnold Bayley recognized that taste is not immutable and that a future curator might see these objects with a very different eye from his. He had rescued some charming Victorians despised by his predecessor Sinnett, while Sinnett had brought back to light a Fuseli and a Mulready exiled in disgust by old Cobbleston. An interest in such vicissitudes, examples of which abound in the history of art, had made it a matter of conscience with Arnold to get the Cemetery cleaned, tidied, and properly conditioned for its purpose.

But in a shunned corner, shrouded by dust sheets that were like the robes of penitents, was a batch of pictures for which it was quite certain that no resurrection was possible, the spurious and semi-spurious productions of which, whether through bad judgment or bequests of a mixed character, every public collection must possess some specimens. Elderfield was rather exceptionally well supplied with them, certain directors having been incautious, and several—especially in the early days when there was little to exhibit—ready to accept gifts or legacies of doubtful quality. Yet latterly there had been much more selectiveness both in making purchases and admitting gifts, and one hardly expected to find any acquisition of the last fifteen years in this section, least of all one which had the good word of Sir Harry Maximer.

'What makes you think it's in the Rogues' Gallery?' he inquired, raising his eyebrows incredulously at Miss Bosworth as the attendant removed the dust sheets.

'Because it was one of the things Mr. Sinnett had X-rayed. He was so fond of getting things X-rayed,' she added with the almost maternal indulgence she felt for the idiosyncrasies by which each curator was distinguished in her mind. 'And he was simply amazed when it turned out to have something wrong with it. So was Sir Harry. I can distinctly remember there was a correspondence about it. But the artist's name just escapes me—though I think it begins with a W.'

'Surely no Italian names begin with W?'

'Then perhaps it's not an Italian. Yes, on second thoughts I believe it was something else. No, no, it won't be among those!' she cried to the attendant, who was manoeuvring a large canvas out of the rack. 'It's a small thing, that I'm certain of!'

The fact that the picture, when identified, was of medium size and bore a plaque ascribing it to Jan Brueghel made Arnold doubt at first whether Miss Bosworth's recognition could be valid, but as she instantly dropped the W and pronounced emphatically in favour of B, and as, moreover, the fake was of a most skilful and deceptive order, and one he had determined to investigate the first time he had noticed it, he allowed it to be carried up to his office; and soon he had before him the dossier it was now a simple matter to produce.

The first letter bore a date eleven years old, in Cobbleston's time, and was from Maximer himself:

Dear Cobbleston,

I thank you sincerely for your very gratifying remarks about *Milanese Painters*. I sent you the book with some diffidence because the colour reproduction is not all I could wish; but I am glad you think the text will be helpful. That is the kind of appreciation one works for.

Since our pleasant meeting last Christmas, I have been wondering, à propos of our conversation on Flemish painting, whether you are still without a single example at Elderfield. If so, it has occurred to me that I might be of some assistance. I don't profess to anything more than a superficial knowledge of the Flemish schools myself, but my friend the late John Rennick was, of course, a matchless authority, and I think I can lay my hands on a fine little Nativity by Jan Brueghel with his unqualified certification. It belongs to an acquaintance who is settling in South Africa and anxious to sell, and I fancy on the question of price he would not be unmanageable.

If you would care to see the picture, I can arrange for a meeting between you.

I enclose the letter Dr. Rennick wrote to me personally about this panel when I made inquiry of him a little while before his death, on behalf of the owner. Please return it if you are not interested.

With all kind greetings,

Yours,

H. MAXIMER

Clipped to this was the letter referred to, a typed note in Rennick's well-known staccato style full of those vigorous and incisive phrases which have made him the most-quoted of the post-Victorian critics. No collector could have read the bold opening words: 'An unmistakable Velvet Brueghel and a most seductive one!' without a stirring of the heart.

Cobbleston had responded by return of post, and Maximer's next communication was dated only a few days later:

Dear Cobbleston,

There is no need for you to come all the way to London to look at the Brueghel as I shall be able to meet you better than half-way. I am lecturing in Manchester on the 17th, and Jones (the owner) is willing to entrust me with the picture, so if you would like to come over and see if we can get down to those ugly but useful objects, brass tacks.

Surely it is a case for a grant from the Wellings Bequest! Unfortunately, Jones is being advised by friends to sell at Christie's or Mandell & Strood's, but I think he would be susceptible to a firm offer of cash if only you can speed up your Committee. At any rate, I will use what persuasions I can, for I would rather see it at Elderfield than anywhere. There are some who would say it ought to stay in London, but though a Londoner myself, I am opposed to this pernicious centralization, and, as you know, I never cease to strive against it, by doing everything within my humble power for the provincial galleries.

Matters had evidently moved swiftly after this. To buy a masterpiece praised in the highest terms by so great an authority as Rennick and recommended by Maximer seemed a plunge worth taking even to the Elderfield City Council; and the Trustees of the Wellings Bequest had agreed to loosen their purse strings after a comparatively brief period of deliberation. The receipt signed by S. R. Jones was dated only four weeks after the interview that had taken place in Manchester.

Mr. Jones himself, it appeared, had not met Cobbleston after all. Having a great pressure of affairs to cope with before sailing for South Africa, he had left the whole transaction in the capable hands of Maximer, who had dealt with it, apparently, to everybody's satisfaction.

And then, six years later, when Cobbleston had been superannuated and was settled in retirement, the correspondence had been reopened on the most inauspicious note that could well be imagined. Sinnett's X-rays had shown up the so-called Brueghel as an ingenious piece of over-painting on a composition by a much inferior artist of the same period. Every original feature that could lend verisimilitude to the whole effect had been cleverly put to use, but all that was most characteristic of Jan Brueghel was pure forgery.

Such was Sinnett's unpleasant discovery, and, Rennick being dead and Jones's whereabouts unknown, there was no one to take it up with but the person who had negotiated the purchase; a delicate matter, since Maximer—who had just been knighted for his services to art—had acted without any gain to himself, moved only by the desire to perform a service. But Sinnett, with a judicious mixture of discretion and valour, had written explaining what had been found, tactfully leaving the query implicit in his phrasing.

Sir Harry's reply had come as swiftly as the post could bring it, and gained an additional *empressement* from being written in his own hand:

Dear Mr. Sinnett,

I am shocked—shocked and distressed and bewildered to hear that my dear old friend could have fallen into such a trap. That John Rennick should have been taken in by a fake is something I could not have believed if the details you have given had not made it indisputable.

The news is doubly painful as you can imagine, because of my having been the agent of this imposition. As you must know, I have never pretended to be an expert on anything but Italian art, and without a confirmation from a first-rate source, I would not have dreamed of pronouncing judgment on a painting quite outside my own province, attractive and convincing though it looked. Such a lapse on Rennick's part must be an almost unique instance in the career of one of the finest critics that this or any other country has produced, and I can only account for it by supposing that his ill health at the time must have disturbed his faculties. He was a dying man. I should not have troubled him, but he gave himself so unstintingly to all who made demands on his vast fund of specialized knowledge that we, his friends and disciples, unwittingly abused his kindness.

I am deeply sorry for your justifiable annoyance and the disappointment you will feel at having to remove from your walls a picture which must have been regarded as a treasure— but I hope you will not do anything to reflect on the reputation of one who is no longer here to defend himself.

Yours very sincerely,

HARRY MAXIMER

It had evidently struck Sinnett, as it now struck Arnold Bayley, that in all this loyal outpouring there was no mention of Mr. S. R. Jones, who had received some thousands of pounds for his doctored panel; and he had been pertinacious enough to write again making inquiry as to the good faith of this beneficiary. Maximer's answer, if less vehement than his earlier letter, was in a tone equally firm and unwavering:

I regret [he wrote] that in the perturbed state of my mind when I replied to you the other day, I did not think to touch upon Jones's part in this unhappy affair. I am myself satisfied that it was a completely honest one. I will not say I knew him well; he was an acquaintance rather than a friend, but I saw enough of him to feel convinced that he was incapable of such a heinous contrivance of fraudulence as we have here. The painting must have been tampered with long ago, probably before his grandfather bought it: but whatever his position in the matter, legally or morally, I am afraid he will never be able to make restitution, for he was killed in the first year of the War.

It is not my business to make suggestions, and especially after the fiasco which has arisen from my suggestion to Cobbleston in regard to this picture: but if I dared to hint at what would seem to me a proper course, I would say—the repercussions of shaking Rennick's credit will obviously be serious, while Cobbleston is an old man to whom this will come, I imagine, as a severe shock.

If all the sleeping dogs in the public institutions of Great Britain were aroused, we should hear some very ugly noises. What you choose to do is entirely up to you, and if you decide upon publicity I will not flinch from my share of the responsibility, for, like your Arts Committee and the Wellings Trustees, I was (such is my perhaps prejudiced opinion) justified in reposing on the authority of Rennick.

That was the last letter in the dossier. Sinnett must have taken the hint and let the expensive mistake sink into oblivion. There had certainly been several good reasons for doing so. The simple course, since no restitution was possible, was to remove the offending panel from sight and omit it from the printed catalogue without comment, and this had been done the more easily because at that time there was so little public interest in the Elderfield Art Gallery that its visitors were chiefly those who came in to shelter from the rain.

Arnold Bayley sat for some minutes perfectly motionless, with the documents under his hand. Then he looked carefully at Jones's receipt, but being made out on a printed form supplied by the City Council, it revealed nothing. Finally, he re-read Rennick's brief but glowing tribute to the merits and beauty of the forgery.

He had seen letters of Rennick's before—they were almost as much a kind of trophy in the world of art as Bernard Shaw's postcards in the world of letters—and there was no doubting the genuineness of this one. The writing paper with the engraving of Chadley Hall at the heading, the script in the italic type of the old Darton machine he had persisted in using long after it had become obsolete—these would have been recognized at a glance by dealers, curators, connoisseurs, all over England and indeed much further afield. But for so great a man to be hoodwinked by a pastiche, however cunningly executed . . . what consternation would it not cause if this were known among those who had regarded his verdicts as all but unquestionable!

And if Rennick could fall, Rennick with his even longer store of experience, his even closer application to his subject—for art was his livelihood as well as his pleasure—then must an opinion of Maximer's be treated as sacrosanct? He was glad now, glad to the point of elation in spite of the lost dinner, that he had consented to go over to Charlton Wells that night, and that he would be able to take an open mind with him.

NINE

'I WOULD go to the stake,' said Arnold Bayley quietly, 'swearing that every one of these pictures was painted before the sixteenth century.'

Linda clapped her hands, or at any rate, clasped them with a sound of joyful percussion, and Stephanie, who had been holding her breath, suddenly exhaled it all as if she scarcely cared whether she ever breathed again. Kenneth Dyer began, mechanically, to switch off lights.

'What a moment to leave us in the dark!' cried Linda. 'Really, Kenneth!'

'It's only the contrast. Your eyes'll be used to it in a minute.'

'Our eyes don't want to get used to it. They're celebrating. They need light.'

'All right.' He restored the splendid effulgence in which they had been basking. 'It's obvious you don't know what it costs to burn photofloods,' he added with a candour which his throw-away technique turned to a kind of pleasantry.

'We can pay for them,' she laughed, 'out of the proceeds of the pictures. Stephanie always said they were valuable. What do you think, Mr. Bayley?'

'Valuable! They could hardly fail to be that.' He stared gravely at the three sturdy planks which, laid one above the other, made up the painting of Leda. 'This alone is capable of creating a sensation.'

'Heavens! Do you know, we nearly threw that one away because it was in pieces? What a blessing we didn't!'

'But it's as good as thrown away now, isn't it?' The appalling truth of his words struck him as he uttered them, and he directed at each of them in turn a glance of bleak dismay. For when they had told him, just before he had begun to examine the pictures, of their having yesterday been sold, he had listened only with half his attention. The surprise of finding himself drawn into a secret conclave in a photographer's studio would have tinged with unreality anything imparted to him at that moment; but now the communication came back upon him with a full impact, and he stood aghast.

'Surely,' said Stephanie buoyantly, sustained by the glorious verdict, 'they can't hold Dr. Sandilands to the bargain?'

'I'm afraid they most certainly can.'

'But if he insists on returning the money?'

'He can't insist on their accepting it. They might compel him to hand over the pictures.'

'What? When he's been paid a hundred times less than the fair price?'

'That without doubt is the legal position.'

'Legal position? But Dr. Sandilands has been cheated.'

Arnold began with a nervous step to move about the room. 'It's not cheating, you know,' he admonished her gloomily, 'to buy something at the lowest price you can get it for.'

'Daddy only asked a very little more, after all,' Linda reminded them in a soft and sorrowful voice.

'Suppose'—Stephanie tried in vain to subdue her passionate resistance to a calm persuasiveness—'suppose a man sold a wonderful set of jewels under the impression that they were paste, and the jeweller paid for them as paste knowing all the time that they were diamonds . . . ?'

Inexorably he shook his head. 'The law wouldn't take the view that the jeweller was cheating. The law says it's up to the man who's selling something to know what sort of object it is.'

'And that,' said Kenneth, flinging the words into the open door of the dark-room, 'is exactly what the doctor tried to find out from Maximer the Great.'

'Maximer! Yes!' His eyes travelled frowningly round the room, against the bare walls of which were placed a dozen of the panels, bathed in the radiant light of photo-floods. 'It's inconceivable,' he proclaimed at last, burning his boats, 'that Maximer couldn't have known what these were!'

Kenneth yielded to one of his sudden bursts of forthrightness. 'You think this is a thing an expert couldn't make a mistake about? They do make mistakes, don't they, one way and another?'

'Not that way,' Arnold, once committed, was even more forthright. 'The people who make that kind of blunder are not experts, whatever they call themselves. Oh yes, on the question of attribution there might be plenty of room for dispute, but as to when, and probably where, these pictures were painted, no one who's really handled things of this kind could feel a shadow of doubt.'

'Without any kind of scientific test? No X-rays or anything?'

'I'm prepared to bank on safety in numbers. Each picture is supported by fifteen others.'

'Then Dr. Sandilands *has* been cheated!' Kenneth made a movement of his hands as if he held up a visible chain of logic. 'Maximer must have seen just as plainly as you do that all this stuff was genuine, and yet he told him it was fake. What was he up to?'

'That's what I'm beginning to wonder.'

'Perhaps he took a dislike to my father,' said Linda, 'though really I don't see how anyone could.'

Arnold faintly and sadly smiled. 'I can't quite believe Maximer would let a hoard like this slip through his fingers because he'd taken a dislike to someone. Collectors don't do that sort of thing.'

'I had an idea,' said Kenneth, 'that it was a bit queer the way this man turned up just when he did to buy the pictures, but they shouted me down.'

'Tell me about that!' Arnold commanded, sinking on to a soapbox in which they had brought away some of the smaller panels. The others disposed themselves on a Recamier couch, a gilded tabouret, and a kitchen chair from the darkroom, and while Linda repeated everything she had heard from her father and Beatrix about the transaction with Quiller, he sat with one of his cheeks resting upon his hand, looking, thought Stephanie, like a model for a companion piece to the 'Thinker' that might be called the 'Listener.'

When the brief story came to an end, he remained submerged for a moment in a silence pregnant with speculative thoughts, then he announced impetuously: 'I must go out and walk about a bit and get things clear in my mind. Something must be done. I wish I knew what!' He sprang to his feet, abstractedly smoothed down his already smooth hair, and, turning when he had reached the door, addressed Stephanie in the same shy and hesitant manner as when he had first spoken to her on his own ground.

'You wouldn't care to come with me, Mrs. du Plessis? Two heads are better than one, especially when the second's yours.'

As Stephanie joined him at the door, she caught Linda's smile of congratulation and, deeming it well to keep in evidence those aspects of the adventure that were most congenial to her ally, she returned the look with one of almost equal archness. But, having a much clearer perception than Linda of what his present state of mind must be, she did not suppose for an instant that his invitation had any other motive than the one he had expressed, and was consequently not disappointed when he began in a brisk and business-like tone, after they had walked a few paces:

'I've brought you out so that I can tell you something I don't think I can trust to anyone else's discretion. My position in this matter is awkward to say the least of it . . . but it's my duty to do something, that's certain.' He waved his cigarette case towards her, withdrew it saying, 'No, you've given it up so that you can save money to go to Italy,' and presumed with the flame of a match glowing between his fingers: 'The only lawful way of justifying Dr. Sandilands in a refusal to hand over the pictures would be, of course, to prove some sort of fraudulence, some sort of collusion between the purchaser and Maximer.'

'Could there be the remotest possibility? It did cross my mind, but it seemed too far-fetched. And he's known to be a man of very high principles, isn't he?'

'Of very pompous principles at any rate, and until this morning I never had any reason to question them.'

'This morning?'

'I think I've found out something about Maximer that may lead somewhere. Now you shall have your revenge for my scepticism.'

'Anyone would have been sceptical,' she protested eagerly. 'What could my opinion weigh against his until you'd seen for yourself?'

'It really was a most astonishing thing you were asking me to believe!' His head turned towards her, and the rays of a street lamp falling on his face as they passed showed that he was remembering with a rather sardonic appreciation the scene they had played together yesterday. 'Since I *have* seen for myself, I've come to one conclusion. When such a man is wrong—wrong on this tremendous scale—it must, for some reason, be deliberate on his part. I do him that justice.'

By a mutual impulse they turned as he spoke into the Pump Room Gardens which, since the patriotic removal of their railings in the war, stood open at all hours.

'He has been wrong before,' he went on, 'and perhaps that was deliberate too.' And with this he launched into the tale of his investigations at the Art Gallery.

She listened as intently as if she feared the smallest interruption might make it impossible for him ever to take up the thread again; then, in his first expectant pause, asked with a full sense of the portentous nature of her question:

'Do you think John Rennick really wrote that letter?'

'Oh,' he groaned, 'how cruel of you to steal my thunder! I was just working up to bring it out with such a wonderful crash!'

'Then he didn't write it?'

'You're merely jumping to the conclusion I've had to reach by slow, laborious stages. And if you'd seen it, you wouldn't dare. The paper, the typewriting, the style—everything is pure, unmistakable Rennick.'

'Then what made you suspect it?'

'I didn't at first. But there was a sort of shadiness about Maximer's letters, something artful and unpleasant . . . the way he made sure, behind the façade of devoted loyalty, that all the blame would fall on Rennick's shoulders, the way he practically intimidated Sinnett into keeping quiet! That made me think; but even then, the worst I did think was that Maximer might have known all along the picture was false. That was bad enough!'

They had come to the junction of several pathways and, moving like automata, wandered down a short diagonal road that led to a bandstand. For the greater privacy of his words he had drawn close to her, and even in the midst of her deep anxiety and her wonder, she was conscious of a certain charm in their thus being able to walk together enclosed, as it were, in the intimacy of a problem he had now agreed to share with her.

'Then I went home and, seeing I had time on my hands—the time when I should have been taking you to dinner—I looked again at Rennick's biography by Oscar Robertson, who happens to be a friend and an ex-colleague of mine. And the more I dipped into it, the less I could believe that a man who did so much to advance the technique of detecting forgery could have come such a cropper. So I put a call through to Oscar and had the luck to find him at home.'

'Go on!' she said with frankly artificial calm.

'As soon as I told him we'd got a picture certified by Rennick that had turned out a sham, you could practically hear him pricking up his ears, so I knew I'd got on to the right trail. It seems there have been other fishy instances. Since Rennick's death a lot of money has been made out of dubious works on the strength of his authentication, and yet, when he was alive, nothing he recommended was ever called into question.' And in response to a murmur of incomprehension, he explained: 'It's rather a coincidence, don't you see? If he made mistakes, they were entirely confined to things that didn't come on the market till he was dead.'

'How long ago is it since he died?' she asked slowly.

'Thirteen years.'

'And since then someone seems to have been faking letters—literally forging letters!—in his name to put up the value of worthless pictures. You can't surely think it was Maximer himself?'

'Well, seeing how he lied to Dr. Sandilands—because I'll swear he did knowingly lie to him—I don't think the possibility can be ignored. It's at any rate worth looking into when so much hangs on it.'

'What about this Jones who received the money?'

'What about him, you may well ask! Doesn't it strike you that a very elusive Mr. Jones who first disappears to South Africa and then gets killed in the War is a person who might quite closely resemble Mrs. Harris?'

'But why should Maximer do such an appallingly crooked thing? He's rich, isn't he?'

'I don't suppose anyone's been rich enough in the last dozen years to be able to do what he does out of income. The money that was paid for that faked Brueghel wasn't chicken-feed either. And it was tax-free. A few deals like that would bring in something that would go quite a long way even in the places where Maximer does his shopping.'

'Still, the risk! Would any man in his position take such a risk just for the sake of money?'

'It probably wasn't just for the sake of money.' He broke a twig from some low-branched tree whose leaves had brushed his face, and swished it gently against his cheek. 'He's a man who enjoys being clever. He might get a sort of kick out of pulling off a thing like this—if he has pulled it off.'

'His books contain such diatribes against people who do dishonest things with pictures!'

'Yes, he's very fond of talking about integrity—the integrity of artists, of dealers, of critics, and particularly of Sir Harry Maximer. That alone should put us on our guard.'

They walked on for a while without speaking, each absorbed in complex meditations. Then she said, sighing with the weight of her difficulties:

'If we could link up that man who's just bought the pictures with Maximer, then Dr. Sandilands would have a complete justification for refusing to keep his bargain.'

'Yes, our awful task is to find the connection.'

'But suppose there isn't a connection? You see, he made no approach to Dr. Sandilands. Beatrix, the daughter, went out and found him.'

'Found him, her sister said, in Morris's shop. Didn't you tell me yourself yesterday morning that's exactly where they were intending to take the pictures? Why, it's the only picture shop in Charlton Wells! A man who wanted to come into contact with Dr. Sandilands simply had to hang about Morris's shop and sooner or later he—or as it happened his daughter—would turn up! How do we know that the suggestion of going there wasn't carefully planted by Maximer?'

'It's possible,' she mused. 'It's even beginning to seem probable.'

'I believe if we only had time we could work it all out, fit in every missing detail.'

'Like Dantès and the Abbé Faria in the prison cell,' she said, smiling with pleasure through all her disquiet at his heartwarming 'we'.

'Like Carter and Pollard and the nineteenth-century pamphlets. I'm willing, if it would be any help, to get right down to it in exactly the same way, starting with a little detective work on Rennick's posthumous letters.'

'It's time we need so desperately. Beatrix and Dr. Sandilands appear to be even more anxious to get rid of the pictures than Quiller is to take possession of them. A day or two is the most they'll let me hold out.'

'Suppose I were to see the doctor'—his groping and uncertain tone informed her that he was thinking aloud, and without much confidence in the effectiveness of the process—'and to tell him the transaction's absolutely insane? This Quiller could bring an action against him if he backed out, but it would be some weeks at least before it came into court, and meanwhile we'd have a chance of preparing our case. There may be some useful discovery to be made about Mr. Quiller.'

She did not like to remind him of the words he had spoken yesterday, 'Maximer is a much bigger gun than I am', but she knew they were true, and that it would be futile for him to make an open intervention unless he had clear proof of the collusion he suspected. His offer delighted her, showing as it did how boldly, once won, he threw himself into the crusade, but she answered obliquely: 'Dr. Sandilands is the kindest and nicest of men, only, unlike you, he's not gifted with moral courage. I doubt whether he'd put up a very vigorous fight even if he knew for sure he'd been cheated; and he'd consider it a terrible thing to back out of his bargain simply on suspicion.'

'What? When there's so much to be lost—I should think it's safe to say the most magnificent collection of Florentines any private individual has owned for a hundred years!'

'You mustn't forget they've no aesthetic value for him—really, almost none whatever.'

'Their value in money is not precisely to be sneezed at.'

'He's been told by a high authority who made a great impression on him that their value in money is a hundred pounds. His faith in Maximer won't be shaken without proof. Then there's Beatrix who'd resent my interference furiously. There's a sort of hostility in her to the whole idea of things she doesn't herself understand or care for being potentially so important and so desirable.'

'I know that attitude. In my Army work I saw quite a lot of it. But the other sister, the one I've met, she's not hostile.'

'No, she's our one hope in the Sandilands family. Though I'm afraid if it came to a fight, she might need a good deal of outside support.'

'But she helped to get the pictures out of her father's garage so that I could see them?'

'Yes. Fortunately, it was amazingly easy. Beatrix was listening to a programme she never misses: we chose the time deliberately. The young ones go to the Badminton Courts almost every evening. The maid who was in was plied with a lovely batch of illustrated papers, and she has a radio too—'

'The burglar's friend.'

'Dr. Sandilands actually went out on a maternity case, leaving the garage open. Everything played into our hands.'

'Let's hope you aren't encouraged to take up burgling as a career. You seem quite equal to it.'

She was surprised to find that such very undistinguished jests could give her an appreciable gratification, a tiny sparkle of enjoyment so irrational that it was obviously a symptom of some deeper impulse, the same impulse that made his hand carrying his cigarette to his mouth seem deft and graceful in a very private and inexplicable way, and endowed the arabesques of smoke he breathed into the air with a beauty other lips could not have imparted.

'You might do well if you took to crime,' he went on in a voice so warm and companionable that it seemed to bring them still closer together, for the next instant they were walking near enough for his elbow to brush against hers. 'The way you inveigled me into being practically an accomplice!'

'Are you angry?' she could safely ask.

'I should have been if the collection had turned out what Maximer said it was. Yes, I should have been very cross indeed. But now I feel exhilarated—exhilarated but harassed. What are we going to do?'

'Let's stand still and think,' she said. They had walked round the bandstand several times, and as his stride was longer than hers and she was on the outside of the circle, the exertion began to conflict with her need of cool and unperturbed reflection.

'If we could find an empty seat you could rest a little.' He took her arm with a solicitude which it did not displease her to regard as wilfully exaggerated.

'No, we've been away from the others too long.'

'I don't think they'll mind about that,' he said, 'unless I've forgotten how to read the signs.'

'But Linda may be worrying about when and how we're to put the pictures back. So am I for that matter.'

'Very well, let's stand still and think, but not in the middle of the path.'

He drew her towards the bandstand, and they leaned against the ornamental ironwork enclosing it.

'Think!' he commanded. 'I'll try to think too, though I don't believe I'm nearly as good at it as you are.'

They stood in a silence that suddenly transformed itself into suspense, banishing all thoughts from her brain. Empty of ideas she watched him flicking his hand with the little branch of leaves he had broken from the tree.

'I'm fidgeting,' he said after a time. 'That disturbs you.'

She took the twig from his hand and held it up towards the gleam of a distant lamp. 'It's lilac,' she announced, as if to make that discovery were the sole purpose of their interview.

'Is it? Yes, the leaves are heart-shaped. I shouldn't have expected to find lilac in a public garden here.'

'Oh, but this garden is famous for those trees in early summer. It's dark lilac, the colour of amethysts, and the scent is so delicate and yet so rich and fine, exactly like the colour. I wish it weren't over. You'd be charmed.'

'I am charmed now. Quite, quite charmed, can't you see?'

And before she had even guessed his intention, he had resolutely put one arm round her waist and the other round her neck, and was kissing her.

Her first reaction was complete and breathless wonder. She felt it necessary to release herself and chide him with a remonstrance that was nearly genuine. 'I only saw you for the first time yesterday!'

'Never mind, think how much you're going to see me in the future. You must, you know, if we're really going to save those pictures.'

He laid his cheek on hers, and she found that her second reaction was one of sheer gratitude for his courage, which now seemed a boon conferred on her by providence. For she reasoned that a man who was so far from being a laggard in love would assuredly not prove a coward in war, and there was a battle in prospect that might call for all his daring. Her third reaction was simple pleasure.

TEN

SIR HARRY Maximer was attending what he facetiously called the mass meeting of the anti-da-Vinci societies. In his capacity as great Leonardo authority and enthusiast, he could not have been prevailed upon to attend any such gathering if it had concerned one society alone, lest by his august presence he should seem to be giving it countenance, but the 'mass meeting' was judged to be such a *reductio ad absurdum* that not only he but several other eminent Leonardines had been unable to resist paying their shilling for admission to the Benson Hall and taking seats towards the back of the auditorium, where they formed a group that excited looks of mingled triumph and defiance from the assembled factions.

The notice of this occasion among the lecture announcements in the week-end papers had been worded thus:

OUR COMMON GROUND
Speakers from the Ludovico Society, the Julian Group, the Catherinians, and the New Seekers of the Holy Grail, will discuss the Poyle Cipher and other recent proofs of the Vinci imposture.
Benson Hall, Sat. 3 p.m.

This was the first time these four organizations—which were seldom in accord except as to the necessity of discrediting the person known opprobriously to them all as 'the man from Vinci'—had ever come together. The idea of so historic an encounter had sprung full-armed from the brain of Horace Platt Poyle, the American, whose numerical cipher, which enabled unprecedented revelations to be discovered in the looking-glass writings of Leonardo da Vinci, had, for the time being at least, united all parties. Though no one had as yet worked out incontrovertibly the name for which all were looking, yet it was widely agreed that by the ingenious use of this cipher and its free adaptation according to the result desired, it was possible to produce such illuminating phrases as *Non sono Leo*, *Lion non est*, or the rarefied pun *Vidi non Vici*, which, if translated (as it easily could be) 'I never saw Vinci', might be taken as proof positive of the whole imposture.

Mr. Poyle's suggestion that all who were using his cipher should meet to discuss, not their differences, but the belief they held in common—the fraudulence of the man from Vinci—had been the more warmly received because he had undertaken to finance the project; and even the Ludovicans, largest and oldest of the societies, had assented under this condition to the hiring of the Benson Hall and the publicity that would create a widespread interest.

Not that the Benson Hall was full. No speaker, no subject, had ever been magnetic enough to fill it. Draughts from numerous doors, distracting noises from the street, rigid chairs with unyielding seats, ensured that only the most Spartan and determined characters visited the building more than once, while architecture suggestive of a monastery built for some order pledged to extremest self-renunciation made it certain that even a single experience would leave behind a memory of the most solemn character. It was in fact built on the model most favoured for English civic halls.

Moreover, the anti-da-Vincians were not as strong numerically as their expensive printed publications and the storms of controversy they raised up had the power of suggesting.

But today there was an uncommonly large attendance—nineteen Ludovicans, eight members of the Julian Group, four Catherinians, and five Seekers of the Holy Grail, some dozen of the general public including Leonardines, and even one or two reporters. On the platform sat the Chairman, a very small but none the less masterful man, one representative of each society, and Horace Platt Poyle, a stout benign person with a red face.

Before inviting Mr. Poyle to rise, the Chairman dispassionately, or almost dispassionately, took the audience over the common ground they were about to investigate. The works, he said, passed off as the productions of the man from Vinci (he pronounced it Vinki so as to shed more contempt upon him) were so splendid, so original, so diverse, so full of various kinds of learning that thinking people all over Europe and America had long felt there must be some mystery about their provenance. To have given the world such masterpieces a mind of universal genius was required. Was it possible that such a mind could be found in the son of a petty notary and a village servant girl? Was it possible that the base-born descendant of peasants could have acquired the knowledge of architecture, engineering, mathematics, physics, anatomy, astronomy, military tactics, and philosophy, to be found in the so-called works of the so-called Leonardo? No, it must be absolutely plain as daylight to all rational beings that behind this shadowy and shifty figure there stood another and a much nobler form, the form of one whose education was equal to the astounding tasks imposed on it, who was familiar, as none could be familiar but those accustomed to move in exalted circles, with great scholars, great artists, great generals.

Very well, as to that they were all agreed—there was a muttering of dissent from several Leonardines, and he continued rapidly—all those were agreed who had approached the subject with a fair and unprejudiced eye. But as to the enthralling question, whose was that form, whose was that glorious name usurped by a pettifogging lawyer's son, there was, it must be acknowledged, matter for dispute.

At this point there were exclamations of 'No' from Ludovicans, Julians, and others, but he waved a judicial hand and proceeded as one in full command of the situation: 'Except for a certain element among us which had better be nameless, all of us here today are perfectly open-minded, ready to believe anything except that the hand which gave us those wondrous pictures, those profound writings, was that of the man—or shall I say?—the lout, the boor from Vinci.

Subduing a burst of applause with another firm gesture, he swept his arm gracefully towards his companions on the platform. 'You have before you,' he said, 'besides Mr. Poyle, whom you are about to hear, four distinguished champions, each one of whom comes forth into the lists, if I may for one instant be a little fanciful, with a different blazon on his escutcheon. First, there is the Reverend Thomas Gudgeley, whose book *Leonardo is Ludovico* is the latest and some may think the greatest contribution ever made to the demolition of the ludicrous legend of Vinci.'

The Rev. Thomas Gudgeley, a man with an immense amount of grizzled hair on his face and none at all on his head, looked modestly at his shoe-laces.

'It were superfluous to explain to such an audience as this his arresting theme. Let it be enough to say that Mr. Gudgeley and many other intellectually outstanding men are of the opinion that the sole author of all the works credited to the Tuscan yokel is none other than Ludovico Sforza, Duke of Milan.'

A few soft murmurs of 'Hear, hear!' from the Ludovicans, who did not want at this stage to be too assertive, sounded in counterpoint against a ripple of ironical laughter from the Leonardines, at whom the Chairman glared stonily for a moment before pressing on:

'Everyone present—that is, every responsible inquirer present—will know how ingeniously Mr. Gudgeley and his many predecessors in the field have worked out their theory, overcoming superficial discrepancies as to dates and places, and convicting the hireling Leonardo and his accomplices of what is perhaps the most insolent conspiracy of all time. More than this, they have by their researches discovered a cryptograph of incomparable value by means of which, with a protractor and a pair of dividers, such paintings as the "Mona Lisa" or the "Virgin of the Rocks" may be dissected so as to reveal hidden meanings in every stroke, thus enabling us at last to understand the significance of those words found on the back of a drawing, "Let no man who is not a mathematician seek to know the elements of my work!"'

'Hear, hear!' cried Horace Platt Poyle vehemently; then, realizing that his voice was solitary, he closed his lips tightly and endeavoured to look as if the sound had come from somewhere else.

'Certainly,' said the Chairman, 'the letters of the word "Sforza" or sometimes "Sfortia" or "Sfor" can be made out plainly in various symbolic forms in all the major works when they are turned upside down. But there is a group far from negligible, represented here today by no less an authority than Professor Sligo Muldoon, who take the view—a view not lightly to be dismissed—that the Sforza thus indicated is not Ludovico but Catherine, the redoubtable Countess of Forli. To

some it may seem extravagant to attribute such masculine productions to a woman's hand, but here assuredly is a woman of no common
mettle, and who but the most purblind partisans could doubt that she
was far more capable of executing prodigies than the oaf whose greatest achievement in art was probably the painting of newts, maggots,
toads, and bats for the amusement of illiterates?'

One or two of Sir Harry's neighbours made sounds expressive
of impatience, but such was his own good humour that he merely
chuckled, settling down in his chair—so far as anyone could settle
down in a Benson Hall chair—with an air of being in for a really enjoy-
able time. The knowledge that he would by tomorrow morning be in
possession of a Leonardo of the first order gave all this a rich additional savour, the secret relish that is felt by a lover when he reminds
himself that he will soon hold in his arms clandestinely the beautiful
woman of whom everyone is talking. His slight, very slight fear that the
'Leda' might have been handed over to Dr. Sandilands' friend agreeably heightened his desire, as the fear of a rival, if it be not too sharp,
heightens the desire of a lover. He was fairly sure that no lay person
would choose out of all those pictures the one that was in three pieces
and superficially almost the worst as to condition.

No, the 'Leda' which, encouraged by the company in which he had
found it, he believed to be the lost original of a much-copied work, had
not given him such great anxiety as certain other items more likely,
he thought, to tempt the kind of person he imagined Mrs. du Plessis
to be. For the best part of two days he had been tormenting himself
with visions of her appropriating now the portrait of Lorenzo, now
the wonderful head which he already designated 'the Masaccio', both
of which became more vital to his happiness with every thought he
bestowed upon them.

But this afternoon he was relaxed and cheerful, for he would soon
be out of his suspense. Last night he had telephoned Quiller instructing
him to make some excuse for speeding up delivery of the pictures, and
at lunch-time he had received an unsigned telegram of joyful import:

'Home by evening Pullman with luggage.'

It had at first been agreed that Quiller should remain in Elderfield
without any appearance of undue concern until the doctor's grasping
friend had made her choice, but Sir Harry's patience had failed him,
and he had reasoned that a dealer must betray the importance of a
purchase more effectively by allowing himself to be kept waiting for it

than by normally business-like behaviour. Quiller himself, not being too happy in the prospect of spending the week-end at the Station Hotel, had promised readily enough to bring a little pressure to bear; and it was clear from his splendid announcement that he had been successful. Tonight at ten o'clock, having given him plenty of time to get from King's Cross to his shop, over which he lived, Sir Harry would call and make sure of his treasures, bringing away perhaps half a dozen to rejoice his heart on the morrow. He would have preferred, of course, to bring away the whole lot, but such a burden might excite a taxi-driver's curiosity, besides being a little difficult to keep out of sight at home.

'Caution!' he said to himself, savouring the word with a certain gusto. In the course of many years of dealings that required caution, he had come to take a craftsman's pleasure in his own foresight and discretion. It made him a shade sad at times that there could be no spectator to his cleverness, no wife or confidential friend who might admire his faculty for anticipating every danger; but then it was part of his very cleverness not to have one. There were half a dozen people, all deeply inculpated, who knew a little and might suspect a little more, but there was no one who knew everything. . . .

Sir Harry Maximer did not belong to the common class of deceivers who believe they are victims of circumstance or else assure themselves that what they are doing is not wrong. His mind was very honest and enabled him to recognize plainly the nature of his deeds. But certain ethical lapses in his youth when he had needed money badly had been so well rewarded that he had felt tempted to repeat them on a larger scale, and to elaborate upon them, and the taste for trickery had grown upon him; he enjoyed the profits of it now more than any equivalent sums his business brought him.

He had a natural attraction too towards what was tortuous and complicated and, with a few degrees less of worldly common-sense, might have been on the platform beside Horace Platt Poyle, Professor Sligo Muldoon, and the Rev. Thomas Gudgeley, instead of laughing benignly at them from the back rows of the stalls.

'We know,' the Chairman was proceeding, still wearing the air of judge-like impartiality by which he concealed his passionate adherence to the Ludovican cause, 'we know that, in the words of a well-known historian, Catherine Sforza, was "a sort of wonder at her age, a woman of almost superhuman ability, courage and resolution".

Professor Muldoon tapped his fingers together with a rapid nervous movement. The quotation was exactly the one with which he had intended to begin his own remarks. Now he would have to think up a new opening, and he was very bad at improvisation. But there was worse to follow, for the Chairman, eager to show that he was not bigoted, that he would indeed tolerate any heresy except the damnable heresy of Vinci, continued to quote liberally from various works in which were vaunted Catherine's accomplishments, her knowledge of science, her delight in works of art, her pleasure in the society of learned men, and above all, her interest in warfare, which made it strikingly probable that—if it were not Ludovico—it was she who had recorded or invented so many engines of war formerly ascribed by the simple-minded to the conspirator from Tuscany.

Having briefly but skilfully anticipated almost every point on which the Professor's forthcoming exposition hung and reduced his written speech to an anti-climax, the Chairman next indicated in a courteous but reserved manner Sir Jonas Jones, whose theory was—he hardly needed to remind an educated audience—that Giuliano della Rovere, better known perhaps as Pope Julius II, had concealed his own sublime genius behind the mask of the mercenary adventurer.

'When Mr. Poyle has finished his address,' he announced magnanimously, 'each of the other speakers will have ten minutes to set forth his own case before the discussion is thrown open. Sir Jonas in his ten minutes'—he spoke the words with emphasis, the Julian President having a reputation for long-windedness—'will doubtless recapitulate the interesting points on which he bases his views . . . and one cannot deny it was he who first perceived that the hand which executed the "Last Supper" and the "Madonna with the Carnation" was also the hand that gained renown under the name of Pinturicchio, a fact now accepted, I may say, by all sound critics—'

'Critics of what?' muttered the Secretary of the Connoisseurs' Club, who was sitting next to Sir Harry.

'As to the actual authorship of the so-called Pinturicchio paintings, however, I will merely mention that the application of the Gudgeley Cryptograph reveals the name Sforza, or at any rate, the initial letter of it, in practically every work, not only of Pinturicchio, but also of Lorenzo di Credi, Filippino Lippi, and, in short, a most immense variety of Renaissance creations, showing, as some of us not unreasonably believe, that all this marvellous flowering of energy and invention was the product of a single master-mind.'

Sir Jonas Jones covered his displeasure with a long-suffering smile, and there were some whisperings among his eight followers, who did not feel the Julians had been given quite a fair deal.

'Finally,' the Chairman went on imperturbably, satisfied that he had conceded as much as he could to a group whose ideas he looked upon as somewhat far-fetched, 'I must introduce the—er'—he glanced at his notes—'the Knight Grand Excalibur of the New Seekers of the Holy Grail, Mr. Sidney Stubbs.'

Mr. Stubbs, a large, square, blue-chinned man who looked like a pugilist of the old school, acknowledged the introduction with a stiff bow.

'Now what the devil do you think *he* believes?' the Secretary of the Connoisseurs' Club hissed in Maximer's ear.

'That Leonardo was really a syndicate registered as Round Table, Limited,' Sir Harry genially hissed back.

'The Seekers,' observed the Chairman, sweeping calm but quelling eyes over the entire audience, 'are for their part convinced that the masterworks of the Renaissance were executed not by a single individual but by a brotherhood—a secret religious order versed in mystic doctrine which it was pledged to propagate by means of the most ennobling productions of art. Mr. Stubbs, or should I say'—he glanced at his notes again—'the Knight Grand Excalibur, will tell you that the paintings, the sculpture, the architecture of the Renaissance are full of occult symbolism that was meant only to be understood by initiates, and moreover that France, Germany, and the Low Countries participated with Italy in this great esoteric movement, so that every work may be the product of several hands joined in a fraternity transcending all national and personal barriers.'

'Rubbish!' The word burst out like a small explosion at the end of Sir Harry's row.

He leaned forward and recognized the sharp, handsome, rather sinister profile of 'Juvenal', writer of a column in the *Evening World*. A ripple of disquiet seemed to pass over the audience like wind over grass. The five seated men on the platform stirred uneasily, and the one standing, who was a schoolmaster by profession and not of a meek temperament, said sternly:

'I hear you, sir!'

'I hope you do, sir,' the same voice retorted.

If the Chairman had seen and identified the interrupter, he might have let the interruption go unheeded, since 'Juvenal', besides being the most irrepressible of topical writers, was Member for an uncommonly rowdy constituency and accustomed in and outside the House of Commons to heckle and be heckled with a coolness that was famous. But the Chairman, who was unfortunately both short-sighted and touchy, replied again:

'If you have any dispute with the Seekers of the Holy Grail, sir, you may put your questions when the discussion is opened. And let me tell you, you prove nothing by rudeness.'

'Neither do you, yet you've called Leonardo da Vinci an oaf, a lout, a money-grubbing adventurer—'

'Names he richly deserves,' said the Chairman in the manner of one who dismisses the subject, and perhaps he would have done so if cries of 'Hear, hear!' breaking out in several parts of the hall had not encouraged him to amplify: 'He accepted bribes for passing off another's work as his own.'

'What bribes?'

'The vineyard for one thing that was given him by Ludovico Sforza on the 26th of April, 1499.'

This was a most unguarded riposte, making plain as it did that his pretended impartiality had been a sham, and with the repetitions of 'Hear, hear!' there were now mingled some murmurings of 'No!' and 'Unfair!' and even 'Untrue!'

The heckling meanwhile went ruthlessly on: 'None of you seems to think it wrong to give bribes, only to take them. Your ethics are as muddle-headed as your arguments.'

'It's quite evident that you deliberately came here to be insulting,' the Chairman exclaimed above a wrathful chorus. 'One may guess that from the company you're in.'

He had again chosen his words unhappily. 'Juvenal' was seated amongst the Leonardines, who were, however, perfectly free from any responsibility for his presence. They had come out of an amused curiosity and, apart from putting a few pungent questions when the time came, they had not intended to make any demonstration; but this offensive from the platform released their indignation and brought their united voices strongly into the general clamour.

'I am in the company,' said 'Juvenal' loudly enough to be heard but without losing his composure, 'of those who believe it was far less impossible for a village lawyer's son—'

'We don't want to know what you believe,' cried Professor Sligo Muldoon's wife, an Irish lady of vigorous personality who, from her seat in the front row, had come to the conclusion that the Chairman was not managing the situation with sufficient forcefulness.

The Professor shook his head at her in an agony of embarrassment which was shared in some degree by all his companions on the platform, except the Knight Grand Excalibur who preserved the aloof tranquillity of one on a higher plane. The Chairman, glowering at an abstract object apparently suspended in space, said firmly:

'I have already announced that the discussion will be thrown open at the end of the speeches.'

The journalist rose to his feet and his striking presence and long experience in making audiences listen to him had the effect of commanding at least a moment or two of silence. 'As I'm about to leave, perhaps you'll at least allow me to say this. It was far less impossible for a village lawyer's son to be a great artist than for a statesman to produce a great artist's work in secret in his spare time. Furthermore—'

'Keep quiet!' called Mrs. Muldoon.

'Furthermore, madam,' he went on undaunted, 'the secret must have been rather widely known. Was everyone bribed?'

'Shut up!' Mrs. Muldoon was now driven to shout quite vulgarly. 'We haven't come here to listen to you!' And although the roughness with which she hurled herself into the fray was considered unseemly even by fellow-believers, there was in loyalty a wave of sympathetic sounds, beginning gently enough but gathering strength with utterance.

'If this were a theatre, sir, you would be ejected,' said the Chairman, his piercing tones just audible through the din.

'If this were a theatre the performance would be billed as a farce.'

'Funny without being witty,' the Chairman of the Connoisseurs' Club found courage to throw in.

'At least let's hear it and judge for ourselves!' someone protested from neutral territory in the middle of the hall.

Some applause broke out at this, and 'Juvenal' with dignity picked up his hat and moved into the aisle. 'Very well, I'll go.' He walked towards the nearest exit, whence he turned and asked submissively: 'Mr. Chairman, may I put one question?' The busy pencils of shorthand writers always stimulated him to very fluent expression, and he went on without waiting for leave: 'You all seem agreed that someone went to an uncommon amount of trouble and expense to conceal the authorship of the pictures. Why did he try to undo the good work by planting bits of his name all over the place?'

From relief at seeing the enemy in full retreat, the partisans were quiet and the Chairman vouchsafed an answer:

'A genius who was obliged to conceal his identity in his own lifetime might nevertheless wish to make it known to posterity.'

'Can you explain'—the inquiry was made with a disarming air of serious consideration—'why he was so shockingly bad at it? Here's the man from Vinki, as you call him, still getting all the credit after four hundred years!' He disappeared beyond the portal, but put his head back to add: 'Another thing I'd like to know—why in an age of great painting should anyone go round hiding the fact that he's a great painter? Good afternoon, Mr. Chairman!'

He raised his hat and finally departed, leaving a complication of noises behind him—the plaudits of the Leonardines, the angry buzzing of the controversialists, the scandalized interjections of the men on the platform—still excepting the Knight Grand Excalibur, who remained in yogi-like detachment—and the Chairman's severe voice calling the ladies and gentlemen to order. But the slip which had revealed him as a Ludovican had alienated the members of other sects, and it was evident that the meeting was not going to progress in the quiet and decorous manner that had first been promised.

Sir Harry Maximer had not done as much to sustain the reputation of Leonardo da Vinci as his acquaintances in the audience had expected. Indeed he had scarcely even joined the chorus of mocking laughter, but had sat through 'Juvenal's' duel with the Chairman in a state of indifference almost equalling that of Mr. Stubbs, the Knight of the Holy Grail. This preoccupation was now in some measure accounted for by the movements of a short, plump lady who, before the disturbance had subsided, left a seat at the far end of a distant row, quietly approached the row behind the Leonardines, which was almost empty, walked along it till she came to Sir Harry's chair, and began in a purposeful manner to speak to him. She was recognized by those who had been to his home as his private secretary.

Mrs. Rose had come in by the main entrance at the back of the hall at just about that point in the Chairman's speech when he had been stung by the ejaculation 'Rubbish!' Sir Harry had noticed her tiptoeing down the side aisle, and had immediately been filled with uneasiness, for he knew that she must have come here to find him, and that only a matter of urgency could have brought her. Matters of urgency are seldom pleasant, and it was inevitable that his apprehensions should settle on what had been uppermost in his mind all day, the precious freight that ought in an hour or so to be speeding on its way from Charlton Wells. Mrs. Rose had evidently expected that he would be sitting near the front, and had walked some way down the aisle before beginning to skim the room with her eyes. Then, finding him, she turned back; but realizing that it would not be tactful to speak until the irate interchange between the platform and the hall had come to an end, she had seated herself in the nearest empty chair, and rose only in the commotion that followed.

'Sir Harry,' she said in the softest possible voice, bending over his shoulder, 'there's somebody wanting you to take a very urgent trunk call. I thought I'd better come and fetch you.'

Urgent! Though he had expected the word and known it must come, it seemed to whistle into his ear like a breath of icy air. 'Trunk call from whom?' he demanded in an irritable whisper.

'From a Mr. Black.' For one moment a warm gust of hope contended with the chills of his anxiety, but her next words dispelled it instantly. 'I asked him where you could ring him back when you came home from the meeting, but he said he had no number and would have to ring again himself, and that it was most important to get hold of you at once. He was calling from Charlton Wells.'

'Charlton Wells!' He feigned a mild incredulity. 'Charlton Wells!' he repeated again on arriving with her in the outer hall. He was trying to determine whether it was more prudent to recollect some pressing affair that had slipped his mind or to go on appearing mystified, and decided to keep up, but without excess, his mystification.

'That's what I understood the operator to say.'

'I stayed there when I went up to that "do" in Elderfield last June. At the Royal, wasn't I? But as for Mr. Black—well, I suppose I may have met someone of that name, though why he should consider himself entitled to summon me away from a meeting I can't imagine. Ah, you've got a taxi waiting.'

'Yes, I knew this wouldn't be an easy district to find one on a Saturday afternoon.'

'Good, good!' he said with rather specious enthusiasm. 'Wisely planned!' His brain was working at an even greater rate of activity than usual, and indeed it was a wonder that he could offer any coherent responses at all. Not only was he in a turmoil of conjecture as to what emergency could have caused Quiller to take a step bordering on reck-lessness, but he was tormented with the problem of how to get rid of Mrs. Rose.

There were three telephones in his flat, but they were all on one line, and nothing would be easier than for her to listen to his conversa-tion if she felt inclined. That she was inquisitive he had little doubt; it was the price he had to pay for her intelligent devotion to his interests. A secretary who identified herself so completely with her job that she was willing to give up one of the last Saturday afternoons of summer in order to revise a catalogue naturally liked to know what was going on. There were occasions when he would gladly have dispensed with such extra and unasked for services, giving her as they did a more intim-ate footing in his household than he really desired her to have; but he had grown to place considerable reliance on her loyalty and discretion, which he fostered by a flattering gratitude. There was no loyalty and no discretion, however, that he would trust in possession of his business with Quiller.

'Let me give you a lift to your home, Mrs. Rose,' he said, climbing into the vehicle after her. 'If I'd realized what a fine day it was going to be, I shouldn't have let you stay to work on that catalogue.'

'I've nearly done it now.' She adjusted her hat and the revers of her jacket with neat and brisk little gestures. 'I might as well get it finished.'

'No, no, we shall drop you!'

He leaned forward to tap on the glass, but she checked him: 'I have to go back in any case, Sir Harry, to fetch my things.'

There was no gainsaying such a reason as this, and he was obliged to let her return with him; but as they crossed the threshold of the mansion in Grosvenor Place where his imposing flat was situated, he said with a mixture of authority and solicitude which he knew how to blend effectively, 'Now, there's to be no more work today! You're look-ing pale, and I think you ought to get some fresh air.'

For the next fifteen minutes, he was on tenterhooks in case the expected call should come through while she was still on the premises. Only the certainty that he would reveal his anxiety prevented him from renewing his attempts to speed her departure. If he had been a superstitious man he would have said his guardian demon was at work in the Sloane exchange, for the telephone bell rang at precisely the moment when, carrying her attaché case and umbrella, she opened his library door to ask, as she always rather officiously did, if there was any further service she could perform for him.

'Nothing, thank you, Mrs. Rose,' he said with his hand on the receiver; and simultaneously he heard the outer door close and the operator saying, 'Go ahead! You're through now, Charlton Wells.'

'Hullo!'

'Hullo! This is Black,' said the unmistakable voice of Quiller. 'Who's that?'

'The person you want to speak to.'

'Oh, Sir—!' He could almost be heard swallowing down an aspirate. 'I'm glad your secretary was able to get hold of you.'

'I told you I wasn't to be rung up here.' Maximer could not refrain from throwing out that challenge.

'I thought it would be safe on a Saturday afternoon. In any case I had to get in touch with you. Is it all right to talk?'

'Within reason, yes.' Though he knew there was no one now in the flat but his cook, who was most unlikely to be eavesdropping from the office or the bedroom extension, it was not in his nature to abandon caution totally. 'I hope you're ringing up from a public call box.'

'Yes, with a row of shillings and sixpences in front of me.'

'You should have transferred the charge.'

'I never thought of that. I don't often have occasion to make trunk calls.'

'I was expecting to see you in a few hours.'

'That's just it. I don't know whether to leave or not. The luggage has disappeared.'

'The luggage has disappeared?' Sir Harry's stupefaction was such that only on the last syllable was he sure what Quiller meant by luggage. 'Disappeared!' The word was now vibrant with horror. 'Are you trying to tell me you've lost the trunk?'

'Not the trunk, the contents,' Quiller rejoined in what was for him quite a rapid and staccato style. 'And it has nothing to do with me. I wasn't even over here when it happened.'

Maximer recognized that he was too much in Quiller's power to take a high hand, and, exercising his self-control, he said very courteously: 'My dear fellow, I used a mere turn of phrase. After receiving such a satisfying telegram from you, I was naturally startled. Only tell me what is the matter!'

'Well, I'd better begin at the beginning, otherwise you won't make head or tail of it.' Quiller's voice sank to its usual pitch and tempo. 'Yesterday evening you'd no sooner rung off than I had a letter from Miss S. to tell me this woman, their friend, hadn't made up her mind yet which item she wanted, and if I was in a hurry to get back to London, they could send the luggage after me. She was most apologetic—sorry, you know, to be giving me so much trouble over such a small matter.'

Sir Harry, who did not care for this pointed irony, gave a discouraging grunt.

'That put me in a bit of a spot. You'd asked me to come back at once, but I was pretty sure you wouldn't want me to leave without the luggage.'

'You were right,' said Sir Harry with much emphasis.

'My difficulty was how to get hold of the items and yet not appear to be fussing about them. So I waited until this morning when I knew S. would be busy and the daughter most likely to answer the 'phone, and I rang up and said that, much as I should have liked to oblige, I'd have to take the stuff with me today because the American I was hoping to do a deal with was coming in on Monday morning first thing. I thought it was better to speak to the daughter than the father because it was as plain as a pikestaff on Thursday that she would have liked me to take the things away there and then.'

Sir Harry made an acquiescent sound to show he was listening.

'She raised no difficulties at all, said straight away that she'd get hold of their friend and tell her she'd have to make her choice. And sure enough, after about an hour she rang me back and said the friend had chosen.'

'Chosen what? Which?'

'Your time's up now,' said the operator's voice with what seemed to Maximer a tang of deliberate malice.

'Which?' he repeated urgently. 'Which did she choose. Put it in a few discreet words.'

'I can put it in one—'

'I'm sorry, caller, I must disconnect you now!'

It was hard to believe the operator was not malevolent and Quiller not determinedly lingering over his reply, but after a moment or two of harrowing suspense certain shillings and sixpences enabled him to pronounce the dread name:

'Lorenzo.'

Sir Harry stifled a groan of anguish, reminding himself that there was worse to come. 'Go on!' he commanded, as martyrs are reputed to have said to the headsman, 'Strike!'

'She offered to bring the items to the station for me, but I said I'd be over early and drop in at the house to rearrange the packing. I didn't like all that weight in one trunk.'

'It was reinforced with steel bands,' sighed Maximer, 'but you were quite right to take every precaution. Go on!'

'I came over by the next bus and did a bit more pottering about in the junk shops for the sake of local colour. I bought a nice zinc-lined chest, a sailor's chest, to put the little ones in. Then I had lunch and went up to the house as merry as a grig.'

Even in his anger and dismay, the idea of Quiller as merry as a grig struck Maximer as incongruous, but he was sensitive to the nervous tension which dictated the phrase, and said patiently: 'Yes, what then?'

'Miss S. had had the luggage put in the garage to get it out of the way.'

'Miss S. is a fool,' said Maximer. 'But go on!'

'She hadn't taken out Lorenzo yet because she was intending to do that while I was repacking the others. She'd seen to it that the car was left outside, and she'd got a nice clean tarpaulin laid out ready for me, and she fetched the key from some place where she was keeping it for safety and opened the lid. The tray was empty!'

'Where was the father while this was going on?'

'Lying down. She mentioned that he'd been kept up very late the night before.'

'What was her reaction?'

'To the empty tray? Just what you'd expect. She was puzzled—didn't know what to make of it. Then she lifted it up and underneath there was nothing but an old jack and some bits of scrap metal that she said had been lying about the garage for months. They'd obviously been put in so that the trunk shouldn't feel too light if anyone tried to move it.'

'How did she react to that?'

'At first she seemed to think it was a practical joke—her young sister and brother playing the fool; and she began looking round as if she was sure to find the things hidden somewhere. Then she went into the house, and in a minute or two her brother came out with her—a boy of eighteen or nineteen he is—and he swore on his honour they hadn't touched anything. He said he'd known for years that there was nothing in the trunk but mouldy old—'

'Careful, my friend!'

'Mouldy old items,' Quiller conceded as one who in the course of a game yields a point to a player with a niggling delight in the rules. 'Anyhow, I think you'd have been satisfied if you'd seen and heard him that he had no hand in it at all.'

'I dare say I should.' Maximer's cadence was ominous. 'This was not done as a joke, whoever did it. Well?'

'Well! Miss S. got angry then and went and roused her father. While she was doing that, the son and I had a look round. There was no evidence of breaking in, and the lock of the trunk was in good order.'

'Quite so, I expected that.'

'Presently the old chap—'

'There's no need to describe him.'

'Presently S. came down, and he seemed very much put out—very much put out indeed.'

'Yet he didn't suggest sending for the police?'

'No, but the daughter did. That was another facer for me.'

Quiller paused inquiringly, and while Maximer put a question to himself as to the possible effects of police intervention, the operator struck in ruthlessly again. By the time it had been agreed that further charges should be transferred, he had seen all the fatal consequences that might ensue from reporting the theft, and had even come to a hasty conclusion as to what Quiller's procedure should be.

'You succeeded, I hope, in keeping *them* out!' he said in a manner that made the other very glad to reply:

'I said we'd better make absolutely certain first that it wasn't a joke or a mistake of some kind, and S. seemed immensely relieved at that, and suggested that if I could give him a few hours he'd be bound to get it cleared up, and otherwise he'd return me the money.'

'Did you make it clear you wouldn't accept it?'

'Well, I felt we could come to that later. We don't want to work up any idea that these things are really—'

'Quite! Yes, I take you. Say no more!'

'The problem for the moment is whether I leave by the Pullman or not. Of course, I'd like to stay, but that might show them the—the items are more important than—'

'Yes, yes, I see your dilemma. The position is a very delicate one because S. will obviously do all in his power to protect the culprit.'

'Oh, I don't think so!' Quiller exclaimed in genuine surprise. 'He wants to avoid publicity because it's troublesome, that's all!'

'Do you mean to say you don't know who has done this?'

'I have a fair idea—though I must admit it staggers me to think of it.'

'But she's been able to count on his protection, don't you see? Otherwise she wouldn't have dared.'

'She? What "she"?' drawled Quiller.

Sir Harry was so taken aback that he actually stammered. 'My—my dear fellow, who do you suppose? The woman who was to be given L.'

'Given L.!'

'L.! L.! Lorenzo, if we must be explicit. The woman who put it into their heads to come and see me in the first place. Why, what other possibility enters your mind?'

'M.' Since Maximer seemed to take a childish delight in behaving like a character in a spy story, Quiller would gratify him.

'M?'

'Yes, the man Miss S. first tried to sell them to. I shouldn't have thought him equal to it, but he'd seen some of them and must have found out somehow that I'd bought the lot and put two and two together.'

Sir Harry, who had never met or seen Morris, having despised his shop too much to enter it when in Charlton Wells, had no means of judging whether he was likely to commit a burglary, but he saw that there were potentialities that had not occurred to him and that he could not estimate in a telephone conversation.

'We'd better have a talk about this,' he said, 'under easier conditions. What is your position at this instant with S.?'

'My position?'

'Yes, you had to make some excuse, I presume, to get away and put through this call?'

'I simply told them I had something else to pick up in the town and that I'd come back before going to the station. I think I struck the right note—not too fussy, not too slack.'

'You're sure that interfering daughter hasn't run off to the police?'

'No. S. was very firm about it. He won't hear of it until he's tried what his own efforts will do.'

'Because, in my opinion, he's protecting their friend . . . Now listen, Black! Go back to the S.s and say you've been telephoning London to let your sister know you're coming by the later train. That will seem quite natural in the circumstances. He asked you for a few hours: you give them to him. You remain on the spot till this evening, and you find out everything you can, not only about this M., assuming he has some finger in the pie, but also about the friend—the family friend. Have you heard her name?'

'Yes,' Quiller answered a little sulkily, for he hated night travelling. 'I suppose you don't want me to say it on the telephone?'

'Give me the initial so we may be perfectly certain we both have the same person in mind.'

'I don't know whether to say D. or P.'

'Good. You have it. Now you've got the rest of the day to gather information about this woman—who and what she is, where she lives, and everything that will enable me to pursue my own lines of inquiry in case S. fails with her. She's evidently dangerous and determined.'

Quiller gave an unhappy croak that would have been a protest if he had allowed it to reach full expression. Maximer not having taken him wholly into his confidence, he had remained unaware till now that Mrs. du Plessis was a factor to be reckoned with. To him she had been merely a person who, for some sentimental reason, was to be given a picture, and as such a nuisance rather than an enemy. He had no desire to pit himself against a dangerous and determined woman on behalf of a dangerous and determined man. That sort of thing might lead as far as the police courts, and since those wretched last days at Mandell & Strood's, he had felt a horror of getting mixed up in anything definitely unlawful. So far he had done nothing worse than buying some paintings from a willing vendor at a price scarcely below what he had been asked for them, and he had felt safe if somewhat uncomfortable; but now a perilous element had been introduced, had been sprung upon him in fact, which made him wish very earnestly to embroil himself no further.

'It's going to be difficult,' he said, clearing his throat, 'for you to—how shall I put it?—for you to extract the full benefit from these—these useful items if there's someone who knows, so to speak, that they are what they are.'

'Leave the question of what benefit I get or don't get to me.' To take the sharp edge off the admonition Maximer forced a laugh. 'Your job is to help me recover the lost property. As you are having more trouble than we bargained for, your reward will be proportionate.'

Quiller could not ignore the question of the reward for there was a large claim against him for alimony, and he was far from prosperous. But even without this inducement, he would not have been equal to defying Sir Harry, who, partly by the sheer vigour of a powerful will and partly by a most tangible claim upon his gratitude, had held him in subjection for years. If it had not been for Sir Harry's friendly words on his behalf, Mandell & Strood might have let the law take its course; and without the capital he had supplied for the shop in Islington, it was difficult to imagine how a man so discredited could have earned a living. Of course, he knew now that the other had gained some ends of his own by all this kindness, but the impression it had made upon him at the crucial time had never been quite erased, and he had formed a habit of loyalty.

'The reward isn't the first thing in my mind,' he said, truthfully enough. 'I was glad to save these objects from the clutches of a man like M. who couldn't have failed to buy them if I hadn't put a spoke in his wheel.'

'But now you think he has acquired them without purchase,' Maximer reminded him with a light mordacity.

'That was my first idea, yes. There seemed no other solution. But since you've put this friend in a different light, I don't know what to make of it. You never told me anything about her.'

'It didn't seem material. Perhaps it isn't. That's for you to find out. Whether the luggage turns up or not, come back by the evening train.'

'The night train,' Quiller corrected him dismally. 'There's nothing between the Pullman and the one that arrives in the small hours.'

'I feel for you, Black, but there's no alternative. If the property's still missing, we must meet in the morning. Very discreetly. Is Lyons Corner House open on Sundays?'

'Which one?'

'Say the one at Marble Arch. . . . No, on second thoughts, we might be seen by someone. What about Victoria Station—one of the waiting rooms?'

'I shouldn't say Victoria was any safer than the Corner House.'

'True. We must meet at one of the less frequented stations. What do you say to Clapham Junction?'

'Well, it's not exactly a spot one would choose for a Sunday morning outing.' Quiller took courage for the avowal from the prospect of the night journey.

'Just so. We have as good a chance of a private talk at Clapham Junction as anywhere in London. I'll meet you there at ten-thirty—on the platform near the general waiting-room.'

'You don't think,' Quiller ventured, 'I ought to wait here tonight and meet you tomorrow afternoon?'

'Certainly not. We can't waste time in that fashion. Besides, the longer you hang about getting to know S. and his daughter, the harder it'll be for you to refuse to have your money back if they can't—or won't—produce the goods.'

'Yes, that's a point. Shall I ring you up before leaving?'

'Unfortunately, no. Trunk calls can be traced. They should be used sparingly. I'll tell you what—if the luggage does turn up, you can telephone me from King's Cross when you get in. I shan't mind being woken up in the still watches for that. But if I don't hear from you in the night, I'll look for you at Clapham Junction in the morning.'

Quiller had a very strong suspicion that, though he had reeled under the first shock, though indeed he would fight to possess himself of these pictures as ardently as if right were on his side, Sir Harry had begun, in an almost boyish spirit, to enjoy himself.

ELEVEN

STEPHANIE was waiting alone in a country church situated more or less halfway between Elderfield and Charlton Wells. Though she had come to meet Arnold Bayley and longed to see him, it was with a slight shiver that she seated herself on one of the hard, straight-backed chairs ranged with their accompanying hassocks on either side of the aisle. The deserted building was bleak and humid, and the Victorian stained-glass windows drained the September light of all its warmth. She could not but feel oppressed as she set the austere altar and bare walls against her memories of country churches in Italy, with their ornamental shrines and rich images, their candle flames and votive offerings.

This was the second day of her fortnight's holiday, and the renunciation of Italy went hard with her, the more so as her meetings with Arnold would have to be few and secret. Indeed, the whole affair was anything but the lark she had pretended to think it in order to keep up Linda's spirits. She knew now that thieves, even when they have companions in crime, must spend much of their lives in loneliness and brooding—lying low, waiting for a sign, only intermittently able to enjoy that fellowship which perhaps originally attracted them towards the career of danger.

It was Tuesday today, and she had not seen Arnold since they had lunched together on Saturday, choosing the dreariest of Elderfield's many dreary restaurants to diminish the chance of meeting anyone known to either of them. Her relations with the Sandilands family had become most embarrassing, while Kenneth Dyer was clearly dismayed at having been drawn into the conspiracy and anxious to avoid all contact with her. Arnold's letter, received this morning, proposing the meeting at Mutchley Church was her one comfort—that and the consciousness of a high purpose.

And now Arnold was late and she had nothing to read and felt little inclined in this dour building to pray. He had said he would be coming on his motor-cycle, and it was exasperating to learn how many vehicles could be mistaken for motor-cycles when listened for by eager and unpractised ears. When at last it arrived, she decided perversely to believe that what she heard was only a distant farm tractor and was quite startled to see Arnold's thin shadow fall across the gravestones paving the aisle.

'I'm sorry to be late,' he said, dropping into the chair beside her. 'Things cropped up just when I was leaving my office, and as I'd taken most of yesterday off, it wouldn't have done to be in too much of a hurry today. How are you?'

'Depressed.'

'You mustn't be. I have good news. I would have rung you up and told you if I could have done it safely on the office telephone.'

She followed with soothed eyes the mysteriously captivating small movements of his hands as he brought a notecase from his breast pocket and drew from it a telegram which he opened out and gave to her.

'It came this afternoon. Look!'

She read aloud: "'Transaction B traced to where you expected particulars follow Oscar." Transaction B?' She knitted her brows over the words.

'I'll tell you as much as I know, but not until you've told me what's been happening to *you*. I've been anxious about you—even combing through the papers in dread of seeing the whole thing reported.'

'It's been a horrid time.' The relief of being able to speak to the one person with whom she could be natural and unguarded brought her near to tears. 'I've had to make one excuse after another for not seeing Dr. Sandilands. Of course he knows I did it, but I've written to him denying it. I've told the letter but not the spirit of the truth.'

'You've said you haven't got the pictures? That's true enough.'

'Yes. Beatrix came round to see me. She appealed to me point blank to stop playing the fool. Fortunately she has a manner I can hold out against; but if it had been Dr. Sandilands himself, I think I should almost have succumbed. Now I have to stay out of the way all day in case he should call. I wander about Charlton Wells like a lost soul.'

'My poor darling!' It was the first time he had called her by a word of endearment, and on his lips it sounded entirely new and wonderfully warm and comforting.

'Beatrix spoke of telling the police. I shouldn't mind that at all if it weren't for you and Linda. Publicity is just what's wanted really.'

'But not prematurely. Not before we can prove anything. We shall do that sooner or later, I promise you.' He put the telegram back in his notecase with a smile of satisfaction. 'However, if they do call the police in, I doubt whether they'll find very much—provided the others are discreet.'

'That's what I don't like to count on. I've kept Linda on our side so far by making her think—' she realized that she could not finish as she had intended, 'that she's doing it for the sake of our beautiful flirtation'—and instead went back over her words lamely: 'By making her look on it as a great act of friendship to me. But you see, they're all under the impression—well, at any rate, Dr. Sandilands and Beatrix are—that Quiller will take back his hundred guineas if the pictures don't turn up. When they find it's not going to be as simple as that—'

'Which it certainly isn't.'

'—then Linda's position will become much more difficult.'

'They'll know when Quiller digs his toes in that the things are valuable.'

She shook her head. 'That won't make any difference to Dr. Sandilands' feelings about keeping his bargain. He'll be annoyed and exasperated, but he'll try to stick to his bond.'

'Surely not when he finds what Maximer has been up to?'

'Ah, no, he's not as quixotic as that! But we shall have to prove it up to the hilt.'

'We've made a beginning anyhow. . . . Are you hanging on my words?'

She nodded with a smile that seemed to please him for he took her hand. 'Then let's get out!' He rose and drew her up with him. 'I like to move about when I'm explaining things.'

'Do you think we shall be seen?'

'No one comes to such a dull little church as this except the parishioners, and precious few of them I should imagine. That's why I chose it.'

She was glad to follow him out into the cool-tempered sunshine of an afternoon that seemed to be basking between summer and autumn. In its light, gentle but searching and precise, the uncompromising granite headstones of the churchyard sparkled and the grass that pushed its way up between the crevices of stony graves shone like opaque glass. A sensation of unreality took possession of her. Here she was at this unlikely trysting-place bent upon the strangest of missions with a companion whom she had known five days but who in that time had become more interesting, and even more congenial, to her than anyone she had met in as many years. All that had troubled and disheartened her fell away, for she seemed to be moving upon some new and scarcely substantial plane. Her feet trod the unequal ground lightly, heedless of what lay under it: her hand involuntarily stirred and found itself resting on the sleeve of Arnold's jacket. He laid his own over it and pressed it against his side.

'Well?' she said, but her note of expectancy was half-feigned. Fleetingly at least she had the illusion that it did not matter what he answered or whether he answered at all. Whatever he had to communicate must be secondary to the charm of this entirely personal moment, in which she saw nothing beyond Arnold Bayley and the grey-green churchyard, but saw them as in crystal.

Such moments are seldom shared, though we have a conviction that they should be. He brought her rather ludicrously back to the solid earth.

'On the afternoon of Saturday the 9th instant, acting on information received, I proceeded to the residence of Oscar Robertson, author and art critic, of Steeple Walk, Peterborough, and remained there till the morning of Monday. With the exception of certain intervals for eating and sleeping and thinking about my superior officer, I was entirely occupied during the said sojourn in conferring with the said Oscar Robertson—'

'Now that I'm a criminal, I'm frightened of policemen.' She disengaged her hand.

He was unaware that he had failed to rise to an occasion, and continued pleasantly: 'In other words, Oscar and I really got down to it over the week-end. Do you know, he's kept a systematic record of all the pictures Rennick ever concerned himself with? I mean, everything he authenticated or refused to authenticate or had any correspondence about at all. I can tell you, I enjoyed myself very much with that card index.'

'What is Transaction B?'

He seated himself abstractedly on a tombstone. 'We've made a list of doctored pictures that have been sold on the strength of something written by Rennick, and arranged them in a dated sequence. There are four known ones and a couple of suspects; and all since his death, none before. The Brueghel is C. Two others seem to have been off-loaded first. There was one masquerading as a Steen that changed hands only three or four months after Rennick's death in 1937. It went to Capetown to Sir Hubert Prosser, a retired diamond magnate, and was exposed when he died and his son sold a batch of pictures to help with death duties. The war was the only thing the papers were taking much notice of at the time so it got very little publicity, and Oscar didn't hear of it till two or three years afterwards. That's Transaction A. We still have a good deal to find out about that. . . . Come and sit down beside me.'

'No thank you.'

'Why not? The stone's quite warm.'

'"I do not wish to regard myself nor yet to be regarded in that bony light."'

'Stephanie, what are you saying? Well, if you won't sit down and make yourself comfortable on the cosiest tomb in the place, we shall have to move on.'

He made his way among the corroded marble crosses, the graves enclosed by chains and filled in with broken stone, the graves covered with vast and heavy lids of slate apparently designed to challenge the idea of resurrection. She followed behind him, listening now with all her attention.

'Transaction B is the one Oscar's been working on since I left him. It was a Teniers that was sold to Arcadian Green.'

'Who's he?'

'What? You don't know Green's Amusement Arcades? No, of course, a sedate place like Charlton Wells wouldn't be favoured, but we've got one in Elderfield. They're all over the provinces and several in London, flourishing like the green bay tree--little infernos of rattling music and automatic fun machines. But in private life Mr. Green aspires, quite touchingly I believe, to be regarded as a man of taste and culture: and before the war, when he had a great deal of new wealth and could more or less do as he liked with it, he bought a fine Queen Anne house at Twickenham and took his wife to Chattery's, the interior decorators, with an order to do the whole thing from A to Z, from the books on the library shelves to the last table napkin.'

'It sounds awful.'

'It was probably much better than anything Mr. and Mrs. Green could have achieved by their own efforts, judging from the look of the Amusement Arcades. And you must admit it was creditable that they wanted books on the library shelves at all. What's more, they wanted pictures. They ordered Chattery's to supply them with a selection of warranted genuine Old Masters for the drawing-room. Now a lot of that contract had to be farmed out—one firm supplying the library and another the glass and plate and so on. And the Old Masters were acquired through an arrangement with Lamotte, a Frenchman, a sort of free-lance dealer who bought and sold on commission both in Paris and London—I suppose one could call him a picture broker.'

'Do you mean to say your friend found all this out since Saturday?' she demanded a little breathlessly, coming to a standstill beside him where he paused at a wall low enough to lean on.

'No, no, these facts came to light some time ago—to Oscar's light at any rate. Some reviewer quoted the claim he made in his biography that Rennick had an uncanny knack of detecting falsity at a glance, and he received a very cross letter from Arcadian Green. It had turned out that, despite Rennick's high praises of it, their Teniers was only a copy.'

She was so interested in his story now that she gently removed the hand he had laid on her shoulder. 'How had they learned that?'

'In the most humiliating way. Poor Mr. Green, being very proud of his house and all its treasures, had decided to have a sort of booklet written that he could present to his guests. And as usual sparing no expense, he'd got an expert to write up the Old Masters. The expert was a real expert who was able to tell him that the Teniers was copied—extremely well copied—from an original in some rather obscure Spanish collection. Green wouldn't believe at first that his was the copy—the others were all right, you see—and when it was put beyond doubt, he wrote to Chattery's and requested his money back. Chattery's pleaded that the picture had been vouched for by a first-rate authority, and that they'd sold it in good faith and only made a reasonable profit on it. After that he took legal advice—there's nothing very arcadian about Green—but he was warned that he hadn't a first-rate case.'

'What about the French picture broker?'

'The war was looming up and he had a perfectly good excuse for being difficult to get hold of. In any case, Rennick's letter would have been just as good a protection for him as it was for Chattery's. Nobody ever once thought of questioning that it really was written by Rennick. Why should they? There was the famous paper printed from an early Victorian copperplate, the typing done on an obsolete machine that was a kind of joke in the art world, and the Rennick style which everyone can recognize in the first ten words. That anyone would or could forge such monumental things never entered even Oscar's head until the instances began to multiply. And Oscar himself didn't think of suspecting Maximer.'

'And now you've actually succeeded in tracing this Teniers to him?'

'Tracing a connection between him and it,' he corrected her, 'though I shan't know how till I have Oscar's letter. And the success is all his. I only put him on the track.'

'But it's magnificent, isn't it?' The importance of the discovery brought a solemnity to her face that made him laugh.

'Magnificent, but you mustn't scowl over it!'

'I'm scowling over the problem—ought I to break the news at once to Dr. Sandilands?'

'There isn't enough to go on yet. Enough for us, yes—but remember, we start with the assumption that Maximer's fishy. Dr. Sandilands doesn't.'

'True.'

'We must wait until we have everything cut and dried. Otherwise, you'll convince him of nothing except that we've been meddling.'

'I didn't intend to implicate you.'

'You couldn't help it if you told him about our Elderfield Brueghel.' He rested his chin on his hand, looking somewhat pensively over the wall on to the road, a road bleak and bare of any object capable of distracting the eye except his own motor-cycle and a newspaper fluttering on the ground near it. 'I dare say I seem a coward, but really, if my part in this is made known before we have proof positive, my career will come pretty smartly to a close.'

'You know you don't seem a coward. There ought to be some special combination of the Victoria and the George Cross for what you've done. I'm only troubled about the time factor.'

'The pictures are safe,' he said, and although there was no possibility of being overheard, he dropped his voice to a murmur. 'I told you the safest place to hide pictures was an Art Gallery.'

Stephanie forbore to remind him again that there were others in the secret. No good purpose could be served by worrying him with her fears lest Linda should give way under pressure. It was her business, by every artifice she could contrive, to prevent Linda from weakening.

Kenneth Dyer would, she imagined, keep his counsel. He was a reluctant conspirator but, so far as she could make him out, a discreet one, and he was not, like the unfortunate Linda, in intimate contact every day with the irritated victims of the conspiracy. Kenneth had been torn, in the last stages of the meeting at his studio, by an almost visible struggle between the desire to save a valuable property in which his new friend must rightly have some share and the desire to avoid becoming further involved: but in the end Linda's claims had prevailed and, grudging but gallant, he had driven the fateful burden over to Elderfield Art Gallery in his car next morning, happy that he was not asked to harbour it on his own premises.

Saturday, with its influx of visitors in the public rooms and total quietus in the private ones, was a very favourable day for bestowing the paintings unnoticed under the dust-sheets of the Cemetery, and when Arnold had lunched with Stephanie before leaving to pursue his quest at Peterborough, he had been able to tell her that the treasure was, for the time being at any rate, secure.

Now as he restlessly moved off again, making an erratic path through a sad little colony of anonymous mounds, she inquired anxiously: 'Have you looked at them today? Are they all right?'

'They're all right. It doesn't do to go looking round too much. Nobody's likely to touch anything in the Cemetery—my Cemetery—without consulting me first.'

'What about the portrait of Lorenzo? And Pius II? And the Emperor Johannes? They must be very unlike anything you normally hide in the basement.'

'They're in the Rogues' Gallery, cheek by jowl with our fraudulent Brueghel.'

'Oh, Arnold!'

'It went against the grain, but I was able to tuck a few of them away there as neatly as a conjuring trick. You have nothing to bother about but keeping the Sandilands family from starting up a hue and cry.'

She answered after reflection: 'What they do next will probably depend on Quiller since he can claim to be the legal owner.'

'It's suspicious in itself that he hasn't insisted before now on calling the police in.'

'He went back to London on Saturday.'

'What?' He wheeled round with an expression of the most pained bewilderment. 'The day they discovered the loss?'

'Yes, I only heard that yesterday. Linda and I haven't seen very much of each other, in case it should draw suspicion upon her.'

'Good God, but what you've told me is astonishing—perfectly astonishing! It almost suggests—' He checked himself and with a startled frown seemed to take the full impact of a new and unpleasant idea. 'Wouldn't it be the biggest sell in the world,' he remarked in a changed tone, 'if we'd dreamed it all up, invented it, talked ourselves into it—the whole marvellous scheme? If this man Quiller knew no more about the real value of these pictures than the man in the moon? If he bought them for exactly whatever reasons he may have given for buying them? If he and Maximer had never met in their lives?'

She faced him in the silence of consternation.

'Does it seem likely'—his conviction had mounted with each question—'that a man who'd just been robbed of a fortune would go calmly off leaving other people to deal with the matter?'

'He had some business reason for getting back to London,' she countered feebly. 'He'd already said so.'

'*My dear girl!*' His emphasis turned the words into a vehement protest. 'This Quiller—I've found out about him—keeps a junk shop in Islington. What business could he have that's more important than these pictures if he knows what they are, if he's been put up to buying them by Maximer? No, no, Stephanie!' He turned away with a distracted air and made again for the low stone wall where, resting heavily on his folded arms, he became an image of dejection. 'Let's face it! Maximer may have done some shady things—we've stumbled on that by accident—but as to plotting with Quiller to get hold of those paintings, that's beginning to seem more than a little doubtful.'

'Then the verdict he gave Dr. Sandilands was in good faith?'

He hesitated at this but went on after reflection: 'Even that's more possible than a man's going casually off to London leaving a huge property in the hands of burglars.'

'But what could he do? He wouldn't want to call in the police. You said so yourself.'

'All the same he couldn't help remaining on the spot. I took that for granted.'

'If you're right, Quiller really *is* the legal owner of everything.'

'Yes, except the one they gave you.'

'In that case, we were still justified in doing what we did. In fact, a legal owner who doesn't know the value of such a collection is more dangerous than an illegal owner who'd at least want to make the most of it.'

'Oh come!' he said rather angrily. 'On that principle anyone who happens to acquire a rare thing without knowledge of its value ought to have it stolen from him.'

She did not answer lest in another instant they should be quarrelling. It would be easy to quarrel now, although in her heart she sympathized with him profoundly. She recognized that he was under the strain of having done violence to a respect for law and order which is essentially a characteristic of the disciplined male, and which in her own case was but moderately developed. She weighed too how much more the pictures must mean to her, after her discovery of them, her long and close study of their qualities, than to him who had first heard of them five days ago, and how much greater must be her regard for the interests of Dr. Sandilands, whom he had never met.

The news of Quiller's departure had not struck her as particularly significant, for she had formed instinctively some notion that it was part of his policy. But now Arnold's sudden dismay communicated itself to her, and she stood beside him dazed with the horrid potentialities of their all having, at her instigation, made fools of themselves.

'We could try,' she said at last, 'to buy them back from Quiller. I have a hundred-and-something pounds. . . . I shan't be using the money I saved to go to Italy. He might be content with a fair profit for such a quick return.'

'Now that he knows someone has thought them worth stealing? That's just a little naïve, my dear!' But he gave her a sidelong smile, rueful and friendly, that softened the mockery of the speech. Then his eyes strayed away again to the road and fell on the newspaper, which had blown open and seemed about to fly away.

'That's my paper!' he cried, and hoisted himself over the wall to retrieve it with a deftness that, despite her preoccupation, she found charming. Indeed, to her pleased and partial eye all his movements had the grace we associate with the movements of cats, who never put more energy into an action than it needs and thus have an air of conserved strength that is in itself a kind of elegance.

'I bought this,' he said, restoring the pages meticulously to their folds, 'as I was leaving Elderfield. I had a premonition that there might be something about the burglary in it. I have one every time I see a newspaper boy.'

'Would it be considered important enough to get into the Elderfield papers?'

'I'm afraid it would. The *Evening Courier* has a special column for the doings of Charlton Wells.'

'But that's social stuff, not crimes.' She pointed to the appropriate headlines.

His eye travelled idly down as many paragraphs as were visible and came to rest, uncomprehending at first, on a familiar name. Then with a low but triumphant cry, he held the journal out to her across the wall, his finger marking the place.

'I take it all back!' His voice abandoned its customary restraint and chanted with a rising excitement: 'I recant. I retract. I apologize. I was absurd. The plot's on. The hunt's up. Everything we did was right.'

'What is it? How can I read if you won't keep the paper still?'

He caught her hand and folded it over the paper, exclaiming in a rush of high spirits: 'The trumpet has sounded! We gird up our loins!'

She read slowly and at first almost without trusting her eyes: 'Among the latest distinguished visitors to the spa is Sir Harry Maximer, the well-known art critic. He arrived this morning and is staying at the Royal Hotel. He will be taking the cure.'

TWELVE

IF SIR HARRY had been able to descend on Charlton Wells in deep disguise, he would certainly have preferred to do so, but his large benignant face and five feet eleven of ungainly bulk were too conspicuous to be easily deprived of identity, and he was obliged to adopt another stratagem. Leaning heavily on a stout walking-stick, stiffly shuffling and occasionally pausing as if stricken with some well-nigh unbearable twinge, he submitted himself within two or three hours of his arrival to a rigorous course of treatment for lumbago. He had come armed, in fact, with a letter to Dr. Houston, one of the leading spa physicians—a letter from his London doctor who had received, on Sunday afternoon, an urgent call to attend the crippled sufferer.

Dr. Houston's measures were drastic and included Plombière douches, hot and cold sitz baths, massage performed by a strong and merciless Swede, partial immersion each morning in warm paraffin wax and total abstention all day from wine and the more appetizing kinds of food. These trials Sir Harry endured reluctantly but with fortitude, knowing that his performance must be complete at every point. Having established to the satisfaction of a train of witnesses his pretext for being where he was, he became free within limits to devote himself to his purpose.

He had examined the idea of making a bold contact with Dr. Sandilands, even of inviting his cure for the lumbago instead of Dr. Houston's, but had decided against it. Dr. Sandilands was a general practitioner, not a spa physician, and might be sufficiently surprised at such an approach to put two and two together. Something more casual must be contrived, and in the meantime he could be testing the ground in other directions. Quiller, by a system arranged at Clapham Junction, would keep him informed of any new developments that might transpire from direct communication with the Sandilands.

Acting on instructions, Quiller had written very politely from London to the effect that what was done to recover the pictures was entirely Dr. Sandilands' affair so long as they were got back with all reasonable expedition: there were customers in the offing for them and indeed a good prospect of selling to America had already been lost. The suggestion that the purchase price should be paid back was ignored rather than rejected.

Sir Harry was pretty certain the doctor would turn to the police only as a last resort. His shy and recessive attitude, the privacy with which he had surrounded the pictures lest something concerning their pretensions should leak into the newspapers, and, above all, the fact that his friend Mrs. du Plessis was perhaps the culprit, made the appeal to law an eventuality it was worth while to risk.

Keenly observant and endowed with an excellent memory, Sir Harry had not failed to notice how sharply the daughter had attacked Mrs. du Plessis, how earnestly the father had defended her, and the thought occurred to him that Miss Sandilands' resentment might be the more intense because of some element of jealousy. Beatrix had struck him as one whose animosity might be turned to account: but first he must make sure that his suspicions were well-founded, for now that Quiller had told him in detail about the interview with Morris, he could not deny a bare possibility that the dealer, finding too late that he had been offered a superlative bargain, had instigated the theft.

There was also another possibility and a worse one. Notwithstanding Dr. Sandilands' plea for secrecy, someone might have talked, and it was just conceivable that the burglary was a professional job. Should that be so, to get the things back would be a much longer and more expensive task than Sir Harry had expected to tackle, though not, he prided himself, one that was beyond his powers. But before he need consider so troublesome an extreme, the likelier suspects must be accounted for. He resolved, lying in a cubicle recuperating after the horrid Plombière, to eliminate Morris first.

Later in the day, tormenting himself with half a pint of the obnoxious waters, taken in the Pump Room under a dozen pairs of eyes, he had an inspiration, brilliant in its simplicity, for making a first move towards the Sandilands family. In order to ensure that there should not seem anything furtive about his doings, he had arrived in Charlton Wells with all the publicity an asbestos magnate and an art critic may command: he could fairly assume therefore that his visit would not be unnoticed by the doctor's household, and there was nothing in the least excessive in his writing the note he dispatched by the afternoon post:

Royal Hotel.

Wednesday, 13th Sept.

Dear Dr. Sandilands,

You have perhaps heard that I came here yesterday to take the cure. As you so flatteringly invited me here a little while ago to look at your pictures, I should not like you to think I troubled you to come all the way to London in the knowledge that a week later I should myself be in Charlton Wells.

It was only on Sunday that I was visited with a dire attack of lumbago—an old enemy which I thought I had routed—and, painful as it is to move about under such an affliction, I was obliged to snatch my one chance of getting away at a time when my business affairs in London could be left in other hands. My doctor accordingly consigned me to Dr. Houston, who has put me on a somewhat Spartan regime.

As I hate all forms of discourtesy, I felt I must defend myself against any idea that I had dragged you to London needlessly. If I had known this time last week that I should be here today, I would have spared you your wasted journey.

My greetings to your daughter and yourself,

Yours sincerely,

HARRY MAXIMER

Meditating pleasantly on his own wiliness, Sir Harry strolled out of his hotel to Morris's shop, which was but a stone's throw away. He stared for some minutes at the windows, the contents of which were little changed since Beatrix had studied them a few days before; but whereas she had felt chiefly surprise that there were people who affected to despise such attractive pictures, Maximer examined them with a wincing air that was now all unfeigned. The sight of the spurious Old Masters, signed and dated, brought a spasm to his face which was as good, dramatically speaking, as anything he had achieved in his role of a man racked with physical pain.

He brightened, however, when his eye lit upon Morris's latest cardinal piece. The large and elaborate canvas admired by Beatrix had been removed in favour of a less grandiose subject. Seated at a small table forming the centre of the composition was a nice-looking old cardinal with a rubicund face. On one side of him, in a ray of sunlight, stood a pretty servant girl wearing a short quilted satin skirt, a snowy muslin apron, and a flowered overdress. She leaned forward offering with a coquettish smile a cup and saucer on a gleaming silver tray. On the other side, in a contrasting shadow, stood a solemn-faced priest or monk holding a breviary in one hand, but pouring wine from a decanter with the other. With considerable skill the cardinal was depicted as being in the act of looking from one to the other, humorously uncertain. The title on the gold plaque was 'A Difficult Choice'.

Maximer, who had been wondering what plausible excuse he could give for entering such an establishment—as unseemly to him as a low bordel would be to a great courtesan—decided to play a sort of joke on himself. He went boldly in and asked the price of the cardinal. On hearing from the assistant that it was two hundred guineas, he requested to have it taken out of the window. At this, Morris himself emerged from some fastness whence he judged which customers were important enough to merit his personal attention, and proceeded in strains of uncalled-for rudeness to direct the assistant's movements.

'A beautiful painting, sir!' he exclaimed when it had been placed judiciously upon an easel in a small private salon. 'Lovely bit of colour it is! My word, what a bargain! An investment if you ask me!'

'Certainly a gilt-edged one,' said Maximer, glancing at the ostentatious frame.

'Quality, that's what I call it, quality!' Morris's harsh tone grew lyrical. 'With a thing like this you can't make a mistake—you can't go wrong!'

Sir Harry concluded that he had not been recognized, and pondered while appearing to study the numerous details of 'A Difficult Choice' whether he would gain or lose by revealing his identity. Improvisation being at all times one of his happiest faculties, he made up his mind to act as occasion should dictate, and, after peering at the canvas from various angles, said cannily:

'Perhaps if I'm going to spend as much as two hundred guineas I ought to have something a little more antique. I see this is only dated 1891.'

'Antique?' Morris turned a searching eye upon his customer but could determine nothing about him except that he was a man of substance and seriously eager to acquire something. 'Well, there's others in the same window two or three hundred years old. They cost a bit more, but then they're worth more. What do you expect? They're masterpieces. Rogers, bring out that Huysmans! Get a move on!'

Sir Harry would sooner have bought the canvas before him than anything Morris was likely to call a masterpiece, but he desired the assistant's absence and took advantage of his being in the window to remark, with the clear, straightforward gaze he was wont to assume for throwing out his most cunningly baited hooks: 'I should be willing to invest a few hundred in something exceptional—something, you know, that you could really call a find. It would have to be old, of course.'

He did not imagine that Morris, in the unlikely event of his having the stolen pictures, would forthwith offer them to him on such an invitation, nor would he himself be so imprudent here in Charlton Wells as to buy them. His motive was to observe the other's reaction, to judge whether any temptation rose in him to allude to rare and unprecedented possibilities. It was undoubtedly a hit-or-miss method, but he flattered himself on an acute perceptiveness.

Morris, for his part, had the same belief in his powers but with rather less reason. He now supposed that he had before him what he had learned in his earliest studies of the English tongue to call a 'mug'— that special kind of mug, a godsend to the humbler fraternity of the trade, who believes that there is a virtue in age for its own sake, that wormholes, cracks, and dirt confer value, and that rich bargains await the amateur who shuns the famous dealers and auction rooms of the capital and ferrets around in places which he fondly describes as 'off the beaten track'. His own shop did not cater for mugs of this type, carrying as it did a clean, select, and orderly stock; but if one should stray into his hands with money to spend, it seemed a pity not to reap the benefit. His thoughts flew with regret to Miss Sandilands and her copies of Old Masters, and then he wondered if she had yet succeeded in disposing of them. Unless she had taken them to Elderfield, there seemed a reasonable likelihood that she would have them still.

'Something old,' he said speculatively, 'older even than this Huysmans I'm just going to show you? Maybe I could put you on to a good thing—a very good thing indeed. Maybe. I wouldn't like to promise nothing unless I'm sure.'

'There isn't any Huysmans here, sir,' said the assistant, appearing at the entrance to the little salon.

'No Huysmans? Don't talk such rubbish! What about that Amsterdam street scene, the one that I told you ought to be in an art gallery?'

'It's labelled Van der Heyden, sir.'

'All right! Van der Heyden. You knew what I meant. Why make out you're a bigger fool than you are?'

Sir Harry deemed it time to observe candidly: 'Whoever it's by, I'm afraid it isn't the sort of thing I care about very much. I shouldn't bother to get it out, Mr. Morris.' And having found the hint just offered distinctly interesting, he added, 'What was that you mentioned about something that might be more—more, so to speak, out of the ordinary?'

'About that, I tell you straight out I can't say nothing definite.' Morris was discouraging, for he had realized that he might lose the bird in hand for the sake of the two in the bush. 'If I was to make you a promise I should be deceiving you. Why not try a nice ikon if you want something out of the ordinary? Rogers, fetch up that ikon! Remember where I put it? Look sharp! . . . Personally I recommend you to take this 'Difficult Choice' if you want a beautiful work of art, sir. You only got to keep it long enough and it becomes a real antique as much as the others.'

'Or more,' Sir Harry commented silently.

Morris's sudden caution struck him as significant. It was exactly what he would expect from a man who had yielded to an indiscreet impulse and then perceived his rashness. He longed to pursue the topic, but clearly, there could be no unguarded discussion while the assistant was present nor was it probable in any case that Morris would have much to say until he was better acquainted with his customer.

Leaning hard on his stick, he gazed into the jovial face of the cardinal, his own furrowed with the intricacies of his problem. How was it possible to make any progress without some gesture that would win Morris's confidence and appeal to his cupidity? The gesture most effective would undoubtedly be to make a purchase of some kind, but he boggled—everything that was estimable in his nature boggled —at the idea of paying money for any of the vulgar, puerile, and meretricious productions he saw about him. He must take the trouble to find something that at least was unpretentious, if such an object existed on these premises.

'On reflection,' he said, moving back into the public part of the shop, 'I believe an ikon would be altogether too exotic for me. No, I simply shouldn't feel at home with it. May I just look round a little? It's such a pleasure to rummage out something for oneself.'

Morris, doomed to retain the ikon which he had withheld from Quiller, watched this rummaging with a puzzled and slightly indignant stare. For all his arrogant self-complacency, the man must be a mug of

a prime order if he actually believed he could search out some undis-
covered treasure in this exclusive and luxurious shop. Still, his money
was as good as another's—better perhaps since business was slack
and he had spoken of investing 'a few hundreds'—and to give himself
more scope in case of some inspiration that might need broad and free
treatment, he made a brief sign to the assistant, who was mounting the
basement stairs with the ikon, to take it down again and keep out of
the way.

Sir Harry's alert eye did not miss the signal, which he hoped might
indicate an intention to become more expansive, and while he poked
into corners and probed the depths of the shelves in the back room, he
put out one or two delicate little feelers.

'A place like Charlton Wells should be a happy hunting ground for
a man who's capable of knowing a good thing when he sees one. Not
that the town itself is old, but the residents must have been the sort of
people—until the war at any rate—who were rich enough to hold on to
their possessions.'

'If you got a good pair of eyes in your head, it's wonderful what you
can come across anywhere.' Morris turned the frame Maximer had just
relinquished towards what he considered a favourable light. 'You take
this French picture now. What am I asking for it? Fifty guineas. Yet it
could have been painted by Lancret.'

'If he were working with his left hand and one eye closed,' thought
Maximer, but he only said: 'Modern conditions have no doubt caused
a great number of things to change hands here as everywhere else. One
might expect that a few of them, a certain modest proportion, would
be of some genuine value, though at first, of course, their merit would
easily escape notice. Not many of them, I dare say, would be in such
spick-and-span condition as these.'

Morris wished passionately that he knew whether Dr. Sandilands
was still trying to sell those worm-eaten panels. Obviously, they were
just what this pompous simpleton was hankering after and it would
be a delight to palm them off on him, but in the absence of any certain
knowledge, he could only make it his policy to press the wares he had
in stock and at the same time keep the door ajar, if it were possible, on
the prospect of being able to supply some suitable junk.

'I don't say you can't make a find now and then,' he conceded with
a grudging smile. 'Maybe right now I could lay my hands on something
that would be a sensation if it was properly handled. But to anyone who

likes to know what they're getting, I should say they couldn't do better than a beautiful Millet like you've taken a fancy to now, sir. Better than 'The Angelus' that is, if you ask me.'

Sir Harry suppressed a tendency to recoil. The products of forgery were not altogether novel to him, but he had high standards, and the muddy piece of hackwork in front of him offended his sense of decency.

Luckily within the same instant his eye lighted on something tolerable, no masterpiece but a pleasant unambitious trifle of a period and style too completely out of fashion to be worth faking. It was a late Victorian narrative picture representing a newly married couple driving away in a carriage from a church door: not a young and romantic pair of lovers but an elderly and portly bridegroom with a bride whose prettiness had lost its first bloom and who gazed down at her bouquet as if wistfully aware of the contrast between the fresh flowers and her own faded beauty. The husband clasped one of her hands in both of his own, his eyes fixed on her with a happiness and solicitude portrayed so sincerely as to be touching, and the more so because in the background, watching their departure, two girls in the full flower of youth exchanged a glance half-pitying and half-scornful.

'"A Belated Honeymoon,"' Sir Harry read from the inscription on the frame. He peered into the corner of the canvas and saw the signature of an entirely obscure artist.

'Lovely thing, isn't it?' Morris rhapsodized mechanically. 'Look at the way that wedding-dress has been painted! You could feel the satin! These pre-Raphaelites have been all the rage the last few years. A gold-mine to collectors!' The costumes and the manner of the picture belonged undisguisedly to about 1890, but Sir Harry refrained by an heroic effort from challenging the dealer's accuracy, aware that he would give the painter any label that might improve the chances of a sale. His eyes swept over the whole visible stock and came to rest with relief on this expressive little work, and he asked the price in a business-like fashion.

'Thirty-five guineas—no more and no less,' said Morris vehemently but without much conviction. 'That's nearly what it cost me. It's an heirloom, sir, a picture like this. In a few years you can sell it for double the money.'

'I'll give you twenty-five,' said Sir Harry flatly.

'I should be letting it go at a loss, I'm telling you straight, sir, a dead loss. To be absolutely frank'—he cast about among the various lines of talk he used when selling goods not hallmarked with a famous signature, and found a favourite one—'I intended to hang on to this until I found out whether it was painted by an artist with the same name who's got a big reputation in America. Yes, a lot of American collectors are crazy about him. They'd buy this for four times the money I'm asking.'

Sir Harry, who knew that the price he had offered was more than the commercial value of the canvas, though perhaps much less than it would be worth when the pendulum of fashion had made its reactionary swing, turned away with so uncompromising a shake of the head that Morris capitulated. 'Thirty guineas then? It's a real little gem, sir. Very well, twenty-five! It's giving it away. I couldn't afford to do it if I wasn't sure you'll be a customer for bigger things. It's a pure sacrifice. If I was to run my business like this every day I should be a bankrupt....'

Maximer allowed this litany to proceed unchecked while he questioned himself as to what he could do with his purchase, for, though he was sensible of its modest merits, he had no intention of installing it among the grandeurs of his flat in Grosvenor Place.

He was not long in conceiving the happy idea of sending it as a gift to Mrs. Rose. He had been intending for some time to signify his recognition of her extra services by making her some carefully chosen present, and as her four or five years among the great Italian masters had never weaned her from her taste for what was agreeably trivial and, in her own word, amusing, this 'nineties costume piece would be the very thing. He asked for a card and wrote: 'I hope this will be to your liking and show you that I am not ungrateful for your ministrations.'

Instead of signing his name, he appended only the letter M, feeling sure that his card would be read before the picture was dispatched, and preferring at this stage to remain incognito. Mrs. Rose's home address was in his notebook and as he always carried a substantial sum of money, he was able to complete the transaction in full anonymity.

He had hardly done so when two ladies in cardigans and tweed skirts came into the shop to inquire about a *fête champêtre* after the Watteau style, and as they seemed likely to inspect a large number of pictures before deciding not to buy anything, Sir Harry, who had an appointment with his masseur, postponed his further investigation of this field, satisfied that he had paved the way very adequately for a second visit.

On his departure, the assistant was called up from the basement, and the ladies too having gone, after explaining that they would have to consult their husbands before purchasing the things they had particularly admired, Morris took the opportunity of treating his employee to an improving discourse:

'They'll ask their husbands! You know by now what that means. When a woman wants to get out of a shop, she says she'll ask her husband. A man says he has to see something else before he can make up his mind. . . . The ones who want to "think it over" sometimes comes back, but when they hand you that stuff about husbands and seeing something else first, you can kiss them goodbye. There's some so-called customers you can't sell nothing to, not if you took a course of salesmanship in heaven. Then there's the other kind that come in for something to cover a big wall and go out with a miniature. They're suckers, but naturally you have to have a soft spot for them. They make work a pleasure. Then there's the mugs—and you needn't think a mug is the same thing as a sucker. Mugs can be hard to handle, believe me. They think they know something, they try to be smart. But when you been in business as long as I have, you learn how to manage them.'

He nodded contentedly at 'A Belated Honeymoon.'

'See that! I bought it for the sake of the frame at the Elderfield Mart. It's such trash, I don't even know how I let it get into stock. Yet I just sold it for twenty-five guineas. Why? Because I know how to talk to a mug.'

'Who bought it, sir?' asked the assistant, opening his eyes very wide.

'Who bought it? Don't be an ass all your life, Rogers! How many people have we had in the shop the last hour?'

'Only those two ladies and Sir Harry Maximer, sir.'

'Sir Harry Maximer! What are you talking about? Are you feeble-minded?'

'That was him, sir.' Rogers's air of innocent detachment was hardly convincing. 'He was pointed out to me at the Royal Baths at lunch-time.'

'I didn't know they served lunches at the Royal Baths,' Morris retorted with heavy facetiousness. 'Or are you taking a cure for your big appetite?'

'I was outside, just passing the time of day with the young lady from the bookshop, sir, and he came down the steps, and she told me who he was.' His unholy joy as he perceived the pallid yellow of his employer's skin flush to a dull crimson made it necessary for him to turn aside. 'She said I ought to know, since I worked for an art dealer, that he was the greatest expert in England.'

'The young lady in the bookshop thinks she's entitled to judge, I suppose.' Morris was reduced to sneering stupidly. Seldom in his life had he felt so foolish or so angry. Maximer! The man who was familiar with every trick of the trade, the man whose newspaper articles were aimed at putting dealers like himself out of business! He had tried to sell Maximer an old Dutch Master with the paint scarcely dry! He had actually succeeded—but now he knew there was something fishy about it—in selling him a bit of late Victorian lumber!

Or was it lumber? He picked up the canvas and studied it with feverish eagerness. Was it possible that he had missed behind the unknown signature the touch of Sargent or Boldini, of Solomon or Lavery, artists whose names were still worth money? No, the bravura of these successful painters was entirely lacking, and in any case, Maximer had not come into the shop for this.

What was the fellow up to? What was he after? The last words he had said in crossing the threshold were that he would return in a day or two and would hope to hear of any really old paintings—'on panel for example'—that might be available in the town. He was after *something*, there was no question of that. For a moment, a single second only, Morris entertained the notion that it might be that stuff he had refused to go and see at Dr. Sandilands'. Then he recollected that Maximer himself had told Miss Sandilands there was nothing there but copies—copies that needed a lot of repairs. . . . Not quite the sort of game Maximer was likely to be hunting! What would it be? What *could* it be, here in Charlton Wells? Whatever it was, thought Morris grimly, directing a glare of fury at the genial cardinal, the next time he called he would find things ready for him.

THIRTEEN

MAXIMER drew a most frustrating blank next day when, bent over his walking-stick, he paid his first visit to the Public Library. Quiller had been able to find out quite easily how Mrs. du Plessis was employed and also where she lived, and had supplied him with some slight description of her appearance, and Maximer had hoped to contrive a way of taking her measure. But neither of the two assistants on duty when he arrived had red hair or a delicately fair complexion, and in the course of his ingenious conversation with the dark-haired young lady who showed him the various reference books he pretended to consult, he learned that they were short-handed: the one who could have answered 'simply any of his questions' was on holiday.

He was quite unaware when he left the building, almost forgetting in his irritation to hobble, that he had been speaking to a daughter of Dr. Sandilands. On neither of Quiller's visits to the Sandilands household had Linda been present, and if any reference had been made to her while he was there, he had applied it to the other sister, Valerie, who was home for the holidays and whom he had caught some glimpses of.

The sitz bath treatment, which Sir Harry took in the latter part of the morning, was all that was needed to complete his ill humour. It consisted of sitting first in a very hot hip-bath and then, at the signal of an electric bell, moving into an icy-cold one—a process three times repeated under the pitiless eye of an attendant to whom one's shudderings and gaspings were a matter of candid indifference. What was particularly annoying was that after this session he believed he felt twinges of real lumbago.

His decrepit gait came almost naturally on his walk back to the hotel, and this was fortunate because, as he mounted the steps at the entrance, Miss Sandilands skilfully parked her father's car by the kerb and, springing out, caught up with him outside the revolving door.

'Oh, Sir Harry,' she said, colouring a little for he still carried with him the aura of impressiveness that had so daunted her at their first meeting, 'this will save us a letter!' Then her fine pink deepened because she perceived that such a beginning was not very courteous. 'I mean, my father had your letter this morning, and we were going to answer it . . . I act as his secretary, you know—' She stopped again, and by now her skin was suffused with an unmistakable blush. 'You do remember who I am, don't you?'

His surprise and pleasure at this easy encounter had given his face a rather blank look which she mistook for non-recognition, but he hastened to make amends by saying with a lordly affability: 'My dear young lady, I remember you perfectly. Won't you come in?'

'I was more or less on my way home to lunch,' she answered hesitantly.

'Come in and have a glass of sherry then! It will give you an appetite. I unhappily am not allowed such luxuries, but it does me good to see others enjoying them. I'm not embittered yet, you notice.' As he spoke, he moved into one of the glass compartments of the door. 'Do I go first? Yes, I think that's the etiquette.'

She felt obliged to follow. His lameness would have made it unkind to drag him round again once the door had begun to revolve, but in any case, since he was in such an unbending mood, she was not averse from taking the proffered glass of sherry. Her work as secretary-housekeeper to a busy doctor kept her so much at home that a very small diversion would assume value as a break in her conscientious routine; and as she seldom visited the great hotels of the spa, her social circle consisting entirely of local residents, to drink sherry at the Royal with so interesting a personality as Sir Harry Maximer was almost an adventure.

And so agreeable did he turn out to be when he was not in his official role of critic and arbiter that, in no time at all, she was telling him the whole ridiculous story of those stupid, humiliating pictures.

Sir Harry gave his attention as to an amusing and scarcely credible anecdote. 'You must indeed have eccentric criminals in Charlton Wells,' he said, lifting his eyebrows and shaking his head in humorous commiseration. 'I confess the motive of such a burglary escapes me. What do the police think?'

'We haven't been to them,' Her vexation forced a sigh from her. 'You see, we sort of know who's taken them, and my father would do anything rather than prosecute her. He's sure she only did it because she wants to save them for us. Still, I do think it's a most awful cheek, don't you?' And with that, encouraged by dexterous half-questions and more sherry, she launched into a description of the various circumstances that made Mrs. du Plessis the suspect.

'But could it have been done without an accomplice?' It was the first time Maximer had completely realized how improbable it was that the pictures had been abstracted by one unaided woman. 'She must have persuaded someone else to share her rosy delusions,' he suggested, lightly enough to cover a profound apprehension.

'That's what *I* think. I don't see how she could have done it without Linda.'

'Linda?'

'My sister, the middle one. She works at the Library with Stephanie du Plessis, and I believe they're more friendly than she pretends. Linda's always been terribly gullible—quite different from *me* in that respect. She swallowed all that Medici twaddle hook, line, and sinker.'

Sir Harry's intense alertness was nowhere hinted in his attitude as he remarked idly: 'Of course she would have had access to the key of the trunk?'

'Yes. I kept it in my bedroom. My father can't be induced to admit she had anything to do with it because she's denied it over and over again, and he won't have it that she's capable of telling such bare-faced lies. But I know her a bit better than he does. Anyhow,' she was constrained by family loyalty to add, 'if she's got it into her head that she's doing a noble deed and one day we're all going to be grateful to her, she probably looks on them as white lies.'

'But where,' he asked with the laugh of one who good-naturedly observes the antics of children, 'where would they hide the things? There was quite a stack of them as I remember.'

'That's what we want to know! Then we should soon have the whole silly business cleared up.'

'The obvious place would be where Mrs. du Plessis lives.'

'They can't be there. We had a letter from her simply swearing she hasn't got them, and I somehow feel she wouldn't put that in writing if it weren't true.'

'You don't suppose she'd have sent or taken them away some-where?'

'I can't see her sending them very far!' Beatrix giggled. 'She used to be flapping round them all the time like a hen with sixteen chicks. I don't know who she'd consider good enough to look after them.'

'She might have taken them with her—' He stopped dead just in time to stifle the words 'on her holiday.'

'Taken them where?' she inquired in mild wonder.

He shrugged his shoulders. 'Anywhere. She seems equal to the most extraordinary flights.'

'But she hasn't gone away at all. That's the funny part of it . . . although it's her holiday and she was practically booked for Florence.'

Sir Harry, effortlessly concealing his delicious sensation of relief, said with the most perfect air of detachment: 'Wouldn't that indicate then that the pictures aren't very far off?'

'Yes, my father thinks so too, but the question is where? And what can we do about it?'

'My advice to you is to go to the police, my dear young lady. It may sound heartless, but what other course is open to you?' Nothing could be more convincing than his tone now that, having heard of Linda, he was sure this counsel must be rejected.

'If it depended on me, I believe I jolly well should. I'd like to give that maddening Stephanie du Plessis a good fright, anyhow—poking her nose into other people's business. She's just trading on Daddy's kindness, that's what it amounts to, and she's got my sister under her influence.'

'Well, well, well!' he murmured smilingly, while he tried to weigh the potential gain or loss of taking this discussion any further on the present occasion. 'Who would have imagined anyone could have worked up all this enthusiasm for a batch of pictures which seemed to me, if I dare be frank, hardly worth their house room.'

'You can be as frank as you like with me.' Beatrix was now entirely at ease. 'Nothing that belonged to Mrs. Hovenden was worth house room, that's my opinion. Daddy should have known that better than anyone, because he tried to sell a lot more of her pictures one time when she was in difficulties, and the people who run the auction rooms told him it was hopeless—absolutely hopeless.'

'More of her pictures!' If a large man with a pink face could conceivably look like a pointer in the act of picking up a keen scent, Sir Harry for one fleeting moment succeeded. Then, relaxing, he chaffed her amiably: 'Could more come from one household? Really, Miss Sandilands, I believe your innocent-looking Charlton Wells must have been supplying the market with half the things I've been warning people about for years.'

'Oh, no, the other lot weren't sold. She died before my father could dispose of them. . . . Good gracious!' With her eyes on her watch, she jumped unceremoniously to her feet. 'I shall be frightfully late for lunch. They'll wonder what's happened to me!'

It needed all Maximer's exceptional powers of self-restraint to allow a conversation which had taken such an enthralling turn to end in mid-air, but discretion demanded that he should follow his guest out of the Palm Court without exhibiting any curiosity that might leave an impression on her. As she reached the door, however, he deemed it not imprudent to say cordially:

'A most welcome meeting, Miss Sandilands, a break in my monotonous day of sitz baths and sulphur water. I must say I shall feel quite thwarted if I don't hear how your marvellous saga develops.'

'Oh, you must!' cried Beatrix, finding it delightful that she had succeeded in interesting this potentate who lived in a world so remote from her own and who, a week ago, had proved so immensely intimidating. Then with a daring that left her a little tremulous, she heard herself proposing: 'What about coming to dinner with us one evening? I'm sure my father would be very glad to see you.'

'I should be only too happy!' But the words were no sooner uttered than he perceived there might be certain hazards involved in coming into contact with the Sandilands family at close quarters. This young woman he could twist around his finger because she had that confidence in her own acuteness which is always a distinguishing feature of those who are born to be dupes; but what of the other, the unpredictable Linda? Dr. Sandilands too, incompetent though he was to form an aesthetic judgment, could hardly have built up his practice without some shrewdness in the sphere of human conduct. Would it not be safer to avoid actually inviting his scrutiny, since Beatrix alone would be a sufficient channel of information? The question was asked and answered in less time than it took him to lift his hand to his back in what appeared to be a spasm of sudden discomfort.

'I should be only too happy,' he repeated, 'but alas! my aches and pains remind me that my doctor has made a strict rule against my dining out.'

'What a shame!' Her disappointment was palpable. 'It'll be very dull for you taking the cure all alone.'

'But there is nothing at all against my dining *in*,' he said, giving her the full benefit of his wide, direct gaze. 'Why don't you come and dine with me here one evening, Miss Sandilands? I have rather a weakness— now I'm going to descend in your estimation!—for talking to a pretty woman against a background of Palm Court music. That's the sort of little dinner party I should really prefer with you.'

Beatrix, who was not called a pretty woman nearly as often as she deserved, blushed again, but with pleasure rather than embarrassment, and the appointment for her to dine with him on Saturday evening was soon made. She hurried off in a very good mood indeed: in paying her such a charming compliment, he had dropped about fifteen of his fifty-five years.

Sir Harry felt an even greater elation, but it was tempered by fears and stresses, and his face was full of a predatory intentness which was rather the reverse of cheerful as he took out his notebook and wrote, in case by any unlikely chance the name should escape his memory, 'Mrs. Hovenden'.

The week that followed was a severe trial of his patience, and there were moments when he was tempted to engage a private agent to perform the dreary task of watching to which he was obliged to devote himself. But detective work cannot be done efficiently by one who is not aware of precisely what he is trying to find out nor why the information is required, and Sir Harry could not risk making his purpose known to any third party. It was enough and more than enough that it was known to Quiller.

The person on whom his observations were concentrated was the second Miss Sandilands. He would have preferred to watch Mrs. du Plessis, since everything he had been told of her confirmed his original belief that she was responsible for the daring theft—indeed he quite longed to see the woman whose intelligence and courage were imposing such exertions on him—but her lodging was in a residential avenue where it would not have been easy for a stranger to linger unnoticed, whereas a vigil outside the Library was a simple matter.

It was a building that stood back from the road with a stiff little public garden at the side of it and a much frequented bus stop in front. Built round two shady trees which adorned the wide pavement were benches which, before the days of regimentation, had been intended for the comfort of bus passengers. These were now compelled to stand in a row at a spot marked 'Queue here for buses', and the seats were free for anyone who cared to use them.

Here at least once and sometimes twice each day, after he had endured whatever treatments might have been prescribed, Sir Harry repaired with a copy of *The Times*, behind whose capacious pages he screened himself while he kept his eye on the Library comings and goings. The hours given up to these sessions were lunch-time and closing-time, and as the assistants sometimes came out in twos and threes and, in taking leave, would address each other by name, Linda's identity was not long in doubt. Nor did it require any very advanced technique to deduce her close friendship with the young man who apparently worked at the photographer's establishment just opposite. Twice he was waiting for her outside the Library when she emerged at the lunch hour and they strolled off together softly talking; twice she took a paper bag, which might be assumed to contain sandwiches, over the road to the Portrait Studio and remained there for nearly an hour; three times they met after the Library had closed at six o'clock and drove away in a battered-looking car.

From Beatrix, on a Sunday visit to Charlton Abbey following their pleasant little dinner, Sir Harry had learned that Linda was an irresponsible and light-minded girl whose numerous 'boy friends' were, to her sister, a slightly caustic joke: yet her present conduct revealed no sign of this philandering tendency but rather suggested a serious attachment. . . . A serious attachment—or else the intimacy of two people in some sort of collusion!

Sir Harry, after much weighing of the pros and cons, resolved to pursue his investigation from a new angle. The move he contemplated was, he realized, a shade precarious, but having two excellent reasons for believing no malpractice on his part was suspected, he felt he could afford the risk. First, none of his malpractices ever *had* been suspected; the righteous wrath with which he had denounced all manner of chicaneries had been respectfully accepted from an early stage of his career as an evidence of his own impeccable character. Second, he had by now seen enough of Beatrix Sandilands to make it clear beyond a scruple that the idea of his being concerned in the purchase of what she always called 'those wretched pictures' had not only never crossed her own mind but that no one had so much as attempted to suggest it to her. Even the one person whose keen eyes he feared had not, it seemed, cast any aspersion on his good faith. He came, therefore, to the conclusion that he could go a little further than a man whose reputation was assailable. He decided, in fact, to have his photograph taken.

FOURTEEN

So SKILFULLY had Sir Harry conducted his espionage behind the cover of *The Times* that it had been going on for four or five days before Kenneth Dyer noticed how Linda was being watched.

He did not mention it to her because he preferred not to make her more jumpy than she was already. It must certainly be very uncomfortable for her, being nagged every day about those wretched pictures (for he too gave them this designation), and obliged to he to her father, and not even able to see, except occasionally and by stealth, the friend for whose sake she had entered this wild conspiracy. No wonder the poor girl spoke of feeling utterly guilty and miserable!

For his own part, he had been much happier about the whole business since he had learned that Maximer was in the town. Until then he had been haunted by recurrent qualms. Although he had been the first of the four to suspect trickery, he had not much enjoyed having to counter it by theft, and there had been cold and clammy moments since when he had asked himself whether they hadn't all been leading one another up the garden path into some ugly morass from which they would never be decently extricated. But Maximer's arrival coupled with Stephanie's encouraging note about Transaction B had set the last of these doubts at rest. If he was still ill at ease it was only because he feared Maximer might find some means of getting the pictures into his possession before Arnold Bayley had completed the inquiries that would result in his exposure.

A long course of crime fiction, however, had not prepared him as adequately as might be expected for seeing the girl he was in love with being spied upon by a man with a limp: and the arrival of the villain in person, his walking-stick in one hand, *The Times* in the other, would have reduced him to the most complete confusion if a visiting-card sent in beforehand had not enabled him to steady and prepare himself.

He came into the outer office holding the card in his fingers and looking at Sir Harry with a keen observant eye that betrayed nothing of his inward alarm.

'Do you take passport photographs?' Sir Harry inquired purposefully.

'I can,' When Kenneth was nervous he feared to trust himself to speech and became strikingly laconic, thus acquiring an air of cool and challenging reserve quite worthy of one of the heroes in the books he so constantly devoured.

'I need some rather urgently. Would it be possible for you to do them at once?'

'There's a place in Station Road that specializes in them.' Kenneth's anxiety to know what his visitor was up to gave way reluctantly to his feeling that he was up to no good and ought to be kept at arm's length.

'Did I say passport photographs? How stupid of me! I meant press photographs. I need one or two for my American publishers.'

'There'd be the same fee as for an ordinary portrait sitting,' said Kenneth discouragingly; but the instinct which warned him to get rid of this scheming man contended with a strong desire to pocket his badly needed fee and out-scheme him, and he added, weakening: 'You get one cabinet picture of each position and you can order prints in any style you like.'

'What is the fee?' asked Maximer for the sake of verisimilitude.

Kenneth handed him a small brochure and indicated the scale of charges, still examining him with that keen look which was in reality due to his professional and quite unconscious habit of trying to see each new face from a variety of angles, but which to a stranger appeared somewhat impertinent.

'Could you do them right away? I promised to supply them before my publication date but unfortunately I had no time before leaving London.' Like all the best liars, Sir Harry used the truth whenever possible, and so was able to give particulars with conviction.

Kenneth wavered. All that was sensible and adult in him warned him that he would be playing into Maximer's hands by allowing him to continue his spying on these premises; but all that was boyish and adventurous rebelled against so stodgily prudent a measure as the pretence that he could not fit in the appointment, and after a very little hesitation—just enough, in fact, to stimulate the other's suspicions—he admitted the enemy within his gates.

For some minutes after Maximer had seated himself on the Trafalgar chair which was brought forward for him, a perfect silence prevailed. Kenneth, whose mind could never cover more than one track at a time and whose means did not permit him to employ an assistant, wheeled his lamps into suitable positions and, in distributing light and shadow, became so genuinely engrossed by the technical problem of giving some sort of form to his subject's amorphous features that he almost forgot whose features they were. Sir Harry, so far as he was permitted to turn his head, was looking about him.

'Photography has become a most complicated business,' he remarked at last as Kenneth peered at him through the focusing screen of his camera. 'Besides all these processes we see, there are others no doubt equally elaborate which take place behind the scenes.'

'Just keep your head up, would you!' said Kenneth. 'You've dropped it a little. No, not as high as that! Now you're leaning forward too far. . . . Ah, that's it!'

'So sorry! This is a rare experience for me. The last was eight or ten years ago. . . . I was saying how complex it has all become. A photographer trained in the nineteenth century would be positively baffled by all your expensive apparatus, perhaps hardly able to take a picture at all. The celebrated Mrs. Cameron, if I remember rightly, had no studio but a sort of garden shed.'

'Could you look at some object just about the level of my hand?' Kenneth, holding his arm up, spoke in the rather peremptory tone he was inclined to use with sitters who imagined they could indulge in animated conversations with him while he worked.

Sir Harry did as he was bid but, not to lose the thread he was so assiduously spinning, soon resumed: 'The modern photographer doesn't even, I suppose, develop and print his own pictures? He sends them out, I dare say, to some other specialist?'

'Oh no he doesn't!' Kenneth rejoined tartly. 'At least I don't. Would you mind not talking for a moment? Head up, please! You're dropping it again. Now could you go on looking at the same object but just turning the face a little more this way. . . . The shoulder forward a bit, the elbow a shade back! Let the hand fall quite naturally! Now you've got it. Still! Still!'

The camera clicked. 'Thank you!' said Maximer, gladly releasing himself from his pose. 'How cramped even a normal attitude becomes when one is obliged to hold it!'

Kenneth reddened. 'I'm sorry, I shall have to do that again. I didn't take the shutter out.'

Such a mishap was unusual, for he was really an excellent crafts-man, but the effect of trying to guess whither his client's observations were leading while performing the none too easy task of bringing out his best traits for the camera was to make him slow and inept; and it was some minutes before even the first picture was taken.

Sir Harry, sweltering in the blaze of the powerful lamps, forced into a most oppressive inactivity, brusquely commanded not to talk, felt that he had chosen the hard way of achieving his purpose. He was, however, satisfied that he was not following a false trail.

This taciturn young man with the insolent eyes was, in the view he had formed, a tough customer, one who was fully capable of assisting at, or conceivably even initiating, the stealing of the pictures. His behaviour had from the first moment been highly suggestive of his having something to hide. Sir Harry did not consider whether it might be something to hide specifically from *him*: unaware that even in this very hour Transaction A was taking its place beside Transactions B and C as a completed investigation, he had dismissed the least possibility of his being suspected. If the looted contents of the Saratoga trunk should happen to be actually in this building, then it was a case of having something to hide from everybody. Whether his motive were infatuation for the second Sandilands daughter or, as Sir Harry ungallantly surmised, sheer desire for gain, he would need to be as vigilant as an ordinary burglar.

The likelihood that there were now at least three people besides himself and Quiller who were alive to the value of the hoard was, of course, a serious annoyance, but one that in no way diminished his own ardour. There were among the glorious sixteen five or six which he did not propose, once he laid hands on them, ever to let out of his possession, and as for the rest, he was too confident of his own patience and cleverness to doubt that, in the course of well spaced-out years, he would dispose of them safely and at a profit sufficient to make all his present efforts worth while.

The problems of the future would receive his ingenious attention in due course; for the present he was concerned only to arrive at some excuse for a closer scrutiny of the resources of the studio.

It took Kenneth, occupied as he was, a good while to perceive the drift of seemingly random questions and comments on the methods of modern photographers, and after he had perceived it, to make up his mind how to react. Maximer, he gathered, wanted to know what rooms were on these premises, what chances there were of concealing stolen goods here. Very well, why not give him a little run for his money?

Draping his head under a dark cloth, Kenneth took his time to decide whether any harm could come of such a pleasantry. He could foresee none. The pictures were fourteen miles away; they had only been in his studio for a single night. Surely he could with impunity dangle a few delicious hopes and then enjoy the sensation of seeing the cheat discover that he had been cheated? Still wearing his sable canopy, he moved his camera forward with such an air of swooping down upon his victim that Sir Harry gave a faintly uneasy laugh.

'What now?'

'I'd like to do this one as a close-up.'

'I'm afraid I'm rather a self-conscious sitter. Thank goodness you aren't supported by any glamorous female assistant who would reduce me to idiocy!'

'No, I always work alone.'

'What about the blonde lady outside who took my card?'

'She's the receptionist." He longed to add some statement that would serve his end but all he found himself saying was: 'Would you just straighten the shoulders and raise the chin a little.'

Sir Harry, however, could progress with the minimum of assistance. 'Has she nothing to do but to look alluring, or do you keep her toiling in some dark room full of mysterious chemicals?'

'No, no, she's a receptionist pure and simple.' Kenneth walked slowly up to his client and placed his head at a more favourable angle. 'I share her with the other firm—the car hire people. I do my own developing and all that.'

After this considerable effort, he subsided again into silence, and Maximer, who feared to carry his inquisitiveness to what might seem an extravagant degree, remained still and thoughtful until the close-up was taken. He was very tired of the sitting but it was necessary that he should prolong it until his reconnoitring was complete. He would certainly not be able to make such an opportunity again.

'If you're going to do another,' he said, 'perhaps you'd let me just stretch my legs first. My lumbago seems to grow worse if I sit too long without moving. Would you mind passing me my stick?'

He rose with difficulty not wholly feigned—for the contorted position in which he had carried himself during the past ten days had set up a real stiffness—-and began to stump about the big room as if to relax his cramped muscles; and as he did so, he said with an appearance of intelligent yet casual interest: 'Did you equip all this studio yourself? It counts as a good one, I should imagine.'

'It's fair—plenty of room at any rate for the things that have to be kept out of sight.' Kenneth tried to infuse a sinister significance into the words which, if he had succeeded, would instantly have put the other on his guard, but as he was the worst and most ineffectual of actors, he gave a better performance than he knew, conveying the impression of a man making a strained effort to be natural.

'How much room do you need besides this?'

'A work-room, a store-room, and a dark-room. The store-room's in the basement' he flung out tantalizingly, 'and this is the dark-room,' He opened the door which, as he had noticed, had several times received an attentive glance.

'The pictures are not in there,' thought Sir Harry, but he concluded that it might be politic to accept the tacit invitation to look about, and put his head into the darkness saying: 'May I?'

Kenneth toyed with an insane impulse to push him inside and lock the door on him, but contented himself with the mere impoliteness of leaving the wise fool standing there peering at nothing that was visible while he turned on his heel and busied himself with a new adjustment of his lamps.

'What impenetrable blackness!' said Maximer. 'Quite a bogy hole! Your work-room no doubt is next to the dark-room?' He found the switches as he spoke and, before Kenneth could reply, had produced an illumination very dim compared with the floodlight of the studio, but sufficient to show the shelves of jars and bottles, a sink and drain-ing-board littered with photographic implements, and the banisters of a staircase leading down to the basement. 'This light won't spoil anything, will it?' He stepped into the little room. 'Forgive my curiosity! There's always something so fascinating about other people's "shop".'

Kenneth smiled, envisaging Maximer's frustration at the sight of the basement stairs which he must be longing in vain to descend, and to give a turn to the screw, he called with almost audible bravado: 'I don't mind who looks round the dark-room. The basement's another matter. The dark-room,' he persisted, trying to tease out a response, 'is moderately tidy. The basement's not fit to be seen. It's full of all sorts of things.'

Sir Harry heard the words but they did not have the effect intended. He heard them as a warrior might hear the arrow glancing off his armour in the moment of felling his enemy with a brilliant stroke. His smile was as spontaneous as Kenneth's and much more genial.

Hanging over the banisters he had seen an interesting object, a portion of some soiled white linen garment. Screened from view, he had taken it swiftly and, holding it near the light, had recognized it beyond the hazard of a doubt—the front half of a very out-of-date chemise. That chemise, when he had last seen and handled it a fortnight ago, had been enveloping a painting worthy of Filippo Lippi. His visual memory, always acute, had been heightened by the intensity of that day's experi-ence and, although the linen which had then been white now showed many traces of having been used as a duster, its scalloped edging and the figure 10 embroidered in red thread just beneath the opening of the neck enabled him to identify it with assurance.

No professional detective on the scene of a major crime ever fell upon a clue with greater speed and gusto or with more circumspec-tion. Remarking amiably that the place was 'quite an alchemist's den', he replaced the remnant of the chemise with one deft movement on the banister rail and turned to re-enter the studio with a perfectly unrevealing aspect.

The rapidity of that gesture was his undoing. His walking-stick slipped from his grasp, he made a lunge to regain it, and found himself transfixed as if he had been shot in the back. From some supercharged centre situated just below what had once been his waistline, electric lightnings stabbed out through every muscle, wringing from him a groan he could not have suppressed if life had depended on it. Whether through the uncomfortable posture he had so long sustained or, as he always afterwards believed, through the sitz baths and the ruthless pommellings of his masseur, or whether on account of his making up for wine and other amenities of the table by drinking enormous quantities of strong coffee, he was stricken in the moment of his triumph with a lumbago that was no counterfeit, a doom so infernal that, if the pictures had been where he thought they were, and he himself free to walk out with the choicest of them under his arm, he would not have been capable of descending the stairs to fetch it.

A second groan, more poignant though perhaps less dramatic than the first, brought Kenneth to the dark-room door, whence he beheld what he took to be a piece of exaggerated play-acting. The sufferer's words, as inch by heroic inch he straightened his back, at once confirmed the idea that some ruse was being attempted.

'Mr. Dyer, my lumbago is very bad. I'm afraid I can't continue the sitting. Would you be so kind as to get a taxi for me? I shall never be able to walk to the hotel.'

Kenneth retired with some faint muttering of commiseration on his lips, but his unspoken words were: 'I can see exactly what you're after! You know taxis aren't to be got for love nor money here, and you think while I'm running round the town for one, you'll nip downstairs and start rummaging about. What you've forgotten, my boy, is that there's a car hire agency next door.'

To catch Maximer out in his unseemly little game would be a superb revenge for his having spied on Linda. He ordered the car in a trice, hung back long enough to give his victim time to get well into the trap, and returned flushed with anticipation of an amusing encounter in the basement.

The sight of Maximer making his way slowly and painfully towards the door through a grove of studio lamps came as a deflating kind of surprise. Still more was he puzzled when he was told that, if the proofs were not ready within a day or two, it might be as well to send them direct to Sir Harry's London address since the cure was doing so little good that perhaps he would not stay to complete it.

Kenneth had worked himself up for a particular scene—to which, if he had really been obliged to play it, he would have been hopelessly unequal—and he felt defrauded; the more so as he could not conceive why the enemy was beating or pretending to beat a retreat. But he was compelled to believe, as he saw the wincing and faltering figure begin to descend the steps on the arrival of the car a few minutes later, that his affliction was genuine; and obeying the promptings—rather reluctant in this instance—of humanity, he moved forward and offered an arm. At the same moment, Beatrix, crossing the road from the Library where she had called with some message or admonition for Linda, caught sight of her new friend and advanced exclaiming her distress at his all too obvious plight.

'Why, Sir Harry, you *are* bad today! Good gracious, what are they doing to you? You're worse than you were last week!'

She gave a cursory little nod to the young man recognized vaguely as one of the numerous band who distracted her sister's mind from the duties of home. It was returned in kind.

'I am quite woebegone, Miss Sandilands, quite woebegone. Oh dear!' he moaned as Kenneth opened the door of the car for him, 'why have they this mania nowadays for building bodies so low? If I get into this seat, how shall I ever get out again?'

'Let me help you!' With bright solicitude Beatrix put her firm hand under his elbow. 'I'd better come along with you. You need someone when you're in pain like this.'

Sir Harry was indeed in pain but he had recovered sufficiently from the first grim onslaught to know that he was also in luck; and thinking that there might be things he would like to say to Miss Sandilands, he accepted very gratefully her offer to accompany him to his hotel. Before letting her assist him in mounting to his room, however, he paused at the hall porter's desk to send, as he explained, a greetings telegram to one of his friends whose birthday he had only just remembered.

'Terminus 9987 London.' That was all the address. And the message was simply, 'Many happy returns'.

FIFTEEN

STEPHANIE knew the worst, or nearly the worst, as soon as she saw Linda's face on coming home next evening. It had rained all day and she had tried to kill the lingering time by going to the cinema. The news that the late Sir Hubert Prosser's 'Steen' had joined the Elderfield 'Brueghel' and Arcadian Green's 'Teniers' in the dossier of transactions in which the hand of Maximer could definitely be traced had not yet reached her. There had been no developments for days, nothing but the weariness of wasting her precious holiday in Charlton Wells. Even from the post, which brought her the consolation of frequent letters from Arnold, she had almost as much to dread as to look forward to, since every three or four days it would contain a note from Dr. Sandilands begging her if it were in her power (he always courteously gave her the benefit of the doubt) to end the unhappy dilemma in which he found himself.

Maximer's arrival at the spa, which had seemed to presage at least excitement and the savour of being engaged in an adventure, had not resulted in anything but an increase of tension. Arnold was resolute that no accusation should be made against him until there was abundant material to substantiate it. Indeed, his hope was to avoid open accusation altogether, for he intended to confront him privately with such a wealth of evidence of his misdeeds that he would know himself beaten if it should come to an open fight.

He had arrived at this policy partly because he had no desire to precipitate a sensational scandal in the art world, but chiefly on account of the baffling difficulty of proving collusion between Maximer and Quiller. Without such proof Quiller remained the legal owner of the treasure, and the only way round the situation was to make one of the pair so afraid of exposure on some other grounds that he would submit to calling the deal off—a form of blackmail he justified by the high exigencies of the case. Nothing very helpful had so far been learned about Quiller, and it was on Maximer's vulnerability alone that Arnold placed his reliance.

They knew from Linda that Beatrix was seeing him, and double precautions were therefore taken lest any word should fall which might enable him to be forewarned and forearmed. Since Linda was under the strain of living with those who considered themselves injured parties, it was recognized that her temptation to disclose in self-defence what was known against Maximer would be very great, and Stephanie had refrained during the last week or so from giving her any detailed reports of how investigations were progressing. This guardedness with one of her allies heightened her discomfort, while Linda for her part was plainly as dejected as one of her normally placid and harmonious temperament could be. To lie to so kind a father troubled her deeply, and to report Beatrix's meetings with Maximer gave her a feeling of treachery which she found it hard to reconcile with a conscience which hitherto had borne only the lightest burdens. The fun of helping Stephanie to 'get off' with Arnold Bayley had quite petered out in the subsequent furtiveness, and altogether an eye much less apprehensive than Stephanie's could have seen that it was only a question of time and the degree of pressure before she gave way.

To find her waiting in the drizzle at half-past ten—an hour which in Charlton Wells was equivalent to midnight in a livelier resort—was to know that the race against time had been lost. Linda's plump and youthful face could not easily look haggard, but even under the new fluorescent street-lighting which drained the colour from everything, the redness of her eyelids was perceptible. Her hair, which always framed her forehead in tendrils carefully combed to give the look of softness that she liked, was now merely dishevelled; her coat glistened all over with beads of fine rain.

'Oh Stephanie,' she cried, relief at the sight of her friend momentarily eclipsing her woe, 'thank goodness! I've been waiting so long. I thought you'd never come.'

'You should have gone inside.'

'I couldn't. Your landlady always follows me into your room and talks to me if you're not in when I call. Tonight I couldn't have borne it.'

'What's happened?' Stephanie's hand rested paralysed on the wet ironwork of the gate. She knew the reply perfectly before it was uttered.

'I've done something dreadful. You'll never forgive me. I've told them everything.'

Though these were the very words she expected, their sound still had power to give her an icy shock, and it was with an almost audible gasp she that repeated: 'Everything! You mean—about Arnold too?'

'Yes, I couldn't help it. Honestly!'

'Then he's ruined!'

'Not if he gives back the pictures tomorrow. Honestly, Steph, I just had to. It wouldn't have been fair to let Ken bear the whole brunt alone. He never wanted to be in it.'

The silence that descended was like a pall. She broke out of it. 'Let's go and sit in the shelter at the terminus. There'll be no one there, now. If we go indoors we'll have to talk in whispers.'

'It hasn't really stopped raining yet,' said Linda feebly.

'What does it matter?'

She turned away and retraced her footsteps down the avenue with Linda meekly following, saying imploringly:

'You can't imagine what's been going on. You'd have had to do the same in my place. . . . That beastly Maximer told Beatrix that Ken had the pictures. You remember those chemises and things of Mrs. Hovenden's we cut up for dust sheets? Well, one of them got left in Ken's studio and he wanted a rag or a duster or something, and he used it. And Sir Harry found it there.'

*'Maximer found it there!' Stephanie's incomprehension brought her to an abrupt stop in the middle of the road.

'He went to have his photograph taken. He was spying of course—'

'And do you mean to say Kenneth let him spy?' she demanded fiercely. 'When we knew that was the very reason why he came here, the very reason why he was making up to Beatrix, passing himself off as an invalid!'

'Do be careful, Steph!' Linda pulled her back from the swift path of a car which cleared them by two or three yards. 'I admit it was silly as it turned out, but he meant it for the best.' And as they reached the pavement and walked slowly under the dripping trees, she told what she had heard of the calamitous photographic session. 'Not that Ken had any idea yesterday that Sir Harry had seen anything. But Beatrix was waiting up for me last night when I got home—it was late because we went over to Elderfield to the Dance Hall—and she said Sir Harry had found out who had the pictures, so I'd better confess.'

'Wasn't he supposed to have washed his hands of them? To think that Beatrix doesn't see what it means, his hunting them down like this!'

'He pretends it's a sort of joke, these worthless things being stolen, and that it amuses him to help her get to the bottom of it. He's got her absolutely eating out of his hand.'

They sat down on the hard, stiff-backed, and slightly damp bench that stretched the length of the deserted bus shelter.

'Well?' Stephanie inquired with a cadence of despair.

'Naturally I said I didn't know what she was talking about—though I *am* getting awfully tired of telling all these lies, Stephanie.'

'Yes, everyone's tired of lies. Go on!'

'And when she explained about this ridiculous old chemise, I still brazened it out and said it was all nonsense. So then Beatrix became very firm and older-sisterish, the way she does when she really means business, and she said she hadn't told Daddy yet but she would if I didn't confess the truth in the morning. And she gave me the night to think it over. Of course, I felt awful, because it actually was quite decent of her not to tell Daddy, but still I did stick it out in the morning. . . .'

'Oh, Linda, *why* didn't you come and tell me what had happened?'

'What could I do? I tried ringing you up at lunch-time but you were out. I would have sent Ken to you, but he was away all day. He had a job for the *Gazette*. It's funny the way things always seem to happen like that. Nobody being able to get hold of anybody!' Linda burst weakly into tears. 'In the afternoon there was a message saying would I please go home the minute I was free because it was urgent. So I dashed off. I had no chance of seeing you or Ken either.' She paused to dab her eyes and nose with a handkerchief that was a mere damp little ball.

'When I got home there was a most frightful crisis. Quiller had turned up. At least they'd had a letter from him. He said he was back in Elderfield and as it appeared the pictures were still missing, he was going to the police. He said they were his property and he felt he couldn't neglect the matter any longer. It was quite a blunt and business-like sort of letter, different from his last one.'

'When was it posted?'

'This morning, in Elderfield. And, mind you, all this act at the studio only happened yesterday afternoon.'

'He must have travelled up in the night.'

'Yes, that's what Ken thinks. Sir Harry probably telephoned him in London and got him to leave post-haste, but it wouldn't be any use trying to make Daddy or Beatrix believe that. When I told them it was a conspiracy and Maximer was a cheat, they just got furious. Even Daddy got furious! Anyhow, they were waiting to see me and it was dreadful—just like schooldays over again. Beatrix had given the show away about Ken, and Daddy warned me that unless I got him to hand the pictures over at once, they'd be found by the police in his studio and he'd have to take the consequences.'

'As there were no pictures in his studio, you might have risked the consequences.'

'Oh, do have a heart, Steph!' Linda's voice was low and gentle even in dismay. 'I realize that you're in love with the pictures, but can't you see I'm in love with Ken? Why, it would simply finish things—police and searchings and more and more lies. . . . After all, he did it as a favour. It wasn't like Arnold who felt the same as you did about the pictures.'

Stephanie sighed sharply with misery and impatience. 'I can understand your defending Kenneth, but couldn't you have done it without telling them about Arnold?'

'But it wasn't only to defend Ken. That's wrong. I suddenly thought if they knew the curator of an art gallery had them, because he believed in them and all that, they might be convinced at last—convinced that we were right to do what we did. But it only made them angrier. Maximer must have hypnotized Beatrix. She seems to believe he's about ten times more infallible than the Pope. As for Daddy, do you know what I think? He just doesn't want to find out.'

'Yes, he's overworked and tired. Go on! You told them about Arnold and they were angrier than ever.'

'Daddy asked where he lived and I said I hadn't a clue. That was true at any rate. Then Daddy said it would have to wait till morning. Apparently, he'd rung up Quiller and they'd got an appointment for tomorrow afternoon. I tried to get away to my bedroom then. . . . I was terribly upset, though you won't believe that, I dare say. But Daddy called me back and said we'd all done a most foolish and reckless thing and placed him in a disgraceful position, but that as our motives were not dishonest, he didn't want us punished for it—or words to that effect, you know. And he said I'd better warn you and Arnold Bayley to get those pictures back to him by lunch-time tomorrow because otherwise he wouldn't raise a finger to stop Quiller from doing whatever he saw fit. I'll swear he meant it too, Stephanie.'

'It doesn't matter whether he meant it or not. Maximer will soon have any information Beatrix possesses, that's obvious. He's in a position to do Arnold unlimited harm.'

'No, no, if the pictures come back Beatrix won't tell Sir Harry. She's promised and she doesn't break her promises. I saw her before I came out and told her Mr. Bayley had only done it to please you—'

'That doesn't tie up with the reason you gave first.'

'Oh, I'd got past trying to tie things up, and anyway the real reason simply doesn't go down. I said he'd done it to please you, and that if it came out and he lost his job or anything, you'd never speak to me again as long as you lived. I was in an awful state, crying buckets and all that, and she was in a good mood, having got her own way, so she made me the promise. She said it would be a secret from everyone; and as for Daddy, he'll never breathe a word. He likes you too much for that, Steph, though it's true he's cross with you tonight. Even when he was at his very angriest, the worst he said against you was that you were a fanatic.'

'I'm glad you thought of Arnold,' said Stephanie sombrely.

'Thank you. I shall go over to Elderfield in the morning and fetch the pictures.' She dropped her face into her hands in a gesture of acknowledged defeat. 'Arnold wouldn't be able to go on hiding them even if he were willing to risk his career and his livelihood for it—not now that so much has come out. It wouldn't matter so tremendously,' she suddenly sobbed, 'that Maximer will have them if only he'd keep them together and put them where they can be seen, but how can he do that when he's got to lie low and hide all his life the fact that he's had anything to do with it? They'll be split up, sold here and there—underground. . . . Who knows what will happen to them in the hands of such a wicked man?'

'You'll still have Lorenzo the Magnificent for yourself,' Linda reminded her, as one might comfort a child by a prospect of chocolates or a pantomime.

'That's the most fantastic consolation prize that has ever been given.' Stephanie's laugh was not without a tinge of genuine if ironic mirth. 'What will Beatrix say if I sell it and refuse to share the proceeds?'

She paused. The idea of selling this masterpiece had not occurred to her before because she had never intended that it should be separated from its fellows, but now the question framed itself—what if she took it to London and showed it to the experts in the purlieus of Bond Street? What if she explained that it was one of a batch of sixteen found under such-and-such conditions, that fifteen others had been bought by a man named Quiller. Would not this arouse a curiosity that might have far-reaching results?

The sense of defeat was lifted from her for an instant, then descended again in all its dreariness. Until the fraudulence was proved or the bargain renounced, the pictures belonged in law to Quiller and no amount of surprise that reports of the transaction might evoke could restore them to their previous owner. Maximer's plans for enjoying them might certainly be hampered, but then, she knew enough about those other transactions called B and C to give him credit for a wiliness that sooner or later would find a way round obstacles. She would go to London, she would show the portrait to one or other of the superior dealers, but the only satisfaction she could expect would be the sense of activity and the knowledge that she had done as much as she could.

'You'd be quite entitled to sell it,' said Linda in her soothing fashion, 'and it would serve Beatrix right if you got thousands.'

'No. It won't look very much at home, I'm afraid, in my bed-sitting-room, but I'm going to keep it. Once the others are handed over, it's the only way we shall have of giving anyone an idea of their quality. It's a piece of evidence and we shall need all the evidence we can get.'

'Ken seems to think he has something too. I went to him the first minute I could get out of the house and he was desperately upset about the whole thing, especially about letting *you* down . . . though it was the purest accident, Steph. He hadn't remembered where that beastly bit of chemise came from after he'd begun using it for other things. Still, he felt an awful fool just the same, because he'd thought he was being clever, poor silly! And he told me to tell you if you'd come round to the studio tomorrow morning, he'd try to have something that might sort of make amends. I can't begin to imagine what it is. He wouldn't let me stay. He sent me off.'

'Sent you off?'

'Yes, pushed me out bodily, almost. You'd really have laughed!' Linda's natural gaiety rose above her distress.

'I came on here and waited ages for you. I would have come in any case of course,' she concluded hastily.

'What can he be doing?'

A new hope warmed her, for, like all tenacious fighters, though alert to difficulties and inclined at times to magnify them, she generated hope easily, and she was sure that Kenneth, who always tended to understatement, would raise no idle expectations.

'Let's go and see,' cried Linda. 'He'll still be there. He said he'd be working till midnight or later.'

'If he put you out once, he may do it again.' She summoned, if rather wanly, a smile.

'Ah, but he wouldn't dare to put *you* out!'

Linda was palpably eager for an excuse to return to the studio, and as Stephanie was full of curiosity to learn what Kenneth's way of

making amends might be and would scarcely have time to call on him
in the morning with her dismal errand before her, she raised no objection to an immediate visit, and they set off bearing the discomfort of
damp shoes and ruined make-up with something as near indifference
as any two women are likely to reach under these disadvantages.

SIXTEEN

RESTORED victoriously to his beloved library, Sir Harry Maximer
extended his legs on an Empire sofa, forgetting the last twinges of his
lumbago in the serene delight of his reflections. Everything had gone
off beautifully, really beautifully, and with an ease attainable only
under the hand of a master.

The terms of the telegraph message arranged at Clapham Junction
had brought Quiller so swiftly to Elderfield that no one could suppose
his coming to be in any way linked up with the discovery of the tell-tale
piece of linen in the dark-room; it had seemed a coincidence rather
than a sequel. His own communication of that discovery to Beatrix
Sandilands had been made with exactly the right degree of facetious
interest in an amusing little episode. The plan laid down in London
for Quiller's telephone call to take his instructions had enabled them
to hold a conversation on his arrival which could reveal nothing to
anyone who might happen to be listening in. Thanks to an admirable
code which transformed Dr. Sandilands into a careless clerk and the
missing pictures into some documents that had been mislaid, it had
been possible to communicate all that was necessary for Quiller to
know without a single meeting outside London, or a word of writing
passing between them.

The good offices of Miss Sandilands had, of course, simplified
the affair considerably. The pressure she had brought to bear on her
sister, when combined with Quiller's well-timed threat of firm measures, had proved completely efficacious, and the pictures—minus alas!
the portrait of Lorenzo—had all come back skilfully packed in cartons
and cases less than forty-eight hours after they had been traced to the
young photographer's studio. Quiller had replaced them in the Saratoga trunk and left by the afternoon train with them.

Maximer had been obliged to wait, tantalized, two or three days, not
merely so that his movements might seem quite dissociated from those

of Quiller, but also because his joy, great as it was, had not succeeded in dissolving all his aches; and to ensure that not even the most suspicious mind could connect his attentions to Miss Sandilands with the ends they had served, he had continued to cultivate her friendship and had even taken a Sunday afternoon tea with her at home.

This was the only part of his conduct which had not perhaps been ordered with perfect forethought and discretion—where he might accuse himself bluntly, in fact, of having overdone it. From it had arisen what was, if one excepted acts of God such as lumbago, the solitary snag. Miss Sandilands had accompanied him to London.

It appeared that one of the doctor's nieces, a resident in South Kensington, was about to be married, and his eldest daughter intended to represent the family at the wedding and to take a week's holiday in town beforehand. Sir Harry could not suppress an uneasy feeling that her decision had been influenced by the kindness he had been at such pains to inspire, for she had timed her departure to synchronize with his own, insisting that he was unfit to travel without some helpful companion.

He was not averse from the ministrations of amiable and respectful young women. As long as they did not get between him and his loftier pleasures, women had as much charm for him as for any busy and ambitious man. He might have married if the building up of his double career as art historian and director of a great asbestos corporation had not so completely engrossed his energies. To be made much of by Beatrix Sandilands, whom he considered very personable and who obviously felt a flattering degree of deference towards himself, was rather agreeable than otherwise. Her want of aesthetic culture he accepted without complaint as he accepted the same deficiency in his confrères of industry and commerce, indeed in the majority of his acquaintances: had her taste been sounder, his ingenious schemes would have come to nothing. To court her good graces in Charlton Wells had certainly been no hardship. But to have her on visiting terms with him in London was another matter. Such an intimacy would make it distinctly risky to take possession of his glorious booty.

A very few days, however, should see an end to this last frustration. The wedding, he understood, was to take place on Tuesday, and on Wednesday she would be going home.

It was now Saturday. He had returned from Charlton Wells four evenings ago, and though he had spoken to Quiller every day on the telephone, assuring himself of the well-being of the pictures as if they had been liable to fluctuate in their condition like an invalid, he had not until this morning taken the risk of seeing him. For this occasion, he had contrived an admirable disguise which, despite Quiller's reluctance to adopt it, had been most satisfactory in use. It consisted of the singlet and shorts of a man whose hobby is cross-country running; and they had met by arrangement on the Dover Road where Maximer, driving his own car, had overtaken him—ostensibly a week-end athlete weary of exercise being given a lift by an acquaintance.

Maximer had been able to pick him up, enjoy a full discussion in perfect privacy, press into his hand an earnest of his future reward, and drop him at a convenient point without the slightest fear of any mischance. (Quiller had been less happy: he disliked the costume, and his patron, who seldom handled a car, had turned out a nerve-racking driver.)

The interview had been a great relief to Sir Harry's mind, giving him fresh confidence in Quiller's loyalty and reliability, and enabling him to plan the conditions under which he would take possession of his pictures. The first three were to be brought over to him in Paris next week-end. He needed in any case to see the expert there whom he employed on cleaning and repair work, and this would be an excellent opportunity to put in hand the principal damaged panels, the 'Leda', the profile portrait which was possibly by Baldovinetti, the beautiful 'Madonna and Child' ascribed, on first inspection at any rate, to Filippo Lippi.

On his return the following Monday, he was to have the 'Masaccio', the 'Dead Christ', and the 'Infant St. John', which were to be left for him in a portmanteau at the cloakroom of Victoria Station, the ticket being handed to him in Paris. He loved such neat little expedients, and in the prospect of disposing by a hundred wiles of the works he thought he could bear to part with, the smoke of his cigar seemed to grow more aromatic and to form clouds as light and graceful as if Tiepolo had painted them.

In this beatific mood, when solitude was bliss, to hear someone entering the flat with a latchkey brought to his face a sharply apprehensive frown which scarcely lightened when he recognized the brisk, sure step of his secretary. There had been times certainly when her willingness to work at unorthodox hours had been of great service to him: she had been splendid, for example, when through illness in his office it had been necessary for her to deal with a quantity of his business correspondence as well as his private affairs; splendid again in rounding up after the war the treasures he had lent to provincial art galleries and helping him, over and above her ordinary duties, to establish them in what was then his new flat. Being a childless widow, she was able to give his interests ungrudging priority, and thus in a crisis he could always rely on her.

But lately there had been no crisis, at least none with which she had the least concern, and still she persisted in finding work to do outside her ordinary routine. Unlike most of the business men he knew, he seldom left London at week-ends because he relished the tranquil grandeur of his flat and was able to use the time for furthering schemes which required privacy; and it occurred to him now that it would be pretty hard if he could no longer count on a Saturday afternoon to himself, particularly the latter part of a Saturday afternoon when it was his habit, after drinking three cups of China tea, to luxuriate in one of those cigars sent specially from Havana.

Not that Mrs. Rose thrust her company on him. She always went about the task she had set herself in a quiet and self-contained manner, disturbing him as little as possible. Nevertheless, her presence on occasions of holiday must subtract something from his enjoyment of his little kingdom.

'What is she about today?' he asked himself, quite losing his complacency. 'I told her there was nothing for her to do.' And while she could be heard hanging up her outdoor clothes in the little lobby beside her office, he called in what pretended to be benevolent curiosity:

'Mrs. Rose, why are you here at this very odd hour?'

'I beg your pardon, Sir Harry.' She came to the library door and held it ajar.

'I said why are you here? I thought we decided there was nothing that couldn't wait over till Monday.'

Mrs. Rose gave him the somewhat exasperating smile of a woman who is in the habit of humouring a man. 'Yes, we did, but the office is on my conscience.'

'The office?'

'*My* office. I haven't had time to tidy it all week—there was so much to catch up with when you got back from Charlton Wells—and now, well, it's really a shambles.'

'Couldn't it have remained a shambles till Monday? Your conscience is too susceptible, my dear lady!' His chiding had the playfulness he was wont to assume when he desired to correct her without putting her on the defensive.

'I'm going to a cocktail party quite near, so it's no trouble to spend an hour here first. Then I won't have a muddle to cope with on Monday morning.' She came into the room and he saw that she was not wearing the business-like clothes of every day but a crisp-looking biscuit-coloured dress which he deemed to be fashionable and which was cut and pleated to make the best of her not very satisfactory figure. 'I'll take your tray, shall I?' She approached his sofa table. 'I don't suppose there'll be anyone in the flat just now.'

Sir Harry stirred restively. 'Oh please don't bother, Mrs. Rose!'

'It always worries me to see a tray lying about when it's done with.'

'But it doesn't worry *me*!' Then, fearing the rebuke had been too pointed—for he liked to preserve the smoothest relations with all subordinates, especially the confidential ones—he added gallantly: 'Such a very elegant dress is not quite the thing for housework.'

'You have a bachelor's idea of housework, Sir Harry.' She gathered his cup, saucer, and plate together and restored them to the tray with a studied noiselessness that disturbed him more than if she had rattled them. 'You should have seen what I had to do at home before I came out.'

'All the more reason for not clearing up offices!' His voice sounded in his own ears rather querulously, and for courtesy's sake he tagged on: 'My dear Mrs. Rose,' so that the speech ended with an exaggerated air of solicitude.

'I never get tired if I'm doing something I like.' Assiduously she swept up a few cake crumbs. 'I wanted to make my flat very nice today because I was hanging your picture.'

'My picture?' He blinked at her in pure incomprehension.

'The "Belated Honeymoon."'

'Ah, the little thing I sent you from Charlton Wells!' Since receiving her enthusiastic letter of thanks, he had never thought again about the gift, and it was partly to conceal his remissness, partly to cover ideas of greater moment, that he exclaimed with a semblance of lively interest: 'I do hope you found it not too unsuitable. It can be abominably tactless to give anyone a framed picture, but I thought after five years I must understand something of your taste.'

'Still, I don't know how you guessed it would be so perfect in my little flat when you've never been there.'

'I have studied you well, Mrs. Rose.'

She picked up the tray and then put it down again. 'You look so comfortable, but if you're going to read you must have a better light.'

The evening paper, brought in with his tray, had been lying across his knees, but he had only had a remote intention of reading it. As she busied herself with fetching a lamp from his desk, he shook out the pages with an emphatic crackle, for it was evident that, with her office clothes, she had thrown off something of her secretarial personality; and although he liked his employees to feel a regard for him, he was far from wishing to encourage invasions of his private sanctuary.

He admitted that to send her the picture had been a mistake, since she must imagine he had gone out of his way to choose and dispatch it, and would feel that he had thus made a claim upon her gratitude which she could only repay by special services. Such attentions as she was now offering were a new departure and a very unwelcome one, but it would not be either pleasant or politic to administer a too marked rebuff, and he contented himself with gazing purposefully at the headlines. But as she adjusted the lamp-shade, he seemed to feel her groping for ways of prolonging the conversation, and it was almost a relief to him when a sound that he would normally have considered most untimely gave him an excuse for bringing it abruptly to an end,

'The front door bell! I wonder if anyone is in to answer it,'

'I'll go, Sir Harry. Are you expecting someone?'

'No.'

'Shall I say you're not at home then?' She asked the question with so hopeful a lilt that he found himself strenuously shaking his head.

'Not necessarily. It might be someone I should like to see.'

She went out, leaving him resolved to give no more pictures, and presently returned, announcing with a resumption of her customary cool and efficient manner as she closed the door behind her: 'It's Mr. Arnold Bayley.'

'Bayley? The Elderfield curator? These provincial fellows always think they can see me without an appointment.'

'He says if you can't see him now he can come back whenever it's convenient.'

Sir Harry sighed and then shrugged. His blissful hour was spoiled; he might just as well receive young Bayley as be interrupted in his reveries by Mrs. Rose. 'Let him come in!' he commanded with kingly resignation.

He was aware of no uneasiness. It was a very ordinary thing for art-gallery men with whom he had made contact in provincial cities to look him up when they came to London, seeking, generally, his advice on some potential acquisition or technical problem. Arnold Bayley had struck him as having something more than average intelligence and ambition, just the sort of young man who would desire to cultivate his acquaintance. He prepared to be cordial.

'Ah, Bayley, how do you do?' he said quite heartily as Arnold came into the room. A stranger might have gathered the impression that he was a headmaster receiving an old boy. 'Forgive this decrepitude!' He rose slowly but graciously to his feet. 'I am recovering from lumbago.'

Arnold was glad of this slow rising because it made it easy to evade a handshake. 'You have been up in Charlton Wells?' he said from almost the other side of the room.

'Yes, but I'm a very bad advertisement for the place. I abandoned the cure worse than when I began it. Now I'm nearly better, thank heaven! Wont you sit down? I hope it's not too early to offer you a glass of sherry. Or do you prefer gin-and-something?'

'I won't drink anything, thank you,' said Arnold, seating himself in the elbow chair near the desk where he supposed Maximer conducted interviews.

'You absolutely refuse to be tempted?'

'Thank you, yes.'

'You've brought an attaché case, I see. What's in it? Drawings? A precious little canvas? Something in my department, I'm sure.'

'It contains papers.'

'Oh, forgive me! I must have sounded impertinently curious. People so often bring things here for me to look at.'

'Yes, these are for you to look at, some of them at any rate.'

Such a business-like tone called for a response in kind, and although he thought it distinctly high-handed of his visitor to walk in without a previous engagement and demand that he should examine documents, he lowered himself into the chair behind his desk with an expression of polite attentiveness.

'A question of authenticity, I suppose?'

'Not exactly. We know these things are bogus.'

'Bogus!' A slight, a very slight, apprehensiveness quivered in him. Was it conceivable that one of his profitable chickens was coming home to roost? It was not an eventuality he went in fear of, confident as he was of the subtlety and skill of all his measures; but the young man's gravity was disquieting, and there had been a little correspondence once with Sinnett, his predecessor, which had required extremely delicate handling. The tremor was just sufficient to brace him and enable him quite imperceptibly to arm himself.

'I'll try to put it as briefly as I can,' said Arnold, resting his attaché case on his knees and playing a gentle five-finger exercise on it. 'In 1939 you were instrumental in selling a Jan Brueghel to my gallery. As you know, it turned out to be a fake—'

'Most regrettable! A thoroughly unfortunate incident!' The inflexion was sympathetic rather than apologetic. 'I was deeply distressed about it. My dear old friend, Rennick! Until then I simply hadn't imagined him capable of error!'

'You wrote and suggested hushing the matter up, and that was done. Done very misguidedly, as I think!'

'"Suggested" is a strongish word,' Maximer rejoined dispassionately, 'but use it by all means, if you like. The picture could be removed from the wall a great deal more easily than Rennick's reputation could have been mended once such a crack had been made in it. If I could have got the owner to refund the price, I would—though I am sure he was blameless—but he'd been killed in the war, and there was really nothing to be done. No, no, I can't see that I was in the wrong to say "Let sleeping dogs lie!"'

Arnold had the appearance of considering this view for a moment. Then he remarked quietly: 'A year before that, in 1938, the man who runs Green's Amusement Arcades bought a Teniers for a very high price through the firm of Chattery's, the interior decorators. That was also certified by a letter from John Rennick, and it was discovered to be a copy.'

'I heard something about that,' Maximer acknowledged with a rueful nod. 'Some undercurrent of talk got about. A great pity! These mistakes were made in the last year of Rennick's life. They should not be held against him.'

'I hope they won't be. There was another most unlucky affair. In 1937, just a few months after his death—we go backwards, you see—a

Steen was sold on the strength of one of his famous letters. It was sent out to Capetown and proved to be a forgery in 1940.'

'I hadn't heard anything of that.' Maximer neatly stubbed out his cigar in one of the Empire bonbon dishes, the gift of a lady whom he had obliged by bidding successfully in Paris for an exquisite collection of engravings. 'Poor fellow, he must have gone to pieces at the end more than we realized! Who sold this so-called Steen and who bought it?'

'Well, that's a long and tortuous story, Sir Harry, and as you really know it already, I don't see why I should tell it to you. It's all made out quite clearly here.' He tapped the leather case.

'One moment please!' Maximer struck in sharply; and he did it with so perfectly balanced a mixture of indignation, astonishment, and uncertainty as to whether he had heard aright that, if Arnold had not had the clearest evidence under his hand, he would have been almost convinced that he had committed some ghastly blunder. 'One moment! You may not be aware of it, Bayley, but you've just said something fantastic!'

'I'll give you chapter and verse if you insist.' Arnold resolved by a clear and matter-of-fact style to counter the other's ingenious histrionics. 'Let me begin with the Teniers. It was easy to plant the copy as an original, because at the time no other reproduction was in existence. It had been quietly reposing for a couple of hundred years in a villa belonging to the Count Cobarruvias, who took no particular interest in art, and it was only when the Spanish Civil War caused the place to be overrun that anyone noticed what choice things some of his ancestors had acquired—'

'Yes, yes, one knows about the Cobarruvias pictures,' said Maximer with an excellent parody of the impatience he always displayed when receiving anything that might be construed as instruction. 'It's not in my view an especially important collection.'

'But it was worth saving, and very luckily when the villa was occupied by troops, there was a young Frenchman with them who saved it—who, more or less, prevented the place from being sacked. Later, when order was restored, he went back to Spain with a friend and they were given facilities for making copies and doing anything they pleased.'

'That was all in an article in *Apollo* or *The Connoisseur*,' said Maximer indifferently.

'Yes, an article which didn't appear till a year or more after the copy of the Teniers had been sold as the original. The young man who made it, Pierre Marchand, was a protégé of yours, Sir Harry. You had paid for his art training in Paris.'

Maximer's only reaction was a pensive smile. 'He was one of several students I have believed in and tried to help. None of them, unhappily, have shown any sign of becoming a first-rate artist.'

'But at least one became a first-rate copyist.'

'If he has disposed of copies under false pretences, I am sorry to hear it.' Maximer took up an ivory paper-knife and tested its flexibility with meticulous fingers. 'I lost touch with him years ago.'

'It wasn't Pierre Marchand who disposed of the picture. That was done by his uncle, Baptiste Lamotte, through whom it was bought in all good faith by Chattery's.'

'I see you've been doing some energetic detective work, Bayley, but to tax me with knowing about this transaction is absurd. Merely because I once paid for some lessons for a promising student! It's absurd and most objectionable!'

'Do you deny you had dealings with Lamotte, Sir Harry?'

'Of course I don't. Before the war every collector had dealings with Lamotte. He was a kind of general factotum in the art world, and most of the stuff he handled was outstandingly good.'

'Do you deny the Rennick letter he used for certifying that Teniers was a forgery?'

'How can I either deny it or admit it? I never saw the letter and I haven't been in contact with Lamotte since the war.'

'Well, we can establish quite definitely that it *was* a forgery. It's dated January 1937. The original picture was hanging at that date on the wall at the Villa Cobarruvias in Spain—a country Rennick never visited—and no copy was ever painted, either by Pierre Marchand or anyone else, until 1938, months after Rennick's death.'

'Why was this not exposed long ago?' Maximer gazed over the arched paper knife with a face that showed no emotion other than incredulity and righteous anger.

'Because the forger had a war to protect him. We were cut off from foreign countries and the man who'd been defrauded was not in a position to make investigations. After the war, he let it go. He had no hope of getting his money back and he wasn't interested in clearing Rennick's reputation. But somebody else was.'

'I'm glad to hear it. Naturally I ask who?'

'Oscar Robertson. You may remember him.'

'Oh yes. Some kind of hanger-on of Rennick's.' For the first time the scornful note rang flat.

'He has been working on the problem of these false authentications for a long time; but it was only a fortnight ago that we thought of getting in touch with Count Cobarruvias and verifying the precise date when that Teniers was copied. Sometimes the most obvious thing is the last that comes into one's head. I don't suppose even you troubled to know exactly when Marchand made that copy, Sir Harry? Yet it was an essential detail if people were to go on believing that there was no fraudulence—just an honest mistake by Dr. Rennick in the last months of his life. But perhaps you counted on the copy never being detected?'

Maximer laid down the paper-knife and placed it in front of his inkstand with a very neat and careful gesture. 'You seem,' he said, 'to be making some kind of accusation against me. Would you mind formulating it?'

'Certainly. I am accusing you of having forged letters to promote the sale of spurious pictures.'

Arnold's hands, after he had spoken the words, lay rigid on his attaché case and Maximer's lay rigid on his desk. They eyed each other in a tingling silence.

'You are mad!' said Maximer at last. 'Dangerously and deplorably mad! I shall seek protection against you.'

'You must seek protection against Oscar too. But wouldn't you like to know first what we've learned about the sale of the Steen to Sir Hubert Prosser?'

Maximer extended his large hands in a movement suggesting that if a further outbreak of insanity were impending he would let it take its course.

'The picture was bought for Sir Hubert at Mandell & Strood's, where the bidding was very high on account of Rennick's immensely enthusiastic letter to the owner. She was another Parisian, a Madame Pressigny. There were no currency restrictions then, of course, to prevent a foreigner from buying and selling in the London auction rooms. . . . Now can't you imagine how Oscar and I threw up our hats when we found that Madame Pressigny's address in Mandell & Strood's books was altogether different from the one on the letter purporting to be written to her by Dr. Rennick?'

'People have been known to change their addresses,' Maximer protested with a sarcasm that was a shade over-drawn.

Arnold began to enjoy himself as he saw that his opponent no longer did, and he answered almost genially: '*She* changed more than that. Rennick wrote to her as a chatelaine with a salon full of pictures, but when Mandell & Strood sent her their draft for the Steen, she happened to be the humble concierge of a building at Versailles—a building where you had rented a flat, Sir Harry. Oscar went to see her the other day, and she sent very kind regards to Mr. Maximer.'

'This is all the most slanderous and malignant nonsense!'

'Oh, I don't say the poor old lady had any idea the picture was a fake!' In his triumph he stooped to the artifice of deliberate misunderstanding. 'She was under the impression that you were selling it in her name because you were hard up and anxious to conceal the fact. But time loosens all tongues, and after thirteen years, hearing that you were honoured and prosperous, she didn't see any harm in telling of the little favour she'd done you. Not speaking a word of English she was perfectly ignorant—that goes without saying—of the correspondence she was supposed to have had with Dr. Rennick from a chateau she'd never seen and which probably never existed.'

Maximer pushed his chair back from the desk, folded his arms, and directed his eyes to the parquet of his floor with the fixed frowning stare of a man who wishes to think without the smallest possibility of distraction.

'What is the object of all this research?' he asked calmly after a substantial pause.

'There are several objects. For one thing, there's to be a new edition of Oscar's book on Rennick and he's writing an appendix with the plain facts about these posthumous letters.'

'I'm grateful for your warning, Bayley. Tell Robertson that if one breath of suspicion is cast on me I shall apply immediately for an injunction.'

'You'd be taking a very great risk to do that when you've been mixed up in three such shady transactions.'

'*You* are taking a great risk, let me tell you, to jump to the conclusion that I forged those letters—if they were forged, and I have no one's word but yours for that.'

'Not even Rennick could write letters from the grave. Out of the three we've been discussing, one was produced after his death. You won't argue about that when you've seen Count Cobarruvias' statement,' he put in firmly as he saw Maximer raise a protesting hand. 'One was written to you, and one was about a faked picture that was sold at your instigation by your concierge. The facts when published will speak rather loudly for themselves. There was no one in a better position to forge the letters. You used to stay at Chadley Hall and it must have been simple for you to come by the engraved paper. You are a man of exceptional literary skill and you have a profound knowledge of painting—'

'The compliment is gratifying, whatever its intention.'

'It was entirely in your power to imitate Rennick's style of talking about a picture, a thing impossible for Lamotte or any other foreigner.'

'But to commit that particular crime—since you lay your unseemly imaginings before me—I should have needed to have not only the paper and the skill you mention, but also, my dear young man, a very peculiar typewriter which is more likely to be found in a museum of antiquities than a household such as mine.'

Arnold made no reply. All Oscar Robertson's efforts to find out what had happened after Rennick's death to his old double-keyboard Darton machine had been futile. The contents of Chadley Hall had been sold by auction, but if the typewriter had been among them so little had its ripe age and quasi-primitive structure enhanced its value that it must have figured in the catalogue only as one of the odd and unnamed items that made up the miscellaneous lots. The indefatigable Oscar had striven in vain to establish that any of these had been bought by Maximer, and though both investigators were convinced that the instrument had been either in his possession or accessible to him for at least two years following Rennick's death, it remained the missing link in their strong chain of evidences.

It was time therefore to change the subject. He rose, laid his case on the seat of the chair, and stood lightly grasping the back. 'There is another matter,' he began in the measured and compelling tone of one who knows the force of what he has to say. 'A man called Quiller has just acquired in Charlton Wells fifteen Florentine panels which are, I suppose, the most important discovery of its kind that's been made in this century. I have every reason to believe that you were responsible for that transaction and will profit from it.'

For a long moment Maximer sat frozen, shocked out of his pretended unassailability. Nothing is more devastating than to find, after we have congratulated ourselves again and again on a transcendent piece of good fortune, that we have utterly miscalculated; and it is harder to be deprived of that which we have won than that which we have laboriously earned. A man gambling beyond his means who secures the first prize in a great sweepstake will feel more rage and dismay if it is confiscated than if he had lost his life savings: and Maximer, whose winnings were nothing less than the Hovenden pictures, was in the frame of mind when he would have parted sooner with almost any treasure lawfully gained.

He saw them threatened and with them his reputation, his career, his freedom itself, and at last he trembled.

The various ruses by which he had exploited the name of Rennick had been, of course, highly unethical—he was not in the least insensible of that—but he could not seriously believe that after so considerable a lapse of time any very dire punishment would be exacted. A prosecution would be immensely complicated, the foreign witnesses difficult and in certain cases impossible to get hold of, the bad faith of any single individual concerned in the negotiations a most baffling thing to try and prove. Undoubtedly Robertson and this menacing Arnold Bayley would be capable of stirring up ugly rumours, but he would not be without some power to take counter-measures, and he was fairly sure, even in this unprecedented crisis, of an ability to live down attacks upon his character based on events a dozen years old. But if at the same time as old transgressions were being raked up, a new one, on a scale exceeding all the others, were to be brought to light, here was ruin.

Standing to lose the pictures and everything else as well, he was obliged to steady himself while he contrived his astonished reply:

'Charlton Wells! Florentine panels! You can't really be trying to tell me that you—the director of an art gallery—have allowed yourself to be carried away by this opium dream of Medici masterpieces? Good God, there must be something in the atmosphere up there that sends you all into trances!'

Exhilarated by the enemy's discomfiture, though he guessed rather than perceived it, Arnold relaxed into a laugh. '*You* can't really be trying to tell *me* that you—the ace of experts—could look at those pictures without knowing what they were? There were sixteen of them, recollect!'

'I knew very well what they were and told Dr. Sandilands what I knew. Who are you to set your opinion against mine?'

'Come, Sir Harry, we can call that bluff. We've brought the portrait of Lorenzo to London.'

Considering the dreadful difficulties under which he laboured, Maximer's nonchalance was a piece of acting not without merit, as Arnold recognized. 'Ah, that was an excellent pastiche! You may easily take someone in with it. But don't be taken in yourself, Bayley! You might end by looking extremely foolish.'

Arnold clasped his hands together with an air of slow and patient thought—and indeed the situation was one in which he felt the necessity of weighing his words.

'We are tremendously anxious,' he said on an impulse of candour that could not be mistaken, 'to set all this right without the great blaring scandal that's otherwise bound to be the upshot. If you insist on making us take the obvious course—'

'Excuse me, but might I ask you to elucidate this "we"? Are you referring to yourself and Oscar Robertson?'

'Us two certainly, and also Mrs. du Plessis, who is responsible for the fact that either you or I ever heard of the pictures.'

'Mrs. du Plessis? I know of her of course from Dr. Sandilands and his daughter. So it was she who launched you on this mission? She must be a most redoubtable woman, gifted with powers of persuasion and self-persuasion that I personally find quite enviable, a kind of younger Joanna Southcott.'

'I have no desire to hear your views on Mrs. du Plessis.'

The energetic rebuke was not without a glint of enlightenment for Maximer, who smiled rather disarmingly as he answered: 'Please allow me to have some ordinary human reactions, Bayley! Here is a lady who sets all this train in motion against me—'

'Why do you assume that?'

'A very strong instinct tells me that these two totally different accusations—hers and yours—haven't come together by accident. I defy you to pretend that you were trying to fit me into the role of a forger until Mrs. du Plessis drew you into this dangerous plot of hers. All worked up because I couldn't endorse her opinion of some objects she had no qualifications to judge! You must pardon me if I go on regarding her as at least a very wrong-headed person. But I admire her for the force of her personality. It must be considerable. When I heard that she'd actually prevailed upon two other people—three if you were in it—to steal those pathetic pictures, I laughed, but I also found something admirable in it. I should have liked to meet her.'

Arnold had refrained from interrupting in the hope that the other might slip into some unguarded utterance. Now, as Maximer ended his disingenuous speech, he responded with a sense of effect fully worthy of his antagonist: 'To meet her? That's easier than you think. She's sitting downstairs in your outer hall.'

Maximer rose to the occasion. 'My dear fellow, how could you let me seem so inhospitable? In the hall! What on earth was your motive?'

'We thought it would be easier for you to come to some decision if you and I were alone.'

'I don't know what decision I could come to,' said Maximer in almost humorous protestation, 'but I should be glad to meet the lady.'

'Very well, I'll fetch her.' He picked up his case from the chair.

'Are you afraid I'll impound the papers?'

'They're all copies,' Arnold informed him wryly. 'I might as well leave them.'

With his departure, Maximer struggled against a sensation not far from panic. He was tempted to lock the door of his flat upon these insolent intruders and shut himself away with the documents so that he might estimate the strength of the hands that were against him. But his disposition, which was essentially sanguine and self-confident, was not long in reasserting itself. He could not be outwitted by a provincial curator who had barely been heard of and a library assistant who had never been heard of at all. Besides, Mrs. Rose was in the flat, and to leave two visitors beating, so to speak, on the portals would excite her always active curiosity. As to that, he felt no little curiosity himself, for he had hardly lied when he spoke of admiring Mrs. du Plessis.

Sir Harry was not much given to praising the discernment and sagacity of others. His self-esteem made it more congenial to him to tear down the pretensions of those who dared to pass judgment in the sphere where he was arbiter than to uphold their findings; but there was a sort of courage that could win his plaudits even when it took the form of an obstacle in his own path, and all that he had heard of Stephanie from Beatrix's gossip, all that he had learned of her through the annoyances she had inflicted on him, combined to evoke in him an appreciation deeper than he had been able to avow. The respectfulness of his greeting and his almost courtly bow as, after a longer wait than he had found comfortable, Arnold held open the door for her, were only superficially ironical.

She crossed the threshold warily, averting her eyes from the beauties of the walls and the great bookcases as if they might seduce her from her purpose, and stood facing her adversary with a gaze of perfectly frank hostility.

Arnold resumed his post beside the desk. 'I have been telling Mrs. du Plessis,' he said, 'that you maintain Dr. Sandilands' pictures are of no value.'

Sir Harry motioned her to a chair, but with a slight shake of the head she rejected it and, as he had expected, remained standing.

'I advised him to the best of my ability,' he said with dignity, 'and this is indeed a most extraordinary sequel. To be charged with . . . but I must really ask you—one or other of you—to make it clear what I *am* charged with!'

'You pretended the pictures were no good and then sent a man to Charlton Wells to buy them,' cried Stephanie with an even fiercer anger in her eyes than in her voice. 'You must give them up or we shall do things that may surprise you.'

'My dear young lady, you've already done things that surprise me! Will you resent it very much if I say that, until today, you've both surprised and amused me! But your conspiracy against me is not amusing. It's merely tiresome.' Stationed in front of his empty fireplace, he surveyed them with his headmaster's manner in its most consummate form. His hand seemed to brandish an invisible cane. 'You are going to force me to take boring precautions against you. I shall have to warn Dr. Sandilands that you're still meddling in his affairs, warn the Arts Committee at Elderfield that their gallery is in the hands of a crack-brained mischief-maker, warn Oscar Robertson's publishers that I shall seek an injunction against his book. And if you persist in your baseless slanders—I'm sorry to use such blunt words but they are the only apt ones—I shall be obliged to protect my reputation by taking whatever legal action my solicitors may advise.'

Arnold and Stephanie exchanged a glance, a glance with raised eyebrows that seemed to say: 'See how he blusters!' Maximer could not have acknowledged even to himself how it deflated him.

'We came here,' said Stephanie, 'to offer you a truce. . . .'

'I was not at war.'

'But we are!'

'You are attacking a bogy of your own creation. I know nothing of this man Quiller, nothing of any of the offences you've been inventing for me. You are reckless to speak in such terms without being able to substantiate them. I defy you to prove the slightest shadow of a connection between me and this picture dealer. If you can, if you do, I will—'

'What *will* you do, Sir Harry?' she broke in with a fiery eagerness very different from Arnold's cool and circumspect style.

'I will build an art gallery for your famous pictures,' he answered sardonically.

'And if we can't?'

'Then I shall expect you to apologize.'

'To apologize and leave you to enjoy the plunder!' She moved a step forward, refusing to see some small restraining gesture made by Arnold. 'Ah no, never! Never, I promise you! You don't know how mistaken you are if you think you can own Leonardo's 'Leda' or even half a magnificent Botticelli and conceal how you came by them!'

As she spoke, she opened the attaché case with swift retributive fingers and subtracted triumphantly from papers clipped together in business-like order and marked with disquieting little dockets a thick sheaf of unmounted prints held together by an elastic band.

She flung it on his desk as if it had been a steel gauntlet and, coming to meet the challenge, he took it up disdainfully.

'What absurdity is this?'

'Look, Sir Harry! Everything is recorded! Every picture in the collection with enlargements of the details! You won't find it as safe as you imagine to dispose of those panels, or to keep them either, when we've published these.'

It cost him the greatest effort he had yet made to retain his look of lofty forbearance as he removed the elastic and strewed over his desk four or five dozen photographs, as clear and workman-like as those which commonly appear in art journals—a labour that had kept Kenneth Dyer up till dawn on the one night when he had so reluctantly harboured the stolen goods.

'Look!' she insisted, picking up one by one the prints nearest her. 'Here's the dead Christ! And here's the hand and the drapery of the bier! And here's the head that couldn't be mistaken for any other head that was ever painted! And this is the head of the Emperor Johannes. And this is the Muse Urania!'

Maximer, still endeavouring to sustain a kind of derisive condescension, examined the photographs attentively. 'The reproduction of pictures,' he said after a long pause, 'is always a most unpredictable business. Good ones, I find, often appear so poor, and poor ones so wonderfully good. These are extremely well done. Your idea, no doubt, Bayley?'

'No, I'm afraid it never even occurred to me. The credit belongs entirely to Kenneth Dyer.'

'Ah, the photographer. He's better than I should have guessed judging by his portraits of me. But then he was able to take his time.'

'No,' said Arnold. 'Except for one night, the pictures were over in the Elderfield Art Gallery the whole two weeks.'

Maximer's false insouciance dropped away from him at this. He went on studying the squares of pasteboard diligently, but it was as if his hand fumbled over a house of cards that had been blown down.

The implacable Mrs. du Plessis was right. He would neither be able to sell works of which so exhaustive a record had been made nor to add them, except in deepest secrecy, to his own collection. And the most ardent and covetous virtuoso can derive little pleasure from possessing what no one but himself may ever see.

Sir Harry had not calculated, even when he had supposed the panels to be in the keeping of a photographer, on their receiving so professional a treatment. He was aghast, in fact, to realize that he had not really calculated on their being photographed at all. If any vague notion of such a risk had flickered into his mind when he had discovered Kenneth Dyer's complicity, he had dismissed it as a needless qualm, all unaware as he had been that he and Quiller were under suspicion of fraudulence.

In his then jubilant humour, the forlorn little band of burglars in Charlton Wells seemed vanquished from the moment when he had found the means of making them give up their booty; and, vain as he was, he had never credited them with any ability to hit back at him.

It was an appalling stroke of luck that an extremely obscure young photographer in a North country watering-place had turned out capable of providing these first-rate reproductions, and worse still that a man like Bayley, who had handled Old Masters, had been able to make a close scrutiny of the pictures. It had cut the ground in the cruellest way from under his feet: and in a position of such hideous insecurity, he was tempted to deeds of shame.

Yes, he was tempted to have the paintings altered so drastically as to render perfect identification impossible. Cleaning in any case would make a good deal of difference to their appearance, and if in the process some features stressed in the photographs should vanish and others, in keeping but diverse, should take their place, there might be certain ingenious ways of explaining the resemblances. . . .

He pulled himself together, shocked at the contemplation of so base an extremity. He might have passed copies off as originals or caused mediocre works of art to be turned by skilful hands into 'Old Masters', but never, absolutely never, had he committed any act of vandalism upon an Old Master that was genuine.

With the recognition of this high scruple and the self-applause that accompanied it, he won back something of his normal resilience. He was precluded now from enjoying the pictures but at least he would not suffer for them. On that he was resolved. Though the presumption that he and Quiller had been acting in concert might be strong to one who was as knowledgeable as Bayley or as passionate in her conviction as Mrs. du Plessis, a court of law would require very definite evidence, and he felt pretty sure that this would not be forthcoming.

More than that, a court of law would require a prosecutor, and was the mild and diffident doctor in Charlton Wells likely to assume that role?

He began to stack the photographs together with a resumption of his former blend of contempt and tolerance. 'Have you laid your morbid fancies about me before Dr. Sandilands?'

'We've been hoping you'd make it unnecessary for us to do so,' said Arnold.

'How, for example?'

'By instructing Quiller—'

'Instructing Quiller? On what authority? I have no power over him.'

Arnold replied only with an obstinately sceptical gaze.

'The truth is you've come to me to do something about Quiller because you know full well that Dr. Sandilands never will. You've been counting on blackmailing me with this tale of forged letters and all the rest of your concoction, but I'm impervious—utterly impervious to such suggestions. My integrity is established. It stands beyond question. No critic or collector or dealer of repute in the whole of England will give credit to your stories for a moment. As for Dr. Sandilands, I'm much mistaken if he would risk laying himself open to being taken for a madman.'

Arnold and Stephanie looked at each other again, and this time their eyebrows were not raised but lowered. He was sensible that, if he had not in the least shaken their belief in his guilt, he had reminded them vividly of the difficulty of putting it to any practical use.

'Now,' he ended with a victor's politeness, 'if you will excuse me, I have an appointment to keep.'

The ormolu clock on his mantelpiece told him that, by telephoning at once to the house where Beatrix Sandilands was staying with her relatives, he might be able to catch her before she set off for the theatre. She had called in yesterday to bring him a home-baked cake, and had mentioned that she was seeing as many plays as she could afford seats for. He had not taken the hint then, but now he would make amends and would invite her to sup with him at the Savoy after the show. She would like that, for she had complained that staying with cousins was dull when no one was thinking of anything but wedding preparations, in which she had small share.

Her friendly relations with him had been invaluable. Without them he might easily have been bluffed into imagining that all the Sandilands family was ranged against him, undoubtedly a most serious position for him if it should come to pass. For the moment his firmness had succeeded in perplexing his enemies, but they were formidable and might become more so.

His only safety lay in a very close alliance with Dr. Sandilands' daughter.

SEVENTEEN

IN THE back room of the Islington antique shop, Quiller sat drinking tea and reading the *Evening World*, making first for 'Juvenal's' column as of late he had been morbidly compelled to do.

No other newspaperman in London could have succeeded in turning the story of some faked pictures and forged attributions into such first-rate popular journalism. From the appearance of the first headline, THE MYSTERY OF THE MISSING TYPEWRITER to yesterday's WHEN MR. GREEN WAS NOT AMUSED, his Rennick stories had been handled with a touch that delighted his eager readers and even made some impression on that great mass of the public addicted to more violent dramas. His presentation of each phase of discovery as if it were a new chapter of a detective serial was masterly in its compression and vigour; and in a fashion that was particularly sinister to one who had some inkling of what had gone on behind the scenes, the name of Maximer was woven in and out of the pattern with a brilliant suggestiveness.

Few topical writers understood the laws of libel better than 'Juvenal'—indeed they were a speciality among all the editorial staff of the *Evening World*—and those who disliked him feared him most when he was flattering. Quiller could picture his patron's impotent rage faced two or three times a week with an apparently sympathetic account of his own gullibility.

> So skilful was this fake that Sir Harry Maximer, most distinguished of experts, was completely taken in, and had no hesitation in acting as the owner's agent. . . .

This of the Elderfield Brueghel. And of Mr. Jacob Green's Teniers:

> . . . According to the Spanish Count's statement, only one man was ever allowed to copy the paintings at the Villa Cobarruvias. It must have come as a grievous blow to Sir Harry Maximer, doyen of art critics, to learn that this young Frenchman whom he had befriended and singled out for great things, had been mixed up in the unsavoury business of passing off a copy for £8000. Sir Harry has been unlucky in his protégés, one of whom was convicted in New York of adopting the signature of Picasso. In this branch of forgery he was quite untrained and easily detected.

And again, so damagingly yet so guilelessly worded:

> I called on Sir Harry Maximer, celebrated for his exposure of forgeries, with the bogus Dutch masterpiece that Sir Hubert Prosser had bought in 1937 for a price running into five figures. Sir Harry had an extraordinary tale to tell about this painting and the reason why he sold it in the name of his French caretaker. He is quite sure it is not the picture he dispatched from Paris. The fake, according to his theory, was substituted at some point in transit. . . .

Quiller had winced at that paragraph. It was he who had valued the Steen for Mandell & Strood's and passed it as authentic, the first service he had ever performed for Maximer, the first descent from conscious integrity. How wily were the persuasions that had been used! Of course he had thought the Rennick certificate genuine and believed that the canvas belonged to the ostensible vendor, Mme Pressigny. Maximer, who was extremely well-known and respected at the auction rooms, had dropped some hints to him about her pitiable need of the sum that might be raised from the sale. It was all so long ago, he couldn't recall the details, but he did remember that, though he had suspected the picture and guessed that Maximer suspected it too, he had kept his misgivings to himself.

Now it was clear, in the light that 'Juvenal' had been so suavely yet so unmercifully shedding, that Rennick's encomium had been a forgery and the forger not far to seek. Quiller felt profoundly uneasy, for in his cellar were fifteen works of major importance acquired in circumstances by no means open to investigation. And such were the scandals beginning to creep about the name of Maximer that he feared to be involved with him at any moment in a terrible *éclairissement*.

'Juvenal's' articles for the *Evening World* were syndicated in several provincial and overseas papers. Though Maximer's reputation was always treated deferentially, it could not remain unaffected even in the eyes of laymen. If no worse consequences followed, his prestige must yet suffer a serious decline.

Maximer himself had taken fright at the very first sign of the fray and had put through one of his cryptic telephone calls to cancel—'for the moment' he said—the trip to Paris and the delivery at Victoria Station of the three small panels he had planned to have left there. It was not like him to postpone without abundant reason any pleasure his heart was set on, especially the pleasure of acquisition. There was evidently something in the wind—something of graver import even than this unburying of old and unknown misdeeds. For Quiller the situation was most uncomfortable and a severe test of loyalty which lately had been hard tried.

But today, to his relief, 'Juvenal's' column was devoted entirely to the latest landscape that had been selected for open-cast coal-mining. He took a draught of tea and was turning back thankfully to the front page when his eye was caught by a conspicuous paragraph at the head of the section of topical items called 'London Mixture'.

ANOTHER CLEANED PICTURE

In the laboratory of the Quattrocento Gallery the experts have been disclosing under the grime of centuries a painting which is believed to portray Lorenzo the Magnificent, fabulously wealthy banker and ruler of Florence, connoisseur of art, letters, and beautiful women. The picture is to be exhibited but will not be for sale. Gallery Manager Frank Grimsby estimates value at not less than £25,000, and more if pundits decide that it is the work of one of the top-ranking painters of Lorenzo's court where some of the most highly-priced masterpieces of the world were painted. Owner of the panel is a library assistant who earns under £8 a week. 'I would rather she spoke for herself,' said Mr. Grimsby when asked to disclose how the portrait was found. 'All I can tell you is that it is a genuine and sensational discovery.'

Quiller let the paper sink slowly to his knee. The hue and cry had begun. Within a few weeks or days the story of how a London dealer had bought fifteen such pictures for a hundred guineas would be news even in the monster-circulation press. There would not be the slightest difficulty in tracking him down. . . . Already perhaps the existence of fabulous wealth under his roof was known not only at the Quattrocento Gallery but to dealers and agents, to newspaper reporters, to Scotland Yard. . . .

Yes, if now that Maximer's honour was blown upon, someone succeeded in demonstrating that there had been connivance between them, even Dr. Sandilands might not be too weak to claim redress, and Scotland Yard was bound to take an interest.

But what, he asked himself, what if on the other hand no link could be traced? He, Quiller, would be to all intents and purposes the legal owner! He could refuse to hand over the panels. Maximer would have no remedy: he could do nothing except by incriminating himself. For a moment or two Quiller toyed dizzily with the idea of double-crossing the man who had made him wear running-shorts.

It was not the first time it had entered his head, but it was the first time it had taken any shape less vague than the figments that may float in the background of a dream. But with the assumption of a realistic form it came heavily down to earth. What was the use of speculating on such desperate deeds? He could no more have defied Maximer than he could have flung himself in the path of an advancing tank or heckled a speaker in the Albert Hall. It took 'Juvenal's' moral courage to make war on Sir Harry.

Quiller was a resourceful man, a sensitive and intelligent man, but courage had never been his portion. And fundamentally he was honest; he would not betray his benefactor, the man who had put up the capital for his business and never been paid back.

He poured himself out another cup of tea and gulped it with the relish of one who makes the most of his creature comforts to soothe a harassed mind. Slowly, carefully, he read the alarming paragraph again and, ruminating over one of his sister's currant buns, decided that the gossip writer's information was not, as he had at first feared, a new move in 'Juvenal's' ingenious campaign against Maximer, a campaign set going, he could readily imagine, by some impetus from hands in Charlton Wells. It was a real piece of gossip, picked up with no helping hand from anyone concerned.

If Mrs. du Plessis and those friends of hers who had helped to steal the pictures had wanted to call attention to the portrait of Lorenzo, they could have done so weeks ago.

On the contrary, it became clear when he took thought that this was exactly what they had *not* wanted. To arouse curiosity as to the provenance of that panel, to admit that it was one of many, was the last thing they would desire while he or Maximer had possession of the rest of the treasure and might take hurried measures to get rid of it. No, someone had talked out of turn, someone in the laboratory perhaps—one, he hoped, who did not know the name of Quiller.

He started and put down his cup with a clatter. There was a noise in the shop. Since he had brought home that portentous Saratoga trunk, he had become so jumpy that his sister was making him take phosphates. He had developed a neurotic horror of having a fire on the premises, and all small noises made him think of flames licking round the cellar staircase; so that, instead of stepping out of his sanctum to meet customers like a dignified antiquarian, he was inclined to dash at them with a wild haste.

Neither a fire nor a reporter awaited him among the groves of desks and console tables, only a young man who wished to examine a snuff-box that was in the window.

The sale, after a little bargaining, completed, Quiller returned to the *Evening World*. Striving to banish his troublesome speculations, he poured himself one last half-cup of tea—dregs unfortunately and cold ones at that—and refolded the paper so that he could start on the front-page news. There was a trial which he was following every day with close attention, at one with the rest of the public in finding it better reading than the speeches at Westminster and the notes exchanged by foreign governments; though he could have wished that it were not a trunk murder.

By the time he had reached the announcement 'Back Page, Col. Five', he had managed quite to immerse himself in the drama of the obviously guilty man struggling to explain away damning circumstances, and it was almost with a wrench that he directed his eyes to the headline of the adjoining column:

ASBESTOS MAGNATE WEDS

Asbestos magnate! Didn't that description apply to someone he knew? He had read all the eight lines describing Sir Harry Maximer's marriage to Miss Beatrix Sandilands in an obscure Belgravia church before he had taken in the significance of it.

He rose, forgetting the murder trial in an inrush of buoyant high spirits. A load like a tangible burden seemed to have been lifted from him.

'By God,' he said—and he was within a breath of saying it aloud—'he's a clever devil!'

Whatever happened old Sandilands would never prosecute now.

EIGHTEEN

MAXIMER did not dare to take Beatrix abroad for a honeymoon; he felt obliged to remain where he could study all the London papers day by day. The story in the *Evening World* about the portrait of Lorenzo had set him more than ever on the *qui vive*, and fabricating a crisis that might brew up on the asbestos market, he contented himself with engaging a suite for the week-end at Bray—where he surprised his bride not altogether pleasantly by his assiduous reading of the Sunday newspapers and the great refreshment that he seemed to derive from them.

Beatrix had her own preoccupations, however, because she had to follow up the brief note she had sent to her father with a long explanatory letter, and it was not an easy one to write.

When a woman who normally puts prudence before everything at last decides to throw her bonnet over a windmill, it will invariably be found that she chooses a windmill of no small stature. For Beatrix, who had dominated her father, two sisters, and a brother all her adult life,

there was something irresistibly captivating in the idea of being dominated. She had a strong-minded woman's secret yearning to be a weak
one, a managing woman's illusion that it would be delightful to yield up
her will to the dictates of another, a being whose superior wisdom she
could reverence and defer to. She whose tendency had always been to
belittle and deflate the pretensions of others had been impressed from
the first by one whose powers in this respect seemed greater than her
own. The fact that he was eminent, labelled for all the world to see as
an important person, was distinctly an attraction, ignorant though she
was of the subject in which he excelled.

Success of almost any kind commanded her admiration, for though
she never would have admitted it, she herself was undermined by an
inward sense of failure. To be good-looking and lively and a skilful
housewife, and yet to have attained the age of twenty-seven without
winning even transiently a single heart—it was not exactly conducive
to serenity.

How wonderful it had been then to win Sir Harry's! Or at any rate,
how interesting! He was such a fascinating man with all that he knew
and all that he had seen and done and his masterful way of dealing
with people. And then of course there was also all that he had! It was
not her first consideration, but it was not her last either. She was by
no means mercenary, but several years of making ends meet in the
doctor's household had rendered the prospect of being a wealthy man's
wife uncommonly agreeable.

Yet she had returned to Charlton Wells after accepting Sir Harry's
proposal without breathing a word of her good fortune. It was not
destined to be appreciated, as she realized all too well, by her family,
and she did not intend to spend the days that must pass while Sir Harry
was procuring the licence in daily arguments about her chances of
future happiness. Her father would be bound to object to her marry-
ing a man double her age, and Linda had never forgiven Sir Harry for
telling them the truth about those miserable pictures, over which she
had made such an utter fool of herself. She was certain to take very
unkindly to him as a brother-in-law.

And there was another obstacle to candour. Ever since her father
had learned that the curator of the Elderfield Art Gallery had disputed
Sir Harry's verdict and thrown himself whole-heartedly on the side of
Stephanie du Plessis, he had been silent and troubled, veering back
to Stephanie's point of view and obviously repenting, though he had

refused to go back on it, of the bargain with Quiller. Poor vacillating man! As if a young upstart like Arnold Bayley had any right to set up his opinion against the ripe judgment of a famous authority!

Then there had been some article or other in the *Elderfield Courier* mentioning Sir Harry's name in a way that seemed to deepen her father's feeling that he was not as reliable as they had been led to think . . . something about his having recommended a bad picture to the Elderfield Art Gallery. She shouldn't wonder if it had been all trumped up by Arnold Bayley. Perfectly obtuse to the significance of 'Juvenal's' revelations, which had been taken up in the Elderfield press, she dismissed unquestioningly what little she saw of them, but they had the effect of strengthening her intention to refrain from discussing her plans until they had been fulfilled. It was easy to get back to London after a fortnight at home because there was at the moment an unusually competent domestic staff with a housemaid who had the rare virtue of being able to take telephone messages; and a very small excuse sufficed for a parent who was not, perhaps, left alone quite as often as he would have enjoyed.

But being left for a long week-end is one thing and finding one's devoted daughter has abandoned her home to make a clandestine marriage is quite another, and Beatrix had her work cut out to paint what she had done in bright, acceptable colours. She tried various methods, from genially sharing the astonishment of the *fait accompli* ('I just can't believe that I'm now Lady Maximer and the owner of a mink coat!') to calmly and realistically laying cards on the table ('After all, I'm twenty-seven, and though you may not think Harry very suitable for a son-in-law, I haven't exactly had a wide range of choice. I shall now have an opportunity of doing things for Linda, Valerie and Geoff, but first we must go into the question of a secretary for you, Daddy darling. Personally I think . . .').

She was unaware that even as she wrote, on an October Sunday morning, her father, with the *Evening World* from London on his desk, was suffering similar perplexities in drafting a letter. The news about the portrait of Lorenzo had not yet reached her ear or eye. It had been simple for Maximer to keep the evening paper from her on their wedding day.

They had been married on Friday. On Monday morning they returned to London in Sir Harry's car, driven by his chauffeur.

'I ought really to go straight to the city,' he said, 'but perhaps it would be as well to take you home first and introduce you to Mrs. Rose.'

'But I met her before, Harry, when I came to see you with Daddy.'

'Yes, I mean—introduce you as my wife. She may have to be handled rather tactfully after about five years of more or less managing my domestic affairs.'

'You didn't tell her about the wedding?' said Beatrix lightly. She felt quite equal to coping with a private secretary who might have got a bit above herself.

'My dear, a secret that has been told even to one person is a very imperfect secret. I of course would have been delighted to announce our marriage to the world, but you were so anxious that your family should be kept in the dark.'

Beatrix was silent and thoughtful at this. Her behaviour to her family was beginning to gnaw uncomfortably at her conscience.

'I think, my dear,' Sir Harry suggested as they mounted the steps of the mansion where he occupied the first and second floors, 'it would be courteous for me to see Mrs. Rose alone for a moment beforehand. Would you care to go into the drawing-room while I talk to her?'

Beatrix could raise no objection, and he went into his library and rang, not without a faint trepidation, the bell communicating with his office. As he waited for his secretary to appear his eye was struck by an envelope propped upright on his desk, and, what was much stranger, a picture balanced against one of the legs. He knew the letter was going to be troublesome the moment he looked at the picture. It was 'A Belated Honeymoon'.

Sunday.

Dear Sir Harry,

I read the announcement of your marriage on Friday evening and am taking advantage of your absence today to come and clear up my things. I think, the position being what it is, you will be willing to waive the usual notice. You will be able to get a shorthand-typist at once if you ring up one of the agencies, and I dare say Lady Maximer will deal with many of the things you usually leave to me.

May I remark that I consider the gift you made to me only five weeks ago showed the greatest want of taste in the circumstances? But it seems from what I have read and heard lately that want of taste is not the only thing you are guilty of.

Sir Harry flung the letter down with an incredulous gasp. Mrs. Rose must have taken leave of her senses! Such insolence! Such presumptuousness! He had thought her the most rational of women, but since his recent visit to Charlton Wells there had been an indefinable something in her attitude towards him, a something in which a kind of guarded possessiveness was the chief element, that he had found rather disquieting, and now he knew exactly whence it sprang.

That picture—what a mistaken kindness it had been to send it! Modest as was its price by his accustomed standards, it had been too costly a gift to be dispatched so casually to one of his employees, especially an employee who had evidently been nurturing some ill-judged ambition.

Now that he looked at it again, he could see that if she had deluded herself with hopes which he had never had the slightest intention of raising, the subject of the painting was capable of being misinterpreted. The irony of it would be altogether lost on so matter-of-fact an eye as hers. She could observe only that it was an elderly man gazing with rapt affection on a not very young bride. The title might seem to her almost a declaration.

Of all the absurdities! She had probably been waiting ever since for him to follow it up, reading meanings of her own into every little compliment framed only to keep her in a good humour. There is no one who is deceived or who deceives herself more easily when a romantic chord is touched than a woman who prides herself on having no nonsense about her. His life had turned into an object lesson on this theme.

Mrs. Rose had, as she would have put it herself, turned nasty; but fortunately, the degree of confidence to which he had admitted her had been restricted. He had not given her any weapon likely to inflict serious injury on him. Still that dragging-in of things she had read and heard was highly unpleasant.

He picked up the letter again, for there was more to follow; and now for the first time he noticed something odd about it—something that turned his pink face as unlovely a colour as if it had received a coat of bad varnish. The page was typed—that might have been expected—but the type was not that of his familiar Underwood. It was italic type done with a green ribbon.

He had to sit down and spread the letter out before him, on his desk, his hand felt so unsteady as he went on reading:

> You must excuse any mistakes I make as I am not used to typing on such a very old machine as this. Perhaps you don't remember that when I first came and you were just getting settled here, I took in some of the furniture you had been keeping in store during the war. The old Darton that went down to your luggage room in the basement made quite an impression on me, being the kind my grandfather had in his office. I took the liberty of getting it up this morning because I had been reading how the late Dr. Rennick's friends are looking for a typewriter just like this.
>
> There is one last matter I might mention while I am about it. I overheard your conversation on the telephone with the man who rang up from Charlton Wells on Sat. the 9th Sept. In fact I took down some of it in shorthand. I couldn't help recognizing the voice of Mr. Quiller though you called him Black. He really has a voice no one could ever forget, and three or four years ago he was ringing up a good deal about one thing and another. I suppose I ought not to have listened, but remembering how Dr. Sandilands had arrived from Charlton Wells a few days before with that huge trunk of pictures, I couldn't help feeling inquisitive. It was only because I have always had your interests so much at heart.
>
> I wonder if Miss Sandilands, now Lady Maximer, knows about your instructions to Mr. Quiller and how you called her a fool. She did not strike me as a lady with a great enthusiasm for pictures, but I dare say you will train her to your way of looking at things.
>
> I know you are not fond of long letters, so I'm afraid this one will not be much to your taste, but as your conduct lately has given me quite a lot to think about, I felt I might as well return the compliment.
>
> Yours very truly,
>
> JEANETTE ROSE.

The magnitude of the blow, now that he had received its full impact, was such that for a moment it stunned him, and he could only apprehend how odiously commonplace Mrs. Rose's prose was when she wrote a letter that he had not dictated. 'Quite a lot to think about' . . .

She wanted to give him quite a lot to think about. What did she mean by that? What threat was she veiling or unveiling? With the slightly struggling movement of a man who drags himself out of a swoon, he rose and began to pace from one end of the rose-strewn carpet to the other. His was not a character that weakly succumbs. Already he was asking himself in a rational if not a composed manner precisely what harm it was in her power to do him.

Much harm had been done before she had joined the forces against him. He had not known until 'Juvenal' had called to interview him that this man, whose private name happened to be George Robertson, was Oscar Robertson's brother. That frowning glance between Bayley and Mrs. du Plessis which he had interpreted as a mutual admission of defeat must in reality have signified their resolution to wage the war *à outrance*. The campaign against him, the repercussions of which had not as yet been fully felt, had been a bitter experience; but without the slightest evidence that he had ever been in possession of Rennick's typewriter, even the most hostile journalist must confine himself to very guarded utterances. There would not be much need for guardedness once Mrs. Rose had told her story.

And the publicity that was obviously likely to be accorded to the portrait at the Quattrocento Gallery would be a new and most potent means of wrecking what was left of his reputation, for the fact that he had pronounced the superb picture to be worthless would not be long unknown. Until now he had cherished a forlorn hope that when the question of the other fifteen was raised, he could maintain—though the cost to his pride would be excruciating—that he had made an honest mistake. But with Mrs. Rose able to produce a shorthand report of his conversation with Quiller . . . He was not a violent man, but at the thought of this revolting slyness he assumed at least the expression of one.

He had warned Quiller so particularly not to telephone him. She must have played the old trick of pretending to go, opening and closing the door, and then creeping back to listen. How stupid, after years of contending with her curiosity not to have taken precautions against that!

It had probably been then, with the knowledge that he was or might be in her power, that she had first flattered herself with the hope his marriage had dashed down. She had been watching him for weeks with the predatory stillness of a spider in the centre of a web! A profound determination gathered in him that, whatever trouble might yet be brewing, he would never be prevailed upon to be a spider's banquet. To yield the victory whole and entire to Mrs. du Plessis would be a noble fate compared with that.

* * * * *

Dr, Sandilands received his first news of the wedding from the reporter of the local paper who rang up next day to ask for information and instead found himself imparting it to an entirely incredulous household. Reporters from Elderfield followed and were given a very bleak reception. By the afternoon post there arrived Beatrix's first note, telling him in a few affectionate and defensive lines of her marriage, and the *Evening World* with the notice of the wedding marked in ink. This had been sent not by Beatrix but by one of his London relatives. The paragraph headed 'Another Cleaned Picture' could not be passed over unread when pictures were so perpetually on his mind, and the news that Stephanie's portrait of Lorenzo had all the value, even the monetary value, she had always ascribed to it did what little still needed to be done to open his eyes to Maximer.

That eye-opening had been a slow and reluctant process, but it was now so complete that he could very adequately divine the motives of the marriage.

After a night of mourning for the folly of his prudent daughter, he allowed himself to take a little infection of cheerfulness from Linda, who could not conceal her tendency to regard the whole event as the best joke that Beatrix had ever initiated. If she had been given any chance of expressing her opinion beforehand, she would certainly not have approved the match, but since it had taken place she could only enjoy the wonderment it provided and speculate on the astonishing possibilities of the future. And Dr. Sandilands, who had begun by being shocked at her seeming callousness, came by degrees to find her attitude comfortingly realistic.

'There's one good thing,' she dared to say at last. 'We know he's got the pictures, Daddy, so they'll come back into the family now.'

It was the first time she had indicated the persistence of her belief in Maximer's dishonesty since that painful scene when she had wept so much and her father had been so angry with her. But he had since shown his remorsefulness in many little ways.

He sighed. 'He's never likely to confess he's got them. Ah, if I'd only let them stay over at Elderfield with Bayley this frightful marriage wouldn't have taken place!'

'*Something* would have taken place, you can bet your boots, with a man like that plotting and planning.'

'There seems to have been a trifle of plotting and planning on your side too.' He gave her a smile of pure contrition.

'Oh, that was all Stephanie's and Arnold Bayley's doing. They've been plotting like anything since we had to—since Quiller took the trunk away. They don't tell me what goes on any more,' she added with a rather sheepish laugh, 'at least not much, but of course, I know who's behind these articles that have been appearing in the papers—"The Mystery of the Missing Typewriter" and all that. I should think Sir Harry's sorry he got Arnold so hopping mad. I'd hate to fight with him and Stephanie, wouldn't you?'

'I'm afraid I have been fighting them, and very much to my own disadvantage. Oh, dear me! The way I've treated poor Mrs. du Plessis makes me feel very foolish. And it seems she won't even sell the picture I gave her! What a strange young woman she is, to be sure!'

Linda's face assumed an unwonted gravity. 'Daddy, Beatrix being married to Sir Harry is going to be an awful blow to Stephanie, won't it? I mean, it'll absolutely tie her hands.'

'It shan't tie mine at any rate,' said the doctor resolutely. 'I owe her an apology and I shall certainly send it.'

Thus it came about that, on Sunday morning, he was sitting at his desk laboriously composing a letter at the same time as his errant daughter was poring over her explanation of the unprecedented concealments of the past three weeks.

'Do you think,' the doctor inquired, looking up from a sheet which contained so many erasures and corrections that he prepared to discard it, 'do you think you could stay in one evening this week and put on a dinner?'

'A dinner *party*?'

'Well, a decent little dinner for four. I think rather than make a lot of excuses which don't sound very loyal to Beatrix when I read them over, I'll just ask them both to dinner. This young Bayley as well.'

'Now that's the best idea you could have had, Daddy. You wait! I'll give you a dinner such as you've never tasted. After all, you won't have

Beatrix as housekeeper any more, so I'd better be getting my hand in, hadn't I?'

'Don't make it too unlike anything I've ever tasted,' he pleaded, taking a fresh sheet of paper.

'There's just one thing,' said Linda after a silence big with decision. 'I don't think it's fair to invite Arnold Bayley without having Ken.'

'Ken? Who's he? Oh, your photographer fellow!' He pursed his lips doubtfully. 'You want to make it a dinner of all the conspirators, a regular Guy Fawkes evening.'

'But, Daddy, Ken did an awful lot, honestly! He stayed up all night taking photographs of the pictures, and then, another time, he worked nearly all night again doing prints of them, just to make it hard for Sir Harry to dispose of them.'

'It's that kind of thing that's brought about this fatal marriage,' he rejoined with another heavy sigh. 'You meant it well, no doubt of that—'

'The marriage is likely to be a good deal more fatal for him than for her,' said Linda, emboldened by the success of her confidences to become still more candid. 'Can't you imagine what a dance she'll lead him when she's seen through him? She only married him because she looks up to him and think's he's wonderful. Oh, good gracious! I don't envy poor old Sir Harry Maximer when she finds out that Stephanie's been offered twenty-five thousand pounds for that one picture!'

'Yes, there's something in that,' he agreed with a certain gleam of amusement. 'There's decidedly something in what you say, my dear. Now I'll write my note and perhaps you could take it by hand. I should like not to lose any time in making amends.'

NINETEEN

THE CONSPIRATORS' dinner, as Dr. Sandilands insisted on calling it, was not until Thursday, but the glorious news of the return of the pictures was communicated to everyone concerned the moment it was received on Wednesday. So the meeting, instead of being merely an occasion of mutual commiseration, became a festivity which the shadow of Beatrix's rash conduct was hardly allowed to mar.

Before they entered the dining-room, the doctor read aloud to his three guests the letter that had come by the previous morning's post.

Dear Dr. Sandilands,

Further to my visits to your district and the items I bought from you on the 7th September, namely fifteen paintings on panel including one which was incomplete, I write to inform you that subsequent examination has shown that these works are not what I took them for at the time of the transaction.

You will appreciate that I was given to understand both by Miss Sandilands and yourself that the paintings were copies of Old Masters, and that I bought them under this impression and paid a suitable price, considering the amount requiring to be spent on them in order to make them acceptable to my customers.

Having now closely inspected the said items, I am of the opinion that they are genuine Old Masters, and that you sold them to me under a misapprehension.

As I have always had a reputation for fair and honest dealing, I do not care to keep the pictures, which are worth a price out of all proportion to what I gave for them, and on learning that the portrait described as 'Lorenzo the Magnificent', which I also saw at your house, is now in process of cleaning at the Quattrocento Gallery, where I am acquainted with the manager, I inquired whether they would be prepared to put the other fifteen pictures in their strong room pending your decision as to what you want done with them. Accordingly they were taken there today and registered as your property. I enclose receipt herewith.

I shall be much obliged to receive your cheque for one hundred guineas in due course, being refund of the amount paid by me.

Trusting this proposal will meet with your approval,

    I am,

        Yours faithfully,

           E. QUILLER

'It's quite, quite incredible!' said Arnold. 'Well, of course, he doesn't expect it to be credible. It's just a completely unanswerable get-out and that's all he means it to be.'

'Are you sure—oh please! are you absolutely sure there isn't a double-cross somewhere?' cried Stephanie almost wringing her hands.

'How do you know the receipt from the Quattrocento Gallery is really a receipt for *our* pictures?'

'They're very clearly listed.' Nevertheless the doctor's voice betrayed a faint tremor.

'It wouldn't be easy to put others in their place when there are all Ken's photographs to compare them with,' said Linda.

'I hope Quiller knows about the photographs,' the doctor remarked nervously. 'We shall be going down to London tomorrow, but I had to have twenty-four hours to make arrangements for my patients—apart from the pleasure of this dinner.'

'Whether Quiller knows about the photographs or doesn't, the man who's instructing him does, and that's the thing that matters.' And as they went in to dinner, Arnold began to tell the story of how he and Stephanie had bearded the lion in his den.

'You are certainly responsible for the fact that these pictures have been restored to us,' said Dr. Sandilands, going round the table to fill their glasses with champagne.

He forbore to add that they were equally responsible for the elopement of his daughter, for even that calamity was beginning to have its compensatory aspects. Linda, on her mettle, had put up an unexpectedly good performance as housekeeper in her sister's absence, and they had decided yesterday that she was to leave the Library and look after him altogether in future. In getting special leave to go to London, she had already given notice. Of course, she would never really be as efficient as Beatrix, but then she was very good-natured, and in his retirement, which was not far off, her amiable and easy-going companionship would—yes, he admitted it—would, in some respects be more agreeable.

'Everybody behaved marvellously except me,' said Linda, with a mixture of laughter and apology.

'And me,' Kenneth reminded them less gaily. 'I can't tell you what a first-class fool I felt when I saw I'd given the whole show away.'

'But, Ken, just look how you made up for it!'

'Your photographs were certainly one of our trump cards,' said Stephanie.

'And we mustn't forget,' Arnold went on, 'the credit due to Oscar Robertson. Without his work on the Rennick forgeries, we should never have been able to bring anything home to Maximer. We really had no evidence that he'd sent Quiller here, nothing a court of law would have accepted for a moment. Even now, I can't think why he's made such an unconditional surrender after brazening it out so long. We never were able, after all, to prove any connection between him and Quiller.'

'Oh, it *would* be nice to think there wasn't one!'

Arnold remembered that Dr. Sandilands had just acquired Maximer for a son-in-law, and deemed it well to take a new line. 'I'd like you to meet Oscar Robertson, sir. I'm going to be in London while you're there, and with your permission I could perhaps fix something up. Oscar and his brother, 'Juvenal', who's been such a valuable ally—'

'It's a little difficult for me, Bayley, seeing there's been this marriage, you know.'

'It was just on that account, sir, I suggested it. We shall have to call off the pack, you see, and Oscar's champing to run these Rennick forgeries right to earth.'

'You mean, have Maximer prosecuted? Oh dear me, I hope not.'

'Prosecution? No, that's not likely. My Committee won't bring one, I think I can promise that. Sir Hubert Prosser's dead and his executors over in South Africa have never shown much interest in our investigations. Arcadian Green might be inclined to bring an action, but it would have to be against the firm who sold him his picture and they, fortunately or unfortunately, are in liquidation. Still, it's just because Maximer always seems to get away with it that Oscar would like to have him utterly discredited. . . . A pity, seeing that he really is a great authority and the author of books that are invaluable.'

'Well, if you think that my meeting these brothers will avert any catastrophe . . . Since we're all going to London, I should very much like Mrs. du Plessis—or Stephanie, since you all call her so—to come with us as my guest.'

Arnold placed his hand boldly and possessively on her shoulder. 'I'm afraid she can't do that, doctor. She's going with me as my wife. As a matter of fact, it will be our honeymoon.'

Marriages take precedence, at least in the code of politeness, even over historic hoards of pictures, and everyone talked about Stephanie's wedding, which was to take place in Elderfield the following morning, as if it were the only topic they had any interest in discussing. But at last, with the meringue glacé and the second bottle of champagne, Kenneth Dyer flung at a fruit-dish on the sideboard the question that everyone had been longing for somebody else to ask.

'I suppose if one of these panels is worth twenty-five thousand, the whole lot together must come to a pretty tidy fortune?'

'I should like to hear your opinion on that, Bayley,' said the doctor with a restraint that was well-managed but deceived no one.

'If you break up the collection, it's worth a great deal of money,' Arnold replied gravely, gently rotating his glass. 'There's no doubt about that.'

'And what if it isn't broken up?' A dry little cough hinted at the doctor's dismay, for he did not need to be told that Arnold and Stephanie would aim at keeping it intact.

'Then it's worth more than anyone is likely to pay. Its value is fabulous and therefore can't be realized.'

'Oh *Lord*!' groaned Linda with such a childish spontaneity that everybody laughed. 'What a sell! Just when I'd practically chosen my fur coat!'

'In terms of fur coats I dare say you'll do very well. I only mean you must be prepared to accept a much lower price if you keep the collection together than if you sell it piece by piece—one picture fetching thirty thousand here and another forty thousand there, and so on.'

'Why, such sums as that are beyond our wildest dreams,' said the doctor as Linda gasped and Kenneth went so far as to whistle. 'Are you sure you're not getting just a bit carried away, Bayley? I mean, one doesn't want to lose touch with reality.'

'No, it's quite true that if you want to ensure a proper future for all these pictures together you must be content with smaller figures. That's what I'm saying. But you'll certainly be offered great temptations to do otherwise.'

Dr. Sandilands was by no means sure that he desired to resist these temptations, but he recognized that he must be guided by the wishes of those whose efforts to save the treasure had been so nearly thwarted by his own to get rid of it, and he inquired: 'What's your idea then of how I ought to dispose of them?'

'Stephanie and I have been sketching out a sort of plan.' Arnold picked up a salted almond and gazed at it with great intensity. 'It's only in an embryonic stage at present, but for what it's worth . . . the idea is that you should have each separate picture valued independently, and that when we're in a position to publish a thoroughly reliable estimate of the total, you should announce your willingness to accept half—that should be at least a hundred thousand pounds—if the collection can be bought as one entity. I can then get busy with the Arts Council, the National Art Collections Fund, and every other organization likely to be interested, and we can launch a nation-wide appeal. When the pictures have had what's necessary done to them, we can send them on a grand tour to help earn their purchase price. They'll arouse immense curiosity.'

'Are you sure?' said the doctor somewhat incredulously.

'I couldn't be more sure. You mustn't under-estimate their importance now that it can be told. Stephanie and I were most anxious that it should be kept dark until they'd been got somehow or other out of Quiller's hands. We were horror-stricken, as you can imagine, when some idiot in the Quattrocento laboratory got talking about the portrait of Lorenzo—which, incidentally, is by Piero di Cosimo. But since we can unbosom ourselves at last, you may as well know that Stephanie's theory has been tested and proved right.'

'Her theory about these things belonging to the Medici?'

'To Lorenzo the Magnificent himself.' Arnold's smiling gesture begged her to take up the story.

'It's simply,' she said with a diffidence that would have surprised Beatrix, and that was indeed rather a new thing in her, 'it's simply that most of them can be identified from the 1493 inventory that was found when the Laurentian Library was brought back to Florence after being moved for safety during the war. When I made the first suggestions in our "Medici dossier" I had no direct evidence about the contents of his palace but the 1492 inventory, the one that was published by Eugene Muntz in Paris in the 'eighties. That was a very cursory document. The descriptions of each picture only amount to a line or so, and very often the artist isn't named. The 1493 inventory is most careful and precise, obviously written by a proper custodian. Arnold was able to get a copy of it made for us in Florence, and it's been possible for us to put it all— well, beyond conjecture, really.'

There was a murmur of applause from three of the listeners, and she went on: 'Even your cinerary urn is there—only it wasn't in fragments then. The "Leda" is by Leonardo—we always knew that—and you've got one of the two Masaccios that were on either side of the fireplace in the first room, and then there's the head of the Emperor Johannes, that Gozzoli used as a model, perhaps, when he did his fresco in the chapel. . . .'

Her voice, which had grown tremulous, suddenly broke, and as she covered her eyes with her hand, two or three tears splashed on the polished table.

'It's only,' she explained amidst a susurration of embarrassed little noises, 'that I feel so overwhelmed when I think of the magnitude of it. Imagine that poor old Mrs. Hovenden living with them all her life, almost, and dying in difficulties not knowing . . .'

This was so solemn a thought that for a moment or two nobody seemed inclined to speak; then Kenneth, in one of his happy impulses, restored the sense of celebration by saying: 'Let's drink to her!'

Linda clinked her glass against his, delighted to be released from the necessity of appearing serious. Dr. Sandilands smiled privately into his wine, conjuring up there, so far as his restrained imagination could achieve it, the image of the old lady framed in her doorway, the wintry twilight falling on her face, behind her the deep gloom in which the marble pierrette simpered and the mahogany coat-and-umbrella rack stood rigid and forbidding—sentinels, had he but known it, of an Aladdin's cave.

Arnold held his glass in both hands as if it had been a chalice. 'I really do drink to Mrs. Hovenden,' he said earnestly. 'I even drink in the most heartless way to her not having known anything about pictures.'

He turned to Stephanie and laid his lips to the rim.

TWENTY

SIR HARRY'S offer to build an art gallery if the Hovenden pictures could be housed together in Charlton Wells and maintained by civic funds did a great deal to stimulate the energies of the distinguished Committee which had undertaken to raise the purchase price. Not less did it help to restore a reputation injured by widespread and most unpleasant rumours. His article in the *Sunday Times* condemning the policy of centralization of the nation's art treasures and pleading the cause of an enchanting resort which might, if its merits as a depository were recognized, become a new cultural capital and a place of pilgrimage, was received with acclamations in Charlton Wells and the North country generally.

His description of the beauties of the collection in a special feature for *Apollo* caused the exhibition arranged at the Tate Gallery to be awaited with the most eager interest. His exposition for *Picture Post*, illustrating, with a series of excellent photographs, the pictures at various stages of cleaning, ensured that this interest was not of a rarefied and restricted order. His reply to a *Times* letter-writer who had suggested that they should be sent back to Florence was generally reckoned to have made short work of that proposal.

He was the leading spirit in organizing the tour the collection was to make on leaving the Tate Gallery, and he succeeded in arousing so great a curiosity in America that he was able to secure the guarantee of a considerable sum in dollars. All this disinterested activity made a most favourable impression and very nearly extinguished the scandal.

A woman who said she had been his secretary tried to engage the attention of certain newspaper editors with a story of his having first pronounced these pictures to be copies or fakes, but was given so little credence that even the few lines she managed to get published in the *Plain Dealer* were promptly rescinded when Sir Harry called for that journal to produce some vestige of support for the insinuations. The difficulty of interviewing Mr. Quiller, who had gone to America on business concerned with the export of antiques, made it quite impossible to check the woman's almost fantastic statements.

On her writing to 'Juvenal' to inform him that she knew the whereabouts of John Rennick's typewriter, he had replied that he knew it himself: the machine was in the hands of his brother, having recently been dispatched to him in one of Pickford's vans.

Sir Harry was at peace with 'Juvenal' and almost at peace with Oscar Robertson, who had made a treaty with his friends that he would remove all aspersions from the name of Rennick without aspersing any other name in the process. The price was dear, nothing less than the art gallery he had promised to the avenging angel who was now Mrs. Arnold Bayley; but he did not altogether begrudge it.

While he was still capable of doing so, it was well to make some provision for his own superb collections, since it was quite certain that his widow would be the last person to arrange their proper disposition. Now that he had been obliged to confess to such a monstrous blunder in connection with the Hovenden pictures, she had developed a rooted conviction that all his judgments were worthless and his favourite canvases valuable in inverse ratio to the value he placed on them. He could only resolve that, if she were still his wife at the time of his decease, the masterpieces on which he had lavished so much of his love, his knowledge, and his substance would be dealt with by other hands than hers. He had therefore, in making his new will, left Arnold Bayley as the executor of his artistic property, since he was the obvious choice as custodian of the new art gallery.

And perhaps if, largely through his own ingenious efforts, Charlton Wells could be built up into England's great shrine of Italian art, the glories of the Maximer collection would be housed more honourably there than if they were squeezed into the already crowded treasure houses of the capital.

The glories of the Maximer collection! Alas, there would be little chance of adding to those when his capital had been depleted by the price of an art gallery, even if it were only a miniature one. Still, it might be that long before that bounty had been given, he would have acquired something to compensate him for the splendours he had lost. He had not breathed a word of it to Beatrix—he never did of his own volition breathe a word of anything touching on the painful topic of pictures—but her other Hovenden paintings that her father had once made some effort to sell had not failed to arouse his longing for possession, and before leaving Charlton Wells in September he had visited the shop with the cardinals for the second time and empowered Morris to negotiate on his behalf for any works of art that Mrs. Hovenden's heirs and assigns might still have at their disposal. Morris had seemed to him an excellent choice as mediator, being too ignorant and stupid a man to use discrimination.

Discrimination was just what he did not want and what, in fact, he had forbidden Morris to attempt. It was through his fatuous belief in his power to discriminate that he had, so fortunately for Dr. Sandilands and the nation, rejected the 'Madonna and Child' by Filippo Lippi and the 'Dead Christ' by Verocchio; and he had therefore been strictly enjoined to leave his own taste and judgment in abeyance.

From time to time there came from Charlton Wells reports of progress. It was slow because Mrs. Hovenden's step-grandson, the owner of the Old Rectory, lived in New South Wales. He had been in the habit since her death of letting the house furnished through a firm of agents, and though it was true, as Morris had ascertained, that there were numerous old pictures on the premises which the tenants had stored away in the attics, it was difficult to get access to them. According to Morris, Mr. Hovenden, who had never seen his property since boyhood, was uncertain whether he wished to sell.

Maximer was extremely anxious that a bargain should be struck before the immense value of the pictures acquired by Dr. Sandilands had been made public. Though he realized his impatience might operate to his disadvantage, he was obliged to press for an early decision, and at last, fearing to be confronted with rival candidates, was driven to make a blind offer. Provided the transaction were no longer allowed to hang in the balance, he would pay Morris an agreed sum for any pictures whatever that could be certified by affidavit as part of Mrs. Hovenden s estate.

At this, he was given to understand, Mr. Hovenden had been led to do business, and a day came—not a moment too soon, for the papers were beginning to talk of the great find from Charlton Wells—when the bargain was struck. There was yet some delay in arranging with the tenants of the Old Rectory to take possession of the property, but that was eventually done, and the obsequious Morris assured him that he would have the entire consignment in time for Christmas.

He had been informed that the works were all on canvas, and he had brilliant hopes that the same ancestor who, in the eighteenth century, had brought the Medici hoard back to England might have had the discernment to buy Titians, Correggios, and Veroneses. From Morris's description they sounded wonderfully promising. A tomb with a mourning figure beside it and an angel hovering above—that surely was a subject for Tintoretto. A shepherd in a valley—this was doubtless a pastoral scene by one of the seventeenth-century classicists. These pictures were not necessarily, he realized, all Italian. Some might certainly be French. The landscapes, of which there appeared to be a substantial number, might well be by Claude or Poussin. From what Morris said of them in his ignorant way, it seemed highly probable that they were.

It was on the 21st of December that the vast crates were delivered, transported at Maximer's especial request by Messrs. Bourlet. The day promised to be altogether an auspicious one, for while he waited, quivering with excitement, for the porter to fetch a hammer and pincers, Beatrix came in with a letter from Linda which contained the extraordinary news that the missing half of Botticelli's picture of the Muses had turned up in a convent in Italy. A priest had identified it by the photographs of the Hovenden portion which had appeared in an Italian art magazine, and there seemed little doubt that the work would ultimately be presented to the public in its entirety.

Though it would never be his, Sir Harry was too sincere an enthusi-ast not to rejoice in these tidings, but Beatrix was always so very scathing and disagreeable when she had any occasion to talk of her father's pictures that, after the first delight and wonderment had been expressed, he wished she would go away and leave him to do the bliss-ful task of unpacking without her comments.

She insisted, however, on bringing newspapers to protect the parquet floor from straw and shavings, and remained to give advice and a quite superfluous helping hand to the porter.

'More Old Masters, I suppose,' she said in a special tone she now always used for talking about the objects of his passion. It was very much the tone she had acquired from that vanity-crushing nurse on whom she had unconsciously based her personality.

'I trust so, my dear. I have some reason to believe they might be.'

'From Charlton Wells!' she remarked, glancing with surprise at one of the labels. 'I thought Daddy had snaffled all the Old Masters in Charlton. These are much bigger. I hope they're prettier.'

'The great masters of the sixteenth and seventeenth centuries painted larger works, generally speaking, than those which were done on panel. And I think you are likely to find them prettier, as you call it.'

'I could do with something decent-looking for a change in my bedroom. I'm sick to death of that circle of pudding-faced angels float-ing around the sky on cushions.'

'Very well, my dear,' he said handsomely, anxious to keep her in her present comparatively good humour. 'If there's anything you find among these new acquisitions which takes your fancy, you may certainly put it in your room. They're quite ready to hang, you see.'

'Heavens, what a frame!' Beatrix exclaimed as the porter and Sir Harry together removed the wrappings from the ornamental gilding.

'Late Victorian plaster painted gold,' he murmured with a slight sinking of the heart. 'Very heavy and ornate, and hardly what I should have expected. If these pictures were framed seventy or eighty years ago, they'll be covered with brown varnish, I fear. Yes, yes, I see they are! This one is at any rate.'

Nevertheless, though Morris's assurance that the pictures were absolutely in their original condition was evidently of doubtful validity, his hands were almost painfully eager as he stripped away the copious packing materials.

A shriek of laughter, not his own, greeted the unveiling of 'The Guardian Angel'. A mourning figure by a tomb, an angel hovering above . . . but not by Tintoretto.

'This is only the first,' he said with effortful courtesy. 'Have the goodness to repress your mirth, if you please, until you know what's here. There are twelve others.'

'Well, I shan't have that in my bedroom, you may be sure. Why, it's just like that awful junk that Daddy told us about—the stuff he tried to sell for Mrs. Hovenden.'

A silence fell upon Sir Harry. Grimly and with a full sense of his impending doom, he uncovered a canvas larger than the first and yet more tawdrily framed. His wife's light giggle sounded in his ears like the laughter of a fiend as he laid bare in all their starkness the shivering expanses of 'Snowbound in a Yorkshire Dale'.

THE END

FURROWED MIDDLEBROW

Lightning Source UK Ltd.
Milton Keynes UK
UKHW040133210322
400364UK00003B/18